PRAISE FOR *LILA*

Heart-wrenching and uplifting family saga. This series is a compelling, inspiring story of an immigrant family's trials and tribulations. It is so well told and moving, and the detailed landscape made me feel right in the story. A great book club read.
—*Martha Conway, author of The Underground River*

Lilacs in the Dust Bowl is a triumph of family story-telling. Stevan's remarkable achievement is to have brought to vivid and believable life a family saga of immigration to western Canada that, in the annals of Ukrainian-Canadian stories, covers exciting new ground.
—*Myrna Kostash, author of All of Baba's Children*

Diana Stevan has written a powerful and compelling portrait of a Ukrainian farming family. A tale of family, faith, endurance, and determination, Lilacs in the Dust Bowl is an inspiring testament to the strength and resilience of the human spirit.
—*Manuel Matas, author of Borders of Normal*

What makes this novel compelling is the factual telling of what life was like during the Depression for a family with little resources but big on hope. Told in clear, crisp prose, it's a novel which when you start, you might want to hide your to-do list.
—*Allan Hudson, author of Vigilantes*

A well written and timeless saga. Stevan has woven together, in a seamless fashion, historical events, geography and strong character portrayals based on extensive background research but most importantly, on the close and loving relationship she had with her ancestors who are the root of this story.
—*R G Johns*

The plight of the Canadian immigrant farmers, who endured harsh winters, poor soil conditions, swarms of grasshoppers, and scorching summers are described so closely as if the author was one of the family members herself

—*Uliana Hlynchak, TV producer*

Lilacs in the Dust Bowl is a captivating story and account of personal and Canadian history. What makes this book and the previous one particularly poignant is that the stories are based on author Diana Stevan's grandmother.

—*Patricia Sandberg, author of Sun Dogs and Yellowcake*

LILACS
in the
DUST BOWL

ALSO BY DIANA STEVAN

LILACS
in the
DUST BOWL

A NOVEL

DIANA STEVAN

Peregrin
Publishing

LILACS *in the* DUST BOWL
Copyright © 2021 Diana Stevan
All rights reserved.

Library and Archives Canada Cataloguing in Publication

Peregrin
Publishing

ISBN: 978-1-896402-29-1 (paperback)
ISBN: 978-1-896402-16-1 (Mobi)
ISBN: 978-1-896402-17-8 (Epub)
ISBN: 978-1-896402-18-5 (PDF)

Grateful acknowledgement is made to the trustee of The Margaret Millar Charitable Trust for their permission to use the quotation from the works of Margaret Millar.

"Oh, You Beautiful Doll" is a ragtime love song published in 1911 with words by Seymour Brown and music by Nat B. Ayer

Cover design by Ares Jun
Formatting and layout by Polgarus Studio

Printed and bound in the United States

For Baba
Lukia Mazurec

*The smell of moist earth and lilacs hung in the air
like wisps of the past and hints of the future.*

Margaret Millar

1

No Turning Back

1929

The iron wheels hitting the stones sounded like a death knell. Lukia Mazurets stifled a cry as she sat with her children in the back of the old wagon rattling over the dirt road, away from her life in Kivertsi. She clasped her hands so tightly her knuckles turned white. Seared in her mind was her mother's face as they waved goodbye—her mouth set in a tight line, her eyes glazed over. She had lowered her head; then her legs buckled. She would have fallen had Lukia's brother Pavlo not stepped forward to catch her. When he grabbed her, she leaned into his chest and sank further. A neighbour who'd come to see the Mazurets family off helped Pavlo settle her on the wooden bench by the door.

Afraid that image of her mother crumpling would haunt her the rest of her life, Lukia crossed herself and said a silent prayer: *Please God, take care of her and Pavlo, his wife, his girls ...* There were so many names, so many to remember and pray for.

The wagon rounded the corner. A tall row of bushes blocked Lukia's view of her farm. She moaned, then stared ahead at her neighbours' fields—row upon row of golden wheat stalks swaying in the gentle breeze. She would see them no more.

A lump caught in her throat. Was leaving a mistake? Would she ever see her mother and Pavlo again? She bit her lower lip. There was nothing she could do about it now. Their farm and all their stock and implements had been sold. There was no turning back.

Up front and driving two horses, her brother Petro was telling her son Egnat that he hoped to join them in Canada within a year. Unlike Lukia, Petro had some wealth to manage—some rental property he had to take care of before he could emigrate.

There had been some tense moments when Lukia prepared to leave. The cut-off age to emigrate was fifty, and she was four years older. To fool the authorities, she dyed her hair and lied about her age. In the government office, she'd been afraid the agent suspected.

Egnat also had problems. He'd become a father just one month earlier, and emigration rules stated no child under three months could leave the country. Like his mother, he chose to lie. He added two months to his baby's age on the emigration papers.

Lukia turned to gaze at her granddaughter, contentedly nursing in her mother's arms. It was a good thing Genya was a healthy baby and, though delicate, could pass for being a little older. She glanced at Elena and wondered what her daughter-in-law was thinking. Leaving her own mother and father behind couldn't have been easy, yet she hadn't complained.

They passed another golden field of grain and a farmer working his scythe, reaping his wheat. Had they stayed, they'd be out on their land as well, bringing in an early harvest. It had been a good year, one that would benefit the new owner, a relative of one of their neighbours.

"My God," Lukia said aloud, "will we ever see this land again?"

Elena shrugged, but her wet eyes suggested she didn't believe they would.

Lukia said nothing more. She didn't want to add any more sadness to the layers of grief they carried. Instead, she gazed at her other three children, sitting across from her.

At least Eudokia, now nicknamed Dunya—after a song her brothers sang—seemed excited about their new adventure. She wriggled in her seat as she talked incessantly about the ship they were going to take across the ocean. Michalko, twenty, and Havrylo, sixteen, sat grimly, half listening to their sister, their eyes moist as they passed one familiar place after the other for the last time.

Taking a second look at her daughter, Lukia realized that amid her busy preparations to leave, she hadn't noticed how quickly Eudokia had grown. She was only fourteen, but the white blouse she wore over her already mature breasts would have to be replaced in the fall. The black-and-white checkered skirt might last longer if Lukia moved the button. She sighed. It was a good thing she was bringing her sewing machine, even though Egnat had complained it was too heavy. She'd make her daughter a new dress once they got settled in Canada.

Lukia closed her eyes. *Oy, Gregory, if you could see us now. Leaving the motherland. Would you be angry with me? I hope not. Despite how much we love our country, there's no future here. Our children would starve, and I with them.*

Egnat had agreed with his mother about the future. The Polish government, that had taken over the western part of Ukraine, was not allowing farmers to add any more land to their property, even if they could afford it. With the birth of her granddaughter, Lukia knew her farm could not provide for them all. As if that wasn't bad enough, the Poles had converted all the Orthodox churches to Catholic ones. Losing her place of worship had been a blow. Her faith had bolstered her all the times she felt she couldn't go on.

But it was Michalko who had sealed her decision to leave their

3

homeland. Seated across from him, she admired his handsome face, his dark, curly hair and dancing eyes. He had threatened to move to Argentina after he'd heard that the Polish government was considering drafting young men into the Polish army. Lukia couldn't blame her son for wanting to avoid a military commitment. With the Bolsheviks threatening the bordering countries, nothing was stable. War could break out at any time. And he, like most in their country, had seen enough of war. *But Argentina?* A neighbour's son had immigrated to Argentina and the poor woman never heard from him again. Lukia didn't think she could bear losing another child.

It was a stroke of luck—as if God had been looking out for her—when she heard two men talking on a street in Lutsk about Canada's offer of farmland to outsiders at a fraction of what it would cost in Volhynia. It was more land than she'd ever dreamed of having. Rushing home, she shared what she had learned with Egnat. Itching for more hectares himself, he welcomed the opportunity.

Now, here they were, on their way to a place they knew little about, with only what they thought they required: kitchen wares—including a large steel basin for mixing bread dough and bathing Genya—a couple of two-handled saws for cutting trees, and a metal trunk packed with their sheepskin coats, felt boots, and goose-feather perinas for Canada's cold winters.

The wagon shifted, and she looked down at her feet. Between them were gifts of love—food for their journey from the relatives and friends who came to see them off. She recalled the warm hands of those who had pressed hers and asked her to write. Since she didn't know how, she promised that Egnat would. He'd keep them all connected.

2

A Stop in Warsaw

At the Lutsk station, they watched their train roll in. Clouds of steam rose from its engine to meet the sky. When the whistle blew and the conductor yelled, "All aboard," Lukia's stomach sank.

Petro placed a hand on her shoulder. "Sister, you'll be fine. Remember, if the others could emigrate, they would, too."

"I don't know. I hope you're right. Give my best to Anna."

"I will. We'll try to come as soon as I can find someone reputable to manage our apartments."

After their goods had been loaded on the train, Lukia kissed her brother firmly, picked up her wicker basket, and climbed on board with her family.

The train to Warsaw was crowded, but they found seats together. After some small talk with a Polish woman sitting in front of her, Lukia took the lunch out of her basket. She passed slices of kybassa and bread to her children, who made sandwiches for themselves on their laps. The familiar smell of garlic mingled with cigarette smoke from a passenger nearby.

Lukia felt like pinching herself. She couldn't believe they were finally on their way. Though tired after packing most of the night, she couldn't tear herself away from the window. She wanted to preserve images of her homeland: farmhouses with thatched roofs and mud-plaster walls painted white, cows grazing on green pastures, farmers toiling on their land and towering sunflowers swaying as if they, too, were bidding farewell. She kept looking until her eyelids could no longer stay open.

After four hours, they arrived in Warsaw. Lukia approached an official in the train station and asked for directions to a hotel for emigrants. They would stay there a couple of nights, then board a train for the seaport of Danzig.

Lugging her basket and bags, Lukia led the way down Chmielna Street and across a busy intersection with modern cars and streetcars on tracks. Behind her, Egnat and Michalko carried their heavy trunk with the saws between boards on top, tied together with a rope. Dunya and Havrylo hauled their mother's sewing machine, and Elena held Genya with one arm and with the other, a burlap bag of clothing.

As she walked, Lukia admired the architecture and activity on the streets. Compared to Lutsk, Warsaw had more stately buildings, many constructed of brick and embellished with wrought-iron balconies. There were also more cars than horses and carts, including a few luxury vehicles. She supposed it was because Warsaw had been kept out of enemy hands. The Great War hadn't ravaged the city, nor had its civilians suffered through a civil war like the people in Volhynia. How could anyone back home make progress when they were always busy defending themselves?

What surprised Lukia most was the fashionable clothing on the men and women she passed. The men wore trim wool suits with padded shoulders and fedoras; the women wore beautifully sewn outfits and stylish hats. She passed a stocky woman around her age wearing a mid-calf length dress, a bell-shaped straw hat with a ribbon around the crown, and sheer stockings made of silk or rayon. Lukia was tempted to run back and ask the woman if she'd bought her outfit or made it herself, but she didn't, for fear of sounding foolish. She made mental notes on clothes she'd like to make once they got settled in Canada. One day, she'd have a fine hat to wear to church. A fine straw hat would be more flattering than the babushkas she wore.

At the hotel, Egnat told his mother he had heard on the train good vodka could be purchased at a local bar. Not knowing what they'd find on board their ship, Lukia gave him thirty-five zloty to buy a few bottles. It would be comforting to have their customary shot of liquor with their meals.

While her other children went off to explore and Elena settled on the middle bed to nurse Genya, Lukia dozed off on the bed by the wall. She slept soundly, and would've slept longer if not for the sound of Egnat's footsteps jarring her awake.

Startled to see him standing by her bed, she abruptly sat up. "Egnat, what are you doing?"

He sputtered, "Two thieves robbed me. One bumped me, the other had a newspaper hiding a gun."

"What?" cried Lukia. Her forehead crumpled with the news. "They took the money?"

"I would've fought if it wasn't for the gun he pointed at me."

Elena's mouth dropped open. "You could've been killed."

"Oy, oy, oy!" Lukia said, angry not only with the thieves but also with her son. He'd lost the money. She studied his face to see if he'd been drinking. It was redder than usual, and she smelled alcohol on his breath. "Don't lie to me. I'm not some fool. This is what happens when you go drinking and you're not careful."

Bowing his head, Egnat avoided his mother's eyes.

Groaning, Lukia shook her head. "This is our misfortune." She silently vowed to think twice the next time Egnat asked her for any money—especially for vodka. Was it an omen, a sign they weren't meant to go? Four other families from her village had wanted to emigrate but couldn't. One family's farm had been cursed so it wouldn't sell; in the second, the head of the household was barely a teenager and couldn't qualify; the third was run by an adult son whose mother refused to sell; and the fourth family was held back because the wife had glaucoma. Maybe Lukia and her family weren't destined to go, either.

3

PLEASE SIR

By the time they reached the seaport, the family had been travelling for a week. They excitedly took turns gawking out the window as the train pulled into the Danzig station—an ornate red-brick structure with the tallest clock tower they'd ever seen.

After gathering their belongings, they struggled off the train with the other emigrants and traipsed down the street to an austere government building where they would have to stay until their ship arrived. A burly woman who ushered them in said that each passenger would be examined for any contagious condition; if they did not pass, they would not be allowed to board. Her gruff voice suggested that getting through the examination would be a feat in itself. Since there were hundreds of emigrants—Germans, Poles, Slovaks and other Ukrainians like themselves—the wait was long.

Lukia understood the necessity for medical scrutiny but disliked how they were made to line up like cattle for a lice check. The male doctor in a white lab coat examined each head with a magnifying glass under a bright light and reported the results to his female assistant, also in a white lab coat, who wrote the information down. Again, Lukia worried that an official would notice she had dyed her hair. She stood ramrod straight while the doctor studied her scalp. It took only minutes, but it seemed much longer. She breathed normally again when he said, "Next," and waved her on.

After that, one by one, they entered a private room and stripped in front of the shipping line's blind female doctor who—with the help of a nurse—assessed the health of each passenger. Although Lukia silently questioned how a blind physician could be in charge, she thought nothing more of it until Elena came out of the examining room with tears in her eyes.

"What's the matter?" asked Lukia, bouncing her fussy granddaughter in her arms.

"The doctor said I have to return home."

"What? Why? What's the problem?"

"Mama, I ..." As Elena struggled to talk, Lukia handed her Genya and barged ahead of the next person into the examining room.

"Why can't my daughter-in-law go?" Lukia asked the startled doctor.

The doctor, a matronly woman with severe features, scowled. "Who's speaking?"

"Panye Lukia Mazurets." Lukia had identified herself as a married woman. "You examined my daughter-in-law and refused to sign her papers."

"The woman with the hard lump in her breast?"

"Yes."

"Panye," the doctor said, "it could be cancer or something contagious. We can't take a chance on others getting sick."

"Oy, what are you saying? We can't leave without my son and his family."

The doctor's face softened. "I'm sorry, but those are the rules."

Lukia's mind swirled with the news. She stammered, "Yes, I

understand, but she just had a child. This is nothing. Maybe you didn't see, she's a young mother."

"I don't have to see to know she's young," the doctor said sharply.

"Of course, I didn't mean ..." Lukia said, adopting a calmer tone. "Then you must know this is normal. Her breast will soften with time. Please let me talk to the agent responsible for immigration."

The doctor hesitated, then said, "It won't do any good, but you can find his office on the second floor."

Lukia grabbed the doctor's hand and shook it. "Thank you."

Without hesitation, Lukia and her family marched upstairs to the second floor. In the corridor outside the immigration agent's office, half a dozen people were waiting for a hearing. A few of the emigrants made room for Lukia and Elena on the bench by the door, while Egnat and his brothers and sister stood with the others nearby. After what felt like an interminable wait—made more anxious with Genya's crying—Lukia and Elena entered the agent's office.

The middle-aged man sitting behind the desk didn't look up. He finished arranging the papers in front of him in a neat stack, folded his hands and sat back. He regarded Lukia and Elena. "How can I help you?"

While Lukia explained the situation, the agent occasionally glanced at Elena, who was jiggling Genya to soothe her. When Lukia had finished, she said, "Please sir. One month and she should be fine to leave."

"That's impossible," he said, leaning forward and squinting as if he needed glasses. "They must go to the end of the line. They must wait a year. As it is, once you get to Canada, you'll have to sign an affidavit allowing them to join you the following year. For now, they'll have to go back to their village. I'm sorry. There's nothing I can do."

Stunned, Lukia stood there with her legs trembling. She exchanged sorrowful looks with her daughter-in-law. How could she go on without them? She'd come to rely on Egnat for more than just his help on their farm. After Gregory had died when Egnat was only sixteen, he'd acted more like a father than an older brother to his siblings. And yet, she couldn't go back to Kivertsi with her family because she'd sold everything. At least Egnat, Elena, and Genya could stay with her parents until Elena healed.

The agent cleared his throat. "Panye Mazurets, there are other people waiting."

"Please sir," she said again, her voice cracking. "Let my son and his family emigrate a month later. I beg you. I have no husband. My son is like a father to my children. I don't know how we'd manage without him."

He threw his hands up in the air. "Panye Mazurets, there's nothing more I can do. Canada has its rules."

"Then let me speak to the Canadian Consulate. Give me an interpreter."

The agent stared at her for a few moments, then said with an exasperated sigh, "Come with me." Along with her family, she followed him down the long corridor to another office, where they were told to wait outside the door. Before long, she was summoned inside.

In the largely empty room with cream-coloured walls, Lukia stood with Egnat and Elena in front of the Canadian consular official, a short, squat man in a wrinkled brown suit. Bent over his desk, his bald head shining under the harsh ceiling light, he studied their immigrant applications. Beside him sat the translator, a plump woman with greying hair pulled back in a bun. She kept glancing back to Genya in Elena's arms. Michalko, Havrylo, and Dunya fidgeted as they stood behind their mother.

After a few minutes, the official raised his head and said in English, which the translator immediately repeated in Polish,

"Panye Mazurets, your papers are in order. If your daughter-in-law heals as you expect her to, she and her family can follow you in a month's time. As long as they have the money, you understand? Your son will need five hundred zloty to emigrate with his family."

Lukia blinked. That was a lot of money, but if Egnat couldn't come, what would she do? None of her other children could replace Egnat. Without him, they would not survive.

The consular official shook his head and said to Lukia, "Panye—"

"Wait, please," Lukia said, interrupting. She mentally calculated what five hundred zloty would mean. It was half of what she had in her brassiere. Egnat stood beside her, his face drawn, his mouth curled downwards. She put a hand on his shoulder and turned back to the official. "No problem. He'll have the money."

Egnat's eyes widened.

Upon hearing the translation, the official smiled. "That's good." He wrote something on her application and signed it before handing it back to her.

Lukia thanked him and put the paper in her purse. She said to Egnat, "See, our family won't be broken."

Egnat whispered to her as they were leaving, "But Mama, the money?"

"Never mind," was all she said.

Soon after returning to the waiting area for ship passengers, Lukia said to Elena, "Come with me." They went to the toilets, where Lukia removed the banknotes she'd stitched into her brassiere and handed half to her daughter-in-law. "After what happened in Warsaw, it's better you should hold on to it."

Elena didn't question her mother-in-law and tucked the zloty into her brassiere. She said with a solemn face, "Don't worry. I'll keep them safe."

When they came out of the toilets, Elena caught Egnat's eye and patted her chest, indicating she had what they needed. Raising his eyebrows, Egnat said to his mother, "Why didn't you give me the zloty?"

Lukia cocked her head and said in a matter-of-fact manner, "You know how you like your drinks."

"I wasn't drunk when I was robbed."

"So you say. Drunk or not drunk, that money's gone." Seeing his glum face, she added, "I know you're a hard worker. No one works as hard as you, but I want to be sure you'll have the money to join me."

Looking sheepish, Egnat didn't reply.

"Oy," Lukia said softly. "I don't want to leave you."

"Don't worry, Mama. We won't be far behind."

For fear of breaking down, Lukia averted her eyes. She would pray she was right, that Elena's lump had to do with the adjustments that came with breastfeeding after childbirth. But what if she was wrong?

Egnat jutted his chin. "What are you thinking?"

"I'm thinking it won't be long before we're together again." She nodded, trying to convince herself as well.

When it came time to board the Polish steamer headed for Rotterdam, Lukia could barely tear herself away from her eldest son and family. No one was dry-eyed as they hugged and kissed each other on the dock. Before turning to go up the gangway, Lukia looked at their faces longer than usual. She wanted to commit them to memory in case she never saw them again. She shuddered; her body was in a duel with itself. One half wanted to leave; the other half was desperate to stay. She forced herself to walk away on legs that didn't want to move. Michalko, Havrylo and Dunya followed her like baby ducks. As she lumbered onto the deck, she tried to swallow the fear that had grown since she'd been told her eldest son wouldn't be able to immigrate with her.

Would Elena's lump subside? And if it did, would the authorities really allow Egnat, Elena and Genya to leave for Canada in a month's time? Could she trust the government? There were two to consider: the Polish and the Canadian one. Would the same agents be sitting there processing emigrants or would someone else take over, someone less willing to bend the rules?

She stood at the railing with Michalko, Havrylo and Dunya. On the pier below, a crowd of well-wishers was seeing loved ones off to sea. Egnat's family appeared tiny from this distance, as if they were already on the path to disappearing from her life. When the ship's bell rang, signalling their departure, Lukia bit her bottom lip to keep from sobbing aloud.

Nearby, a seaman shouted, "All ashore." The visitors on board quickly said their goodbyes and scurried down the gangplank. Since they were dressed in the latest fashion and she hadn't been allowed any guests on-board, Lukia presumed they were the friends or family of first-class passengers.

She choked back a sob as two seamen hauled the bridge back from the dock. There was no way to get off the ship now. Should she have returned to Kivertsi with Egnat? No, she couldn't have. There was nothing to go back to. Back when they returned from the refugee camp, they'd at least had their land waiting for them. Now, even that was gone.

She leaned on the rail. The dark, churning water below was as much a mystery as the land she was going to. Perhaps she'd been too hasty to leave. Governments come and go. Maybe the Poles would relax their rules. Maybe they'd be able to buy more land. Maybe Ukraine would win back its sovereignty. So many maybes! Her stomach sank further as she considered what she'd done. Leaving without Egnat, Elena and Genya had to be the biggest mistake of all. Lukia's eyes watered.

"Mama," Dunya said, snuggling against her. "Don't cry. We'll see them soon."

"Yes, daughter. We'll see them soon." She said the words, but she wasn't convinced. Doubt and fear invaded her thoughts, pushing any hope aside. She put her arm around Dunya and squeezed.

As they left the harbour, she momentarily lost sight of Egnat's family. The panic that ensued quickly abated when she spotted them again in the crowd on the dock. She waved frantically; they waved back just as frantically. Others on shore jumped and yelled at their loved ones: "Safe voyage!" "Don't forget to write!" "We'll miss you."

With Egnat, Elena and Genya fading into the distance, all Lukia could think of was: *What have I done?*

4

A MIGHTY SHIP

The small Polish steamer skirted the northern coast of Germany, past windswept cliffs and barren beaches. With little room to manoeuvre, Lukia felt the other immigrants' anxiety as she stood side by side with them on the deck and stared at the stark, unpopulated land.

Her mind drifted to her home in Kivertsi and the livestock that used to greet her daily, like the chickens that squawked when she walked by. She could get more livestock in her new country, but she wouldn't be able to replace the family she'd left behind. Memories flooded in—Gregory grabbing her breasts by surprise when she was at the stove cooking, laughing with her at their children's antics, and in the evening, sitting with her outside on a clear night, the moon for company. Those days were gone. Like the dreams she couldn't hold onto in the morning. She'd left him there, buried with their four sweet, lost children—Natinka, Fedor, Ivan and Hania—with no family to visit their graves. *But maybe I'm wrong,* she thought. Perhaps Gregory's brother would stop by and say a prayer. Maybe he'd arrange for the annual blessing. Her mother would go, but she was not long for this earth. And once she passed, who would make sure the ones who'd gone before her weren't forgotten?

"Oy, Gregory," she said under her breath. "I've given up so much."

Her mother had caught her talking to Gregory once, six years after he passed away. She said it was time to let him go. She told her mother that talking to him gave her comfort. Her mother replied, "God has to give you comfort now."

Turning to the west, Lukia let the wind caress her face. She knew her mother was right, yet she continued to reach out to Gregory, as if he could hear her. She had to stop pining for what once was. She couldn't afford to sink into despair. More than ever, she needed to be strong.

Lukia had never seen Dunya so excited. When they neared the Rotterdam port, her daughter jumped up from the bench and hurried the family along. She helped gather up their belongings on the deck before the ship had even docked. After four days of enduring the smell of unwashed bodies onboard—hers included—Lukia was looking forward to the next leg of their journey. Maybe there would be an opportunity to bathe on the ship. All she needed was a cloth, soap and some water.

After a few minutes of confusion on the dock which was sorted out in exchanges with a fellow passenger and a seaman, Lukia ushered her children to where the Nieuw Amsterdam, their ship to Canada, was anchored. Struck by the immensity of the vessel, she stood there gaping until a dock worker noticed her and said, in Polish, "She's a big one. Biggest one Holland America has ever built. She carries over a thousand passengers and has two decks." He smiled at Dunya jumping up and down. "That's one passenger who can't wait." He pointed to the ship's gangway, where a line of passengers was already forming. "You check in over there."

Lukia and her children hauled their goods to join the others in line. When they reached the front of it, she showed the family's immigration identification cards to the seaman standing beside a middle-aged woman who was acting as an interpreter. The woman examined the cards and said in Polish, "You're in third class. Make sure you don't lose these cards. You'll need them when you arrive in Halifax."

"How long will it take to get there?"

"Six or seven days, depending on the weather."

Everything was so new. The crew's efficiency made her reflect on all the years she'd spent on the farm while the rest of the world had moved ahead. And yet she couldn't imagine a life that didn't get its bearings from working the land. It was still early in the morning, but by this time back in Kivertsi, she'd have laundered the clothes in the creek and bread would be baking in the oven.

Lukia and her children stood by as their belongings were loaded into a crate, which was then hoisted and dropped into the hold of the ship. They took on board only what they needed—clothing, herbal remedies, and the icon Lukia's mother had brought back from one of her pilgrimages to Pochaev, the Ukrainian Greek Orthodox monastery famous for miracles.

At the top of the bridge, an official directed them to the bottom deck where Ukrainians and other Slavic immigrants crowded the passageways, jabbering with one another. It was comforting to hear her own language, but for how long? They weren't all going to the same place in Canada, a country bigger than the one they were leaving, with a language they didn't understand.

Squeezing through the throng, Lukia and her children found their room. It was narrow and windowless, with two bunk beds, a metal sink and, beside it, a thin towel draped over a bar. A steward walked from door to door instructing the immigrants not to take the towels with them when they reached their destination, as the passengers before them had done. The towels were to remain with the ship. They were also told to keep themselves as clean as possible, washing at the sink regularly to avoid infecting one another with disease. The steward said there was a doctor on board, but because of the many passengers on the ship, they couldn't rely on his help if someone got sick. It was therefore everyone's responsibility to stay clean.

Lukia was thankful they were all together and not crowded into one of the dormitories on board that held up to thirty people. There were approximately six hundred third-class passengers. With one toilet and one tub assigned to each group of fifty immigrants, the waiting lines were long. Outside of the cabin passageway, there was a day room and a dining room for third-class passengers. The rest of the ship was off-limits; the staircases between decks were closed off to prevent one class from mixing with the other. But no one complained. Some had heard from a seaman that conditions had been far worse only a few years back. Back then, there were no third-class passengers, only first-class, second-class and steerage. Immigrants were herded into the belly of the ship where hundreds slept together, and bathing and toilet facilities were almost non-existent.

When Lukia had her turn in the bathroom, she discovered the toilet had a flushing mechanism, something she and her family hadn't seen before. The novelty delighted her children. She, however, found it startling when she first pulled the handle and sea water ran through the bowl. She couldn't get used to the loud whoosh and the speed with which everything in the bowl vanished. Toilet paper was another surprise.

Since the lines to use the facilities were long, she worried about how she might manage in case of sickness. But despite her apprehension, using this modern bathroom made her smile for the first time that day. This kind of travel was a luxury.

Back in their cabin, her children babbled with pleasure over what they'd found and were eager to explore more of their surroundings. They grumbled when Lukia insisted they get organized first.

After they'd stored their bags under their beds, Lukia led them in prayer, asking God to give them a safe journey and unite them with their brother Egnat and his family in Canada.

"Come on, we're leaving," someone shouted in the passageway outside their door.

"I'm coming, I'm coming," a small voice replied.

Within seconds of hearing the voices in the hallway, Dunya was out the door, followed by her two brothers. Lukia joined them on the deck in time to hear the ship's whistle blow as they departed from Rotterdam. The North Sea, with its ripples of navy blue, stretched before them like a story without end. The vastness of the open water further underlined the enormity of their decision to leave everything they knew. Lukia's heart skipped a beat as they drifted farther and farther from the dock, the buildings and the land shrinking under her gaze.

That evening, in the third-class dining room, they were pleasantly surprised to find their meals served at long tables, set with quality crockery on white tablecloths. The wood benches allowed families to squeeze in together, and though there wasn't much elbow room, the arrangement was otherwise lavish. Following dinner, an orchestra comprising an accordionist, a drummer, saxophonist and a violinist played waltzes and polkas for about an hour. The conductor even encouraged some passengers to play with the spare instruments on board.

But the warm memory of a merry evening cooled the next day when they learned too late that they had missed a safety drill on deck. One passenger, a Czech woman with dyed red hair and a faint moustache, told them not to feel bad about missing it, as attending the drill wouldn't have helped. All the instructions had been given in English or Dutch. And besides, the deck had been so crowded and noisy, it was hard to see and hear the seaman demonstrating what needed to be done in an emergency.

Lukia wondered why the Czech woman had bothered to reassure her, as she didn't find any of this recount reassuring in the least. None of her children could swim, and neither could she. And even if they could, one would have to be a very long-distance swimmer to get to shore if the ship capsized in the middle of the ocean. Land on either side of the ship was barely visible.

Feeling vulnerable at sea, Lukia found it hard to digest her supper. The gentle swaying of the ship didn't help, and she grew queasy and retired early to her room.

During the night, the ship headed into a storm; fierce winds tossed the vessel, rocking it from side to side. Lukia and her children slept fairly well, but in the morning, she and Havrylo had difficulty standing without feeling seasick. The rest of the day brought no relief, and they didn't feel well enough to get out of bed, even for supper. This was not the case for Dunya and Michalko. Lukia heard them laughing and kidding one another as they bounced down the passageway towards the dining room.

Lukia and Havrylo weren't alone in their suffering. Quite a few passengers had succumbed to seasickness. Their retching sounds, along with the sour smell of vomit and the odour of unclean bodies, filled the air in the third-class quarters, which added to Lukia and Havrylo's nausea and discomfort. They stayed in their room, moaning and taking turns throwing up in a bedpan near their beds and using the sink to clean up as needed.

Steady at sea, Dunya and Michalko ventured out every evening and returned late, their cheeks rosy, their eyes sparkling, and their talk full of stories of how much they had danced and how much they had eaten. They told their mother they'd had soup, nuts, meat, vegetables, fruit and desserts. One day, they even had pickled herring. But their talk of food turned Lukia's stomach, and she tried not to heave while listening.

Michalko said, "It's like being at a dance hall on water."

Havrylo's face scrunched up in sadness.

"You don't even like dancing," Michalko said to his brother. "You're only missing the food."

"Don't tell me," Havrylo said, on the verge of crying.

Lukia gave Michalko a stern look. "Stop teasing him."

Dunya patted Havrylo's arm. "I'll see if I can bring you back something."

When the sun came out the following day, a ship's attendant asked them to leave their rooms and go up on deck so the crew could hose down the passageways and the rooms to get rid of the stench. Unsteady on their feet, Lukia and Havrylo climbed the stairs to the open deck where they immediately sat down with their backs to the water. The fresh air was exhilarating, but Lukia could not look at the sea without feeling woozy. A quick glance showed the ship tossing and rolling as it plowed through the turbulent waters. An empty metal pail had been left next to a lifeboat for anyone needing to vomit. She made a mental note of its position in case she needed it later on.

After supper the following evening, Dunya returned to the cabin with a couple of oranges and a banana for her mother and Havrylo. Her brother's pudgy face lit up when he saw the fruit.

"Who gave that to you?" Lukia asked from her bed. "You didn't steal them, did you?"

"Mama!" Dunya said, indignantly. "The cook gave them to me for helping him."

"Helping him with what?"

Dunya beamed. "I was walking by the galley and peeked in. When he saw me, I asked him if I could help. He asked if I knew how to peel potatoes. I laughed and said, of course. He put me to work and afterwards gave me oranges and bananas." She gave Havrylo an orange. "Have you ever seen anything so wonderful? You peel it."

"Eat slowly," Lukia said to Havrylo. "This may not agree with you. Your stomach is tender from all that throwing up."

Lukia took small bites of a peeled orange and welcomed the sweet taste. When the juice dribbled on her chin, she said to her daughter, "Get me a towel."

While Dunya dampened a washcloth at the sink, Michalko entered the cabin. "The captain said we're heading into a squall and we should stay in our room."

"Oy. Not another one!" Lukia crossed herself. "What hell is this? I'm not used to lying like a lazy cow. You children better get to bed, too. We don't know what tomorrow will bring."

"I want to see the waves," Dunya said as the ship pitched.

"It's not safe."

"I'll go with you," Michalko said. Ignoring their mother's warning, they dashed out of the cabin. Too weak to run after them, Lukia prayed.

Not long after, the noise of the storm intensified, along with the pitching of the ship which continued to sway back and forth. The bedpan slid out from under Lukia's bed and across the floor; a glass fell off the shelf above the sink and broke into pieces. Lukia and Havrylo held on to the sides of their bunk to keep from falling out.

"Oy, oy, oy," she moaned, while imagining Dunya and Michalko being thrown overboard into the Atlantic. If they drowned, the villagers back home would think she threw them over herself. After she and Egnat had skirted the law by lying, a few jealous villagers had nattered about Lukia, saying she planned to keep the money from the sale of her farm for herself by finding some way to kill her children during their voyage to Canada. How ridiculous! And yet, the villagers did more than gossip. Stating they wanted to preserve the children's inheritance, they had organized a referendum, a vote on whether Lukia could sell her farm. When she heard about the upcoming vote, she told Egnat to bribe the young men in the village with vodka so they would vote in her favour. The enticement worked and she won. Though she'd miss the support given by some neighbours and family, she wouldn't miss the pettiness of those who resented anyone trying to better themselves.

A sudden groan of the ship jarred her thoughts.

Where were Dunya and Michalko? What was taking them so long? "Pray with me that your sister and brother return soon," she said to Havrylo.

They prayed, and with every howl of the wind, Lukia crossed herself. Her heart pounded heavily, and she feared she was in danger of having a heart attack. Just then, Dunya opened the door, with Michalko right behind her. They stumbled into the room with their clothes drenched, their hair wet and their faces glistening in the low light from the passageway. The wind's lashing had reddened their cheeks and noses.

Trembling from the cold, Dunya said, "Mama, it was so scary!"

Michalko stuttered with excitement. "The waves were as angry as bears."

"And as high as a house," added Dunya.

"I'll give you angry if you go out again. You want me to die of a heart attack? Is that what you want? What would you do with no mother?"

Chastened, Dunya and Michalko quieted immediately.

Foolish, foolish children, thought Lukia, as she watched them ready themselves for bed.

Upon returning from breakfast, Michalko reported what he'd heard in the dining room. "The captain announced the storms have blown us one hundred and fifty miles off course."

"Don't say," Lukia said, groaning. Breathing in the smell of vomit on their deck, she feared coming down with something more serious than seasickness. How many more days could she endure?

And yet, it wasn't all misery. On this occasion, she welcomed the distraction of her daughter's incessant chatter about the folks she'd met, especially about the new friend she made while walking on the third-class promenade. "Mama, Stefka is twenty and engaged to a Canadian. She has such a beautiful white dress for her wedding. She showed it to me."

Though pleased her daughter had a companion on board, Lukia fretted about Stefka's influence. And for good reason, it turned out. Later that same day, while Lukia waited in line to use the toilet, a fellow passenger told her that Stefka had flirted boldly with several young men on the ship, even Michalko. Concerned, Lukia quickly shared the gossip with her daughter. "It's not nice, Dunya. What is Stefka thinking? Would she act that way if her fiancé was here on board with her? You can imagine what else people are saying about her." Dunya agreed, but it didn't stop her from seeking Stefka's company.

The rest of the journey turned out to be more of the same: days of calm punctuated by hours of anxiety brought about by more rolling of the ship. Whenever the ship rocked violently, Lukia was sure she'd never see land again. Because of her misgivings, she was astonished when they arrived in Halifax on August 21, only one day later than scheduled. It had taken them a month to reach Canada from their village.

5

MANITOBA BOUND

W ith the ship in dock, Lukia's seasickness was finally over, but her stomach, worn out from all the heaving, churned once more, this time with fear. The realization they were thousands of miles from home hit Lukia like a freak wave coming out of nowhere. If what they wanted in Canada didn't materialize, what then?

Eager voices and bustle outside their cabin door meant their fellow travellers were already on their way off the ship. She swallowed her fear and rose from the bunk bed. She washed her face, smoothed her hair and straightened her dress. She gave her children the once-over, stopping at Michalko to adjust his shirt collar, which was sticking up on one side, and then at Dunya, whose face showed signs of a recently eaten meal. Lukia took a handkerchief out of her sleeve and, after moistening it with water from the tap, rubbed the stains around her daughter's mouth. Havrylo needed no adjusting; he crouched to retrieve his bag from under his bed. After checking they had their belongings, Lukia and her children jostled down the passageway to the staircase leading to the main deck.

As Lukia made her way with the others towards the bridge, she inhaled deeply. The day was cloudy but warm, with barely any breeze. Across from the vessel stood a long, two-storey red-brick building, where many immigrants stood in a line waiting to go in. She took another deep breath, squared her shoulders, and said to her children, "We made it to Canada. With God's help, we'll make this land our home."

Their ship wasn't the only one arriving at Pier 21 that day. A couple of other large vessels were tied up further down the wooden boardwalk. As Lukia walked down the gangplank with her children, she wondered where in Canada Manitoba could be. She'd been told by the Canadian agent in Warsaw she would get land near a city in that province.

She stepped onto the pier and welcomed the solid ground under her feet. The pier teemed with immigrants scrambling to find out where to go next. Like her, some women wore babushkas, long dresses, and black leather oxfords. Those who had travelled in first class wore fashionable hats, shorter skirts, and shoes that would have no business in the countryside. As for the men, their attire also reflected their class. The well-to-do stepped off the ship wearing fedoras and freshly pressed suits, whereas the farmers looked as if they'd slept in theirs. Their head covering wasn't much better—a dusty tweed cap or a shabby hat with a crumpled brim.

The crowd moved slowly, but after weeks of rocking and swaying with the waves and throwing up repeatedly, Lukia didn't mind standing in line. She took off the sweater she'd worn on board and turned her face to the sun. After a few moments of savouring the sunshine, she turned to Havrylo to see how he was doing. On board, they had taken turns with the bucket. His face was still pale, but he was now laughing about something with Dunya. Lukia turned her attention back to the crowd. Though looking tired and bedraggled from their long journey, the immigrants were jubilant and expectant as they waited for their goods to be unloaded. Hope for a better future was something they all shared.

After identifying her goods and ensuring she could retrieve them after seeing the immigration authorities, Lukia and her children headed for the imposing structure in front of them.

Along with the other immigrants, an official ushered them into an immense hall on the second floor, where many newcomers—every one of them looking apprehensive—sat in rows of wooden benches waiting their turn. Two agents, middle-aged men in white shirts, ties and dark suits, sat at a table facing the seated immigrants. Lukia assumed the woman sitting next to the men was an interpreter, by the way she talked to each applicant who came forward.

One by one, people rose when their numbers were called. While Lukia waited, she played with her babushka, hoping to hide any greying hair. After a few weeks of travel, the dye she'd used to cover them had faded and recent growth had exposed her grey roots.

Lukia nudged Dunya beside her. "Have a look. Do you see any grey showing?"

Dunya scrutinized her mother's face and tucked a few loose strands under the scarf. "It's all covered. You look fine."

"Good." Lukia settled in for the wait. But fatigued from the rocky voyage, she soon fell asleep on the wooden seat.

Before long, Michalko jolted her awake with his elbow. She'd been dreaming about Gregory singing a sad song at the kitchen table. "Mama, he called our number."

"What?" She forced her eyes open. An official at the front of the hall held up a card with their number on it. "Let's go," she said as she rose. She was thankful there had been no instructions this time to go into a room to strip before meeting the agents.

One agent had narrow eyes that narrowed further when Lukia and her children approached the table. The other, a lean man with steel-blue eyes, a large forehead, and a reddish scalp under thinning hair, stared at Lukia while he peppered her with questions. He wanted to know where she was from, what her occupation was, how many children she had, and her age. While the woman seated next to him translated, the squinty-eyed agent filled the columns in his ledger, writing down numbers and words in English.

Lukia addressed her concerns to the interpreter. "My oldest son couldn't come with us. His wife had a minor problem after she delivered her child, and they had to stay back for a few weeks until she healed. I don't want to pick a farm without him."

"Not to worry," the translator said in Ukrainian. "First things first."

"Can I wait for him here?"

"It's not possible."

"Oy," Lukia said, rubbing her index finger against her thumb.

"Listen, Panye Mazurets. You have to go where they send you." She examined a paper on the table. "Winnipeg. You're going to Winnipeg."

"I was told Manitoba."

"Winnipeg's in Manitoba. It's the capital city. Your son can meet you there. He must deal with whatever happens on his own."

"Oy," Lukia said again, not even trying to hide her distress. She said no more, sensing they didn't care. But then the agent who had been squinting at them grinned. The lean one stamped her passport. The sound of the stamp on her book sounded like a musical note to her ears. At least she'd passed their scrutiny. They weren't sending her back. She'd lied about her age and gotten away with it. At fifty-four, she was four years older than the cut-off age. She couldn't help but grin.

Her smile widened when the lean agent said in Ukrainian—a pleasant surprise— "Welcome to Canada."

"Thank you," Lukia said and tucked her passport into her purse.

Hoping to exchange her money, Lukia headed to the Annex, next to the immigration building, and stood in line for the wicket with a caged opening, where a young woman sat next to an agent dispensing cash. When Lukia got to the wicket and presented her zloty, the woman took one look and said in Polish, "I'm sorry, Panye, the only currency we can exchange are bills and coins from America, Britain, France, and Italy.

Lukia harrumphed. "What kind of system is this? What am I supposed to do? How am I supposed to get to Winnipeg with no Canadian money?"

The young woman sighed out loud as if she, too, couldn't understand it. "You can change your cash at the immigration building in Winnipeg. There are lots of people going back and forth to Poland. I've been told there's been no problem exchanging money there."

Lukia frowned. The young woman had better be right, as she had only a little Canadian money, exchanged with a traveller at the train station in Warsaw. He'd just returned from Canada and willingly traded his dollars for zloty. But what if she'd been tricked? What if the money she got wasn't Canadian? She leaned forward and said, "Can I see what your money looks like?"

The clerk opened a drawer beneath the wooden counter and pulled out a couple of bills. She passed them under the bars of the wicket for Lukia to see. The bills with a picture of a king were like the ones she possessed. She had heard nothing bad about this royal, but that could be because she didn't understand the language, nor did she know anyone who knew anything about his rule. For all she knew, he could be another tsar only looking out for himself and his family. Still, she was satisfied to have the right currency.

Lukia and her children gathered their goods and headed to the Canadian National Railway platform by the Annex. A few nuns were standing by the passenger cars and giving each immigrant family a bag full of food. Peering inside the bag she received, Lukia discovered a loaf of bread, a few cans of sardines, and a long sausage marbled with more fat than she'd seen in the old country. She smelled the sausage; it was fresh enough. Though grateful for it, she missed the garlic aroma of sausages made in Volhynia. Once again, the pangs of homesickness threatened to overwhelm her as she realized how different the food would be in Canada. She gritted her teeth and pushed forward with the throng lining up to board the train. While making her way, she noticed Negro and Japanese porters ushering the immigrants into the cars. The varied races suggested Canada had opened its arms not only to Ukrainian farmers but also to others from around the globe. It was a good sign.

The Mazurecs—their name *Mazurets* had been anglicized on their Canadian documents—boarded a coach and found a couple of wooden benches with slat seats. They placed their belongings around their feet and settled down. With everything so unfamiliar, Lukia's heart raced, as if her body was expecting to do battle soon. She let out a groan so loud that Dunya, seated next to her, asked, "Mama, are you feeling all right?"

Hiding her anxiety, she patted Dunya's hand. "I'm fine."

When the train moved, Lukia clasped her hands, and once again ruminated on her decision to emigrate. So far, it had been a disaster. From the robbery in Warsaw, to leaving Egnat, Elena and Genya behind, to their ordeal at sea, it had all been hellish. Could it get any worse? The fact they were moving even farther west tied her stomach in knots. Four more days of travel. Who would have thought their eventual destination would be at such a great distance from Kivertsi, from her mother and brothers, and from the family graves?

Lukia paused her brooding when Dunya opened the window, then abruptly snapped it shut to keep out the soot from the steam locomotive. The coach was oppressively hot, but the heat was preferable to dirty air.

Within a short time of leaving the port of Halifax, Lukia

became riveted by the landscape. Not having travelled much in her life, she revelled in one extraordinary scene after another. They chugged along a coastline, rocky and dotted with seaside villages and lighthouses. They travelled over trestle bridges with expansive views of low mountains and forests similar to the ones back home. The sight of poplars brought comfort, but when they passed long stretches of tall grey rocks bordering the tracks, she worried again. Behind the granite slabs rose mountains that made her question how anyone could grow wheat on this kind of terrain. She had no guarantee the land near Winnipeg was flat, fertile and free of rock.

Dunya's babbling caused Lukia to look over at the Polish woman seated next to her daughter, who could talk anyone's ear off. She had been talking for a while and, despite the Polish woman's fidgeting, carried on with her story about the ocean crossing.

At length, the woman crooked her head and said, "That's lovely, dear, but if you don't mind, I'm going to have a nap."

"That's all right. I was finished anyway," Dunya replied. She folded her arms and stared out the window.

Lukia smiled to herself. That was one child she didn't have to worry about.

The repetitive clickety-clack of the wheels put Lukia to sleep in short order for the second time that day. She wasn't sure how long she'd slept, but when she awoke Michalko had wandered off and a young woman was sitting in his seat across from her. The woman introduced herself as Nadia from Warsaw. She was friendly enough, but from the way she sat, with her short skirt exposing too much leg, and the way she giggled and flirted with a young man who walked by their seats, her manner reminded Lukia of Stefka, the young passenger they'd encountered on the ship. The woman who had told Lukia about the missed fire drill said that Stefka had slept with a few sailors during their crossing.

And Havrylo had hinted that Michalko had taken a turn, too, which not only annoyed Lukia but also made her worry about her son's judgment. Wayward women could carry disease from one man to another. Because of Michalko's roving eye, Lukia knew he'd be one son at risk of catching something or getting some woman pregnant. If that happened, no matter who she was, he'd have to marry her. It was only right. As soon as Egnat joined them in Canada, she would ask him to explain to his younger brother the pitfalls of going after wild women.

She tried not to stare at Nadia, who talked so loudly other passengers turned to gawk. "I hope he's as cute as his photo," the young woman said.

"What if he isn't?" asked Dunya innocently.

"Well," Nadia said, "a promise is a promise. He paid for my trip over, so ..." Her voice trailed off.

Watching Nadia flirt with passersby made Lukia consider her own looks. It had been a long time since she'd fussed about her hair. She'd developed the habit of simply combing her hair back and twisting it into a bun, fastened by bobby pins. It was the most practical hairstyle. The wind couldn't get at it and obscure her vision when she was out in the fields. And there would be no hair found in her cooking and baking, either. Dreaming about a new hairdo was pointless, as it was one luxury she couldn't afford. Besides, why change now? She wasn't looking for a new husband.

They passed through a mountain tunnel and, soon after, arrived in Montreal.

"This is where I get off," Nadia said.

The tall buildings in the cityscape resembled the ones in Warsaw.

"They speak French here, you know." Nadia straightened up as if to underline the importance of this information. "My fiancé speaks both French and English."

"I thought everyone spoke English in Canada."

"Not in Quebec. This is where the French settled. That's what he told me in his letter."

Lukia digested this information and wondered what other surprises were in store.

When Nadia disembarked, her young man was waiting for her. Lukia and her children strained at the window to see them greet one another and embrace. After they'd hugged, he said something that made Nadia back away. Then he left without even looking back. She froze for a while, then vanished into the crowd.

His action was startling. Lukia had been critical of the young woman's behaviour, but what could have possessed him to abandon her so soon after she'd arrived? Had he received news from his former village in Poland that she'd fooled around with other men? Was he disenchanted with her looks—not that he was any prize? He had a stooped posture and, though fairly young, was already losing his hair. His demeanour suggested he carried his problems on his back, not a good indicator for a happy marriage. Perhaps there was another woman in his life and he had come to tell Nadia that his life had changed since he'd last written. What was the Polish girl supposed to do now? How many young women's hearts were broken because they hadn't taken the time to know someone first before making a commitment?

Lukia hoped her daughter was paying attention. Nadia's perkiness and worldly nature had enthralled Dunya, but the young woman's tragic meeting was a lesson on the affairs between men and women. One that should give anyone pause.

As the train chugged away again, an older woman with wavy blond hair began passing out slices of white bread. When she got to Lukia, she took a quick look at her children and gave her two slices.

The colour of the bread was shocking. Lukia had never seen bread that white before. It tasted fine, but the soft texture made it hard to chew and pieces of it glued together in her mouth.

The well-groomed man across the aisle asked the woman who was handing out the bread if he could see the wrapping. She handed the loaf to him—only half remained—and waited while he read the print on the waxed paper.

Lukia admired the man not only for his facility with the English language but also because she'd heard him speak Ukrainian to a fellow passenger. She cleared her throat. "Excuse me, what kind of flour is it made of?"

"White flour." He grinned. "It's a new kind of bread called Wonder Bread."

Lukia chortled. It was a good name for a loaf so unbelievably white. "What a country!"

"Yes."

"Are you going to farm in Manitoba, too?"

"No. I have a grocery store in Winnipeg. I emigrated from Ternopol twenty years ago." That was an oblast south of Volhynia. "I'm returning from a visit to my parents in the old country. I wanted them to immigrate, but you know how it is. They're too old now."

An image of her mother, standing in the doorway with her head bowed, filled her mind. She was too old to immigrate as well. He was right. She knew how it was.

He pulled a book out of his satchel and began to read. She said nothing more. She wished she could read. It would be a good way to pass the time. But outside of travelling, when would she ever have time to read, even if she could?

It wasn't long before they passed a rolling landscape, more promising for farming. There were lakes hugging the tracks and orchards with fruit ready to pick. A day later, when they stopped at a depot called Port Arthur, she and her children got off the train to stretch their legs. The Ukrainian grocer joined them on the railway platform and pointed out a grain elevator nearby. He told her there would be many more in Manitoba, another day away by train.

6

A MATTER OF TRUST

As the train approached the border of Manitoba, Lukia and her children looked in awe at the spectacular vistas of crystal-clear lakes amid rocky terrain and woodlands of oak, pine, and birch. An hour later, the land flattened and became endless fields of grain. Hope surged in Lukia's heart as she viewed the golden stalks of wheat. If all went well in Winnipeg, she'd soon have a farm of her own and could put aside her doubts about immigrating once and for all.

When they finally arrived at Union Station in Winnipeg—a structure that looked like a palace—a Dominion Lands agent was waiting to escort the immigrants to the Immigration Hall near the tracks on Water Street.

Along with other women and their families, Lukia and her children were put up in private rooms with bunk beds on the third floor, which also included laundry and bathroom facilities. Men were given accommodations on the second. After the long trip, clean clothes and a bath did much to brighten their spirits. Meals took place in the communal kitchen on the main floor as well as at a lunch counter. In addition, if desired, staples for cooking could be purchased at a reasonable cost at a shop in the vicinity. If this was what the government was willing to provide for new immigrants, she thought the future might be rosy indeed.

Lukia's initial excitement about reaching her destination didn't last long, as she began to worry anew about Egnat and his family back in Volhynia. She immediately asked Michalko to write to his brother, informing him of their arrival in Winnipeg and where he could send a reply to their letter.

She didn't want to pick a farm without her eldest son's counsel. But what if he never came? The thought was terrifying, especially since the Dominion Lands agent had said all immigrants had to find something within days of their arrival. She hadn't considered that she might have to manage on her own in the next while. Her other two sons were not as knowledgeable or as hard-working as Egnat.

She took some comfort from the fact that other Ukrainian immigrants seemed just as anxious. They gossiped among themselves, trading any information they had. Lukia quickly learned that all the farmland close to the city had been taken by the earlier immigrants, which meant that any grain grown on the land still available would have to be transported by railway at great cost.

It wasn't what the Canadian government had advertised. The posters in Lutsk had made it sound as though there was plenty of good, arable land available for anyone willing to make the trip overseas. Lukia berated herself, thinking she should have known governments can't be trusted. She'd had her trials in the old country, so why had she assumed this one would be any different?

With good farmland seemingly in short supply, she wasted no time in the morning. She hurriedly ate her breakfast, then went downstairs to the immigration office on the main floor. Though it had just opened, the cavernous room was already teeming with immigrants waiting to talk to one of the staff standing behind the glass-topped, polished wood counter. Festooned above were thick garlands of dried wheat, and on each of the three supporting posts rising from the long counter hung framed pictures of farms at harvest time. The décor gave the impression Manitoba's crops were bountiful in a land of plenty. Behind the counter were at least ten desks, at which sat officious-looking men and one woman in a high-necked blouse with puffy sleeves and a locket around her neck. Behind them, under the high, arched windows, stood uniformed men in peaked caps. Overwhelmed by the grandeur of the place, Lukia stood gawking in the sunlight streaming into the room.

After catching her breath, she approached a uniformed man by the room's entrance and asked where she could find the Dominion Lands agent. Fortunately, he spoke Polish. He pointed to an older man in a brown tweed suit, white shirt and tie, standing in the hallway, talking to a hopeful homesteader who kept gripping the brim of his cap as he listened. The agent seemed pleasant enough, with his kind brown eyes and a reddened, pear-shaped nose, which probably came from too much drinking.

While she waited her turn to speak to the agent, she couldn't help overhearing him say in Ukrainian, "You can take however long to decide, but we can only support you for a few days here. If you can't find anything, you and your children will have to stay in a hotel and find some kind of work in the meantime." Placing his hand on the immigrant's arm, the agent added, "We can help you with that as well. Many farmers need hired hands, and there are city residents who could use household help. Your wife and daughters can find employment there."

"Thank you," the homesteader said and nodded to Lukia as he left.

She stepped up to the agent. "I'm Panye Mazurec. We arrived yesterday. I've heard all the good land close to Winnipeg is gone. What do we do now?"

The agent ran his fingers through his fine brown hair. "Panye, it's true, but Canada is large. There's plenty of land left."

"When can I see one of these farms?"

"You can see one tomorrow. There's a good one near Ethelbert."

"Ethelbert," she said, the foreign word struggling on her tongue. "Where is that?"

"Two hundred and thirty-five miles north of here."

"Oy. That will take most of the day to get there. Nothing closer?"

"A lot of Ukrainians have settled there. There's both a Catholic and Orthodox church in town." At the mention of an Orthodox church, Lukia warmed to the idea. "The CNR has a train that'll take you right to the village. I can arrange for a real estate agent to go with you."

"If that's the best you can do, I'll have a look."

He flipped a page in his notebook and ran his finger down a list of names. "I see you have an older boy. He could start earning money while you look for a homestead."

"How?"

"Since you've arrived at harvesting time, there's plenty of work available for strong young men like your son. Pan Meronek has a farm near Stonewall, twenty miles from Winnipeg. He needs a couple of hired hands."

"Our people?"

"Yes. The Meroneks came over with the last wave."

"I'll tell my son." An uneasiness settled in her stomach, one she expected would stay until Egnat and his family could join her.

7

ETHELBERT

W hile Lukia waited in the immigration office to meet the agent who would take her to Ethelbert, Michalko reassured her about his new job as a hired hand. "Don't worry, Mama. If Dunya and Havrylo have a problem, the agent will know how to find me."

"Good," she said, despite her discomfort at leaving her two youngest while she travelled a fair distance. It was what the government had advised. Dunya and Havrylo would stay in the Immigration Hall and watch over their possessions.

A young woman in a pale blue chemise—a new style Lukia recognized—and a middle-aged man in a fine wool suit approached Lukia. The young woman said in Ukrainian, "Panye Mazurec, this is Pan Tachiuk, a real estate agent. He'll be showing you the property in Ethelbert." She batted her blue eyes at Michalko, then turned back to Lukia. "We'll make sure your children are comfortable."

"Thank you."

As the immigration worker walked away, Michalko followed her with his eyes.

Mr. Tachiuk said, "Nu, Panye Mazurec, are you ready to go?"

"Yes, but give me a minute, please."

She beckoned Michalko to her side and said, out of the real estate agent's earshot, "Remember, we're strangers here. People will judge us before they even know us."

Michalko tapped his foot. "I know, Mama, I know."

"I'm not just talking about that young woman," Lukia said. "It's important you show up on time for work and do your job well."

"I know," he said irritably. He gave her a quick kiss, then went over to the immigration worker in the blue chemise who was back at her post behind the counter. Her middle son could charm anyone. Up to now, his older brother had kept him on a straight track. But Egnat wasn't here, and Michalko, who'd always had a mind of his own, was now twenty—an age at which he listened to no one. He was his father's son. Gregory hadn't listened, either.

It took most of the day to get to Ethelbert. The train rolled by one homestead after the other, stopping along the way at various small towns. Outside these settlements, the land went on forever, blending with the horizon in the distance. The fields full of golden wheat swayed with the late summer breeze, as if keeping step to a fiddler's waltz, their last chance to party before being cut down.

The sight of farmers threshing their grain made her wonder how the new owners of her farm in Volhynia were faring, and whether they were content with its yield. Winter was still a few months away, but would Egnat get here before the snows came? And would she be able to find land that would satisfy their needs? Or would she and her children be set adrift, like a boat with no anchor and no shore in sight?

After a stopover in Dauphin, a small city featuring a majestic train station built with dormers, turrets, stone and brickwork, they pulled into the town of Ethelbert. Lukia immediately noticed a grain elevator farther down the tracks. It was a promising sight, but the most heartening one was a Ukrainian Greek Orthodox church with its gleaming onion-shaped domes—a place to find solace in a strange country.

Mr. Babiak, a Ukrainian farmer from the district, greeted them at the station. The government's provision of a local farmer who spoke her native language eased the pain of being so far from all that was familiar.

The three adults sat in the front of his wagon as they trundled down roads as bumpy as those back in the old country. Mr. Babiak said, "There's a quarter section close to town that hasn't been settled yet." While they rode, they exchanged information about the oblasts they had come from. The farmer had been in the area for ten years and said that at least in Canada he was free from worrying about which army was going to march next over his land.

They'd been driving for about a mile, past fields ready for harvesting, when the agent pointed to a dilapidated house ahead. "That's the one."

Mr. Babiak said, "The house is old but well insulated. With a little fixing and paint, it'll make a fine home."

"What happened to the man who owned it?"

"Pneumonia. After he died, his children moved to Ontario. They weren't interested in working the land." He made a face. "It's different here in Canada. It's hard to keep your offspring on the farm when there are good jobs on the railway or in the city."

It saddened Lukia to hear about a family breaking up like that. She'd grown up with the idea it was a child's duty to stay with the land. It was a corner of the earth that was yours; it gave you security when all else failed.

The agent pulled the wagon to a stop before they reached the house. Mr. Babiak climbed down first and gave Lukia a hand. Together they crossed the gravel road to the fallow field. In every direction, there were sections populated by stumps and bushes that would have to be cleared.

"This land doesn't look like it's even been tilled."

"He wasn't much of a farmer," Mr. Babiak said, "and his son was lazy. They had only dug up part of the field before the farmer got ill. Can't blame him for the house. It's much the way he found it."

Lukia picked up a handful of the brown, coarse soil and let it slip through her fingers, leaving behind a fist full of large pebbles. Her chest tightened. This earth wasn't black like the earth in Volhynia.

"Well," the farmer said, turning his gaze on her. "What do you think?"

She cleared her throat and said, "I'm sorry. I'm going to wait until my oldest son arrives. I don't want to buy anything without him."

He tilted his head. "Then why did you come all this way if you were going to wait?"

"Listen," she said, "I don't buy anything without seeing it first. There's a reason this one is still for sale. I'm not going to jump into anything. I expected to find some land that was promising, but ..." Her voice trailed off. Sure, the government was offering a quarter section of land for ten dollars, but the authorities expected a good return for their generous offer. Immigrants had to promise to spend at least six months of each of the first three years living on the land and making improvements. That meant not only maintaining a house, a barn, and a barbed-wire fence, but also cultivating land—in many cases, land that hadn't been plowed by anyone before them. Poor soil filled with stones wasn't mentioned on the posters advertising for farmers to come to Canada.

Frowning, Mr. Babiak left her side and joined the agent who was standing by the wagon. The sun was so bright she had to shield her eyes while she waited for the men to finish talking about her decision. The agent took off his fedora and wiped his brow with a handkerchief he'd taken out of his pants pocket. Replacing his hat, he mumbled something.

Moments later, Mr. Babiak motioned her over. "Panye Mazurec, it's the only acreage available around here." When she hesitated, he added, "Think carefully. All good land is going fast."

She snorted. *This isn't good land.* As if agreeing, the wind whistled plaintively around her ears.

"You know, Panye Mazurec," Mr. Babiak said, "the authorities expect immigrants to find something quickly. That's why they only put you up for four days."

Her forehead pleated. "I won't quarrel with you, but this is a big decision. I need to consult with my son."

Mr. Babiak rubbed the back of his neck, then looked at the agent, who crooked his finger, signalling he wanted to talk to him once more. Mr. Babiak left Lukia's side to huddle with the agent, their faces so intent that Lukia speculated they were going to force her to buy this horrible land. While she waited for them to finish talking, a black and white dog that had wandered up the road caught her attention. In time, she and her children would get a puppy of their own. One that knew how to herd cows.

Mr. Babiak returned to Lukia. "We understand. It's hard to buy a homestead on your own, but the problem is, you need to work while you wait for your son. There's a poor family near here, the Olynyks; they would welcome some help. You and your children can stay with them until your son and his family arrive."

"That would suit us fine," Lukia said, grateful they'd accepted her decision.

She could see the men were disappointed. But did they know how afraid she was about her family's future? What if there was no arable land left in Manitoba? What if this was all there was? If so, she could expect more sleepless nights. Her sleep had first become troubled when Gregory joined the Tsar's army fifteen years ago and left her to fend for herself. After that, there had been no rest from uncertainty. *Please God,* she said silently, *please help me find a better farm in Canada.*

Mr. Tachiuk arranged for Lukia to meet Dunya and Havrylo the next day at the Ethelbert train station. Her children brought all their belongings, and the Ukrainian farmer once again met Lukia with his wagon.

Mr. and Mrs. Olynyk turned out to be gracious hosts, but because they were poor, the only sleeping arrangement they could offer was a spot in their barn. There, Lukia and her children slept on a bed made of hay covered with the heavy cotton cloth they'd brought from the old country. Lukia could not believe how desperate they'd become. They had lived meagrely in Volhynia but never had to sleep with animals before. The smell of cows defecating close to their beds was particularly unsettling, but there was nothing that could be done. She kept telling her children they were fortunate to have a place to lay their heads at night.

While Lukia and Havrylo helped with chores, Dunya got work for fifty cents a day as a live-in housekeeper for another Ukrainian family, a few miles from the Olynyks. It was on a well-to-do farm with twenty-three cattle. With her family split and no word from Egnat, Lukia's dream of security in Canada faded with each passing day. She dismissed the temptation to write Egnat and tell him to stay home, because then what would she do if he didn't come? What would he do? He couldn't rely on Elena's parents to support his family. The shame of that would be too great. She felt as if she'd climbed onto a merry-go-round that wouldn't stop. She'd bought her ticket, but it wasn't for the ride she'd dreamt of.

Several days later, Michalko showed up unexpectedly at the Olynyk farm. He told his mother he had a few days off and wanted to see how she was managing.

Lukia wasted no time telling him of the job Dunya had secured. She also mentioned she'd had no word since his sister left. Concerned, Michalko offered to go check on her.

A few hours later, Lukia was outside beating a rug when she saw a black car pull up at the end of the farm road. Michalko got out of the sedan, nodded to the driver who had given him a ride, and walked towards her with his head bent and his shoulders stooped.

"Michalko, what's the matter?" asked Lukia. "How's Dunya doing?"

"Mama, they're going to kill her." The grave look on his face was one she hadn't seen before. "They make her scrub their floors with a brush and then, an hour later, the men come in for lunch and stomp on the floors with their muddy boots. They soil them so badly she has to wash them all over again after they leave." His forehead creased further. "Not only that, but they have no pump. She has to fill all the troughs by hand from a well for twenty-three cattle, then haul water into the house for the kitchen as well."

"Oy, they're so rich and they have no pump?"

"I also saw the food they're giving her. Scraps, after all the others have eaten."

Lukia didn't ask him to elaborate. Without hesitating, she said, "Go bring your sister home."

After that, Lukia found other work for Dunya and Havrylo, picking low-bush cranberries—each filling a pail daily. The grocer in town gave them little for their efforts, but it was better than nothing.

Less than a week later, Mr. Babiak drove up the Olynyks' farm road in his wagon. Seated on a bench outside, Lukia looked up from her work, separating the ripened cranberries from bits of twig, leaves and green, unripened berries. Beside her, Dunya and Havrylo were cleaning the berries as well.

Mr. Babiak got out of his car and waved a letter. "Panye Mazurec, I have something for you."

With trepidation, she took the letter from him. The postmark was from their village of Kivertsi. The handwriting was Egnat's. Lukia waited until Mr. Babiak went inside the house to talk to Mrs. Olynyk, then swallowed hard. Expecting the worst, her hands shook as she tore open the envelope. She handed the letter to Havrylo. "Read it."

"Dear Mama, I hope you and my brothers and sister are well. We are finally on our way. The doctor said it was fine for Elena to go."

"Thanks be to God," Lukia said and crossed herself.

Havrylo continued to read. "You were right, Mama. The lump went away. And more good news. Uncle Petro found someone to manage his properties, and they'll be coming with us. By the time you get this letter, we'll be on the ship. Your son, Egnat."

"Such good news."

Dunya kicked up her heels with such exuberance that Lukia cried out, "Dunya, watch the pail! You'll spoil all our hard work."

Even if the pail had spilled, Lukia wouldn't have been upset for long. They had no farm yet, but at least they'd all be together soon.

8

UNITED AGAIN

Lukia's heart pumped wildly as the steam locomotive pulled into Union Station. She strained to see into the passenger cars, but the smoky haze from the train's engine impaired her view. However, it wasn't long before the visibility improved and the windows showed people rising and gathering their things. But no Egnat, Elena and Genya. Where were they? Her palms sweated. Did they miss the train?

Dunya and Havrylo ran ahead, searching each car for signs of their brother and his family. Lukia looked up and down the platform, hoping to see her son in the throng disembarking from the train. Young and old struggled with their possessions as they met familiar loved ones or headed out of the station on their own.

Dunya returned breathless, with Havrylo close behind. "They're not here," she said.

Lukia stood on her toes to see past a couple of tall men blocking her view down the track.

"Mama!" It was Egnat's voice.

"There they are!" shouted Dunya.

Lukia turned. She couldn't believe her eyes. Egnat was walking towards her, loaded down with a battered suitcase and a heavy sack, followed by Elena, carrying Genya in one arm and a carpetbag in the other. Joy rippled through Lukia and she laughed out loud.

"Thank God!" Lukia said, clutching Egnat tightly. After they embraced, she held her son at arm's length to have a good look. His short brown hair and full moustache had been neatly trimmed, and his brown eyes shone; the strain of the past month barely showed on his handsome face. Overcome at seeing him, she unexpectedly teared up.

"Mama, why are you crying?"

"Oy, I thought I'd never see you again."

"I believed that, too."

"My God, my God, you're here. And my dear Elena." Lukia kissed and hugged her. "You've come a long way. How was your trip?"

"You know," Elena said, "I only threw up once on the ship."

"Only once? You did well. I don't care if I ever go on one again." She fondled Genya's skinny arms and legs. "Look how she's grown. She's delicate. Is she getting enough milk?"

"I was small-boned, too."

"You still are." Lukia furrowed her brow. "Are you trying to lose weight? You're so thin."

"I'm like I always was. I lost all the weight I put on in pregnancy."

Lukia took Genya and bounced her in her arms. "Such a pretty baby."

From behind her, a scratchy voice bellowed. "Sister. I hope you have a fine dinner waiting for us."

Turning, she beamed. "You haven't eaten?" She poked Petro's broad belly. "What are you hiding in there?"

"This is how you greet me?" Rocking his head from side to side, he said to his family, "It must be the new Canadian way."

"Ha." Lukia handed Genya back to Elena and hugged her brother, then stepped back to admire his long, black velvet coat.

"You're dressed like you were expecting to meet the king."

"Of course," Petro said, twisting his moustache and twirling in front of her. His blue eyes twinkled. "Have I missed him?"

Lukia laughed. If there had been room, she would have danced just to show her family how happy she was they'd arrived.

Her sister-in-law stepped forward, carrying six-month-old Tony. "Lukia, you're looking well."

Pleased with the compliment, Lukia said, "You know, I do what I can." She turned her attention to Tony. "He's so big now."

"Yes. I'm developing muscles I didn't know I had."

"Good you're all here," Lukia said. "Maybe we can get settled soon."

"We'll see," Anna said, in a tone suggesting nothing had changed between her and Petro. They stayed together because, as Lukia's mother often said, you make your bed, you lie in it.

Lukia's gaze shifted to her children. They were kibbitzing with their cousins—six of them, ranging from five to eighteen. At least they got along. There was nothing like family to ease the discomfort of being in a new land.

"Let's go," Lukia said. She and her children grabbed some baggage. When she spotted the large pot tied to Petro's trunk, carried by her two oldest nephews, she added, "Such a great banyak! You can make a lot of holupchis in that one." If they ended up living close to one another, she would borrow it for special occasions.

As they proceeded to the station's exit, Lukia fell into step beside Egnat. "Did you see Babcha?"

"No. Babcha went back to live with Djajo Pavlo. She's still running around curing people."

Upon hearing her brother was taking care of their mother—in the Carpathian Mountains, about four hundred kilometres from Kivertsi—Lukia breathed a sigh of relief. If anything happened, he would write and let his sister know. "And Dmitro? How's he doing?"

"You know Dmitro. He still pines for you. He told me to tell you if you ever change your mind, he'll be waiting."

"Ha," she said. "Too bad he never found himself another wife." Dmitro had proposed only a few months after his wife, Irina, had died. Gregory's sister had been an angel. She had given them shelter and food when they returned from the refugee camp in the Caucasus. But his too-short mourning period wasn't the only reason she rejected Dmitro. "How could I marry him? He drinks too much."

The surrounding commotion was growing. Tired of shouting over the station crowd to be heard, Lukia grew quiet and steeled herself for a later talk with Egnat and her brother. Though dreading their reactions, she'd have to tell them what she'd discovered since landing in Manitoba.

On their way out of the station, Lukia's newly arrived family stopped to admire the waiting room with its grand rotunda, glass-panel ceiling, and intricately designed marble tile floor. Anna and Petro were surprised to find such opulence in Canada. He grunted and said, "So, this is Veeneepeg!"

"Yes," Lukia said. "Like Lutsk. Some fine buildings, but some not so fine."

More astonishment followed as they exited the station onto Main Street, its avenue wide enough to accommodate six lanes of traffic and streetcar tracks down the middle. The excitement of being reunited buoyed them as they made their way down the sidewalk to the Immigration Hall. Weighed down with bags and valises, Dunya, Havrylo and their cousins lagged behind. The children's enthusiastic conversation and occasional laughter competed with the traffic noise—the clackety sounds of the streetcars, automobile horns, and a peddler's cries from his horse-drawn cart.

Walking alongside Egnat, Lukia asked, "Does Elena have the money I gave for safekeeping?"

"Of course." He patted the chest pocket of his jacket. When she raised her eyebrows, he said, "I made a mistake once. It's safe with me. You know, the authorities wouldn't have let us come otherwise."

"Good. We'll need it to set up a farm." She adjusted the bag in her hand. "How did you manage when you returned to the village? The people must've been surprised when you came back."

"They taunted us."

"What? Who did?"

"You know, the ignorant ones. They kept saying, 'Oh, Canada, oh Canada,' in a singsong voice. I didn't pay attention. I knew if they had a chance, they'd emigrate in an instant."

Lukia muttered, "If they only knew. It's not exactly what I expected."

"What do you mean?" Egnat stopped walking and stared at his mother.

"Keep walking. I don't want Uncle to hear." She turned to see where he was. Petro was several steps back, walking with Elena. Lukia suspected he was bothering her daughter-in-law. He tended to say foolish things, as if every young woman fancied him.

"Why would it matter if he heard?" Egnat asked.

Lukia dismissed her son's question with a wave of her hand and resumed her pace. "I've tried, but it hasn't been easy to find good land. I was tempted to write and tell you to stay in Volhynia."

"Is it that bad?"

"Oy, son. The agent sent me to Ethelbert, a day's ride away by train. A nice community. Lots of our people. They even have an Orthodox church. But the land was awful. Full of stones. I don't know how the government expects us to grow wheat in that soil."

"What's this about the government?" asked Petro, coming up beside her.

Not wanting to admit she might have made a mistake coming

to Canada, she changed the subject. "Did you get your property settled?"

Petro grimaced. "I did what I could. It's a good thing we left when we did. They're hanging aristocrats now. It would have been our turn next."

"No! The Bolsheviks? And they say they're for the people."

"They can't wait to get their hands on any wealth. They want everyone to be at the same level so they can control them."

Egnat glanced behind at the Korneluk children, talking with Dunya and Havrylo. "Where's Michalko?"

"He's working as a hired hand north of here. At the Meroneks' farm."

"Ukrainians?"

"Yes," Lukia said, smiling.

No more was said, as they'd arrived at the Immigration Hall. She'd given Egnat some idea of the challenges they had faced since arriving. She knew he was disappointed. It wasn't what any of them had expected. Next, she'd have to tell her brother. Petro would not take such news lightly.

While her brother and son and their families rested from the long trip, Lukia went downstairs to the immigration office. Tomorrow was Sunday, and she wanted to find a church. She hadn't been to one since leaving Kivertsi. She was unhappy with their predicament, but she wanted to at least thank the Lord for bringing her family safely across the ocean.

She approached the clerk who spoke Ukrainian and asked if there were any Ukrainian Greek Orthodox churches in Winnipeg. The young woman's blue eyes crinkled. "Yes, there are three."

"Three?" Lukia couldn't believe that a Canadian city had three where she could practice her faith. Her heart pounded as if she'd struck gold. "Do you know anything about the congregations?"

"Just a moment." The clerk approached a willowy man sitting

at a desk under a tall, arched window. As the young woman talked, he peered at Lukia over his reading glasses, then wrote something down on a piece of paper.

With the note in hand, the young woman returned to the counter. "They're all quite different. Saint Michael's congregation, north of here, on Disraeli Street by the Red River, is full of people from Bukovina. Ivan Suchavsky is on Main Street, but we know little about it except that it has roots in America. And Saint Mary's the Protectress Sobor, on Sinclair Street and Burrows, has immigrants from Volhynia."

"Volhynia. That's the oblast I'm from. Is Sobor far from here?"

"Maybe an hour by streetcar. You can catch one on Main Street, a half block from here. You have to go north."

Lukia could hardly contain her glee as the young woman wrote the directions. She couldn't wait to tell her family about the church she'd found in Canada.

Unfortunately, the next day, no one in her family was as enthusiastic as Lukia about attending the divine liturgy. Egnat complained that they were still tired from their cross-country trip. Petro said he and his family never went to church in the old country and they weren't about to start in Winnipeg. Lukia grumbled about his lack of faith. Gregory had turned his back on religion as well. If he hadn't, she believed he'd still be alive. When she repeated the story of how Gregory hadn't paid attention to her bad dream and hadn't crossed himself before he went into the woods, where a tree felled him, Petro said that was foolish thinking—that crossing yourself changed nothing. She clucked her lips. No one would convince her otherwise.

Lukia boarded a streetcar with Dunya and Havrylo. As instructed by the immigration clerk, she gave the conductor the right change—twenty-five cents for six tickets, enough for going there and back. She sat across from her children on one of the two wine-coloured plush benches that ran the length of the car on each side. Above the benches hung straps for passengers to hold while standing, but this morning there was no need, as the car was half empty. The half dozen well-dressed passengers looked as if they, too, were going somewhere to worship. The driver, who stood as he drove, pressed a pedal by his feet and a gong sounded. He waved his arm at someone outside the front window. An old man in a horse and cart was taking his time crossing the tracks. The streetcar driver complained loudly before moving on.

Lukia and her children appreciated the view as they crossed the intersection of Portage and Main—two extraordinarily wide streets busy with streetcars, bicycles, automobiles, and horses and buggies. Farther down the route, the City Hall on Main Street resembled something out of a storybook, with its red and grey striped exterior, brick and stone construction, turrets on all four corners and an ornate clock on top. They passed commercial establishments and were astonished to see, on the right side, the palace-like Royal Alexandra Hotel with its stately train station, a rival to the one they'd used. When they turned left—after about six blocks—onto Selkirk Avenue, Lukia straightened up. The immigration clerk had told Lukia that this street was an Eastern European shopping mecca. She craned her neck to view shops, banks, a synagogue, a church, schools, and doctors' offices all along the street. This being Sunday, the stores were empty and dark. Perhaps, one day, she'd have time to explore the area.

Getting to their final stop took longer than she'd expected. Once they got off the streetcar at Sinclair, they had to run three blocks to Sobor. When they finally arrived at St. Mary's the Protectress, half out of breath, Lukia blinked twice. There was no handsome building with grand double doors and five golden domes, like the ones in Volhynia, or even like the one in Ethelbert.

Instead, there was only a concrete finished basement with a roof on top. The only sign this was a Greek Orthodox church was the Orthodox cross with its three bars engraved on one of the corner concrete blocks.

Lukia hated being late for the religious service and took a deep breath before opening the side door to the basement. They stepped down to the underground hall, where the service was already in progress. What struck her as unusual were the rows of folding chairs filled by the congregation. Back home, the parishioners had to stand for the three-hour service, as there was no place to sit. Obviously, Canadians had to be pampered. She also noticed the men wore suits, and the women were more fashionably dressed than those back home. There were a few babushkas like the one she wore, but they were mostly on older women. The others wore lovely straw hats with flowers. Lukia was sure her daughter would make a fuss about her babushka later and beg for a hat.

After they'd seated themselves at the back, Lukia went up the centre aisle towards the brass candle holder in front of the iconostasis, the partition separating the nave from the sanctuary. Though uncomfortable walking up the aisle in front of an unfamiliar crowd, she had to do it. She always lit candles for dead loved ones when attending the divine liturgy, so they'd burn while the priest led the congregation in prayers. She took a few Canadian coins from the side pocket of her dress, dropped them into the ceramic dish near the candlestand, and took six beeswax candles out of the wooden box. As she lit each one, she prayed silently for her four departed children, her husband and her father.

On the left side of the hall, the choir stood to sing the Nicene Creed. Back in her seat, Lukia mouthed, "I believe in one God ..." She sang the rest of the prayer along with the choir and admired the beautifully painted iconostasis. Behind its three arched doors, bordered in gold and surrounded by images of Christ and his disciples, the priest was blessing the wine and bread.

She missed her church in Lutsk but found comfort at the end of the service when the congregation sang Ukraine's national anthem with passion: "Ukraine hasn't died yet, nor its glory and freedom. Upon us, my young brothers, fate shall yet smile. Our enemies will perish, like dew in the morning sun. And we too shall rule, brothers, in our own land." As long as she could remember, Ukrainians had fought for independence. They'd had it for about a year after the Great War, only to lose it again. Now Poland ruled the west, and the east had returned to the rule of Russia. She'd left that constant turmoil behind, but the land was in her blood. It would always be.

After the service, she lined up with the other congregants to kiss the ornate gold cross in Father Sawchuk's hand. He welcomed her to the parish, then beckoned to a sturdily built man in a loose-fitting grey suit, who was busy scraping the dripped wax off one of the brass candle holders.

"Panye Mazurec," Father Sawchuk said, "this is Arkadi Karpinsky, president of the Men's Auxiliary. He can answer any questions you have about the parish." She guessed that Arkadi was around her age, because of his thinning hair combed neatly across his shiny scalp and the fine wrinkles around his eyes.

Lukia followed Arkadi to the right side of the nave, where they could talk without holding up the line of congregants waiting to kiss the cross.

"When did you arrive?" he asked. "Are you settled yet?"

"Nu, you know how it is. I've been waiting for my son to come. We had our troubles. We have yet to find some suitable land."

"I know. My wife and I have been here half a year now, and we're still looking."

"Don't tell me," she said, frowning.

"Ah, here she is." He gestured to a pleasant-looking woman with tightly curled brown hair and wide-set, warm eyes, walking towards them. She wore a button-front print rayon dress similar to Lukia's. "Maria," Arkadi said, "this is Panye Mazurec."

"It's lovely to meet you, Maria. You can call me Lukia. Your husband said you haven't found a homestead yet."

"No. We're staying with friends."

Lukia sighed. "This is news I didn't want to hear."

"What can we do?" Maria said, shrugging.

"Well, at least I found this church. Thank God for that. Are there any plans to finish the building?"

"Of course," Arkadi said. "You know, the congregation dug the basement by hand. Now, we're raising money for further construction. The Ukrainian National Home Choral and Dramatic Society puts on concerts and plays to raise funds. This month, they're mounting the operetta *Black Sea Cossacks* by Starytsky and the play *Don't Go to Parties, Hryts.*"

"That's a good title!" Lukia said, laughing. "You know our people."

"You and your children should come."

"If I could contribute, I would, but you know how it is. I don't know if we'll have enough to buy a home, let alone help here."

"I understand," Arkadi said. He pulled a piece of paper and a pen from his jacket pocket and wrote some numbers. "If there's anything my wife and I can do for you, please phone us." He handed her the note.

"If you hear of a good farm, we'll be at the Immigration Hall."

Maria said, "Let's both hope and pray we find one to our liking."

Lukia smiled. "Till we see each other again."

Would they see each other again? It all depended on where Lukia ended up living. If she bought a farm near the city, perhaps she could come to this church once in a while. It would be reassuring to be with people who shared a common history. She put the note in her handbag. She'd gone to church to find solace. Instead, she was left with more questions, the answers to which remained in doubt.

9

THEN THERE WERE THREE

Over supper, Lukia learned that her brother already knew about her ordeal in Ethelbert. Gossip moved fast in close quarters. When Egnat overheard new arrivals at the Immigration Hall complaining about being misled, he shared what he knew with his uncle. She was relieved to have missed that conversation. Petro had had time to calm down, especially after a few drinks in his room.

After the meal, her daughter-in-law and sister-in-law took the little ones to bed, while the older children left to play cards at an empty table on the other side of the dining room. Egnat and Petro stayed at the table with Lukia. She ate the remaining peas and carrots on her plate, then pushed it away. "You know," she said, wiping her mouth with a napkin, "they promised us 160 acres for ten dollars."

"I know," Petro said, massaging his moustache. "You don't have to tell me. What are we going to do now?"

Lukia clasped her hands. "Look at real estate ads. See what's for sale. I've only seen one, and that one was good for nothing." She thought of mentioning they could also look at farms far from Winnipeg, but she liked the idea of being close to a city where the opportunity to barter and sell dairy products was best.

With glum faces, they gathered again in the morning and proceeded downstairs to the immigration office, where they explained their predicament to the female clerk who had helped Lukia find a church. She listened patiently, her gaze darting from one to the other. "Let's have a look," she said, and got a city newspaper that was lying on a desk.

She unfolded the paper on the counter and turned the pages to the advertisements in the back section. After perusing the ads, the only farm she could find close to Winnipeg was a 240-acre property with a fully furnished seven-room house. It was five miles from the outskirts of the city in the district of Rosser and listed for $9,600. When the clerk said they could buy it with a down payment of $3,000, Lukia's face fell. It was considerably more than any of them could afford on their own. She thanked the agent and stepped away with Egnat and Petro.

As if paralyzed by the news, they stood in one spot in the open hall by the office for a good ten minutes, watching other immigrants come and go. Finally, Lukia said, "We can't stay here indefinitely. They won't let us. If we can't find a farm, they expect us to make other living arrangements. Like the Karpinskys did. But they have friends here, we don't." She wrung her hands.

Petro eyed the lineup to see a clerk. It had grown since they'd left the office.

"We have to do something," Lukia said. "We can't stay in a hotel; all our money would go." She bit her lip. "Petro, I have a thousand dollars towards the down payment. Could you manage the rest?"

Petro frowned. "I can only give the same as you. No more."

"We're still short a thousand." She expected as much and yet, she hoped for some kind of miracle. Until his departure from Volhynia, he'd earned income from the rents he'd collected in his apartment building, but now he counted on a fellow countryman to manage his investment. The man was supposed to send him the rent money while he sought a buyer for the apartment building. With Petro unable to contribute enough, there was no point in driving out to see the place advertised.

Crestfallen, they climbed the stairs to their rooms. Halfway up the stairs, Lukia stopped. She said to her brother. "I have an idea."

"Ha. I hope it's better than the last one."

"No, listen. I have to make a phone call."

His eyes widened. "To who?"

"You'll see," she said.

While her brother and son stood with their jaws open, she opened her purse and hunted for a piece of paper. When she found it, she waved it at them, turned on her heels, and went back downstairs.

The Ukrainian-speaking realtor met Lukia, Egnat and Petro the following morning at the Immigration Hall, then drove them in his black Ford car—a treat for the trio after years of travelling in wagons—out to the countryside. Petro sat up front with the agent and Lukia in the back with Egnat. They zigzagged their way through the wide intersection of Portage and Main—which impressed Petro and Egnat—and turned down Notre Dame Avenue. They motored past tall brick buildings, then smaller ones, even a couple of factories farther down the avenue. It took quite a while to get outside the city, causing Lukia to wonder whether she'd ever be able to navigate these streets on her own.

Arkadi and Maria Karpinsky were waiting for them at the 240-acre farm in Rosser. They'd arrived with a short, bald man in an ill-fitting jacket over mismatched trousers. He had dark circles under his eyes and kept looking at Lukia, as if he knew her from somewhere. If she hadn't been so intent on finding out more about the property they were viewing, she might have found his scrutiny disturbing.

After meeting the Karpinskys and their friend, Petro pulled his sister aside. "You did good. Pan Karpinsky seems like an honest man."

"Yeah, yeah, yeah," Lukia said, "but don't count your chickens yet. Let's see if this property meets our needs."

One matter they all agreed on: this was a gentleman's house, large enough to accommodate them all, and well-constructed for the harsh winters ahead. It was a two-storey home with a peaked roof and horizontal wood siding, painted white with dark green trim around the windows and doors. After examining it and the barn, they surveyed the fields.

Egnat immediately bent down and grabbed a handful of dirt. He shook his head in disgust as the soil slipped through his fingers, leaving a row of pebbles in his palm. Countless stones would have to be removed before ploughing and seeding could begin. The only advantage this property had over Ethelbert was its proximity to Winnipeg. And maybe the stones were a bit smaller.

With the prospect of months of backbreaking work, Lukia said to the realtor, "The posters boasted that Canada had the best farmland in the world. This looks like land that's been abandoned by all who came before us."

The agent repeated what she'd already heard. "What you'd hoped for is long gone. All the good land was taken up while you were still thinking about emigrating."

Her brother's sour expression mirrored her feelings. He bent down to pick up a handful of soil, as if he knew what to look for. She pressed her lips together. He wasn't a farmer, nor was he interested in becoming one. If he sold his property in Volhynia, he planned to buy an apartment block in Winnipeg. But with the continuing political turmoil in the old country, the Bolsheviks could overwhelm the Poles, and if that happened, he could end up with nothing.

Her stomach churned as she gazed at the vast prairie landscape. Volhynia had vistas of gentle hills in varying shades of green with patches of yellow sunflowers woven throughout, but here the land stretched out, flat and wide with no end in sight, as if a mighty hand had ironed it. The only break in the picture before her was a stand of trees near the house.

The wind picked up, blowing around bits of dry grass and debris. Overhead, a flock of honking geese in a V-formation headed south. Lukia blinked away a speck of dirt as she watched the birds fly by. Egnat, who had been pacing out the length of the field, returned to stand with the others.

Seemingly impatient, the agent said, "Well, do you want it or not?"

Lukia spoke first. "Can you give us a few moments to discuss it?"

The agent nodded. "I'll wait in the car."

When the agent walked away, Lukia said, looking first at Egnat, then at Petro and Arkadi, "Nu, what do you think?"

Arkadi shook his head. "I've already rejected half a dozen farms like this. Why would I want this one?"

"What are we going to do? There is no better land."

"I'm not a farmer," Petro said. "I'll go by what you all say. If my luck turns, I won't be here for more than a couple of years."

Folding her arms, Lukia said, "Egnat, what do you think?"

Egnat kicked the dirt. "It'll take a lot of work, day and night, to remove the stones and improve the soil."

"It'll also take a lot of manure," Lukia said, "but what else can we do? We need to get settled somewhere."

While the men ruminated, Lukia considered what she was proposing. She was asking them to join her in purchasing this property. That would mean living together as equal partners. She had no concerns about Egnat, or Arkadi, who appeared to be a decent man. She hadn't heard him say a cross word to his wife, which counted for a lot in Lukia's mind. And most important, he was a man of her faith, a religious man. Someone she could trust.

It was only her brother who made her hesitate. Though he'd rescued her when she was sick with typhus and lying on a cold, concrete, hospital floor in Lutsk, she had too many bad memories of him mocking her, or worse, when she was still a child, mercilessly teasing her about her developing body. How could they manage a farm together, let alone live in the same house? They'd be arguing in no time.

Petro said, "Lukia, if this is the best we can get, we should take it."

Arkadi nodded in agreement.

Lukia picked up a handful of soil again. She opened her hand and stared at the stones in the dirt. What was she getting herself into? Each family head had promised to give $1,000, which meant they'd each have eighty acres to plant their crops and vegetables. It wasn't much, but if all went well, each would have enough to feed their families and produce enough grain, dairy, and vegetables to sell to merchants in the city.

As Petro and Arkadi walked ahead to tell the realtor of their decision, Maria took Lukia's arm. "That went well," she said.

"Yes. Thank God I met you that day in church."

"You've made an impression." Maria pointed out the short, bald man, who was standing by his car and talking to Arkadi. "Our friend wants to meet you. He's been a widower for a year. He's a good catch; he has good property not far from here."

Lukia stopped walking and patted Maria's arm. "Listen. I'm not interested in anybody right now. I was married a long time. It would be hard to get used to another man."

"I know," Maria said. "But it's not good for a woman to be alone. Your children will grow up and leave—"

"I'm sorry to interrupt you, but I've heard this many times before. After my Gregory died, my brother-in-law became a widower, and he courted me. I wasn't ready then, and I'm not ready now. You tell him I'm sorry."

Maria smiled. "He can't say I didn't try." She gave Lukia's arm a squeeze and went to join her husband and the short, bald man.

Lukia grunted. If she *was* interested, she wouldn't be going after someone who couldn't speak for himself. A man like that would need more care than she was prepared to give. Besides, didn't he ever look in a mirror? If he was so well off, why was he wearing such a lousy suit? He could at least buy a new one.

With the purchase of a homestead settled at last, Lukia breathed easier, but her heart ached for what she'd left behind in Volhynia. This wasn't what she bargained for when she heard the two men talking about golden opportunities in Canada. She almost laughed at her own foolishness. She had taken her children halfway across the world on the back of some strangers' conversation. How many others had been duped like her?

It wasn't only the lack of good land that bothered her; it was also the people. Though unfamiliar with the language, she could see the disparaging looks English speakers gave her when she approached; the sideways glances tossed her way when she couldn't converse in their tongue. When she tried the odd English word, she was met with derision. She quickly learned from the Ukrainian immigrants who had been in Canada for a while that the words hurled her way—*Bohunk, dumb Galician*, and *garlic-stinker*—were slurs against her nationality. This form of disrespect wasn't foreign to her. She'd experienced much the same under the thumb of the Tsar and later the Poles. It's no wonder Ukrainians stuck together. They believed in the old saying: An ox should keep company with oxen, and a horse with horses. There was comfort in being with your own in a new land. What stung Lukia the most was the fact she'd traded all she knew for a land with little promise, and a community who gave the impression they wished she and her kin had never come.

A full-throated sob threatened to pull her down, but she

stopped herself. She'd had enough of crying in her life. She told herself there was always hope, for here there was peace. There were no marauders hiding in the forest, and no sounds of gunfire coming closer and closer. She took a deep breath. She'd sacrificed too much to give in to the grey clouds that hovered over her. She had to keep going, if not for herself, then for her four remaining children. She owed them that much. And as she'd done in the past, she prayed. Prayed for the strength to continue.

10

SETTLING INTO ROSSER

None of the three families had had the experience of living with another household. There were seven in the Mazurec family, eight in the Korneluk family, and six in the Karpinsky family. Twenty-one in one house! Ten were adults, and two of the twenty-one were babies. It was common knowledge that every family had trouble getting along at times, so how were they going to manage living with two others? The lack of privacy, the bustle of people coming and going, doors opening and shutting at all hours, the endless chatter of the young, the howling of babies in the middle of the night, and the crowding in the kitchen at mealtimes—these were the challenges they all faced.

They'd barely moved in when Lukia began regretting her decision to live with her brother and his family. Petro chose the best living arrangement for his wife and children—the two largest rooms upstairs and another room on the main floor. She understood there were more Korneluks than Karpinskys or Mazurecs, but his ways could be so irritating, such as announcing, without discussion, which rooms he was taking. Lukia had to bite her tongue. She didn't want to start her life in Canada bickering in front of the Karpinskys, who were little more than strangers.

She and her children ended up in a room with two double beds on the second floor, and Egnat, Elena and Genya took a first-floor room next to the living room as their bedroom. As for the Karpinskys, they also made do with only two rooms, one up and one down, which must have been a hardship. Arkadi and Maria had to share their rooms with two grown sons, a married daughter and a son-in-law, who was a deacon.

Each family had brought some basic cooking utensils and tools. They agreed to share the cast-iron stove and take turns keeping its firebox full of coal or wood. It was too late in the season to seed any crops, but it wasn't too late to buy livestock and at least prepare for next year's harvest. Horses and cattle, and various equipment needed to run a farm, would be bought at auction.

After the realtor mentioned that local newspapers listed farm auctions, Egnat bought a copy of the *Stonewall Argus* at the Rosser grocery store and brought it back to the house for Boris, the eldest son of the Karpinskys, to read. According to his mother, Boris had spent every spare hour learning how to read and write in English. He was only seventeen, but he commanded attention because of his size. Close to six feet tall and broad in the shoulders, he could have been intimidating, but he wasn't the least, thanks to his mild demeanour.

The three family heads and Egnat gathered around Boris at the kitchen table. The first auction notice he read aloud announced a sale in a couple of weeks, one block north of Lindsay's Store in Stony Mountain, a town not far from them. Mr. H.L. Grant was selling some mares, geldings, yearlings and cattle plus a bull and forty hens. As well, there was a wagon and box, a hay rake, two sets of sleighs, a walking plow, buggy, saw jack, ten stanchions—which they learned were wooden milking stalls—a gang plow, binder, six milk cans, fifty milk bottles, a cream separator, coal heater and various furniture.

The other auction listed, to be held a week later at Mr. Frank Scott's farm outside of Stonewall, had similar equipment and livestock for sale, as well as a 1923 Ford touring car in good running order, a gas lantern, a churn, a shotgun, 150 bushels of oats, twenty tons of hay, a stack of straw, and a quantity of potatoes. Sales were to be concluded in cash.

Lukia heaved a heavy sigh. While the ads were promising, no prices had been listed. Nor the condition of the goods being sold. Since it was impossible to know what they could afford when they didn't know how much anything cost, they decided to attend both sales and do it with a sharp eye.

They needn't have worried. At the first auction they attended, they found out that haggling wasn't much different in Canada than it was in the old country. Canadians wanted the best price, too, and were willing to wheel and deal for it. The Mazurec family, like many of the newcomers, bid low, but it paid off. After two auctions, the three families had enough horses between them, a dozen black and white Holstein cows to milk, two bulls, pigs, turkeys, chickens for eggs and the occasional supper, and another sleigh to add to the equipment that had come with their property. As for feed for the animals, the last occupant of the Rosser property had left some hay and seed. They were on their way to establishing a farm.

Any fears Lukia may have had about not getting along in this large household were diminished in the glow of having a common purpose. Besides cooperating in their living quarters, each family took care of their own sections, clearing the fields of rocks and stones.

It was arduous work. Lukia and her children began before daybreak, picking up stones and tossing them into the metal flatbed hooked to their horse. She glanced at her sons and daughter as they concentrated on their work, heads down. What were they thinking? This wasn't the dream she'd promised them, but there was no point in dwelling on their plight. To linger in despair would only delay getting the land in shape. She ignored the heaviness in her body and picked up more stones.

They hadn't been picking long when she noticed Egnat heaving too many at a time. She shouted, "Be careful, Egnat. You're going to pull your guts out if you keep doing it that way."

He waved his hand as if to say, *Don't bother me, I know what I'm doing.*

It didn't stop her from worrying. She'd seen enough countrymen laid up because they'd ignored the pain that came with backbreaking work.

Rocks weren't the only concern. The rough ground also sprouted plentiful quack grass that threatened to choke anything planted. Taking turns with the spade and pitchfork, Dunya and her brothers tilled the soil while Lukia pulled the rake through the unforgiving earth. Elena remained in the house to take care of Genya and cook the meals.

It took weeks to turn over the earth. They worked from sunup to sundown, their backs aching as they bent over the weeds and pulled their implements through the dirt to get at them. Though the work was gruelling, the great outdoors gave them room to breathe; it was an escape from the suffocating closeness to the other families in the house.

The other job they completed before the cold weather hit was whitewashing the milk house. Dunya, Havrylo and their cousins swished on a mixture of thick lime and water with brushes made of twigs tied together. Listening to their chatter and laughter soothed Lukia's mind and warmed her heart as she fed the chickens in the barnyard.

But it wasn't all harmony in Lukia's family. Havrylo moped periodically because he missed Kivertsi, where he could fish in the creek nearby. The Rosser municipality had no creek, or river, or lake that promised the excitement of a large catch. There were places he could go, but they were too far to even consider. She didn't want to add to his misery, so she didn't admit to missing the creek as well. She missed bathing and the smell of laundry freshly washed in the cool, clear waters. The well on the land provided water for their daily needs, but it couldn't give them the joy of splashing outdoors under a cloudless sky.

Though anxious about Havrylo, he was the least of her concerns. Michalko was the one who troubled her sleep. Nothing had changed since they'd emigrated. He seemed to take every opportunity to shirk his duties. When he took breaks to relieve himself, they were longer than the ones Egnat took. Lukia worried when he didn't come back to the field as quickly as he should have. She hoped he wasn't bothering Elena while she was nursing her child or making meals for the family. Lukia had seen the looks he'd given his sister-in-law, who did nothing to encourage him. Michalko fancied himself a catch, and he certainly was one, with his black hair, dancing eyes and swagger. He had the charisma that charmed many, but he wasn't the worker his older brother was. Michalko was unwilling to miss a good time if the opportunity presented itself. His behaviour caused a lot of tension between them. She kept hoping he'd grow up.

Michalko was taking too long of a break again. She was tempted to go see what was keeping him, but that would mean leaving the fields, and there was too much work to complete before the sun went down. With the fall days getting shorter and shorter, they had to finish before the snows came.

She laid her rake on the ground and stretched her sore muscles. Egnat worked feverishly nearby, carrying on as if he had the strength of two men, and only raised his head to grunt when Michalko returned to help. To get ahead, the brothers would have to pull together like a team of horses.

The preparation of the soil went reasonably well, until the day they began plowing. Elena had placed baby Genya in the shade of a poplar tree about twelve yards away from where she and Lukia were working the soil. Their heads were down when Egnat unexpectedly came by, driving the plow. Lukia stood up to wipe her brow. It was then that she saw the big black horse suddenly stop with his hoof in the air, prompting Egnat to shout, "What the hell?"

Lukia's heart stopped. Genya lay on the blanket, right under the horse's hoof.

"Egnat, the baby!" Elena cried out and hurried over to pick up her daughter.

Relieved to see Genya in her mother's arms, Lukia crossed herself. "My God. To think ... so close."

"What the hell were you thinking?" Egnat snapped at Elena.

"I couldn't leave her in the sun." Elena's pale face showed she'd suffered the same fright.

"It's a good thing the horse stopped before he trampled her."

"Enough!" Lukia said. "No harm was done."

"Only because the horse had more sense than my wife." Egnat glowered as he patted the animal, who was stroking the ground with the hoof that had hung in the air.

"I'm sorry," Elena said. Still angry, Egnat refused to look at her, and kept his eyes on the animal.

"We have to thank God for His mercy," Lukia said gently to Elena. "It wasn't her time. Take Genya back to the house. You've worked hard enough for one day."

Though Lukia had barked at her son, she understood his fury. She blamed herself as well. She knew that Genya was lying in the field but, like Elena, she hadn't seen the danger. They'd assumed there would be lots of time to move Genya before Egnat came their way. Luckily, the horse stopped. Her grandchild had been spared. Having lost four children herself, Lukia knew how quickly God could snatch a child away.

The three families exercised their need for space in the fields, but they couldn't avoid one another in the house, or when they had to wait their turn for the outhouse. With little privacy, the women suffered more than the men who could go behind the barn if they had to. In the kitchen, the women divided up the cooking responsibilities, but with so many children underfoot, there was bound to be constant complaining and scolding. To add to the commotion, the two babies took turns crying. When one stopped, the other started up, which caused impatience all around. It was easy to overlook the demands of one's own children, but to put up with those belonging to the other parents was one stress too many.

Tony—Petro and Anna's youngest—was a fussy baby. His mother had little patience with him or his three-year-old brother, Roman, so the job fell to her five-year-old daughter, Rita, who cooed and cuddled her younger brothers whenever they wailed.

Because of her earaches, Genya also howled, at least once a week. To ease her agony, Lukia or Elena would wrap grain in a piece of cheesecloth, then heat the cloth packet in the oven and put it over Genya's ear. Michalko helped calm his niece by putting a record on the gramophone he'd bought with some of his earnings as a hired hand. Lukia hadn't complained about the extravagant purchase, because she loved music. If she'd known the hardship they were going to face, she would have said no.

But now Lukia smiled at the family picture before her. Her son snuggled Genya as he sang along to the record in his rich tenor voice and twirled her around the living room floor. The only one who wasn't happy about Michalko's support was Egnat. He questioned how his brother had time to help the women, but not him in the fields.

The Karpinskys, with their grown children, largely kept to themselves. They weathered the Mazurecs' and Korneluks' periodic family storms, and for that Lukia was grateful. She understood each family wished they were on their own. It was only desperation that had brought them together.

School had started in their district, but none of the Korneluk or Mazurec children attended, because they were needed on the farm. Lukia and Petro were more concerned about survival than education for their young. They informed their children they could attend once the snows arrived. But even then, Lukia and Petro would have to find more ways to earn income.

Thinking locals would know what work was available, Lukia asked Egnat to drive her to the Rosser General Store a few miles away. It was a white wooden building, with a gas pump out front and a sign on the side advertising Coca-Cola, the same sign she'd seen on storefronts in towns she passed during her train ride from Halifax to Winnipeg.

Egnat parked their horse and wagon near the blacksmith shop next door. Lukia got down from the wagon and smiled at the six children in the back box of a parked Ford truck before going into the store.

After exploring the goods on the shelves, Lukia found a customer who spoke Ukrainian. She explained her need for work, and he guided her to a bulletin board that had a note pinned on it by a local farmer seeking help. With the customer's aid, she learned where the farm was located.

Encouraged, she said, "Thank you," the only English words she knew besides hello.

11

BENTLEY FARM

Dunya complained when her mother came home with the job notice she'd found on the community bulletin board. She reminded her mother of her terrible experience in Ethelbert. They had treated her like a slave! she said. Lukia sympathized, but tried to assure her that this farm would be different and that she would go, too.

Mr. Bentley, a tall, lean man in overalls, hired them as soon as they showed up. Dunya's cousins—the three oldest Korneluk children—and Elena were also given work on his vegetable farm, harvesting corn, potatoes and beans. He said he'd pay each of them $1.75 a day and provide supper.

The next morning, Dunya and her mother rose with the sun and the rooster crowing, and after milking the cows and packing a lunch of cheese, bread and berries they'd picked the day before, they set out for the Bentley farm—a good forty-five-minutes walk away. No one said much as Dunya and her cousins walked behind her mother and Elena, who took turns carrying Genya. Alex, Dunya's twelve-year-old cousin, had woken up in a foul mood. Grumbling, he kicked at the gravel on the road as he tramped behind the group.

Up ahead, Lesya, a neighbour's daughter around Alex's age, was herding cows to pasture near the road, with the help of a brown dog that tried to keep the cows together by barking and running around her.

Alex yelled, "Lesya, why don't you join us? Why work for free for your father when you can get $1.75 for the day and a free meal?"

"Maybe tomorrow," she yelled back. Her smile lit up her freckled face, and her honey-coloured braids swayed as she spun around to take care of the cows.

After that exchange, Alex skipped along, whistling. His brothers teased him, but he didn't seem to mind. Dunya figured he liked the attention.

When they got to the farm, Mr. Bentley explained what he wanted done, but since no one's English was that good yet, he had to show them what to do instead. It was simple work. Dunya didn't mind; she'd worked since she was little on their farm in the old country. Harvesting was second nature to her. Picking vegetables was a time to daydream about her future, one that didn't include farming. She enjoyed working outdoors—inhaling the fresh air and appreciating what the sun and water had contributed to each seed— but she wanted more than her mother had. Farming was brutal work; you were too reliant on the weather. And yet her mother never complained about the morning-to-night chores that only a farmer understood; she'd accepted her lot in life. Dunya looked over at her mother, whose head was down, her mouth set in a determined line, her hands busy pulling up one potato after the other. The work thrilled her mother because they were adding to the family income, while her brothers stayed at home to prepare their section for the coming year.

The next day, Lesya joined Dunya, Alex, and his brothers digging up potatoes down one row while the adults worked in another.

After working an hour, Dunya heard Alex and Lesya giggling behind her. She turned to see Alex throw a potato at Lesya, who laughed and threw one back at him. Within minutes of those first throws, Alex and Lesya were scooting down the rows, laughing and throwing more potatoes at each other. The dust flew from under their feet as they ran further down the row.

Alarmed, Dunya hollered, "Alex! Come back."

Paying her no heed, Alex continued to goof around. Dunya kept working. Her mother, who was a few rows over, would have said something if she had noticed the commotion. No one saw Mr. Bentley drive by in his old truck and stop.

Charging down Dunya's row, Mr. Bentley bellowed, "What the hell is going on here?"

Fear whitening their faces, Alex and Lesya slipped behind some corn stalks on the edge of the potato field. Dunya kept her eyes on Mr. Bentley. Her mother and Elena, clutching a potato, came over to see what was going on.

Mr. Bentley counted heads. "There's two missing." Some rustling sounds got his attention and he turned in that direction. Dunya held her breath for a moment, worrying for her cousin. Mr. Bentley stepped over the potato plant row to where the corn stalks were and began hitting each tall plant with his hand. "No use hiding. I've been watching you from the house with my binoculars. I've seen more than I want to see." His hand hitting the stalks made an eerie sound, as if it was only a matter of time before something exploded. "Fine. You keep hiding. I can wait." He stood still for the longest time. Dunya was afraid to move.

Her mother scowled as they all waited to see what would happen. She broke the silence. "Children, come out immediately! We can't wait here all day."

Alex and Lesya sheepishly came out from behind some corn stalks halfway down the row, their faces lowered, their eyes avoiding Mr. Bentley's.

He glowered. "I think you've done enough for the day. You can both go and don't come back." He waved his hands at Dunya, her mother, Elena, and Alex's brothers, as if he was shooing flies. "In fact, you can all go."

Elena dropped the potato in her hand.

Dunya's jaw dropped.

"What does this mean?" her mother said.

Lesya, who had some command of the language, said, "Panye Mazurec, Pan Bentley is firing us."

"No! Such good work; such good pay!"

Frustrated, Dunya spoke up, "Please, sir. We work hard." She wanted to say more but didn't know the words.

Mr. Bentley knitted his eyebrows. "The rest of you should have told him to smarten up. If I have to stand here and supervise, I may as well do the work myself. Now get your things and leave." In case they hadn't understood, he waved his arms again and pointed to the road that had brought them there.

Dunya looked over at her mother and Elena, who shifted Genya from one arm to the other, then picked up her bag from the ground. It was humiliating to leave with their heads bent under the furious gaze of Mr. Bentley.

Her mother complained as they walked home, the bounce in all of their steps gone. She held nothing back from Alex or Lesya, who followed and kept their distance. Silence had replaced their playful banter. Only her mother's voice rang out. "I never should've let Alex come. He doesn't listen. And why did he ask Lesya? She doesn't have to worry about where her next meal is coming from. What are we going to do now? Such a good job, and we lost it." She muttered all the way home.

12

BUMPS IN THE ROAD

That evening, Lukia lingered at the table with Egnat and Petro. She rubbed her thumb against her index finger repeatedly, as she said, "It's terrible. It could hurt our reputation. Now what kind of work will we be able to find? If Bentley tells others in the community, no one will hire us."

Petro said, "Keep your voice down."

"Why should I keep my voice down?" She peered behind to see if any of the Karpinskys were around. They weren't. "It was the only job posted and now that's gone, too."

Egnat said to Petro, "You should punish Alex for the problems he's caused our family. If it wasn't for his recklessness, we'd still have work."

Petro mumbled into his almost empty glass. He topped his glass off with more homebrew.

"Petro," Lukia said, "Alex did wrong. How is he going to learn if you don't say anything?"

"Sister, this is between me and my son. Mind your own business."

Lukia harrumphed and stood up from the table. He had no right to talk to her that way. She was older; he should show more respect. Egnat stood as well, almost knocking his chair over, causing Elena, who was darning in the corner, to say, "Watch what you're doing."

After that, the two men avoided each other as much as they could in a house where every move was noted. It was just as well. There was no talking to her brother.

As fortune would have it, Lukia didn't have to worry about her family's reputation. There were no other farmers looking for help, so any gossip about their failure at the Bentley Farm was of little consequence. Her biggest concern was survival. Since they'd purchased their acreage so late in the season, she had no harvest to count on. The coming winter looked grim.

After a few sleepless nights, considering how she could bring in some money, Lukia decided to look for work in the city. When she shared the idea over supper, Anna and Elena—who had young ones to care for—said they would stay home and manage the household. As Maria Karpinsky was going into Winnipeg the next day for some supplies, she told Lukia she'd bring back a copy of the *Ukrainian Voice*. The weekly newspaper, published in her native language, was bound to have a list of positions in its Help Wanted section.

And with the land finally cleared of stones and stumps, Dunya and her three younger male cousins prepared to attend East Rosser School, a one-storey white clapboard building two-and-a-half miles away. Michalko and Havrylo, along with their cousin, Ted, would stay on the farm and help the men mend fences, repair equipment and care for the livestock.

The other new development came from the Karpinskys' married daughter. She announced that she and her husband had found a living situation in Winnipeg and were moving. She explained that, with her husband being a deacon, they needed to live close to Sobor.

With plans for how they'd all pass the winter completed, Lukia spent the evening embroidering an apron with a bib she'd sewn for herself. She was thankful she had her handwork to keep her from dwelling on the future.

On the children's first day of school, all three families were up early. The sun hadn't risen yet, but already the house was fully lit with kerosene lamps. The children bustled from room to room, worrying about the day before it had even begun.

Lukia was in the bedroom upstairs fashioning her daughter's long brown hair into a single braid when one of her nephews yelled from below, "Dunya, we're leaving. Are you coming?"

"Pretty soon," she yelled back.

Lukia arched her eyebrows. "Don't keep Uncle waiting. You don't want to make your cousins late the first day." Petro had offered to take the children to school that morning, but after that, they'd have to walk there and back on their own.

Dunya pressed her lips as she observed herself in the mirror over the walnut bureau. She twisted and turned, flattening the front of her white percale blouse with her hands.

It was obvious her daughter was uncomfortable with her maturing shape. Putting her hands on Dunya's shoulders, Lukia said, "You look lovely."

Dunya groaned. "Why do I have to go? I'm only going to be teased."

"You don't know that. You have to learn English," Lukia said, firmly. "If you learn how to read and write, you can help me."

"What about Havrylo? Why isn't he going?"

"Havrylo's needed on the farm."

Grumbling, her daughter left for school with Victor Karpinsky and the three Korneluk boys—Alex, Leo, and George. Lukia couldn't blame Dunya for being apprehensive. Her daughter had had a dreadful experience in Kivertsi, where the boys in her school had bullied her and the teacher had called her names. Initially, she'd stood up to the boys, but being only twelve, she couldn't tolerate their torment. She developed headaches for which neither the doctor nor her baba could find a cure. They didn't go away until Dunya had left school entirely.

Lukia couldn't help thinking she'd failed her daughter. She had talked to the teacher in Kivertsi, but to no avail. He neglected to discipline the boys who bullied Dunya and—even worse—raped her niece, Hanyuta. After Hanyuta's mother had refused to press charges, knowing her daughter would be interrogated mercilessly in court, there was nothing more that could be done. Lukia believed that someday those involved would pay for their crimes, if not in this life, then in the afterlife. But that didn't help Hanyuta then, nor her daughter.

More than ever, Dunya would need to use her wits in these changing times. Education was critical. A woman could no longer be reliant on a man to take care of things. Lukia had learned the hard way when her husband volunteered to fight for the Tsar's army. No matter how much she'd pleaded, Gregory would not listen. He was determined to go fight, and nothing she said could stop him. Lukia hoped her daughter was beginning to understand how strong a woman had to be to survive.

13

SELKIRK AVENUE

L
ukia and Maria sat in the living room, listening to Egnat read the Help Wanted ads in the *Ukrainian Voice*. There was one ad for a naymichka—a maidservant—that appealed to Lukia. The ad said: Wanted maid, light housekeeping, small family, sleep in, weekends off.

Maria decided against applying for any position. Since her daughter had moved to the city, she said she had more than enough work to keep her occupied on the farm. Lukia wanted to say she also had enough work to do here, but she didn't bother. Maria's situation was different. Arkadi could afford to keep his wife at home.

The next morning, Lukia put on a navy crepe dress, then checked her purse to make sure she had enough money to get to Winnipeg and back. She could catch the Canadian Pacific morning train at the Rosser station or the bus that travelled Highway 221 parallel to the railway, but she hated to spend the money. The train cost sixty cents one way to Main Street and Higgins, which was expensive, and the streetcar to Selkirk Avenue cost another ten cents. She didn't know the price of a bus fare, but she suspected it was also costly. If she was lucky enough to get one of those housekeeping jobs for six dollars a month, that money could go quickly if she used the train or bus going back and forth on weekends.

She kept looking at her watch as she hiked the gravel highway. It was at least a two-hour walk to the outside of the city where she could take a streetcar the rest of the way. Was she making a mistake in thinking she could hitch a ride? She'd been walking for about fifteen minutes and was about to give up and walk north to the Rosser train station when Ihor Chimiuk, whose homestead was only a couple of miles from theirs, appeared, driving his wagon up the road towards the city. He stopped beside her. "Good day, Lukia. Where are you off to?"

"Winnipeg. I'm going to Selkirk Avenue."

"You're in luck. I'm going to the markets near there."

At the beginning of the ride, they exchanged a few pleasantries about each other's families, then fell into silence. Lukia had never been much of a talker; she'd always preferred to let others babble on. It seemed Ihor was of a similar bent.

She relaxed as much as she could on a wooden seat that bounced with every rut the wagon hit. On each side of the road, the prairies glowed under the morning sun. Since each farm's acreage was much larger in Canada, the homes were few and far between. She assumed neighbours would have to travel some distance for advice or help.

He turned to her. "How are you managing? Are you getting settled?"

"You know how it is. We arrived in the country too late. Aagh, what can I do about that?" She paused. "I didn't want to say, but I'm going into the city to look for housework. Maybe a rich family will hire me for the winter."

He grunted. "They'd be lucky to have you. No one works as hard as our people."

In the old country, she never had to work for anyone else. In

Canada, with money scarce and her expectations dashed, Lukia had to swallow her pride and clean other people's houses. She was sure Gregory would disapprove. Well, if he did, she'd say: *Never mind me. Look what your volunteering for the Tsar's army got you. Nothing but grief afterwards. Did you get the land the Tsar promised? No, you didn't! So don't criticize me now.*

Stewing over the imagined argument, she didn't realize she had adopted a sour expression until Ihor said, "Are you all right?"

She tightened her lips. She didn't want to explain what she was mulling over. She'd earned the right to be upset. Forcing a smile, she said, "Yes, yes. I'm just thinking about how I'm going to talk to any employer. I don't understand the English language. I can speak Ukrainian, Polish, Russian, some Czech and Yiddish, but the English language is beyond me."

"Not to worry. There are so many of us here now, you won't have any trouble. Not on Selkirk Avenue, that's for sure. That's the heart of the Jewish community. Lots of Slavs there as well. You'll have no trouble at all."

Ihor let her off on Selkirk Avenue near Salter Street. Before she left her neighbour, Lukia pulled out a piece of paper from her coat pocket and showed him the large letters and numbers Egnat had printed.

Ihor peered at the note. "That address is only a few blocks away. Keep going east towards Main Street." He pointed down Selkirk Avenue, where a line of cars and a ragpicker's horse and cart waited patiently while two men carried a couple of crates from a wagon bed to a shop nearby.

"This is fine," Lukia said. "You were kind enough to get me this far. I owe you."

"You don't owe me anything. Good luck." He hesitated, then said, "Will you need a ride back? I could come by here in three hours. Will you be finished by then?"

"May God bless you. That would be wonderful."

"Good. We'll meet at three o'clock at this corner."

After Lukia climbed down, he clicked his tongue and tapped the horse's rump with his switch. Lukia didn't wait for him to leave. She skirted the wagon and the horse dung on the road, but couldn't avoid getting some manure on the bottom of her shoe. As she scraped it off on the curb, a peddler drove by with his wagon full of clothes and bottles and a few live chickens in cages. He wore a shabby wool jacket and a tweed cap with a torn brim over his dark eyes and bushy eyebrows. His heavily wrinkled face showed a man used to working long hours in adverse conditions. They exchanged glances. He grinned, exposing a mouth with a few front teeth missing. His warm expression, coupled with his sad situation, tugged at her heart. It was easy to recognize those who worked hard, even at great personal cost.

She pulled her coat tighter and headed in the direction Ihor had pointed out.

Mrs. Hrushowitz and Lukia took an immediate liking to one another. The employer complimented Lukia on her dress's fine stitching and craftsmanship, and invited her to sit down on one of the gold brocade tufted chairs in the living room. She asked about Lukia's family and how many days a week she could work. She wanted someone who could do light housekeeping and cook meals for herself and her husband. They were a busy couple. He owned a dress shop on Selkirk Avenue, and she volunteered in two Jewish charities. For her work, Lukia would get twelve dollars a month, which would include board and room during the week, and she could go home on weekends. When Lukia mentioned she'd have to return to her farm in the spring when the ground thawed, Mrs. Hrushowitz said it wasn't easy finding good help but she'd worry about that when the time came.

Given the beautifully decorated living room, Lukia suspected the

Jewish couple were doing very well. Mrs. Hrushowitz didn't even have to help her husband in the shop. Besides the brocade side chairs, there was a matching sofa, a glass-topped coffee table, two mahogany side tables adorned with delicate bone china ornaments of young ladies in old-fashioned garments, and a grand British wool rug with tassels on the polished hardwood floor. On the wall over the sofa hung an oil painting of a country landscape in an ornate curlicue wood frame and, to each side, beautifully cross-stitched pansies in walnut and gilt frames. The artificial pink roses in the blue glass vase on the coffee table looked so lifelike, Lukia was tempted to smell them when the lady left to get her a key for the front door.

Lukia told Mrs. Hrushowitz she could start the next day. After some cookies and tea, Lukia headed down the street to Oretzki's department store to buy some flannel fabric and matching thread for a dress for Dunya. Pleased with securing a position, Lukia stepped lightly the whole way.

Mrs. Hrushowitz turned out to be a fair boss, complimenting Lukia on her cooking and baking and ensuring she cooked enough to have three good meals a day herself. For a few weeks, Lukia had no worries. But one evening, when she was washing dishes in the kitchen, she overheard the couple talking about their finances in the dining room. Mr. Hrushowitz's voice cracked as he continued to talk, showing some deep anxiety. Lukia gathered that Mr. Hrushowitz had invested in some stocks and had lost a lot of money. The stock market crash, as he called it, was affecting people all over America and Canada. He said it was a calamity for the entire nation. Mrs. Hrushowitz cried softly when her husband told her they had to cut back on their expenses.

Lukia rubbed her thumb against her forefinger. *What did this mean? What if they couldn't afford her help anymore?* She wished she could ask them about it, but feared they'd be angry if they knew she'd overheard their private conversation.

The bigger question was, what did this news mean for her family's future? The way the couple had talked in hushed voices, you'd think the world was ending. She peered around the kitchen door into the dining room. Mr. Hrushowitz lifted his newspaper and, after reading a bit more, told his wife that a man had jumped to his death after hearing about his losses.

Lukia would have to tell Egnat about the stock market crash. He'd have to talk to the people at the Winnipeg Grain Exchange to see if this calamity meant anything dire for farmers. Already, she'd been told the grain price had dropped dramatically from the previous year. An alarming fact. They hadn't even farmed, and already the prices were ridiculous. *Had they arrived too late to support themselves?* Her throat went dry with the news. She poured herself a glass of water, but it did little to ease her throat or the turmoil in her stomach.

Putting the last dish away in the cupboard, Lukia again questioned her move to Canada. The government's offer of a good-sized homestead had seemed promising, so rosy, but ever since she'd arrived in Manitoba, she'd seen nothing to match that promise. Though there was freedom to speak out and she could practice her religion without fear, what good was that freedom if you couldn't support yourself?

"Lukia," called Mrs. Hrushowitz. "Can we have some tea, please?"

"Yes, Panye," Lukia said, raising her voice to be heard. She hung up the tea towel and put the kettle on.

Lukia woke up with pains in her chest. She'd had them before, but they'd gone away almost as quickly as they'd come. The sharp pangs probably had to do with the awful news she'd heard the evening before. She made her bed, then went to the kitchen to prepare breakfast for the Hrushowitzes. After putting the coffee on, she stewed some prunes and made porridge.

"Smells good," Mrs. Hrushowitz said as she entered the kitchen. She went to the cupboard by the fridge and took out a pin cushion with needles and a box of coloured threads.

Stirring the oats on the stove, Lukia grimaced.

"Lukia, what's the matter?"

"It's nothing. Just some indigestion." Lukia continued to stir the porridge.

"You look pale. Are you sure it's nothing?" Her employer's lined forehead and gentle voice showed her concern.

"It's my chest. I've had this before. It'll go away shortly."

Mrs. Hrushowitz put the pin cushion and thread box down on the table. Taking the spoon away from Lukia, she said, "Sit down. Please."

"Oy." Lukia twisted her mouth and sat down.

"Have you seen a doctor?"

Lukia shook her head. She wouldn't know where to find one. In the old country, the doctor from the village was never available; he was at the hospital or at home, drunk. Most people managed on their own or consulted a herbalist like her mother.

"I want you to see Dr. Reznowski. He's just down the street. I'll call him."

Lukia tensed up. She didn't have money for a doctor. "No, thank you, Panye Hrushowitz. I'll be all right."

"Is it about the money? Are you worried about the cost?"

"Of course."

"Listen," Mrs. Hrushowitz said, taking the pot off the stove, "I'll take care of any charges. I'll notify the office to send me the bill." When Lukia hesitated, she added, "It has to be done. I insist." Mrs. Hrushowitz wrote the address down on a piece of paper and handed it to Lukia. "It's just a few blocks down Selkirk Avenue."

While her employer called the doctor's office, Lukia went into her room to get her purse. She glimpsed her hair in the bureau's mirror. Her dye job had faded and her grey hairs had multiplied since then. "No matter," she mumbled and opened the door.

Outside of that one visit to Oretzki's, Lukia hadn't had time to appreciate the activity on Selkirk Avenue. Despite the bitter wind and the slippery street from the snowfall the night before, the sidewalks had been shovelled and were busy with stylish pedestrians. Several women wore the latest fashion: long, wool velour coats in shades of brown, navy or wine. Each coat sported a large shawl collar made of mink, fox or beaver and had decorative buttons. One lady even had a matching fur hat and wore leather boots and gloves.

Lukia pulled her sheepskin hat down over her ears and raised the collar of her bikasha. The long quilted-cotton coat she'd made and lined with cotton and wool batting served her well in the old country, but here it was the outerwear of a poor woman.

Refusing to dwell on her condition, Lukia checked the address Mrs. Hrushowitz had given her. She had another two blocks to walk before she got to the doctor's office. Was she making a mistake going? The pain had subsided. But then again, it had subsided in the past as well. Since her employer had been kind enough to arrange and pay for an examination, she forged ahead.

The avenue had a steady stream of vehicles of all sorts. Shops up and down the street sold everything you needed. There were two grocery stores, butcher shops, chicken and egg dealers, barbershops, a watchmaker, a sign painter, and a store selling gramophones and records. Besides the shops, there were synagogues, churches and a couple of banks. She stopped to look in the windows of a furniture store. The first-floor displayed chesterfields, dining tables and chairs.

Just ahead, a two-storey red brick building with five glass doors opening onto the sidewalk piqued her curiosity. Lukia stopped to admire the brass door handles and examine the posters on the outside walls. She'd never seen a movie before, but she recognized that these were advertisements for the films being shown inside. On one poster, a photo of a couple in an embrace illustrated a love story. This building had to be the Palace movie theatre Petro had gone to when he was in the city. Maybe once her family got on its feet, they'd be able to afford to go. Her brother had told her it was like real life. Watching the story unfold on a large white screen made you forget your troubles. He also said it was better than watching a play or hearing a story told around the kitchen table. She didn't understand that comparison. She'd always enjoyed the few plays she'd seen in Volhynia. Her son Michalko had acted in a few and wished to play a role again. As for the other, there was nothing better than hearing a story directly from the person who'd lived through it.

Dr. Reznowski's receptionist, a stout woman with hazel eyes and light brown hair swept back and pinned in a roll, greeted Lukia when she arrived. She said in Ukrainian, "Panye Hrushowitz phoned to tell us you were coming." She pointed to two side chairs in the hallway. "You can wait here."

When another patient exited the doctor's office, the receptionist ushered Lukia into the examining room, where she waited a few minutes more. Dr. Reznowski, a slight man in a crisply ironed white coat over a herringbone suit, entered abruptly.

"Panye Mazurec?" he said, shaking her hand.

"Yes."

"What can I do for you?"

She wondered what Mrs. Hrushowitz had told him or had she only talked to his receptionist? "I've had pains in my chest."

"Please undo your buttons."

She undid the top row and slipped the dress off her shoulders. While she did, he said, "I hope you're finding your way here."

"Nu, you know how it is." But did he? He was a doctor with a pleasant office and an assistant. What did he know about want?

He checked her heartbeat with a stethoscope and took her blood pressure. Putting aside his instruments, he said, "Panye Mazurec, your blood pressure is a little high. If you lost weight, that would help. You need to watch the salt in your diet, too."

"Oy," she said. This wasn't news she expected. She loved to salt her food liberally, but now she'd have to be more careful. As for the weight, he didn't have to tell her she had to lose some pounds. She'd tried to cut her portions down, but that was hard to do. She thanked him and proceeded to the front desk, where she was told Mrs. Hrushowitz was taking care of the fees. At least there was that.

14

FAMILY UNREST

Dunya's school day started off with the Lord's Prayer and the singing of "God Save The King". Pretending to know the English words to both, she mouthed them as she stared at the framed photo of the monarch hanging over the blackboard at the front of the room. Near the end of the anthem, she caught the eye of a girl looking at her. When the girl smirked and whispered to her friend behind, Dunya realized she'd been caught pretending. Humiliated, she wanted to run out of the classroom and never come back. Instead, when the anthem was over, she sat down and shrank in her seat.

As the day progressed, Dunya sank lower in her seat. She didn't understand one word of what the teacher said. Ridicule from girls her own age was the hardest to bear. The hurt was like a large nut stuck in her throat, and there was nothing she could do to dislodge it. Even thinking of a happy folk song did nothing to alter her mood.

At recess, Dunya stayed in one corner of the yard, away from the group of girls who giggled in her direction. They were around her age but in a higher grade. Since the teacher taught all the grades in one classroom, Dunya stood out, being fourteen in Grade 1 and sitting at a desk at the back of the room with the lower grades.

She couldn't have been standing long, gazing at the long grasses beyond the schoolyard, when a girl around her age joined her and said in Ukrainian, "Hi. I'm Olga. What's your name?"

"Dunya."

Olga said, "They're a stupid bunch. I wouldn't waste time worrying about what they think. They laughed at me, too, when I first arrived. Did you just move here?"

"Yes. We arrived in August."

"Welcome. We can hang out together."

Dunya said "Good" in English and laughed. "I have to try."

"You'll be fine."

When Dunya had first seen Olga in the classroom, she had seemed unapproachable because of her long, stern face, mousy brown hair, and sad hazel eyes. But now that they had talked, she found her warm, soft-spoken, and a good listener. It turned out that Olga was an outcast, too. She'd immigrated a month earlier and spoke a little English. The other girls in the schoolyard stared at them, but Dunya turned her back.

The only good that came out of attending school was a new friend.

On Saturday evening, after a trying week at school, Dunya sat down beside her mother on the green chesterfield and picked a pair of holey grey socks from the basket on the floor. Her brothers wore through the toes and heels of their socks faster than she and her mother could darn them. She was anxious to talk about school and wished there was more privacy, but it was impossible with so many in the household.

Rita was on the floor, smelling her little brother Tony's toes and pretending they stank. He laughed every time she did it, which only encouraged her to do it again and again. Dunya and her mother couldn't help laughing along. Alex and Ted were also on the floor, munching roasted sunflower seeds and playing cards with Victor Karpinsky. Their chatter was boisterous, causing Dunya to look over. "I won for a change." "Deal me a good hand this time." "Don't cheat. You always cheat."

The men in the house had retreated to the barn to have a smoke and catch up on the news of the day. Aunt Anna and Mrs. Karpinsky were in the kitchen, baking peanut butter cookies for their children's lunchboxes; Lukia had made hers earlier. The smell of the sugar treat wafted into the living room.

Dunya took a large darning needle from the red pin cushion on her mother's lap. Threading the needle with yarn, she said, "The teacher makes me exercise my hand. I do circle after circle. How is that going to help me read and write?"

Her mother didn't look up from her mending. She was barely listening.

Alex piped up. "It's penmanship. The teacher is teaching you how to write."

"Write what?" Dunya whined. "I don't know the language. I can't read. Why doesn't she show me how to read?"

Her mother murmured. She remained intent on her darning.

Frustrated, Dunya pulled the thread through the heel of the sock too hard and it broke. "How would you like it if they couldn't even say your name?"

"What now?" her mother asked.

"The children call me Dolly."

Alex said, "That means cute girl. Like a doll. That's good."

"I don't care." Dunya pouted. "Why do I have to learn their language when they can't even say my name properly?"

"Oy," her mother said. "If that's the worst thing you have to complain about, you have nothing to complain about."

Dunya wasn't happy with her mother's answer. She wanted more sympathy. Secretly she liked the name Dolly, especially after Alex said it meant a doll. She'd only had a small cloth doll when she was little, but she'd seen beautiful dolls in Oretzki's department store. She had gone there a week ago with her mother to buy a pair of shoes. When they walked through the toy section, Dunya had stopped to pick up a doll to examine its construction. It was beautiful and lifelike, with a painted head, feet and hands made of china; its muslin-covered legs and arms were bendable, so the doll could sit upright and look natural, like a real baby.

But her most exciting time in the store was when she tried the X-ray shoe fitting machine. She had put on new black oxford shoes, then put her feet into the opening at the bottom of the tall contraption. The shoe clerk peered through the porthole at the top and asked Dunya to wiggle her toes to see if there was enough room. Dunya and her mother took turns looking at the bright green image of her skeletal feet, showing there was plenty of room for growth in the shoes.

Dunya admired Canada for its modern ways. But she didn't like discovering that a change of country didn't mean a change in bullying. She kept darning but knew she'd have to approach her mother again if nothing changed at school.

In the morning, Dunya twisted her chestnut-coloured hair into a long braid down her back and donned the same white blouse and checkered skirt she'd had on the day before. Her mother had promised a new flannel dress, but so far, she hadn't found the time to sew it. Dunya wished she could wear her bronze velveteen dress, but it was for special occasions only.

School depressed her. She wasn't learning how to read and write; the other girls remained aloof; and a new torment sprung from a boy in the fifth grade.

Walter, big for his age, sat behind her. His shiny black hair fell over his forehead in a long, tangled curl that occasionally obscured one eye. His teasing started at the end of her first week at school, when the teacher stepped out of the room. He poked her in the back and said, "Dolly, I like your tits."

Not understanding, Dunya turned around and said, "What?"—one of the few words she had confidence to use. When he repeated, "I like your tits," the other children snickered. She was about to ask a girl what the words meant, but just then, the teacher returned to the room.

At recess, Dunya told Olga what Walter had said.

Olga rolled her eyes and whispered, "Tits means your breasts. He said he liked them."

"Oh!" Dunya said, knitting her brow. She scanned the schoolyard and spotted Walter standing with a few boys. Their eyes met, and she glared at him. He laughed back. She turned to Olga. "How do you say he's a pig in English?"

After learning the word, Dunya shouted, "Pig!" Seemingly unbothered by the slur, he mocked her by putting his hands on his chest and pretending to lift big breasts. One of his friends guffawed and mimicked the gesture.

Back in the classroom, Dunya noticed she'd lost a button on the placket of her blouse. Horrified, she hunched her shoulders forward, trying to hide the exposed skin. She blinked back tears and turned her face away from the other students. The bank of six windows revealed nothing but brown prairie grasses disappearing into a grey skyline. She wanted to disappear as well into the brownish-grey blur of the world outside. Anything to escape the ridicule.

The week before Thanksgiving, Dunya told her mother the teacher wanted to know if anyone in the house would help at a dinner planned for the holiday. The English women in the district needed help to wash dishes in the school kitchen and would pay two dollars and provide a supper. Pleased with another opportunity to add to their income, Lukia and Elena volunteered. When the day arrived, they were picked up in a wagon, treated well, and even given plenty of leftovers to take home. It was good to see the English could be welcoming.

"Mind you," Lukia said, afterwards to her daughter, "We were servants for the day. I'm not so sure they'd like us at their own tables."

On Halloween, it snowed and snowed, leaving a four-inch blanket of white on the ground. It turned out to be one of Dunya's better days at school. For a treat, the teacher let them spend a longer recess outside, where they threw snowballs at one another and built a snowman. All the students took part, and for the first time, Dunya felt like she was part of the class.

Because of the heavy snow, Uncle Petro drove her and his boys home in his horse-drawn sleigh. The temperature had fallen and the wind was brisk, making Dunya shiver in her fake fur coat. She moved closer to her cousin, Alex, so she could feel the warmth of his kazshook, a brown leather coat with fur on the inside.

She said to Alex, "How can you be friends with Walter? He's such a jerk."

"It's none of your business who's my friend. You just can't take a joke." Then he pulled her braid.

"Ow. You're just as bad," she said, poking him with her elbow.

Alex snarled but did nothing more until they got back to the farm. As soon as he and Dunya had stepped off the sleigh, he pushed her down in the snow. Laughing, he ran off.

"Dumbbell!" she yelled. It was a new English word she'd learned. "Alex, you're going to get it!" He kept running. After she got up and cleared the snow out of her boots, she trudged to the barn where Egnat was cleaning up the dung the cows had dropped. She stormed towards him.

"What's lit you on fire?" he asked. As soon as she told him, he put down his shovel. "We'll see about that."

Together, they found Alex by the front door of the house, banging snow off his boots.

Dunya smirked as Egnat said, "You're supposed to stick up for your cousin. What right did you have, hitting a girl?" He pushed

Alex hard in the chest, toppling him over into the snowbank nearby.

Before Alex had a chance to get up, her mother and uncle came rushing out of the house. Uncle Petro hollered, "What the devil? How dare you hit my son!" He grabbed a shovel that was resting against the outside wall.

Her mother yelled, "Run, Egnat! Run!"

Dunya's heart pounded. What had she done? If she hadn't complained to her brother, he wouldn't have hit Alex and Uncle Petro wouldn't have got so upset. Besides, Alex was nice to her most of the time. He was just being goofy, horsing around. Why had she taken it so seriously? Why had she complained to her brother?

Luckily for Egnat, he was considerably younger. He easily outran Uncle, who, after a hundred yards, had to stop and grip his chest. Leaning on his shovel, he doubled over and inhaled deeply to catch his breath. Egnat was out of danger for the moment, but that didn't stop Uncle Petro from waving his fist and swearing, "I'll kill you."

Dunya stiffened with fear. She was sure her uncle had been drinking. She'd smelled alcohol on his breath when she got in the sleigh for the ride home. It was nothing new. He could be a madman when he drank.

Mr. Karpinsky, who'd come out of the outhouse, hurried over and grabbed Uncle by the shoulders. "Petro, that's family. You can't hurt your sister's son." After talking to him quietly for a few minutes, he calmed Uncle down.

"What got into him?" muttered her mother. "Crazy fool!"

An uneasy truce ensued, but the tension between Egnat and her uncle remained. Thankfully, the two men's occupations ensured they would be working in different places tomorrow. Egnat had to be in the fields at sunup, and Uncle Petro had secured work in Winnipeg as a carpenter.

Dunya could not believe how quickly the argument had escalated. Like gasoline on fire. And she was the one who struck the match.

15

CRACKS IN BLOOD

The whole fight between her son and her brother played over and over in Lukia's mind, disturbing her sleep. To think Petro had threatened to kill Egnat! She shuddered. Beside her, Dunya stirred. She should have known living together wouldn't work. Petro was someone who wouldn't listen to reason. Rather, he was one who invited chaos and confrontation. The fact he had saved her life when she had typhus had kept her playing the peacemaker in the family. But now the threads binding them together had worn so thin, another cross word from his lips might tear them for good. Her son's happiness was at stake. She knew it was only a matter of time before her son or brother would crack and she'd be forced to choose. Until then, she would bite her tongue and pray for civility and reason in the house.

Farmers gathered one Saturday in mid-November at the Rosser General Store to complain about their poor yields. They blamed the government for the emotional rollercoaster they'd endured at the hands of those setting prices and guaranteeing shipments. Lukia, Petro, Egnat and Arkadi got an earful. Canada had produced one hundred million fewer bushels than the previous year, yet the grain marketers had withheld wheat sales to raise prices. Initially, it seemed like a good idea, but quickly the farmers discovered higher prices meant you sold less. And what was the good of that? 1929 had been a poor year for all farmers in the northwest. The change in pricing had done nothing to improve a farmer's lot. No one could afford to wait for payment. They all agreed the Wheat Pool had blundered. Argentina and some countries in Europe had stepped in to fill the vacuum Canada had created.

With trouble in the house and trouble in the land, Lukia performed her tasks at the Hrushowitzes' house with difficulty. She often paused her work to consider her plight. There had been no wheat or other grain to sell that fall, and they were already worrying about next year's prospects. She was thankful to have work in the city. But for how long was anybody's guess. She caught snippets of anxious conversations between Mr. and Mrs. Hrushowitz. The stock market had shown signs of recovering, but after the shock of the dramatic downturn the month before, they and the rest of the world were holding their breath, hoping there wasn't another dark slide around the corner.

The other matter troubling Lukia was her need to lose weight. The doctor had recommended it for her heart. That shouldn't have been hard, given that times were lean. But so far, evening meals of meat, potatoes and bread had changed little. She had a good appetite. Especially on the farm, after a shot of homemade vodka before supper. It was one of the few comforts she had. With liquor warming her belly, a hearty meal, and the singing of folk songs afterwards, she could forget for a while what she'd given up and the dilemma she and her family were facing.

Because of the grim outlook, Petro and Anna pestered her about finding another husband. As if that would solve her problems. But as she'd told Maria, she wasn't interested. She'd learned to live without a man all these years. Sure, she was lonely, especially at night when the house was dark and her mind wandered back to Gregory. She'd remember their lovemaking, the smell of tobacco on his clothes, his husky voice, his bruising moustache on her lips, and his warm embraces. No matter how many times suitors had shown interest, there was always something about them she disliked. They were either drunks or so frail they needed a nurse, not a wife. Or a mother for their children. She had enough work with her own. She didn't need another man's family to take care of.

When Gregory died, she had thought she wouldn't be able to go on, and yet, remarkably, she had. Perhaps God had prepared her for her husband's death by first putting her through the misery and pain that came with losing children. There was no pain like that of losing a child before their time.

Maybe she'd change her mind about getting married again. Some women hopped from one man to another with little time in between. She couldn't understand how they could do that, but they probably wouldn't understand her, either. Even her daughters were different. Hania, her beautiful daughter, shy and retiring, had been unlucky in love. Lukia's heart tugged again with the memory of how Hania had died, three years after Gregory. After so many losses, Lukia almost gave up her faith. She couldn't understand why God was punishing her, but then she reasoned, it was not up to her to question Him. She prayed Dunya's life would be different. She was mature for her age in mind and body, and more of a flirt than her older sister. She had a knack for it. Already, she was attracting boys like flies to honey.

She'd lost Hania, but also her grandson. Kolya was just a baby when his mother died. Lukia had sewn him a sailor suit before he immigrated to Argentina with his father and stepmother, only months before she and her family left for Canada. Everything happened so fast that no one thought clearly. Perhaps she would have chosen Argentina too, if not for the wonderful land Canada promised.

And that wonderful promise had joined her family with Petro's in the same household. Now, she churned at night, thinking of ways to resolve Egnat's and Petro's disputes. In the past, she'd prided herself on sorting out any dissension, but there was nothing she could do to resolve their conflict. The cracks in their relationship were widening with each day. Surely, the bad blood between them was affecting the Karpinskys, too. How long before it became impossible for the three families to live under the same roof?

16

Too Many Circles

D unya's torment continued at school, even though her mother had made her a new flannel dress. When she wasn't drawing circles, she was staring out the window, wishing she was somewhere else. She didn't know why the teacher wasn't giving her any other instructions. Dunya suspected the teacher couldn't be bothered, or maybe she believed her new student wasn't capable.

The only exchange Dunya liked at school was the new name the students gave her. 'Dolly' made her feel like less of an outsider. Her family kept calling her Dunya, but Michalko and Havrylo were called by their new English names, Mike and Harry. Her mother had adapted to the change, showing some pride in accepting what she said was the Canadian way. She even liked that there was an English equivalent for her name—Lucy—but was not in favour of anyone calling her that. She couldn't give up everything, she said.

Dunya was surprised to learn that one of the Ukrainian farmers had anglicized his name. Kolinsky became Collins. And yet she didn't blame him. Slurs could cut more than knives. You couldn't see the wounds, but they were there.

Dunya might have been able to endure the teasing, but with

her mother working in Winnipeg and Elena occupied with Genya and housework, there weren't any sympathetic ears at home. She also felt lonely. Olga's house was too far to visit spontaneously and there were no invitations from the other classmates to get together after school—not that Dunya had any time, given her chores of milking the cows, helping with the cooking and the baking, and cleaning up after supper, but she would have liked some social time with girls her own age.

The Jonesky girls across the road from their farm offered to take her for a ride in their family car, but she declined because her mother had heard the Jonesky girls were wild and everyone knew what happened to wild girls. Dunya wouldn't have gone for that ride, anyway. She'd seen the younger Jonesky girl lean out the car window and swig a bottle of beer, giggling as if to show the alcohol was already doing its job. Her cousin in the old country had been a wild one, too. She'd shown her junyou to the boys in the school outhouse, and not long after, a couple of them held her down while the other two had their way with her. Dunya couldn't risk anything like that happening to her.

With no time or opportunity to socialize, Dunya stuck to home. That meant putting up with the boys in the house—three brothers, five male cousins, and two Karpinsky boys—and their ferocious male energy. And with no locks on any of the bedroom doors, Dunya was always mindful when she dressed in their family room.

One day, Mrs. Karpinsky took her aside and said, "Watch Boris. Don't let him make a baby."

Taken aback, Dunya said, "You don't have to worry, Mrs. Karpinsky. That won't happen." Dunya wondered what Boris's mother thought of her. She wasn't that kind of girl. She'd known how babies were made from the time she was five, when she'd seen a bull go at it with a cow.

Mrs. Karpinsky said nothing for a moment and simply stared at her. "All right. You're a good girl."

After his mother's warning, Dunya regarded Boris as someone to be cautious around.

Not long after that conversation, when Dunya thought she was the only one in the house—the others were busy with chores in the fields or barn, or had left on some errand—Boris showed up in her bedroom doorway. She was putting away some newly washed underwear in the bureau drawer.

Alarmed by his sudden appearance, she said, "Boris, what are you doing here?"

"I saw you go to your room, and ..." He moved to come into the room.

"Stop, Boris. Don't touch me." She put her hands up as if preparing to do battle if she had to.

His eyes widened. "Don't worry, Dunya. I was only going to sit on the bed."

Not sure whether to continue putting her undergarments away or wait until he left, she kept her eyes on him.

"I just wanted to talk to you."

She sat down on the bed and said, "So, talk."

He mumbled, turned on his heels, and left as quickly as he'd come.

Relieved, she returned to her chore. While she folded her clothes, she reviewed her conversation with Boris. He was a gentleman, after all. She was closing the bureau drawer when she heard footsteps.

He stood in the doorway again. "Dunya, I meant to ask you. Do you want to be my mother's helper?"

Her forehead furrowed. That could only mean he wanted her to marry him when she came of age. Flattered to have a proposal at fourteen, she considered what that would mean. She couldn't see having Mrs. Karpinsky for a mother-in-law. She believed that Boris's mother wanted a daughter-in-law who was compliant, someone she could boss around. Dunya picked at a sore on her hand as she thought about a life with Boris.

"Do you?" he asked, shifting from one foot to the other.

She cleared her throat. "No thank you. I have enough to do for my own mother."

His face fell. He was probably surprised she didn't jump at the chance. His family was better off.

"Is there anything else?" she asked. "I have to feed the chickens."

He shook his head and left.

She felt proud of herself. She'd handled a delicate matter maturely. It would've been unfair to say yes when she had no feelings for him. He was nice enough, but not the kind of man she was looking for. She couldn't say what kind she wanted, but she knew it wasn't him.

School became even more unbearable, and by the end of November, Dunya decided she'd had enough. But to quit, she'd need her mother's permission. Instead of going directly home from school, she decided to visit her mother in Winnipeg and plead her case.

It was a two-hour walk to the edge of the city and at least an hour by horse and cart. Soon after setting out, she realized it was colder than she had expected. She stopped to raise her collar and button her fake fur coat up to her chin.

She'd been walking for a while when she spotted a police car coming up the road. She stuck her thumb out to hitch a ride. The police car slowed down and came to a stop beside her.

The dark-haired cop leaned over and rolled his passenger-side window down. "Where are you headed?"

"You go to Winnipeg?" asked Dunya.

"Not all the way, but get in. I can get you closer at least."

Dunya didn't fully understand what he meant, but got in the car. The policeman tried to have a conversation but gave up when he realized she spoke little English. They drove for a few miles before they came to a crossroad where Highway No. 7 and Highway No. 6 met. It seemed familiar, like the place she'd stopped at with her mother on a previous trip to Winnipeg, so she said, "Please, sir. I get off here."

He peered out his window. There were no other cars coming. "Are you sure this is where you want to get off? There's nothing here."

"Yes. Very good. Thank you." She got out of the vehicle, assuming she was at the north end of Selkirk Avenue, where it connected with Keewatin. Within minutes of the police car leaving, she realized she had no idea where she was. The more she hiked, the more confused she became. There were no cars in either direction. She decided not to wander too far in case she was headed the wrong way. Slowing her pace, she considered her predicament. Her breath formed white clouds in the frigid air. The wind had picked up and snow started to fall. She stopped walking for a moment to watch the crystals dot her sleeves and marvel at their intricate beauty. To keep warm, she periodically stamped her feet and flapped her arms across her chest. With the light dropping, she prayed a car would come soon. Her fingers had turned white with the cold and she attempted to warm them by blowing on her hands. Looking up, she saw the headlights of a vehicle coming towards her. Again, she stuck out her thumb.

Relieved to see a car with an older couple pull up and stop, Dunya opened the door and said, "Thank you," before climbing into the back.

"What are you doing hitchhiking at this hour of day?" the woman said. "There's nothing around here. You could easily get hit and no one would see you. In fact, my husband was coming right for you when I pointed you out. Isn't that right, Henry?"

"Yes, that's right," he said, not taking his eyes off the road.

The woman peered out the windshield. "It's coming down fast now. Good thing we saw you, that's all I have to say."

Dunya said, "I'm okay."

The woman continued to jabber as they zigzagged down the gravel road with the driver trying to avoid the ruts. Dunya wiped the steamed-up side window with her sleeve. She couldn't see any city lights.

Alarmed, she said, "Stop, please."

"What's the matter, honey?" the woman said, as her husband slowed the car down.

"I want go to Winnipeg."

"No, honey. Sorry. We're going to Stony Mountain."

"Oh no," she said, her voice breaking. "I am lost."

"Where do you live?"

"Rosser, but Mama's in Winnipeg," she muttered, glad she knew that much. "I go see Mama."

Henry said, "Oh, sorry. We can't drive you there. We have young ones at home we have to get to. It'll be their bedtime soon." He applied his brakes.

"Okay," Dunya said, opening the car door.

"Are you sure you want to get out here?" the woman said.

"Yes, please."

As Henry and his wife pulled away, Dunya had second thoughts. All she knew was she had to walk back to where they'd picked her up, and that was a long way. The woman was right. With the heavier, blowing snow hitting her face and legs at a slant, it was hard to see for any distance in the darkening sky. She was tired and cold—on top of being angry about the teasing at school. This was no life. Her mind wrestled with images of the English girls at school and how they'd laughed and whispered behind her back, and how the boys had made jokes about her breasts, sometimes right in front of her, as if she were invisible. Did none of them think she had feelings? Had none of them experienced loneliness? She considered lying down in the ditch by the side of the road and freezing to death—the kids at school wouldn't care—but thinking of her mother and how many children she'd lost kept her moving. She walked for another ten minutes before a dark sedan approached with its lights on. She stepped out into the middle of the road and raised her arms. She prayed they would stop. She felt she could go on no longer. All she could think of was: *Hit me or take me.*

The dark sedan stopped.

Breathing a sigh of relief, she opened the front passenger door. "Hello," she said to the driver, a man with a pockmarked face. "You go to Winnipeg?"

"Climb in. You could've got yourself killed standing in the road like that. You need your head examined."

Dunya's legs and body shook with the cold.

He turned up the heater. "What's a young girl like you doing out on the road so late at night?"

"Sorry. I speak little English."

"Okay. You just let me know where you want to get off. I'm going as far as Arlington Street. Do you know where in Winnipeg you're going?"

"What?"

"What street in Winnipeg do you want?"

"Selkirk Avenue." She took a piece of paper from her pocket and showed him the address.

"Well, I'd like to help you out, but I'm only going as far as Arlington and Selkirk. The place you're looking for is further down. About another five blocks, I'd guess."

"Okay," Dunya said.

When he dropped her off, he pointed her in the right direction. The sidewalks were empty and there was only the odd car passing down Selkirk Avenue. The street lights were on and the snow, melting as soon as it hit the ground, gave the sidewalk a glassy sheen. Having warmed up during the car ride, she found the walk to Mrs. Hrushowitz's home not as bad as being out on the country road at night. By the time she arrived at the house, it was eleven o'clock.

Mrs. Hrushowitz answered the door wearing a robe over her nightgown. "Yes, what do you want?"

"My mama. Lukia Mazurec."

Mrs. Hrushowitz looked startled for a moment, then said, "Come in. I'll get her."

Dunya waited in the hallway which was fancier than any she'd ever seen. Its cream-coloured wallpaper resembled some expensive taffeta material. There was a walnut clothes rack in the corner, a walnut-framed oval mirror over a hat stand, and on the floor, a wine and navy blue patterned wool rug. There were no icons hanging on the wall, not that Dunya expected any. Her mother had told her she was working for a nice Jewish woman.

What was taking her mother so long? Her boots were wet, and she was reluctant to move for fear of muddying the floor, but her curiosity got the best of her and she stepped lightly over to the mirror to have a look. She looked like a poor waif. Frowning at her bedraggled reflection, she took off her wet hat and patted her damp and matted hair.

Her mother appeared in the hallway, wearing her nightgown; she seemed drowsy, as if she'd just woken from a deep sleep. Her eyes widened at the sight of her daughter. "Dunya, what are you doing here?"

"I had to see you."

"Oy, what happened to you? Come here. Let me get you out of those wet clothes."

Mrs. Hrushowitz said, "Would you like me to make some hot tea?"

"Thank you, Panye. That would be lovely."

After Mrs. Hrushowitz left, her mother said, "My God, what were you thinking?" Shaking her head, she put her arm around Dunya and guided her down the hallway to a room with a narrow bed and dresser.

17

SLAVING AWAY

After settling Dunya in her bed—which was barely wide enough for one person, let alone two—Lukia lay awake for hours. It was no good working so far from home. Anything could have happened to her daughter on the road. She was so headstrong, there was no stopping her once she'd made up her mind about something. Lukia had to agree that school sounded terrible. She didn't understand these teaching practices and wished she could help her daughter, but not knowing the language, she could do nothing except allow Dunya to leave school.

What a shame. She'd become another uneducated woman, vulnerable to the deceit of others. On the other hand, her daughter was no fool. She'd shown an aptitude for numbers. She'd learned how to barter for what she needed and could strike a good bargain when pressed. Once she learned the language, she might find some meaningful work, but for now, she could get work as a housekeeper in the city.

In the morning, Mrs. Hrushowitz told Lukia that the Novaks, who lived across the street, hadn't found household help yet. Dunya immediately went over to ask about the position. When she returned, she told her mother that, like Mrs. Hrushowitz, they had a well-appointed home with imported carpets and fine wood furniture, and she was to start in two days. Mrs. Novak had hesitated about hiring someone so young but, after hearing why Dunya wanted to quit school, she said the job was hers.

Though Dunya was now working across the street, Lukia barely saw her. Dr. Novak's wife kept her busy from early morning until midnight—washing, ironing, and cooking. The pay was reasonable—fifteen dollars a month, three dollars more than her mother—but Mrs. Novak wasn't. She complained that Dunya used too much soap in the washing machine, so she made her wash the clothing, linens and bedding by hand. When Lukia learned about her daughter's heavy workload, she offered to help in the evenings when she was free, but Mrs. Novak wouldn't allow it. Lukia guessed she didn't want her to see how hard she worked her daughter. It was absurd what some people expected. They were so high and mighty, and yet they treated those less fortunate coldly.

Dunya grumbled to her mother, and after a couple of weeks of hearing complaints, Lukia said, "You'll make yourself sick if you keep this up. Tell Mrs. Novak you can't work for her anymore. There are lots of positions for housework. You don't have to work like you're a slave."

The next housekeeping job Dunya secured wasn't much better. As a result, Lukia agonized over the work they had to do to make ends meet. How had she missed the fact they'd be moving to Canada in the middle of the summer, too late to do any planting of grains that could sustain them over the winter?

Lukia was ill-prepared in other ways, too. She'd experienced cold before, but not the kind she had to endure in Manitoba. November brought biting snow and wicked wind, which whistled like some demon and lashed their faces and turned their fingers white, even in mitts. In Volhynia, the temperature dipped below freezing, but not as low as here, nor were the winds as severe. From what Mrs. Hrushowitz had told her, the worst was yet to come. January was the killer month, with temperatures rivalling those of Siberia. One day, she and her daughter would have to buy fur coats.

Lukia had always relished returning home for the weekends, but since Egnat and Petro had quarrelled, the atmosphere in the house had changed.

Petro had always prided himself on being a ladies' man, so when Elena dismissed his attempts at flattery, he pouted. Lukia understood the attraction. Her daughter-in-law was pleasant to look at, kind, always willing to lend a hand, and never complained. Her rejection added to his irritation with Egnat. Petro had difficulty sharing center stage with another man in the house. In his mind, there was room for only one cock of the walk.

It seemed no matter what Egnat said or did, Petro would say, "You think you're so smart." "You're a pipsqueak." "Let a real man do that." Provoked, Egnat would snap back and stomp out of the house.

Unable to stand the constant bickering, Lukia confronted her brother one late afternoon. He'd come into the house to roll a cigarette and, having finished, was heading back to the barn. Wanting privacy from the others, she put on her coat and stepped outside to follow him. The snow-covered ground took on a blue tint in the fading light. He barely noticed her presence and marched ahead. "Petro, wait! I need to talk to you."

Petro stopped and wobbled as he stood near the front door. His glassy eyes showed he'd had more than a few shots of homebrew. Lukia immediately regretted she had chosen this time to talk to him.

"Why are you picking on Egnat?"

"He's still wet behind the ears. He thinks he knows everything."

"He's a grown man. He has a wife and child. You've seen how he works. He takes nothing for granted."

"Listen," he said, staring at her intently. "He doesn't show me the respect I should have. I'm his uncle. I'm older than him and he contradicts what I say." What her brother said was true. They'd been taught the young should bow down to the older generation. But how could her son show respect when his uncle's behaviour didn't command it?

"I know," she said. To appease him, she added, "You deserve respect."

"Talk to him then."

"Oy, Petro. I can talk to him, but it doesn't help when you bark at him every chance you get. He's not a child anymore. He deserves respect, too." She exhaled sharply. "And leave Elena alone. Go after your own wife. Enough already."

Petro's eyes darkened. "Are you finished?" He didn't wait for an answer and stormed off.

Later that evening, he yelled at Anna about something.

At bedtime, Lukia prayed to the icon of the Virgin Mary that hung over the bed she shared with Dunya. The icon was one her nephew had tried to burn after he'd joined the Young Bolsheviks in the old country. He and the other hoodlums had roamed the Ukrainian countryside burning anything religious. She had hidden the burnt edges of the icon under a simple wooden frame she bought in Lutsk. With the help of her faith, she had weathered wars, typhus and losing four children and a husband. Now, she pleaded with the Holy Mother to give her strength to endure the winter in Manitoba and show her the way out of the gloom she'd brought upon herself and her family. She also asked for the strength to bear the strain between her son and her brother. Outside, the wind howled as if mocking her request.

The snowstorm outside did nothing to calm Lukia's nerves. She shivered and buried herself under her goose-feather–filled perina. It was going to be another dreadful night, a night when she tossed and turned, reviewing the past and worrying about the future.

Lukia's talk with her brother did little to change the emotional temperature in the house. In fact, another incident the next day added fuel to the slow-burning fire between Petro and Egnat. She was clearing the supper dishes off the table when Egnat entered the house carrying his rifle. He sat down on a chair in the corner and began to clean it. Nearby, Rita and Dunya were playing a card game of Pig on the floor. Lukia had just placed the dishes in the sink filled with hot, sudsy water, when she heard a loud thud, then a shot. Dunya screamed. Rita started crying. Lukia turned to see a section of the ceiling rain down, scattering specks of cream-coloured plaster over Egnat, Rita, Dunya, and the surrounding area. The smell of gunpowder and smoke filled the air. Her son's mouth fell open.

Petro burst out of his room and took in the damage. "Durak!" he shouted at Egnat.

Egnat's face turned red. His uncle had called him an idiot.

"What happened?" asked Lukia.

Egnat said, "I thumped the butt of my rifle on the floor to loosen some dust."

"The fool didn't have his safety catch on," Petro said.

"Oy," Lukia said, staring at the ceiling. "What are we going to do now?" Elena came out of the bedroom. She must have had her nursing interrupted, because she was buttoning up her dress.

Mrs. Karpinsky rushed down the stairs into the living room. Seeing the destruction, she shook her head. "That's your room up there, Lukia."

"I'll fix it, I'll fix it," Egnat said, brushing the plaster off his pants with his hands.

"Yes, like you fix everything else," Petro said.

"There's no need for that kind of talk," Elena said, rushing to her husband's defense.

Fortunately, it was just the plaster that had fallen. The bullet had gone through the floor upstairs, but nothing else was damaged.

Petro continued to mumble "durak," causing Egnat to mutter under his breath as he swept up the pieces of plaster.

He later told his mother he realized his mistake. "I know it was stupid, but Uncle doesn't know how close I came to hitting him. He keeps needling and needling me."

"It's good you held on to your temper."

Egnat snorted and said it was only her presence that had kept him from lunging at his uncle and throttling him.

With the ongoing turmoil at home, Lukia thanked God she'd found a church to lean on. She appreciated Sobor's enthusiastic parishioners, who planned to build a grand cathedral with five domes like the one in the old country. Egnat and Mike, with their pitch-perfect voices, would have been welcome additions to the church choir, but they lived too far away to get to the city in time for evening practices. Lukia and her family had attended one theatrical production put on by the parish and found it as good as anything they'd seen in Kivertsi and Lutsk. The fundraising committee also had plans for concerts and poetry recitals featuring work by the poets Taras Shevchenko and Lesia Ukrainka.

Mike was, of course, thrilled about the drama staged and wanted to act in a production. If he proved to be successful in the upcoming audition, Lukia knew he'd put rehearsals ahead of any work demanded of him on the farm, which would infuriate Egnat, who depended on his brother's help. But she needn't have worried. His talent, though obvious, was rejected. Roles went to young men who had already established a presence in the congregation. Rebuffed, Mike declared himself to be Russian, much to the consternation of his siblings.

Lukia couldn't understand her son's announcement, which was a betrayal of sorts. Back in the old country, Lukia and her family had been under Russian rule longer than they'd been under Polish rule, but neither occupier had treated Ukrainians well. Then again, Mike was a hothead. He was rejecting his Ukrainian heritage as though it had something to do with his failure to get a role. He continued to attend church services, but the frown on his face suggested he wouldn't be going long. Lukia agonized over her son's extreme reaction, but she'd learned long ago Mike was not one to listen to reason.

Mike's failure to get a role wasn't the only problem at the church. Though Lukia valued Reverend Semen Sawchuk's fervent and uplifting sermons, he wasn't universally liked in the parish. The equally passionate Wasyl Swystun—the choir director and founding member of Sobor—challenged the priest on the running of the church. Besides being a gifted leader, Swystun was training to be a lawyer and used his persuasive talents to convince many of the parishioners their priest was overstepping his boundaries. Swystun made this accusation after noticing his name had been left off the fundraising brochure. The priest explained it had been simply an oversight, but the choir director was not about to be mollified. Lukia found the whole dispute unsettling. She went to church to pray and thank God for His blessings; she didn't go there to wage war on the priest who dispensed what she needed during these hard times.

Because of the endless gossip, Lukia avoided joining the Ladies' Auxiliary and told the rest of her family to stay away from those who wanted the priest gone. She'd had enough of conflict and political upheaval in the old country.

Christmas came with more uncertainty. Petro, Arkadi, and even Egnat told sad stories they'd heard locally or read in the newspaper. The news on the radio Petro had purchased also gave them much to talk about. They learned that a great number had lost their fortunes when the stock market crashed. What this meant for their household was yet to be determined. They had only been living together for three months, but given the poor land and the constant quarelling in the house, Lukia's nerves unravelled. If this was how it was going to be, there was little hope for the future. The Karpinskys had mentioned they were thinking of moving out in the spring. They said they didn't want to farm anymore, but Lukia suspected they'd had enough of the Mazurecs and Korneluks pitching insults at one another.

English Christmas also proved to be challenging. When they were planning to emigrate, she hadn't even considered there would be a different day to celebrate Christ's birth. Canadians celebrated it on December 25. They used the Julian calendar; the Orthodox in her village used the Gregorian calendar, with Christmas on January 7.

At the end of November, the stores in downtown Winnipeg displayed images of Santa Claus, as if his pending arrival was the main reason people would be rejoicing. She couldn't understand this way of celebrating such a holy event. In her faith, St. Nicholas, who brought sweet treats for children, arrived weeks before Christ did, so there was no confusion who to celebrate when Christmas arrived.

For the three families in the Rosser house, English Christmas came and went like any other day, but preparations for Ukrainian Christmas started weeks in advance. That meant forays into Winnipeg to buy special ingredients for cooking and baking. Between the Karpinskys, the Korneluks and the Mazurecs, each family contributed several dishes to make up the twelve meatless dishes required for Holy Supper on Christmas Eve. They planned to have borscht, fried pickerel, herring, varenyky with a couple of different fillings, nalysnyky, potato pancakes, cabbage-filled piroshky, and various vegetables.

One early January morning, when Lukia was making crepes and the sweet cottage cheese filling for nalysnyky, she peeked out the window to see if the winter winds had lessened. They hadn't. The roads hadn't been plowed, and even if they were passable, Petro's truck was unreliable in 30-below Fahrenheit temperatures. Why, just the other day it wouldn't start, and it took hours for the men to get it going again. It hardly mattered as the days had grown so frigid no one wished to go out. Anyone venturing outdoors returned shivering, with a face beet-red from the bitter cold.

The weather had to be as cold as Siberia. She and her children almost ended up there when the Germans invaded Volhynia in the early years of World War I. Fortunately, Gregory had told her to ask the officer in charge to send her instead to the Caucasus, where it was warmer. Gregory's enlistment in the Tsar's army had given her that advantage—the only one she could think of—and her destination was changed. In Siberia's icy landscape, she and her children would have suffered, would have even frozen to death. What would Gregory say now if he knew they'd traded the temperate climate in Volhynia for the extreme winters in Canada? She grunted. She knew what he'd say. His loyalty to their native soil wouldn't have allowed it.

She flipped the crepes in the sizzling butter, and scolded herself for dwelling on what she couldn't change. At least, she and her children were healthy and together. That was what counted.

On Christmas Eve, Lukia rose early to prepare the kolach, the round braided bread, for the centre of the table. After the dough had risen three times, she took her feather pastry brush and brushed melted butter on top before placing it in the oven to bake.

The women, along with Dunya, had worked all day preparing the dishes. With the afternoon light fading, Rita and George pressed their noses against the glass and waited for the first star to appear. Mike brought in the hay to place under the tablecloth and the straw for under the table. Anna buried nuts in the straw for the young children to find later. Harry tucked a clove of garlic under each corner of the tablecloth to ward off any evil spirts that might want to attend the Holy Supper.

Placing a lit candle in the window by the door, Dunya said to Rita, "It's for any poor traveller that happens to walk by. If they see this, they'll know they're welcome to come in for a bite to eat."

Rita said, her nose wrinkling, "What if it's somebody awful?"

"Don't worry. We'll only let in those who come in peace."

Lukia placed her kolach on the table, and Dunya inserted a beeswax candle in the middle. Once all the dishes were on the long table—made with wide plywood boards on saw horses—the three families gathered around. They crossed themselves three times, saying the Name of the Father, the Son and the Holy Ghost, followed by the Lord's Prayer.

Arkadi Karpinsky, being the oldest at the table, recited a prayer for a good harvest in the coming year and threw a spoonful of kutya—grains of wheat cooked with honey and poppyseeds—up to the ceiling. When the grains stuck, a promising sign, there were smiles all around. Following the blessing, each person put a little kutya on their plate.

Lukia said to the children, "Eat the kutya first. The grains stand for members of your family, both living and dead."

Petro poured himself a stiff drink of horilka before passing the bottle around the table. When all the glasses had been filled, everyone clinked them and said, "God willing!"

Lukia relished the warmth of the homebrew settling in her stomach and the beautiful meal laid out before her. But this year, she missed the carollers coming from her parish to sing carols on Christmas Eve. In Kivertsi, they didn't have far to travel, but here in Canada, with windswept roads blocked partly by snowdrifts, carollers risked getting stuck on their way to farmhouses scattered over many miles outside of Winnipeg. The carollers probably visited homes in the city where the streets were plowed. She worried that some of these old but comforting traditions might die with time. She silently asked God to look out for her and her family. She didn't want to lose touch with Him or the land of her birth.

18

WORSE THAN SIBERIA

Lukia had been looking forward to attending church for the Feast of Jordan, the day parishioners received a small bottle of holy water to bless their homes. The service, featuring a large cross carved out of a block of ice in the churchyard, always occurred on January 19, twelve days after Christmas. But when she cleared the frost from the kitchen window, she was confronted by a scene of massive snowdrifts and more blowing snow. It would be madness to go out in this kind of weather.

Petro stepped outside to check the thermometer hanging on the side of the house. He returned shivering. "It's 40 below," he said. "It's so cold, my piss'll turn to ice before it hits the ground."

The first month of a new decade was turning out to be a brutal one. Accepting that she couldn't make it to church, Lukia tore herself away from the window and made some tea. For now, there was enough heat in the house. Luckily, her sons had gone out yesterday with their cousins to cut wood for the stove. They'd left early with the sleigh, the bells on the harnesses tinkling and the air blue with the horses' breath as they rode away. Occasionally, they had to go twenty miles or more to find the forest where cutting was allowed. If they cut enough, they could sell it to others in the district who could not get out for various reasons. What wasn't sold was left to dry over the summer. You could never have enough wood.

Ever since Gregory died in the forest, Lukia never fully relaxed until her boys were back in the yard, splitting wood. She'd spent part of yesterday praying for her sons' safe return. The thwack of an axe sounded like music after hours of fretting. One good thing about chilly days: wood split easily.

Despite the frigid weather, milking had to be done twice a day, animals needed to be fed, and the barn had to be cleaned. After a cup of tea and some porridge, Lukia threw on her bikasha, sheepskin hat and felt boots and trudged to the barn, stepping carefully to avoid the icy patches.

Elena, Maria and Dunya were already on their milking stools. Lukia adjusted hers in the far stall. She didn't mind pulling teats, even when the one she was milking tried to flatten her against the wall. When that happened, she laughed and slapped the animal's rump to make her understand who was boss. What she especially liked about milking was the company of women. They joked and shared stories amid the sounds of milk hitting the pails, cows shuffling their feet, and horses neighing. But this day, the extreme cold deterred the women from lingering long.

They carried their full pails to the house and strained the milk into a separator bowl. They put aside the skim milk for the pigs and poured the cream into a crock. Given the road conditions, it was unlikely they'd be able to take their cream to the creamery tomorrow, so Lukia and Elena churned it themselves. They pressed the butter they made into one-pound blocks, to be traded later for groceries at Dan Balacko's store in Stony Mountain.

The next day, Lukia and Dunya prepared to return to the city for work, but because of the recent blizzard and impassable roads, Egnat was unable to get the sleigh and horses out. Lukia considered walking to the Rosser train station, but there was no guarantee trains would be running. The heavy snowfall, coupled with the wind, had created white hills everywhere. The snow had drifted so much overnight that vast amounts had piled up in front of their door. Her sons had to use all their strength just to pry it open. Shovelling took them another several hours to dig a path to the barn and outhouse. With no phone to contact their employers, Lukia expected they'd understand why she and her daughter hadn't arrived for work. She stared out the window at the unforgiving landscape. She'd traded one hell for another. This was worse than Siberia. At least in Siberia, there were people like her and a system she could understand.

The remaining months of winter dragged, as the brutally cold temperatures kept most people indoors. Fortunately, Lukia and her family had their work to occupy their minds. There was no time to reflect on what they were missing outside. They had tools to maintain, animals to care for, and household tasks that had been neglected when they were getting settled.

When the crocuses finally pushed through the wet snow in the spring, they hoped they would never see a winter like the one they'd had. The warmer weather brought renewed hope, and they made plans to plant grain as soon as the ground thawed.

Though the sight of melting snow raised spirits, the newspapers contained one article after another about the growing unemployment problem. Egnat read that men in need were visiting soup kitchens and standing in bread lines. The family heads in the Rosser house agonized about the days ahead.

The growing desperation in the country reached a crescendo in June, when the electorate—fearing ruin and poverty in the future—voted in R. B. Bennett, a millionaire and a Conservative, as prime minister. They figured, since he had become rich on his own, he'd know how to get the country out of the slump it was in. With 400,000 out of work, Bennett promised relief. Currently, help in Winnipeg was being provided by charities and emergency relief centres. Those who were used to paying their own way shook their heads, wondering if handouts were essential or only encouraged sloth.

Government relief was a foreign concept Lukia and the other adults in the household couldn't fathom. In the old country, no one expected handouts, and the government offered none. Family helped family and neighbours helped neighbours; that was the only help you could rely on. It was a mark of shame if you couldn't pay your bills and had to ask for financial aid. Here in Canada, many seemed willing to trade their pride for some food and a place to lay their heads. But the fact they could get help showed that Canada was a country with some heart.

Summer brought some rain. It wasn't nearly enough, but Lukia and Egnat weren't unduly concerned yet. Wheat required little from nature until it reached a height of six to eight inches.

However, one Sunday, farmers joined city dwellers in St. Mary's the Protectress Sobor, filling it to capacity, to pray for better times. After the service, congregants gathered in the churchyard to gossip and discuss the gloomy news. Concern about crops wasn't the only topic. Rumours circulated that immigrants seeking relief could be deported, but no one knew of anyone who had been.

All the way home in the wagon, Lukia and Egnat reviewed what they'd heard. Though no one in their family had ever stood in line for handouts, the possibility of that kind of desperation hung over their heads like a grey cloud. Anxiety about deportation and hope for a better growing season competed for their attention.

Hope stayed afloat during those early summer days. One bright note for Lukia was the newfound peace in the house. She reasoned the three families had finally adapted to their crowded quarters. The sunny days helped, as did the separate sections on the farm. Egnat and Petro went about their work, spread far apart from one another in the sunshine. The other bright note was the blossoming of the sunflowers she'd planted in the garden—along with the usual corn, cucumbers, turnips, potatoes, onions, garlic, tomatoes, carrots, beets, cabbage, watermelon and cantaloupe. The sunflowers' cheery yellow petals brought back wonderful memories of home in Volhynia, where they bordered mature vegetable gardens and produced seeds for snacks and flowers for bridal bouquets.

Warm days also meant dry days, and too many dry days meant parched fields of grain. Before long, Lukia and Egnat wore identical frowns. The blue sky overhead had no clouds in sight.

"Nu," Lukia said, "what can we do? It's in God's hands."

Egnat scratched his head. "If we don't get rain soon, our crops will suffer. We'll be lucky to have enough to feed ourselves, never mind pay the taxes."

"Oy, that's how it is." There was nothing they could do but pray for rain.

With the country in economic decline, immigration had come to a halt. Egnat wrote to their family and friends in Volhynia to tell them they should stop thinking of emigrating, as Canada's doors were closed. With the rise of unemployment in the cities, ugly signs of discrimination threatened to boil over into violence on the streets. It had happened before, when the soldiers came back after the Great War to find jobs wanting. They'd blamed the immigrants, especially the Ukrainians, whom they called *Bolshies*, as if they were landed Bolsheviks, and other derogatory names, like *garlic stinkers*. Long-buried resentments found a voice in the unemployment lines. With jobs scarce, those who'd been in Canada for a while resented the newly arrived.

When Petro came back from the city carrying the latest *Ukrainian Voice*, the Korneluk and Mazurec families gathered around the kitchen table to hear the news. It turned out the rumours they'd heard in church were true. Egnat read, "More and more Ukrainians are being deported. They can't manage the rent or pay their mortgages. Canada doesn't want anyone who can't manage on their own."

Lukia harrumphed. "The government shouldn't have advertised the best land in the world. Of course, people jumped at the chance."

"We came at a bad time," Petro said. "Businesses have folded. Too many invested heavily, and now they're paying the price. I saw hundreds of people lining up for jobs outside Eaton's department store on Portage Avenue."

"They're hiring?" asked Lukia.

"That's what I was told, but they'd never hire an immigrant. Why are you even asking? You don't speak English."

This was one time she agreed with her brother. New fears of being sent back enveloped them all. Petro left the newspaper on the table for the Karpinskys to read when they returned from the city.

Early fall rains brought some respite. Lukia and Egnat harvested about forty bushels of wheat per acre. In exchange for help with his harvest, their neighbour Ihor Chimiuk sent his men over to lend Lukia and her family a hand. On threshing days—with the work all manual—she and her children were up at four in the morning and didn't get to bed until eleven-thirty at night. The men used scythes to cut the wheat; the women used sickles. They didn't have the money for the machines that would do the work in less than half the time.

At day's end, the men dragged themselves to bed, as did the women. When the women weren't in the fields helping, they were caring for the young, carrying lunch out to the men, cooking, baking and washing up after three heavy meals a day. They served hearty borscht with sour cream and rye bread, varenyky, holupchis, corn on the cob, kybassa and kishka, and for dessert, honey cake and watermelon from their garden.

Ihor's wife, Natasha, also put on a good spread at the end of their harvest, but when Lukia returned home after helping the Chimiuks, she found their farm road littered with broken watermelons from their garden. It was a shame, because she would gladly have given the hoodlums watermelons to eat, if only they'd asked.

With the promise of a decent crop, this should have been a time for elation, but it wasn't. Lukia, Egnat, Petro and Arkadi wore a look of gloom. Wheat prices had fallen yet again. Before they arrived in Canada, farmers were getting $1.40 a bushel; now it was half that. Everything was in decline—milk, cheese, beef, chickens, eggs. The only livestock with any lasting worth was a good milk cow, and no farmer would be foolish enough to give one up.

When it was time to deposit their wheat at the Manitoba Pool grain elevator a few miles away, Lukia told Egnat she wanted to go, too. She was curious about the Canadian system, especially with the unexpected slump in agriculture.

The ride to the elevator was rough. With every pothole they hit, the grain shifted, forcing Lukia to hang onto the sides of the wagon for balance. She kept glancing back at the grain box, as if it was filled with gold and their family fortune could easily slide off on the bumpy road.

When they got to the elevator, the operator in charge weighed the wagon with the grain box, then tipped it mechanically, allowing the wheat to flow through a hole in the floor. Lukia and Egnat watched the grain being conveyed to the top of the elevator and poured into different bins. After that, the operator weighed their wagon again, this time with the empty box, and marked the correct amount of wheat.

The operator, a slight man in dirty cotton pants, gave them a partial payment and said the rest would follow in three installments over the year. He spoke slowly in English. Egnat understood his meaning and translated for his mother. "The government can't guarantee sales. That's why it won't pay for all the grain up front."

When Lukia complained about having to wait for payment, the operator said, "If you don't like it, you can go to a private elevator. They'll give you a full amount there, but in the end, it'll be less in total."

His firm response unnerved her. Lukia left feeling they had no choice. They had to trust that the future payments would come, which was hard, given that she'd grown to distrust any government. They'd all lied to her.

She wasn't alone in her doubts. With low prices for their grain, all the farmers they encountered had deeply lined faces. How were they going to pay their mortgages or their rent? How were they going to feed their families? Was this an unusually poor year? Would the following year set them on the road to prosperity? Hope was a thread they all clung to, even with news of mortgage foreclosures, mounting debt, and daily reports of increasing numbers of men seeking relief to survive. That thread grew thinner with each passing day.

Anna gave birth to her seventh child, Nicholas, on a weekend in early December. Fortunately, Lukia was home. The men vacated the house when Anna went into labour. While Lukia boiled water, she chortled about the men's escape. She supposed they didn't have the stomach to hear a woman scream in agony. She then gave her sister-in-law a shot of homebrew to dull the pain.

Elena and Dunya took turns soothing the expectant mother with a cool, damp cloth on her forehead.

Anna's delivery went well, but she whispered to Lukia, just before she gave the last push, "This has to be my last. I'm going to keep my legs together from now on."

Lukia understood. It was her sister-in-law's only choice if she wanted to follow the church's teachings. Lukia had heard that some women used herbs and other means to end a pregnancy. Did they feel guilty about ending a life? It was never something she considered. And a good thing she hadn't, because she'd lost half of the eight babies she'd been blessed with.

After settling her sister-in-law with her newborn, Lukia left them sleeping. As she scrubbed the blood off the cloths used for the birth—the red quickly staining the water—she thought about Anna's vow. Would she be able to keep her husband off of her? Petro wasn't a man you could say no to. It was true of most of her countrymen. They could stick it in, but they left the resulting children for the women to raise.

19

STORM CLOUDS

For the second year in a row, the severe winter weather forced the families inside, which once again heightened tensions. Everyone was underfoot, not just the children. The women in the house did their best to lighten the mood. They encouraged the children to play cards, sometimes joining them in a game of Pig or Hola. But even that caused problems. In Hola, thwacking the loser's forehead—by releasing the finger against the thumb sharply—was the prize for winning. Dunya won more often than not. Alex complained loudly about the red mark she left behind, bringing his parents into the quarrel. Petro scolded his niece, who listened politely but didn't change her ways the next time she played. Lukia stayed out of it. She suspected her daughter was just getting even with Alex for all his teasing.

But close quarters also brought joyous times. After supper, Victor Karpinsky brought out his accordion to play folk songs. Ted accompanied him on his harmonica, and Egnat took out his black comb and, after wrapping it with a rolling paper, hummed the melody on the comb's teeth. They sang about snow-topped mountains, a poor widow, young girls pining for the boys they love, and boys causing problems by keeping the girls out too late.

They sang about all of life's joys and miseries, from birth to death. There was nothing better to heal rifts than a burst of laughter or an exuberant folk song or a lament they could all relate to. When they weren't singing, they were admiring the latest drawing that Ted had completed. No one knew where he got his talent, but it was one they all encouraged. He did odd jobs for neighbours during the winter months just so he'd have money for paints and paper.

As much as these evenings raised the families' spirits, they couldn't erase the angry exchanges. Clashes erupted once again between Petro and Egnat and also between Egnat and Mike, which frustrated Lukia to no end. Some past slight, smoldering like a hot coal waiting for a spark to ignite, was bound to come up unexpectedly in the middle of what had started out as a pleasant evening of talk and song. It couldn't be avoided, not with so many sharing the warmth of the old woodstove. Petro and Egnat circled each other like two boxers, assessing the best time to get in the first punch. As for Mike, the older he got, the more difficult he was to deal with. He'd never been happy with the idea that Egnat, being the eldest, should have more authority. Lukia was thankful that Harry had the good sense to stay out of the way of both his brothers.

The temptations of the bottle and loose Canadian girls drew Mike further and further away from his duties. What tipped the scales for Egnat was his brother's problems with calculation. Whenever he sold any grain or dairy and cream, his figuring was always less than what Egnat had calculated. It led to accusations that could not be defended easily.

Lukia tried to help. It was another weekend, and she was out in the yard throwing feed to the chickens when she heard Egnat yelling at Mike for returning late from the city again. He accused his younger brother of avoiding his chores. After Egnat had stomped away, Lukia approached Mike while he was lighting up a cigarette. Scowling, he gave her a sideways glance, took a puff, and exhaled a circle of smoke.

"Mike, why are you arguing with your brother? He's older than you. He's been the man of the family since he was thirteen. You need to respect him."

"How can I respect him?" snarled Mike. "He doesn't respect me."

"You have to earn his respect. When you go into Winnipeg to sell milk and cheese and you forget to come back, that's a problem. And when you come back, you stink of alcohol. Where do you go? And how come you don't bring back what he expects? Are you using that money to buy booze or what?"

Mike didn't answer. He lowered his head and took another drag on his cigarette.

"I know Egnat can be rough, but he works hard. I don't know of anyone who works as hard as he does."

"Work isn't everything in life. You need fun, too."

"Fun? Of course you need fun. But first, you need to know how to put food on the table. If you're hungry and you don't have a place to sleep, how will fun help? We all have to do work we don't like."

He gave her a sideways glance again.

"Do you think I like to work from morning till night in the fields? Do you think I like working as a maidservant in the city? Who likes such hard work? But it has to be done." Mike's eyes softened. What was he thinking? Were any of her words sinking in? "You shouldn't shirk your responsibilities. You shouldn't throw money away on a good time. Someday, you'll have a family, and the habits you build now will stand you in good stead."

"I know, Mama, I know." He appeared to listen, but would he change?

She patted him on the shoulder and went back to the house.

The household also had to contend with the ongoing quarrels between Petro and Anna. Lukia's brother constantly picked at his wife, and Anna, in turn, picked on Rita, the only girl in her brood. Their sons wisely stayed out of their father's way. They knew he had a short fuse.

As for the Karpinskys, they minded their own business. It was an unspoken rule in the house. No family head interfered with another family's matters, even if the fighting was impossible to ignore. Still, Lukia found her family's squabbles grating and embarrassing. On more than one occasion, she cringed when she caught Arkadi exchanging looks with his wife.

Nightly, Lukia got down on her knees and prayed for peace. Peace in the house, peace on the land, and peace back in Volhynia.

1931 started out well, with a joyous Ukrainian Christmas celebration, but shortly after, Lukia had an unexpected fright, one that brought back some of the agony she'd faced in the old country. This time it was over Harry.

He went out one Saturday morning in January to hunt a rabbit. As Lukia stood in the doorway to see him off, she thought only of how nice it would be to make a rabbit stew, a dish they all enjoyed. He strode away in the brisk air, his boots noisily pounding the icy crust of the hard-packed snow. She didn't expect him back for a while, because he was a patient hunter and often stayed past mealtime to catch what he wanted. In case he got hungry, Elena had given him a few chunks of freshly baked bread to put in his pocket.

Meanwhile, Lukia turned her attention to the tasks at home. She'd been working the past week in Winnipeg and relished this time to prepare for the week ahead. She milked cows, gathered eggs in the chicken coop, and placed a large pot of water on the stove to boil. It was a good time to cook holupchis, as the Korneluks had gone to Winnipeg to buy staples and the Karpinskys had gone to visit a friend who was in the hospital.

In the kitchen, Lukia removed the rug covering the trap door and went down the narrow steps to the root cellar where she kept the vegetables from the garden. From a wooden basket, she selected four small cabbage heads and brought them upstairs. She felt a twinge in her heart but dismissed it. She'd had this before and knew it was just a sign she'd have to watch her salt intake. She massaged her chest, and the sharp pain vanished as quickly as it had come.

Elena came out of her bedroom. "Do you need some help?" she said as Lukia put a few heads of cabbage into the boiling water.

"No, I'm good, but a honey cake would be nice."

Elena pushed the curtain aside that covered the kitchen shelves and took out the bins of flour and sugar. While she stirred the cake ingredients, Lukia made the filling for the holupchis by mixing cooked rice with fried ground pork and onions. With the smell of fried onions permeating the air, she salted and peppered the filling, sampled a spoonful, and seasoned it some more. She'd have to remember to avoid adding extra salt at the table.

By the time Lukia put the pot of holupchis into the oven to bake, Dunya had returned from selling eggs to a neighbour. The late afternoon sky had clouded over and snow was beginning to blow, signs of a brewing storm.

Soon after, the front door opened again. Mike and Egnat stamped the snow off their boots and entered with their coats coated with a fine dusting of fresh snow.

"It's getting late," Lukia said. "Did you see any sign of Harry?"

"No," Egnat said, hanging his cap on the hook by the door. "He's not back from hunting yet."

Lukia went over to the window. The white landscape, blending with the dullness of the sky, made it difficult to see what was happening at the forest's edge. Her brow furrowed. "He should've been back by now. I wonder what's taking him so long."

"You know Harry," Egnat said. "He might be daydreaming, or maybe he didn't find a rabbit to shoot yet."

Lukia rubbed her thumb with her finger. "I think you better go see where he is. The wind is picking up, and he may not realize there's a storm coming."

"I'll go with you," Mike said to Egnat.

"Oy," Lukia said. "Don't take long. It's enough I'm worrying about one. I don't want to worry about all three of you."

Egnat grumbled and put his cap and coat back on and left with Mike.

Dunya washed the bowls and utensils used in making the cabbage rolls, and Lukia set the table. As she laid out the plates and cutlery, her mind stayed on Harry. She worried about his reasoning, ever since that gun incident in the old country when he'd accidentally shot one of his classmates from school and ended up in jail. Fortunately, the other boy escaped with only minor injuries. They released Harry when the boy's father decided not to press charges. He'd discovered Harry had just wanted to scare the boy after he'd made fun of the way he talked. Thanks be to God, her son had grown out of his habit of drawing out some letters—like saying "pay" instead of "p." His speech had changed, but not his quiet nature.

Dunya put her arm around her mother. "Don't worry, Mama. Harry can take care of himself."

"I don't know," Lukia said. "Oy, tragedy ... I can't take any more ..." Her voice trailed off. She stared once more out the window. Heavy snowfall was blanketing the ground fast. She could barely see the trees, which weren't that far from the house. She moaned when the sound of the howling wind penetrated the walls. The temperature had stayed below freezing for weeks; it was not the kind of weather any reasonable boy or man would want to be out in for long.

"What's taking them?" Lukia asked. If Egnat and Mike didn't find their brother soon, he could freeze to death. "I better go see myself."

"No!" Elena and Dunya simultaneously said. Elena added, "There are already three out there."

Frost coated the windowpanes, and Lukia had to clear a spot to get any view. Her mind wrestled with dire outcomes, but then the sound of a sleigh pulling up caused her heart to leap. She ran to the window, expecting her sons' return, but it was Petro, Anna and their family. The Karpinskys weren't far behind. With the stormy weather, they must have met up somehow and agreed to follow one another home in case of any trouble.

"Oy," Lukia said. "I should've looked at the sky before he went."

"How could you have foretold what the day would be?" Elena said.

"I won't forgive myself if I lose one more." She crossed herself.

The Korneluks opened the front door and brushed the snow off their clothes before stepping inside, with the Karpinskys following them.

Anna took off her coat. Noting Lukia's distraught face, she said, "What's the matter?"

"Harry went hunting. He's not back yet." Lukia continued to stare out the window. Soon, grey figures appeared in the distance. Was it them? Pressing her face closer to the glass, she made out only two figures at first. "Oy, don't tell me," she said, half crying. But shortly, a third figure came into view and her hand flew to her chest. "They're coming. Thank God." As they got closer, she noticed Egnat and Mike supporting Harry. Was he injured? Or worse, had he died? Not another one! *Please God, don't make me lose another one.* Her pulse raced as she waited for them to get to the front door. When they were mere steps away, she opened it wide, letting a gust of icy air fill the living room.

"Shut the door!" shouted Anna. "We have a baby here." She wrapped the small blanket around Nicky tighter and hurried to their room. The others quickly moved away from the door.

Supported by his brothers, Harry stumbled into the house, his clothes wet with snow. His skin was pale, his lips blue, and he shivered uncontrollably.

Lukia said, "Oy, son, son." Elena and Dunya ran to get perinas to wrap him with. Lukia and Egnat took off his bikasha and sheepskin hat and wrapped him in the feather-stuffed bed coverings. "Come by the stove," she said.

"We found him in the bush," Egnat said.

Harry's teeth chattered as he said, "I ate the frozen bread."

Lukia's heart pounded as she checked his hands and feet. *No frostbite, thank God.* Her memory of losing Ivan consumed her mind. He was twelve at the time and had come home wet and cold from hunting for his aunt's lost cow. With the doctor unavailable, she'd tried every treatment she could think of, but her son still died from pneumonia. She crossed herself, raised her eyes to heaven, and prayed, *Please God, let Harry live.*

"Mama," Harry said, his lips quivering. "You're scaring me."

"No, you scared me." Maria brought a comforter and added it to the other coverings on Harry.

"Thank you," Lukia said.

"It's nothing."

Elena gave him a cup of broth from the pot on the stove. "Drink it slowly."

Lukia's fright and ongoing concern darkened the mood in the house. Ill at ease, everyone ate late. Lukia and Dunya took shifts caring for Harry. Even Elena's honey cake did little to sweeten the atmosphere.

That night was a fretful one; Lukia kept checking whether Harry was recovering. Unlike what had happened with Ivan, Harry—except for a few sniffles—rallied quickly. By morning, no one would have known he'd spent several harrowing hours freezing in the woods. Seeing his ruddy cheeks, Lukia crossed herself and mumbled a prayer of thanks.

She made him a glass of hot milk, mixed with a spoonful of butter and two cloves of minced garlic on top—an old remedy for colds. He laughed at his brothers' jokes and devoured the porridge set in front of him. God had let her keep this one.

20

PRAYING FOR RAIN

After a few frigid days in February, the snow disappeared, leaving icy conditions behind. Lukia and her children had to tread carefully to and from the barn. When the ice turned to puddles, they changed from their felt-lined boots to rubber ones.

Egnat griped about the weather. He said it was difficult to get wood out of the forest, now that the muddy roads were impossible by wagon. He suggested they stretch their wood supply by dressing warmly indoors. Mike and his cousins grumbled, but when Egnat reminded them they'd have to go out and chop wood under these harsh conditions, they stopped their complaining and put some extra layers on.

Most alarming was another dramatic drop in grain prices, especially for barley. To add to their income, some locals raised pigs, but hog prices fizzled, too. When Egnat returned from the Rosser grocery store, he told his mother one farmer's grain hadn't sold yet, which was unusual. Typically, by this time of year, all of it would be gone, but who could sell with prices at twelve cents a bushel? Instead of selling, many were hoarding, hoping the prices would rise, or trading their grain for lumber or wood or whatever else they could get through bartering. Trading brought a return of twenty cents a bushel. It wasn't great, but eight cents more than what they could get at market.

They'd also heard that another grain organization, named the Manitoba Farmers Anti-Compulsory Pool League, had formed to compete with the Wheat Pool. Lukia thought it was akin to changing seats at a dance. Your view might be different, but your choice in dancing partners remained the same. Like the Wheat Pool, the new group had no authority over nature. It was the weather that every farmer battled, and so far, there were no signs the battle was waning.

By April, the worst of the winter was over. A gentle breeze, coupled with the fresh smell of the earth awakening after a long sleep, brought renewed hope for a better year. The Karpinskys, who had threatened to leave in the spring, decided to stay. Prospects in the city were no better, they said. But as the days got longer and warmer, the three families faced new challenges. The improvement in weather also brought unexpected dust storms. Thick clouds of black dust swirled across country roads and through farmhouses. The air was so bad, Anna and Elena worried about their children's lungs. Especially when one started coughing. It got so dark in the afternoon; lamps were lit two hours ahead of time. It seemed the sun had taken a holiday and wasn't about to return until the dust clouds dispersed.

The three families did what they could to keep the dust outdoors. They covered up the edges of windows and doors with any rags they could find. Venturing out to feed the livestock, they covered their noses and mouths with handkerchiefs. Trips to the outhouse involved going with heads lowered to avoid eating debris as it flew around. Their eyes smarted from the dirt flying in, and they often had to stop and get the specks out before their eyes turned red.

Lukia found the air so foul it was impossible to work in the garden and the fields. The dust continued to blow until midnight. It blew with a rustling noise, as if all the demons had sprung from hell and released a long, raspy sigh together.

After days of flying dust, the storm abated but left behind dirty houses, dirty barns, dirty chicken coops—in fact, dirty everything that stood in its way. Lukia held her head in her hands and bemoaned her lot. *What hell is this?*

When the sky finally turned blue again, the women aired all the bedding and the heavy winter clothing outdoors. Lukia and Elena, along with the other women in the house, swept and dusted every nook and cranny. They scrubbed the grey surfaces of the kitchen table, stove, and counters. Anna cried as she washed her baby's dirty diapers in a basin by the stove. "They'll never be white again," she said, and rubbed harder.

Once the dust storms passed, they got their crops in. And as they'd done in the old country, Lukia and Egnat rotated their crops. They planted wheat where barley had grown the previous year, barley where oats had sprouted, and oats where wheat had been seeded. Rotating crops, and leaving one section fallow, ensured higher yields. Fallowing kept the weeds down and preserved the moisture in the soil for the coming year. With their minds on crop rotation and not on what they'd endured, they got through each day. But Lukia noticed that her sons drank more than usual, as did most of the men in their community. She understood it was their way of blotting out the misery that had lodged in their stomachs and refused to leave.

Gregory had done the same. His excessive drinking had to do with what he'd suffered on the battlefield. Memories of torn limbs, shattered faces, and corpses left to rot kept him drinking late into the night. Whereas her sons' despair resulted from battles with nature, an impossible war to win. Drought, year after year without let-up, could suck the life out of any man trying to make a living off the land. So far, the drinking hadn't affected her sons' work, so she said nothing. If shots of vodka softened the blows of what they had to endure day in and day out, she wouldn't deny them the only pleasure they had.

But one time, Egnat had the misfortune of getting a bad batch of alcohol from an agent in Winnipeg's North End, one of many who sold home-brewed liquor from their homes. For about fifteen cents, you could get a large Coke bottle full of the illicit booze. It was so strong—one hundred proof—you could put a match to it and light it on fire. If it caught fire, you'd know it was pure and not watered down. Lukia heard that some folks added brown sugar to turn it golden brown, like good rye whisky. That one bottle could last a long time when diluted with water, or ginger ale. Well, that one time, after Egnat and a few friends drank some of that diluted booze and his friends went home, he complained about the fire in his stomach. It must've hurt like hell because he ran outside holding his gut and hollering he couldn't take it. When he continued to run in circles and cry in agony, Lukia asked Dunya to bike over to the neighbours and use their phone to call the doctor.

Fortunately, Dunya caught the doctor before he left on a trip. He had to unpack his car to come over. By the time he arrived, Egnat was feeling better. Embarrassed, he apologized to the doctor for interrupting his plans.

The doctor told them he'd seen this reaction before. After examining the little left in the bottle, he said someone had laced the alcohol with lye to make it stronger. After that painful experience, Lukia figured her son would think twice about drinking again, but she was wrong. His suffering did nothing to slow his alcohol intake. He did, however, exercise caution before he bought any more homebrew. He wouldn't buy it unless the bootlegger tasted it first.

As the year progressed, Lukia knew it was more than farming woes that had added deep circles under Egnat's eyes. Worries about the state of the country and what that meant down the road kept many people awake at night. With so many out of work, hungry and poor, men gathered in city parks and elsewhere to share their frustration. They turned their anger more and more towards immigrants, blaming them for the lack of opportunities. For Lukia, the news of young men mobilizing by the thousands was reminiscent of what had preceded the Bolshevik revolution. Young men in Russia had raged against the established landowners and royalty. Even the church. It was an experience she wished to forget. She had believed that by immigrating to Canada, she would escape that kind of horror.

To ease young men's minds and fill their bellies, the government of Prime Minister Bennett started make-work projects, but the work turned out to be meaningless. How could any man feel good when he spent the day digging holes, only for another man to come along soon after and fill them up again? Same went for road construction. They built roads that started nowhere and led nowhere. The government's meaningless projects kept the masses from revolting.

Then another massive dust storm hit in July, covering everything in a thick layer of dirt. Gritting her teeth, Lukia stood at the window with Maria and Arkadi and watched the wind hurl the earth around their farm. Egnat and Mike were at the barn doors, fighting to pull them shut. As for Anna and Petro, they were in their bedroom arguing, their voices rising in concert with the wailing wind.

It took a full day for the dust storm to die down, but the bickering between Lukia's brother and his wife showed no sign of stopping. Unable to stand the squabbling, Lukia escaped the tense atmosphere by going with Egnat to the Rosser General Store to pick up a hundred pounds of flour, fifty pounds of sugar, tea and some spices, and also to check their mail. There were often patterns printed on the cotton flour and sugar bags, and she liked to pick the ones that, after being emptied at home, could be sewn into lovely pillowcases. Mr. Francis, the grocer, didn't speak Ukrainian, but there was usually at least one customer who did. She scanned the store for someone she recognized. Her neighbour, Ihor Chimiuk, was watching two men play checkers at the end of the counter.

Lukia caught Ihor's eye, and he said something to one man before walking over to her.

"Good day, Lukia. How are you doing?"

"You know how it is. Not so good. And you? How's your place?"

"A mess. The dust storms came from Saskatchewan. We think it's bad here, but nothing like it is over there. We need to pray that beast stays on the other side of the border."

"Oy," she said, "as if we haven't suffered enough. Why is God punishing us?"

"Who knows," Ihor mumbled.

"Give my best to your wife."

He nodded and put on his beat-up fedora and left the shop.

Lukia traded cream and a few dozen eggs for flour and sugar. She waited until Mr. Francis marked down the purchases in a little black book, then asked for her mail. He turned to the wooden mail slots behind the counter and, from one marked with their postal box number, took out a pale blue envelope with red and blue stripes around the border.

"Here you are," he said, handing it to her.

Egnat, who'd returned from putting the bags of flour and sugar in the wagon, looked at the return address and postmark on the envelope. "It's from Pavlo."

She'd been expecting a letter from her brother, who was taking care of their mother. She silently prayed the envelope contained good news.

In the short time they'd been in the store, the sky had turned a sickly yellow, and the winds had picked up again, covering the bleak landscape with grey-brown dust. Lukia and Egnat tied scarves over their mouths and noses again for the journey home. Without the familiar blue of the sky and the green in the fields, it appeared they'd entered a part of the world God had abandoned.

Wishing to blot out the ugliness outdoors, Lukia made tea and sat down with Elena and Dunya at the kitchen table to hear Egnat read the letter. It was a good time, because the house was quiet. Elena said that Petro and his family had gone to visit a neighbour. The Karpinskys were at another church meeting.

It was the middle of the afternoon, but the light was poor; the sun was somewhere behind the sickly yellow sheet in the sky. Egnat lit the kerosene lamp and placed it close to his elbow. Anxiety clouded Lukia's mind as she waited for her son to open the envelope. She couldn't afford any more bad news.

"Dear Lukia and family," read Egnat. "How are you doing in Canada? We hope you are all well. We are like we were when you left. Not much has changed. There are still food shortages, but somehow families are managing."

"Of course," Lukia said. "Our people can make something out of nothing. Go on."

He moved the letter closer to the oil lamp. "So far, collectivization has stayed in the east. We are thankful for that."

"Ha," Lukia said. "That's one good thing about the Polacks. They're keeping the Bolsheviks away."

Egnat read on. "The Polish government is still trying to stop all Ukrainian culture. They've shut down the Prosvita societies in Dubno, Rivne, Kovel and Lutsk. One by one, they're closing all the Ukrainian schools."

"Oy," Lukia said. "Our language and customs will be lost. At least here in Canada, we should try to keep what is sacred to us." She leaned forward. "Is there any news about Mama?"

"Yes." Egnat took a sip of tea and continued reading. "Mama is fine. Just as active as ever, but a month ago she had an accident when she went to Pochaev."

"What kind of accident?" Lukia asked, holding her chest.

Egnat continued to read. "She was walking on the road and twelve horses ran towards her. She tried to get out of the way, but couldn't. She got trapped between them and was badly hurt and bruised."

Lukia muttered. "Of course, she's so thin."

"Poor Babcha," Dunya murmured.

Egnat turned the page. "She peed on her handkerchief and applied it to her wounds. A kind penitent picked her up in his wagon and drove her to the monastery."

"Thanks be to God she wasn't killed," Lukia said, crossing herself.

Egnat twisted his lips and read, "Please send some money. We could use the help. We pray that God takes care of you all. Your brother, Pavlo."

"Oy," Lukia said. "They want us to send money. They think this is like America. Streets paved with gold. You must write them and tell them we're struggling, too." She gave a deep sigh. "This is tragic. They're poor and we're poor, too."

Egnat folded up the letter and put it in his shirt pocket. "I'll write them later."

The news from home had been mixed. It reminded Lukia of why she'd left. She wished she could say it had been for a better country. Perhaps in time, she and her children would get on their feet. She wouldn't admit defeat, not yet.

After two weeks of dust storms, Lukia awoke, hoping the worst was over. But another horror was on display outside her bedroom window. Hordes of grasshoppers—millions of them—were jumping on the road, on the field, in the garden and around the house, as if they were trying to find an opening. Lukia threw a sweater over her nightgown and went into the living room.

"What new hell is this?" she asked Egnat, who'd just come in from the outside.

"I can't take one step to the barn without being whipped by grasshoppers hitting my face."

"Oy," she said, "we didn't need this as well. C'mon. We can't just stand here." She woke her children and Elena, then went to the basket where she kept old rags for fashioning rugs and handed them out.

Lukia and her family—soon joined by the Karpinskys and the Korneluks—marched up and down the rows of their fields, waving rags to fight off the grasshoppers. They flew into their hair and lashed their faces as the three families spent hours battling the insects. After a couple of days of covering the landscape, the pests disappeared. They left behind a sticky residue and had stained their white siding brown.

Egnat and Lukia examined the crops. Though damaged, they had largely survived. The grasshoppers hadn't hung around to feast, as they'd done in Saskatchewan and down south, but they had laid eggs near their cultivated fields, which, if not dealt with, would cause problems in the following year.

To combat a potential disaster, the government offered free poison. At first, Lukia was hopeful this would solve their woes. But when she discovered they were supposed to mix the poison, called Paris Green, with bran, sawdust, and salt—and cover their mouth and nose while doing it—she balked.

"What good is that?" Lukia asked her son. "We kill the grasshoppers, but God forbid you should get sick. And what if our livestock ingest it and get sick and die as well?"

"We have no choice," Egnat said, raising his palms in defeat. "This year, we were lucky. Next year could be a different story."

Petro and Arkadi agreed and set about preparing their own mixture for their fields.

Afraid of accidentally poisoning their animals, every farmer was on alert. They had to keep their livestock from roaming to places spread with poison. But try as they might, they couldn't keep some animals from getting sick. The livestock didn't know this was forbidden food and, being hungry, indulged themselves. Their indulgence wasn't lost on Lukia or the others. The roasted chicken and eggs tasted off. Rita and Dunya said the eggs tasted like grasshoppers. When Lukia asked them how they would know, they both said a grasshopper had flown into their mouths. They had spat it out, but the taste had remained.

After witnessing the effects of the poison and discovering that Paris Green was a fancy term for arsenic, Lukia vowed never to use that concoction again. She shared her concern with the other family heads. Later, Arkadi returned from a trip to Winnipeg with a better solution. He had talked to someone at the Winnipeg Grain Exchange who suggested they plow the grasshopper eggs four to six inches under in the fall to prevent them from hatching the next year. He'd learned that the grasshopper pods laid in grassy areas could contain up to one hundred eggs each. You had to bend down and poke at the soil with a penknife to locate them. Getting rid of the eggs might not prevent the hordes from coming altogether, but at least there would be fewer of them. It meant more work for all, but it was a better solution than taking a chance on fouling their own food and poisoning their animals with arsenic.

As bad as it was, Lukia felt luckier than most. Several farmers in their district had to reseed because the dust storms had blown away their seed along with their topsoil. They had to wait for a day with little wind to replant and avoid the seeds blowing away again. It also made no sense sowing if you couldn't see three feet in front of you.

With the forecast of hot and dry weather continuing into August, Egnat and the others in the household harvested their wheat early in the month, sweat staining the underarms and backs of their shirts as they toiled. This turned out to be a wise decision, because before long, the oppressive heat made it difficult to move. Their eyes became bloodshot and their mouths parched. Even the livestock looked defeated. Their horses plodded with their heads lowered to avoid the sun, and in the early evening they swung their tails like the cows, to keep the mosquitoes at bay.

When Dunya realized the pastures had turned brown and dry, she took the cows down the road to the ditches, where they could munch on grass that hadn't died yet. To further protect their animals and ensure plentiful milk production, Egnat and Mike laid dried moss near their cows and lit it. Smoke from the burning plant drove the pesky insects away. And when they ran out of moss, they lit piles of manure in the stone boats. The smoke rose, hovering over the animals' heads, and for a while they had relief from the bites that made them anxious and affected their milk.

Food safety was also a concern. With high temperatures during the day, the families had to lower their raw meat into the cool well to keep it from spoiling. Even then, they couldn't keep it more than a few days.

Life indoors wasn't much better. The heat from cooking and baking made the rooms unbearable. Beads of perspiration formed on Lukia's forehead as she kneaded bread. At least the grasshoppers had flown away and she could open the windows to avoid suffocation inside.

Every day for two weeks, she looked anxiously at the sky, hoping a cloud would appear. The few that showed up took one look and drifted away, as if hanging around was a bad idea. The remaining crops struggled to survive under the sweltering conditions. Daily, Elena hauled water from the well and carefully poured a meagre cupful on each plant in the garden. Even so, corn stalks sagged and eventually lay on the ground after days of suffering the onslaught of wind and drought. The sunflowers also gave up and drooped their petals; the leaves turned brown and shrivelled; and the stems folded over, as if the load they carried was unbearable.

Concern about the future was etched on every farmer's face. Prices for butter and eggs had plummeted to almost half of what they were the year before. With that kind of price drop and debts mounting, how could any farmer make ends meet? If they weren't working around the clock to keep their plants from dying, they would've had time to crawl into a corner and cry.

And then, near the end of August, it poured as if there was no stopper in the sky. Standing in the doorway, Lukia's stomach churned as the sky opened and flooded her garden and fields. Rain poured down in sheets so thick, everything beyond a few feet blurred. Lightning lit up the sky and the loud thunder made everyone in the yard run for cover. Lukia had never seen thunderstorms like the ones she witnessed on the prairies. The noise made the horses skittish, and the other barnyard animals grunted and groaned as if they were about to be hit.

The puddles turned their road into a river. With the rain relentlessly pounding the ground, Lukia and Egnat could do nothing but wait for it to stop. She was thankful they'd collected their grain—not like some farmers in their district who were still in the midst of harvesting.

But because of the terrible weather, their crop fell short of expectations. The Winnipeg Grain Exchange was paying only forty cents a bushel, and that was for No.1 grade wheat. The grain elevators did the grading, and if you weren't satisfied with their valuation, you could take a sample to Winnipeg and have it graded there. *Fat chance of getting more*, said one of their neighbours.

Given the poor crops and payment, Lukia had no time to lament. With the harvest completed, it was time to preserve food for the winter; vegetables and fruit had to be canned and the root cellar filled. Afterwards, Lukia and Dunya would return to the city to do housework. There were still enough rich people around to hire maids for the long winter months.

Unfortunately, Mr. and Mrs. Hrushowitz were no longer in the well-to-do category. They'd fallen on hard times and had to close their dress shop. However, Mrs. Hrushowitz gave Lukia a reference letter that helped her get employment as a maid for the Bushbys on Selkirk Avenue and, as a parting gift, a string of beautiful fake pearls.

21

MRS. HILL

Compared with her mother, Dunya had difficulty securing a suitable position. All she could find were odd housekeeping jobs in the North End of Winnipeg, but then in February, she secured a position to cook and clean at the Hills Farm, four miles from her home. The pay was $15 a month for three days a week. Decent pay, but the lady of the house was far from friendly. Mrs. Hill, a middle-aged woman who wore drab housedresses and sturdy shoes, presented as a stern schoolmarm; her frizzy brown hair framed her long, angular face like an ill-suited cloche hat. She talked in short, clipped sentences, as if she had more important things to do than waste her time talking to the help.

After setting the work days, Mrs. Hill showed Dunya the room where she'd sleep. There was barely room for a single bed because of the bags of flour and other pantry items stored there. Dunya grumbled to herself. The woman of the house obviously thought little of hired help.

"Oh, one more thing," Mrs. Hill said, after Dunya's first day of work—which involved scrubbing all the floors and the kitchen walls. "Somebody might come and knock on your door." She shook her finger. "Don't let them in."

Dunya wasn't sure who Mrs. Hill was referring to until she met the hired man. He was in his thirties, long-limbed in his grimy overalls, his black, greasy hair unkempt and falling over his large ears. He had a prominent nose and narrow eyes, one of which had a habit of twitching when he talked. He was friendlier than Mrs. Hill; at least, he cracked a smile when they first met.

On her second day of work, when she was clearing the breakfast dishes off the kitchen table, he walked by her to get a drink of water at the sink. Wary, Dunya half-smiled and continued with her chores.

Not long after that, he returned to the kitchen carrying milk cans and placed them on the table. She was in the middle of washing the dishes. Thinking he'd soon leave, she turned her back to finish scouring the plates. He came up behind her and grabbed her bottom. She yelped, "What you doing?"

He snickered. "What do you think?"

Dunya hit him across the mouth with her soapy hand.

He took the towel off the hook and wiped his face. "You're a feisty one."

The sound of footsteps shortened the exchange. Mrs. Hill entered the kitchen. The hired hand nodded at her and abruptly left.

Dunya wasted no time telling her employer what had happened. When she finished, Mrs. Hill said, "That's nothing. How old are you?"

"Sixteen."

Mrs. Hill snorted. "That's old enough. You're a young woman; he's a young man. That's how it is."

Dunya gawked at her employer in disbelief.

Mrs. Hill didn't notice Dunya's shock, as she was hunting in the pantry for something. She picked up an empty shopping bag from the shelf and said, "I'm going to the market with John—"

"The hired hand?"

"Of course, the hired hand," Mrs. Hill said curtly.

"Ha. When you go to the market with him, you can let him

feel you. I want my wages. I quit." Dunya was proud she knew enough English now to not only understand but also to stand up for herself.

Mrs. Hill's eyes widened. "You've got to be kidding."

"No. No kidding."

"That didn't take long."

Dunya stood resolute.

Shaking her head, Mrs. Hill opened her purse and, after mentally figuring out what she owed, paid her. "Tsk." She huffed. "You won't find much better anywhere else."

Dunya ignored her and went into her room to pack.

As she left, Mrs. Hill said mockingly, "Good luck finding something else. Beggars can't be choosy."

Dunya checked her impulse to stick out her tongue and left without saying another word. But within a dozen steps on the snow-covered road, she questioned her decision. She had a four-mile walk home in freezing weather. It had started to snow. Mrs. Hill must've known the conditions, and yet she'd said nothing.

The snowfall covered the gravel in a short time. Dunya had been walking for about a half hour when Mrs. Hill and John drove by in her sedan. They could have stopped and given her a ride. It would have been the kind thing to do. But what could she expect from someone who'd said, "Beggars can't be choosy"?

Dunya's brow creased. *The nerve of Mrs. Hill! She expected me to put up with a pig like the hired man! The bugger!* That's what Olga called men like that.

Shivering, Dunya pulled her fake fur coat tighter. There were no cars coming; the bitter weather and icy roads were keeping motorists home. These weren't conditions for travelling by foot or car. Maybe John's car would get stuck driving and he and Mrs. Hill would freeze, just like her. It would serve them right.

She walked for another hour before she reached the edge of their farm. Deciding to take a shortcut through the field, she clomped through the snow-covered ditch to the barbed-wire fence, then tried to climb through the space under the fence. She was almost through when the back of her coat got caught on a wire. Wriggling, she again tried to move through, but stopped when she realized she could rip her coat, or, even worse, entangle herself even more. She shifted from side to side, but nothing she tried made any difference. How foolish she'd been. What had she been thinking? She envisioned her mother shaking her head, criticizing her for leaving the Hill farm in terrible weather. *Is something wrong with your head? Yes, Mama, something's wrong with my head.* Dunya wiped her nose with her mitts. She should have waited until the end of her day and got a lift home with Mr. Hill. He would have given her a ride in his truck.

The wind continued to blow through her thin coat. Why had she been so stupid? So stupid to buy a stylish coat with her meagre wages. She'd bought it last year and wore it whenever she wanted to make an impression. She should have worn her bikasha lined with cotton batting, but she hated wearing it. It was like a neon sign advertising her immigrant status. She had visions of turning blue with cold, her mother finding her in the morning—an ice-covered statue stuck on a barbed-wire fence. She prayed someone would come along and see her clinging there.

She licked the snow that fell on her lips and blinked the snowflakes away from her eyes. Though not accustomed to praying like her mother, she asked God for help. "Please, dear God. I've been a good girl. I don't want to die like this. I have so many plans."

A quarter of an hour went by with nothing but eerie silence. Then she heard a sleigh's runners swooshing on the road. She hollered, "Help! Help!" A horse-driven sleigh stopped; it was her brother, Harry. Tears of relief fell on her cheeks as he climbed down the ditch, half-falling in the heavy snow. "Thank God you came."

"Dunya, why are you here? What happened?"

She told him the story while he unfastened her from the fence.

Her lips trembled for a good half hour after she got home. Her mother brought her a hot drink of cocoa and a basin of warm water to soak her feet. Luckily, she didn't get frostbite and was thankful she'd worn heavy wool socks in her felt boots. She figured later the angels must have been looking out for her, because she would have frozen to death if her brother hadn't come by.

Struggling to make ends meet frayed Lukia's already fragile nerves. And because of that, cleaning the Bushby home took longer than usual. She kept stopping to reflect on her daughter's horrifying experience with the hired hand. Lukia scrubbed the toilet bowl harder, as if she could scrub away the absurdity of Mrs. Hill's remarks. That woman didn't have a daughter, but she was a woman. She should understand how humiliating such acts were. Because of Mrs. Hill's attitude, her daughter had lost a well-paying position. *Never mind*, Lukia said to herself. Dunya at least had the wisdom to leave before something worse happened. Fortunately, her daughter, being resourceful, found work as a live-in housekeeper at a home on Jarvis Avenue, near the Salter Street Bridge.

Lukia wished they were better off, so her daughter didn't have to venture into strange homes looking for a job. It was hazardous work. If it wasn't a hired hand who attempted to fondle you, it was the husband or son. Even Lukia had to watch out for the wandering hands of men in the houses she worked for. Like Mr. Bushby, who had opened the door of her room while she was getting undressed for bed. She told him point blank that if it happened again, she'd have to tell his wife. He blanched and mumbled something about confusing the door with the closet and left.

Lukia straightened up and inspected her face in the medicine cabinet mirror over the sink. The wrinkles around her eyes and mouth had deepened. There were more grey hairs around her temples. Perhaps she should buy some dye, but who was she fooling? What would Gregory say? She couldn't believe it had been ten years since he passed.

She smiled as she recalled him saying when he came back from war, "You've aged." She replied, "As if you haven't, you old fart." She laughed. They had loved teasing each other. To have that kind of comfort with a man was something she missed. She also missed lying next to Gregory at night, feeling the warmth of his back as she cuddled against him, smelling his sweat and tobacco-scented hair. They'd made love so many times. Wonderful before the war, not so wonderful afterwards. He'd returned a different man. He'd stumble to bed drunk, and after quickly coming inside her, turn away and fall asleep. She understood, as she had gone through a hell of her own. She wondered now how she'd survived those terrible times. She sighed heavily and finished cleaning the bathroom.

22

OY, BROTHER

The spring of 1932 brought more bad news. The newspapers—the *Winnipeg Free Press,* the *Winnipeg Tribune,* and the *Ukrainian Voice*—raised fears with their headlines about protests across the country. There were cries for revolution.

To deal with the growing number of unemployed, the federal government had set up relief camps. These were in addition to the make-work projects established the year before. In exchange for board and room and a minuscule wage of twenty cents a day, men pulled dandelions by the roads and cut firewood. For the majority, it was shameful work, but if they wanted to eat, that was the work available.

That kind of misery was not far from the minds of everyone in the Rosser household. Lukia lamented each time Egnat walked by with anguish written on his brow. It was her fault. She'd sold him the idea of immigrating to Canada. They were now into their third year on the prairies and there hadn't been one crop they could brag about. If they had at least reaped one such harvest, they could hang on to a glimmer of hope, rather than feel they'd traded one bad situation for a worse one. Every day was like trudging miles through mud; the longer you did it, the harder it was to keep going without collapsing. How had it come to this? Egnat had done what he could, practising good farming methods. He listened to the daily weather forecast on Petro's radio and consulted the *Farmer's Almanac*, which Boris Karpinsky translated for him, but he had no control over the weather. It had beaten all of them.

By the end of summer, nothing had improved. Grain struggled to get going. The only plant that thrived was the Russian thistle, as evidenced by its carpet of purple flowers as far as the eye could see. The undeveloped heads of wheat were so dry, it was only good for fodder for the livestock. With another dismal year, they struggled once more to pay their bills. A bushel of wheat that had sold for $1.03 in 1928 now sold for 29 cents, the lowest recorded price in three hundred years. Three hundred years! Just their luck to come to Canada at this time.

Desperate for water, not only for their garden but also for their animals, Lukia told Egnat they had to have another well. Egnat agreed and, remembering what his father had done, made a divining rod out of a forked branch from a willow tree, then spent hours walking up and down the farmland trying to find water. His persistence paid off. He found a water source, and with his brothers' help, dug a new well. To prevent the surface water from becoming contaminated, they lined the top with bricks, which also kept the well from collapsing.

Lukia continued to pray. Surely God knew their situation was enough to make any man cry. What was He waiting for?

The price for grain turned out to be the least of her worries. As she'd feared, her son and brother's dislike of each other reached a boiling point. The fight began over a rack around harvesting time. It wasn't surprising the eruption took place when both Egnat and Petro were exhausted and their defenses down. They'd been working from the time the cock crowed to the time the moon showed its face in the sky.

Prior to their fight, the three families had been sharing a metal hay rack, included with the purchase of the farm, but there was always a problem as to whose turn it was to use it. Especially at harvest time, when all three families needed one to dry their hay.

After two years of sharing the hay rack, Egnat had built his own out of wood during the winter. Petro admired his nephew's craftsmanship and complimented him on his work. Lukia viewed his praise as a turning point, a sign that harmony in the family was possible.

Unfortunately, it was not to be. The day that changed family relations was the summer day Petro took the wood rack without asking Egnat first. Lukia was outside with Elena, hanging up the wash, when she saw her brother filling Egnat's rack with his hay. Elena immediately put a pair of wet pants back in the wicker basket and ran towards him yelling, "Uncle, use the other one. Egnat has plans to use his rack."

Petro bellowed at Elena, "What are you saying, Polish face?"

Lukia swallowed hard. It was obvious, from her brother's speech and his florid face, that he'd been drinking.

Her daughter-in-law blanched. "I'm saying that's Egnat's rack. He built it so he could use it when he wanted to."

"Fuck you, you Polish face! You're going to tell me what to do?"

Egnat suddenly appeared from behind the barn, carrying a bundle of logs for the stove. He stopped when he saw his uncle confronting his wife and dropped the firewood. Mike, who'd been cleaning the animal stalls, came out of the barn doors, not far behind his brother.

Lukia shouted, "Egnat, stay calm."

"What did you say to my wife?" yelled Egnat, as he rushed to his wife's side.

Petro's eyes bulged. "She's a Polish-face prostitute!"

"What?" Lukia said, spitting out the word. "Brother, have you lost your mind?"

"Son of a bitch," Egnat said, as he went for his uncle's throat.

Petro, twice the size of his nephew, grunted as he forced his nephew's arms apart, then grabbed his shirt and, with one mighty pull, ripped it off his shoulders.

Lukia shrieked, "Run, Egnat, run!"

Egnat ran towards the barn with Petro right behind. Elena caught up to Petro and seized his arm. "Stop, Uncle! This is crazy."

He wrenched his arm away and smacked her across the face.

"Aye-yi-yi," Elena said, massaging her cheek as she retreated. Hearing his wife's cry, Egnat turned and picked up a log he'd thrown down.

"My God," Lukia said, gasping. "Look what's started!" Her pulse sped up and she clutched her chest. Taking a few steps forward, she hollered, "Egnat, stop! That's your uncle. Mike, do something!"

The yelling must have brought Dunya, Anna and Maria out of the house to see what was going on. They stood to the side, watching.

With a log in hand, Egnat rushed at Petro, but Mike blocked him. Egnat pushed his brother out of the way. Mike stumbled but stayed erect.

Elena hollered, "No, Egnat, no. He's drunk. He doesn't know what he's doing."

Dunya ran to help Mike hold Egnat back, each gripping an arm.

For a moment, Petro stood dazed. His eyes darted from Mike to Egnat to Elena and to his sister. His eyes briefly settled on Anna before he stomped over to his horse and wagon parked by the barn. She rushed over to him, but he kept his back to her. When he climbed into the wagon, she said something quietly.

"Leave me alone," he said and rode off.

Anna cried out, "Petro, where are you going?"

Egnat shouted, "Go, and don't come back. Piyak!"

Ordinarily, Lukia would have reprimanded her son for calling his uncle a drunk, but not this time. She put her arm around Elena and examined her face. Her left cheek was red and swollen.

Sweating, Egnat approached his wife and stroked her back. "You should've kept out of it. Are you okay?"

Her eyes watered. "It's nothing."

"Oy," Lukia said, "I should take him to court."

"Mama," Dunya said, "what are you saying? You want to take Uncle to court?"

"Go call the doctor." Without hesitation, Dunya ran down the road towards a neighbour's house a mile away to use the phone.

Lukia waited with Elena in the house for the doctor to come. She placed a cold, damp cloth on her daughter-in-law's injured cheek and studied her face. The ordeal had saddened her usually mellow eyes.

"I'm sorry, Mama, for causing so much trouble."

Lukia shook her head. "You're no more at fault than the chickens out there. It's a tragedy, that's what it is."

Elena took the cold cloth from her mother-in-law and kept it on her cheek for another half hour, which was when the Karpinskys and the Korneluk children returned to the house from their work in the fields. There was shock all around at how an argument over a rack could have escalated so quickly.

It took two hours before a doctor showed up. Dunya told her mother that when she reached their neighbour's house, their black dog came running out and bit her. Lukia guessed her daughter had shown up in such a panic, she'd scared the animal. The neighbour bandaged up her wound and called Dr. Baxter, but he couldn't come because he'd had an accident while driving to Stony Mountain to see a patient. His wife called Dr. McKenzie to come instead.

Dr. McKenzie arrived in a black sedan, dressed in a black suit as if going to a funeral. Though Lukia had found the whole incident maddening, the doctor didn't seem surprised to hear about the conflict that had led to Elena getting hurt. Lukia supposed he'd seen and heard more than a few family fights that ended with someone getting hurt.

After examining her daughter-in-law, the doctor told the household that Elena had experienced a good scare, but nothing was broken. He gave her some pills to calm her down. That visit cost ten dollars, ten dollars Lukia could ill afford. Upset, she berated herself. She'd been too shocked to think straight. Had she been in a calmer state of mind, she would not have sent for the doctor. But since her brother was such a strong man, she feared he had broken Elena's jaw.

Later that evening, Anna begged her sister-in-law to forgive her brother. "Lukia, don't say anything to the authorities. They'll arrest Petro. We're family."

"What kind of family is this? He can't treat Elena like that. He can't attack my son."

"Forgive him," Anna pleaded.

Lukia pursed her lips. "If he wants forgiveness, he should ask God first. And then Elena and my son."

Anna clutched her sister-in-law's hands. "Please, Lukia. I'll talk to him. He won't do it again."

"I don't know." Lukia rubbed her thumb with her index finger. "Tell him, next time, I will take him to court."

"Thank you." Anna hugged Lukia, who was so distraught she remained stiff in her sister-in-law's arms.

Sobered up, Petro returned home but didn't apologize to anyone. And no one talked to him about the incident. The adults went about their business, avoiding him as much as they could in a crowded household. They put aside the violent outburst, but this was one fight that would not be forgotten.

The following evening, while Lukia was taking the bobby pins out of her bun, Egnat came to her room. "Mama," he said, sitting down on the bed, "if I could dump Uncle in the Red River, I would."

"Oy, son," Lukia said, "don't say that. God will be angry with you."

"Let Him be angry. Uncle can't treat me or my wife that way."

Her heart broke as she considered the rift in her family. The damage was done, like a rip in a pair of pants. You could mend it to get more wear, but it would never be the same. There would always be that spot that had weakened the whole garment, and if put under strain, would tear again. But what could she do? She did what she always did. She turned to God and prayed for peace between them.

23

A RESPITE

After Egnat and Petro's blowup, the house took a deep breath, aided by the two men going about their business. Lukia thought the continuing bad news from the city had quieted them. The number of unemployed had grown even more; the citizens continued to blame the immigrants for their woes. This was not the time to turn against one another.

Threshing went on. They were now members of a co-op. Since a combine or thresher along with a binder were costly, a small group of farmers shared the equipment. Lukia and Dunya, and sometimes Elena, took lunch out to the men in the field. Lukia liked to spend a few minutes watching Mike and Harry gather the sun-dried sheaves and pitch the wheat into the threshing machine driven by Egnat. It was a wonderful sight: her sons working together without arguing.

The brothers' congeniality extended right into the evening, when they returned to the house, their backs and legs sore from all the heavy lifting. While the women prepared supper, Egnat and Mike took turns relieving one another's pain. They stood back-to-back in the living room and after linking arms, Mike lifted Egnat up and over to get the kinks out. Then they switched positions and did it again. A stranger looking at the two would never have suspected the brothers were at odds as much as they were.

These were the moments Lukia savoured. They gave her hope her family would stay united in a country that had yet to deliver on its promise.

With threshing completed, Lukia and her family returned to their other farm duties. Mike was the one who butchered a pig in the fall. Egnat couldn't even kill a chicken without his stomach turning. He couldn't watch when Mike went into the pen to get the animal. To guarantee the quality of the pork, Mike had neutered the pig when it was young. Unlike Egnat, Lukia had no trouble witnessing her son's butchering skills. He was an excellent butcher. Not one scrap of meat was wasted, not even the bone, which was used to flavour hearty cabbage soups and borscht. Lukia even used the pig's blood to make kishka, a sausage made with buckwheat groats, cooked with lard and seasoning, then mixed with the blood and stuffed into cleaned and ready-to-use sausage casings bought from a butcher shop on Selkirk Avenue. Baked in a greased pan, kishka was a delicious treat for the family.

Mike also took turns with Dunya going into Winnipeg to sell milk and cheese. The last time he went in, he didn't return until the evening meal was over and the dishes had been put away. His uncle and Egnat were still at the table having tea. Lukia went to the stove and filled a plate with holupchis she'd kept warm for him on the stove. She also scooped up some fried mushrooms out of another pot and several slices of kybassa from a frypan.

Pouring a shot of horilka from the bottle on the table, Mike said to his mother, "You know that shantytown on the edge of Winnipeg by the tracks?"

"Yes, I know," Lukia said, setting the plate in front of him.

"It's bigger than before." Mike cut a holupchi and ate a mouthful.

"I've seen it, too," Petro said. "A man has to sink pretty low to live like that."

"I was waiting at a crossing for the freight train to go by when I saw all the shacks. Boxcar after boxcar went by with men hanging on. There were hundreds of men on one boxcar alone. Some were riding on the roof. I even saw one crazy guy hanging onto the rods under the train. I don't know how he didn't fall off."

"Where were they going?" Egnat asked, lighting up a cigarette.

"I got down from the wagon and asked a guy who was watching. He said the men riding the rails can't find work anywhere now that harvest is over. They're hoping to have better luck out west."

"See," Lukia said, "we think we have it bad. At least we have work here. Not good, but it's honest work. We have a lot to be thankful for."

Petro said, sneering, "Oh yeah, so much to be thankful for."

Frowning, Egnat smoked his cigarette.

Mike's tale had dampened the conversation. One matter they all agreed on: farmers in Manitoba were only a little better off than those riding the rails.

The next day, Egnat complained again to his mother about Mike returning from the city with less money than expected for the dairy products sold. Lukia suspected he'd stopped at the beer parlour before coming home. From what she'd heard, he liked to buy people he'd just met a drink.

She immediately went to find Mike, who was in the barn changing the hay for the horses. As expected, he denied the shortfall. He said they'd overvalued their products. She tried to determine the truth by gazing deeply into his eyes, but it didn't make her any the wiser. Without proof he'd squandered the money, she had to let it go. She didn't want to side with one son over the other.

Her decision did not sit well with Egnat. He accused her of

coddling his younger brother, and perhaps that was true. Mike had not been an easy son to raise, with his inclination to party more than work, but he was a good son. He was the most affectionate of the three; he often showed his love by unexpectedly putting his arm around her and giving her a kiss. On chilly evenings, he rushed to get a sweater to put over her shoulders. And besides comforting his young cousin Genya with soothing songs when she had earaches, he was the one who kept candy in a drawer for the young ones in the house. Yes, he was the one who had the tender heart, the one who could easily be bruised. She'd never wanted to choose between her boys, but she was drawn to the one who needed her the most. She suspected most mothers were.

When weeks went by with no further conflict between Petro and Egnat, Lukia believed her brother had learned his lesson. He and her son had even exchanged a few laughs at the table. With a fragile peace, the house returned to its uneven composition, with the odd dissonant notes from Petro and Anna's quarrelling, the Karpinskys going about their affairs as if they were visitors, and Egnat getting upset with Mike for skipping out on his farm duties.

Lukia had her own challenges in the house. She bristled every time she encountered her sister-in-law mistreating her children. Five-year-old Rita, already strong-willed, complained loudly when she was spanked or swatted by her mother for speaking out of turn or refusing to do what was asked. Lukia couldn't understand such harshness, even though she was guilty of disciplining Dunya for minor matters, too. Her daughter would insist she was right about something, even though the evidence proved she wasn't. She'd argue on and on with her brothers, and since she was the talkative one in the family, she easily overrode their objections. Frustrated by the bickering, Lukia would occasionally swat Dunya across the back with a tea towel. Later, she'd take her aside and tell her that if she'd been a boy, her brothers would have struck her. In time, Lukia's admonishment seemed to have an effect. Dunya learned to pout instead of arguing when she felt slighted or didn't get her way.

24
GRAVE THOUGHTS

As the days went by, loneliness crept up on Dunya. There were only three girls in the house. She was sixteen, Rita was seven, and Genya was two. Though nine years apart, Dunya and Rita bonded in a house of boys. They occasionally played card games, but her cousin was no substitute for a proper friend.

Dunya wished Olga didn't live miles away. With no phone, any unplanned visit meant taking a chance her best friend would be home and not doing chores. That was why Dunya didn't bother. Olga came over occasionally with her father when he needed to talk to Egnat about some problem. The last time Olga visited, Dunya had to take the cows to pasture, so her friend tagged along. It was good seeing her again, but with having to move the cows along, they couldn't gossip as much as they would have liked to.

It hadn't been any easier in the city. After the Hills Farm affair, Dunya worked as a domestic for the Pascoe family. For six dollars a month, she cooked and cleaned the drafty, two-storey home on Jarvis Avenue. Because Mrs. Pascoe suffered with the cold, Dunya had to get up before the family and shovel coal into the furnace.

She hated housework but was pleased when she'd earned enough to buy the velvet overshoes she coveted. Much as her mother admired them, she tsked about the expense. She could not believe they cost that much. Four dollars! And so impractical to wear in the countryside, she said. Dunya didn't care about her new boots' practicality; she cared that they were in fashion and was thankful her mother didn't make her take them back.

Still, a pair of new boots was small comfort in a city where she knew no one other than her employer. It was a chaotic house which made Dunya's work even more challenging. There were too many surfaces to dust and too much clutter to work around. The Pascoes' seven-year-old daughter, Lydia, was entertaining, but she was at school during the day, and when she returned, she went outside to play with her friends. As for Mr. Pascoe, he was hardly ever home. Besides his work in construction, he was active in various Ukrainian groups in the community and in Sobor. It was where she'd met him and his wife, who was now pregnant.

Dunya was on her feet all day and didn't retire until she'd cleaned the kitchen after supper and Lydia had gone to bed. Her crowded, spare room lacked any warmth; it was where the family stored some of their belongings. Cardboard boxes and crates lay stacked in the empty spaces between the bed and the chiffonier. She'd lie on the narrow bed and listen for a while to the family's muffled voices—Mrs. Pascoe's soothing words to Lydia at bedtime and her voice rising when Mr. Pascoe came in the front door—before drifting off to her own imaginings.

Dunya wished she lived in New York, a city that fuelled her imagination ever since Olga had told her about the film *Possessed*, starring Joan Crawford and Clark Gable. It's the story of a girl who works in a factory. A fellow worker wants to marry her, but she dreams of a better life. When a train stops in her town one day, she notices the wealthy passengers sitting in the cars. One of them disembarks and, after a casual chat, gives her his name and number and tells her to look him up in New York City. Unhappy with her situation, she goes to Manhattan and finds the man she met at the train station. Through him, she meets a rich lawyer, falls in love, and by the end of the movie they're destined for marriage. Though Dunya had never seen the film, she'd seen the poster outside the Palace Theatre—the one with Joan Crawford and Clark Gable in an embrace, looking into each other's eyes. The possibility of marrying into wealth occupied her mind as she scrubbed the floors and washed the walls. Life had to be better than this. She wanted what the Joan Crawford character succeeded in getting; she wanted to meet a man who'd save her from a dismal future.

One Saturday, when Dunya was home in the kitchen making varenyky with her mother, she brought up her troubles. As she rolled out the small balls of dough into flat rounds, she said, "It's awful being stuck in the city. I've got no friends. There's nothing to do except work."

"I know, but what can we do?" Her mother placed the pot of mashed potatoes on the table and stirred in cottage cheese and fried onions, their pungent smell wafting through the room.

"I haven't seen Olga in weeks. The last time she came over, I had chores. We could hardly talk."

Lukia clucked her tongue. "That's how it is. If we don't do the work, who will?"

Dunya grumbled and rolled out more rounds for the potato varenyky.

Her mother placed a couple of tablespoons of the potato and cheese filling on a round of dough and pressed the edges together into a half-moon shape. "How's Olga doing? Does she have a boyfriend?"

Dunya tightened her lips. She didn't want to talk about Olga. She wanted her mother to know it wasn't fair she had no time for fun. There was always so much to do. Besides her work in the city, she had to help on the farm with the week's baking, cooking, laundry, milking, gathering the eggs, feeding the animals, fetching water, mending clothes, ironing them, darning socks, dusting, sweeping, hoeing, and taking care of Genya. And from spring to fall, there was the added work of seeding and hoeing the garden, taking cows to pasture, stooking during the harvest, picking berries and mushrooms, canning for the winter, and selling dairy products in the city. Exhausted just thinking about it, Dunya sighed and turned her attention back to rolling out the dough.

Her mother tucked a few hairs into her babushka. "Keep the dough balls covered or they'll dry up."

Dunya pulled the tea towel over the exposed dough. "No one pays any attention to me."

"That's not true."

"God made me a mouth and gave me a voice. If I can't use it to talk, then what good is it? They're always saying, be quiet. Be quiet. I'm tired of it."

"Dunya, what's got into you today?" Lukia took another spoonful of filling.

"You've seen how my brothers act. When I try to say anything, they roll their eyes or ignore me."

"Sometimes you start talking and you don't know when to stop. And you repeat and repeat. No one has time to listen. We have work to do."

"If they listened in the first place, I wouldn't have to keep repeating myself."

"Oy," Lukia said, frustrated. "You're the youngest. If they tell you to stop, you should listen."

Dunya made a face and rolled the round too thin, causing it to tear. She picked up the crumpled dough and rolled it into a ball again.

Her mother raised her eyebrows but said nothing.

Dunya filled the next round with potato filling. If she was back in the old country, she'd be going to country dances, berry picking with her friends, and kibbitzing with the young men in the village. Maybe she would've fallen in love by now.

She exhaled loudly, causing her mother to look over. Dunya covered the varenyka she'd made and started another one. Her mother, who'd been so understanding in the old country, had soured. She no longer had the patience she once had. Dunya understood that it hadn't been easy sharing a household with two other family heads—both men—but she wished her mother could appreciate how difficult it had been for her to share a house with so many males. The teasing was endless, and whenever she complained or tried to give her viewpoint on anything, her mother told her to be quiet.

She disagreed with her mother. She didn't talk as much as her mother claimed, but she knew arguing about that point would get her nothing but a swat across the back with a tea towel or a lecture. Her mother would say, "I told you to stay in school. You didn't want to. This is what you have to do now. What else are you going to do?" Dunya sighed and filled another round of dough.

She glanced at her mother, but she didn't respond to Dunya's deep sigh. She was too intent on getting the varenyky finished before the men came in from the barn. There was so much Dunya hated about her life. She hated lugging gallons of milk, sealers of cream, and cartons of cheese to Winnipeg. It was all right if a driver stopped to pick her up, but sometimes she would stick out her thumb only to have a car whizz by, leaving her choking on a cloud of dust. She'd cough and cough and whine about the shoes she'd polished. There was no point brushing the dust off; they'd just get dirty again.

Was this how she was going to live out the rest of her life, wearing out the soles of her shoes on gravel roads, eating dust from motorists unwilling to stop, and massaging the red marks from her hands that held heavy jugs? Her mother was right. She should have stayed in school, but how could she? She didn't think her mother would have put up with the bullying or a teacher who seemed uninterested in helping her.

The last time Dunya trudged the highway to Winnipeg carrying the heavy dairy products, she had thought about jumping in front of a passing car. She had been ready to end it all. But then she remembered it was a sin to take one's life, so she crossed herself and asked God for forgiveness. She considered telling her mother how close she had come to killing herself, but that would be cruel. After losing four, her mother shouldn't have to worry about losing another.

Look at how her cousin in the village had suffered. He couldn't sell the family farm because his father had committed suicide in the barn. His father had committed the grave act to avoid jail for beating up the young man who had bullied his son. And because he had taken his own life, the villagers said his house was cursed. When his widow wanted the priest to bless the house and make it salable, the priest had declined. Said her husband had committed a sin, and this was God's way of showing others his wrongdoing.

Dunya made the last varenyka and covered it with a tea towel. She decided suicide was out of the question. She didn't want to leave her family with a mark against their name. God was not charitable when you broke His laws.

25

ENOUGH IS ENOUGH

Despite Lukia's hopes for family harmony, it was inevitable tempers would flare in a house where men drank at the kitchen table long into the evening. It happened with little warning. The Karpinsky family had eaten early and gone into the city to attend a church meeting. After the Korneluk and Mazurec families had finished their meal, Egnat and Petro remained at the table drinking vodka. The older children left to milk the cows, Anna got Nicky ready for bed, and Rita stretched out on the rug to roll a rubber ball back and forth with her younger brother, Tony.

At first, Egnat and Petro talked amicably about the Communists gathering at the Labour Temple in Winnipeg and what to make of that. They weren't in favour of the party, but they thought the Commies worked hard to strengthen the unions, which was a good thing. With strong unions, workers would have a better chance of controlling their destiny. They were in the midst of this discussion when Elena returned to the table to remove the dish of holupchis. When she leaned in, Petro patted her backside.

"Uncle!" Elena said, abruptly stepping back from him. "What are you doing?"

Petro grinned. "Nothing."

Lukia shook her head in disgust.

Egnat said, "Keep your hands off my wife."

"Ho, ho, ho. She's a queen, your wife." His voice dropped. "Dumb Polack!"

"What did you say?" Egnat's face reddened. Rita and her little brother stopped playing.

"The Poles are not dumb," Elena said, holding the bowl of holupchis. "My father and mother—"

"Polski Mordi," Petro said.

Lukia gasped. Her brother had just said, "Fuck your mother."

"Petro, you've lost your mind! Take that back. Apologize to Elena."

Petro smirked and took another drink.

Egnat stood up and raised his fists. "You want to fight, old man?" Tony sniffled, then burst out crying. Rita put her arm around her brother and took him to their room.

Carrying the bowl of holupchis to the kitchen counter, Elena said, "Leave it, Egnat. He's drunk."

"We'll see about that," Petro said, banging the table with his fist. "No smarkach is telling me what to do." It was another insult—calling his nephew a snot-nosed kid. Egnat clenched and unclenched his fists. Petro got up unsteadily, his eyes wild and his jaw set. He weaved his way to the door and grabbed the axe beside it. Waving it, he said to Egnat, "C'mon. I'm waiting."

Lukia turned to her son. "Don't you move!"

Stunned and also drunk, Egnat swayed at his spot on the other side of the table.

Lukia yelled at her brother, "What are you doing, you crazy fool? Egnat, Elena, go to your room."

Glaring at his uncle, Egnat reluctantly went, with Elena pushing him all the way to their bedroom, which was near the kitchen and just out of sight.

With Egnat and Elena behind closed doors, Lukia said, "Petro, why do you provoke my son? He did nothing to you. And why are you grabbing at Elena like that? She's a married woman; you're a married man. It's not decent."

He wavered a moment, then put the axe back against the doorframe. He sat down once more at the table.

Following a few moments of uncomfortable quiet, Egnat roared from behind the bedroom door. "Has the drunk left yet?"

Petro stared wild-eyed in the direction of his nephew's bedroom door. He lumbered over to the stove as quickly as he could in his condition and picked up a five-gallon tin can on the floor beside it. Banging the can against the bedroom door, he barked, "Come out, you little squirt!"

"Stop it! You'll break the door!" shouted Lukia.

Elena wailed. "Uncle, stop! Please! Enough of this fighting."

"Fuck your mother, Polish face."

"That's enough," cried Lukia. She grabbed her brother's arm and tried to yank him away from the door. He turned and pushed Lukia so hard she stumbled and caught the back of a chair to keep from falling on the floor. "That's it, Petro. Enough is enough. I'm taking you to court."

He sneered at her, but her threat had registered. His eyes narrowed, and he swore under his breath. He put the can down, got his jacket from the coat hooks by the door, and left in a huff.

Lukia pulled the window's curtain aside. Her brother was a sorry sight. He staggered past the turkeys and chickens squawking at him, as if they too wanted to scold him for his actions. When he disappeared into the barn, she knocked on Egnat and Elena's bedroom door. "Uncle's gone."

Egnat opened the door, his face red with rage. "I can't live here anymore."

"I know," she said, her eyes soaking up his pain. "I'm going to take him to court."

"Oy, Mama," Elena said. "He's your brother."

"Brother or not, he has to learn there are limits." Lukia said the words, but they sat in her throat like a lump of indigestible food. The ties between them had been strong. He was the one who'd always helped her when she was in trouble. He'd saved her when she had typhus, and he had gladly given her extra money to come to Canada. And now, she was turning against him. But what could she do? He wouldn't let up. She was sure her brother was jealous. Egnat was a capable farmer, one her brother could never be. It wasn't in his makeup. And Egnat's wife had a nurturing personality, unlike Anna's. He was probably jealous about that, too.

But how was she to proceed? She didn't know how the Canadian court system worked. In Kivertsi, a gendarme helped to resolve family disputes. She deliberated overnight, then decided she'd talk to the agent who had helped them find a farm. He would know the laws and the resources. He'd be the one to ask.

26

X Marks the Spot

The next morning, a warm fall day, Lukia and Dunya hitched a ride to the city and got out at Eaton's, an eight-storey department store on Portage Avenue. From there, they headed east towards Main Street, past a movie house, office buildings and a jewellery store. It was an area absent of hoboes, as if there were no country-wide depression at all. Men wearing fedoras and fine wool suits over white shirts and ties bustled after lunch to get back to their offices. The women shopping must have been from a higher class; they wore fine wool coats, clutched fashionable handbags with their leather-gloved hands, and sported polished leather shoes with delicate straps over their insteps. And their nicely coiffed hair was covered partly by hats adorned with ribbons and feathers. There was even one woman who wore dressy pants and flaunted red-painted fingernails. Lukia and Dunya couldn't stop ogling. They only got dressed up when they went to church, and even there, only one or two women came close in their apparel to what they saw on the street.

When they got to the Immigration Hall on Water Street—a good eight-block walk—Lukia was shocked to find the place had changed so much in three years. The structure was the same, but its purpose was no longer to house and process immigrants. She knew immigration to Canada had been halted, but she hadn't expected the building would change as much as it had. It was now a soup kitchen and a shelter for the jobless. Vagrants and others down on their luck hovered near the doorway or leaned against the walls inside. In their worn and soiled jackets and trousers, their hats askew on their heads, their faces and hands unwashed, their shoes with lifting soles and rundown heels, they shuffled about hunched over, as if carrying the world's troubles on their backs. Her stomach sank at the sight. Not since she'd left the refugee camp during the Great War had she seen this kind of hopelessness. Though she knew of the huge hunger in the country, it was still shocking to see the two realities: the well-to-do and the down-and-out, separated by less than a dozen city blocks.

Determined to carry out her plan, Lukia headed towards the office. She hoped the agent who had helped her in the past was still here, reassigned to work with the unemployed. Dunya lagged a few steps behind. The agent was nowhere to be seen. There was also no one who spoke her language. When Dunya asked the woman at the front desk where the family court was located, she said it was downtown and wrote the address on a piece of paper. Seeing Dunya's puzzled look, she told her to ask any police officer, and he'd direct them.

Lukia and Dunya walked several blocks, looking for a policeman. They stopped the first one they spotted on Main Street. He threw up his hands, showing he didn't understand. But the second one Dunya approached called over a fellow officer who was talking to a shopkeeper.

The fellow officer greeted Lukia respectfully in Ukrainian. "Panye, how can I help you?"

While he listened, his blue eyes shaded under his peaked cap, she explained they were on their way to family court to press charges against someone who was threatening her family at home.

His brow creased with concern. "Should we send some officers to the house?"

"No, no," she blurted. "No police. It wouldn't look good. The neighbours would wonder what's going on. I want a judge to warn my brother. Family is sometimes the worst, you understand?"

"I understand," he said. He retrieved a pad of tickets and a pencil from his pocket. On the back of one ticket, he drew a map and marked a large X where the court was located. "You have to go here," he said, pointing to the X. "This is where you'll find the Court of King's Bench."

"The king is there?" asked Lukia.

"No," the officer said, laughing. "It's just called that."

Was he laughing at her? She dismissed the slight and clutched the rudimentary map. "Thank you for your help." She turned to walk away, but he tapped her on the shoulder.

"Panye, you mentioned you want to lay charges against your brother?"

"Yes," she said, wondering if he was planning on talking her out of it.

"You need to go to the police station first. That's where you file your complaint. Your brother will have time to respond and a hearing date will be set."

"I see. And where is this police station?"

He took out his pad of tickets again, wrote the address down, and showed her which way to go.

27

NO CHOICE

A week later, while Lukia was shredding beets for borscht and Anna was peeling potatoes in the kitchen, the sound of a car approaching caught their attention. Lukia looked out the window and recognized the dark vehicle with the insignia on the side door as one belonging to the Royal Canadian Mounted Police. An uneasy feeling swept through her.

"What do they want?" asked Anna, standing beside her.

Lukia said nothing.

The police officer in the passenger seat stepped out of the car. Dressed in his uniform, a brown shirt and pants with a yellow stripe down the leg, he approached the house carrying an envelope.

Anna got to the door first, with Lukia steps behind. Opening it, she said, "Good morning."

"Good morning. Is Mr. Peter Korneluk at home?"

"I'm his wife. What do you want?"

"It's best I speak with him. Is he home?"

Anna folded her arms. "He's in the barn." As the officer headed to the barn, Anna said, "I wonder what the trouble is."

Avoiding her sister-in-law's gaze, Lukia resumed making soup.

Anna remained at the door. After about five minutes, she said, "I wonder what's taking so long. Do you think I should go see?"

"Maybe," Lukia said. She went on cutting the beets; tiny red slivers of the vegetable piled up on the breadboard. She tried not to think about what was going on in the barn. She suspected it had to do with her visit to the police station in Winnipeg, but not being sure, she stayed quiet.

Soon, she heard the car start again. Not long after the officers had left, her brother entered the house, waving the envelope. "What's this?" he howled at Lukia.

"How would I know? Did you open it?" She took a deep breath and added the beets to the pot of chicken broth on the stove.

"What did the police want?" Anna said.

Petro pointed his finger at his sister. "Ask her."

Anna's brows knitted. "Lukia?"

"Oy," Lukia said, rubbing her thumb with her forefinger.

Petro got a knife from the drawer and slit the envelope open. "Where's Alex?"

"He's out feeding the pigs," Anna said.

Petro opened the door and yelled, "Alex! Come here." While Petro waited for his son, he said to Lukia, "I can't believe you did this. To your own brother."

Anna said, "What did you do, Lukia? Why won't anyone tell me?"

In a matter of moments, Alex entered, his gaze darting from his mother to his father, as if he'd done something wrong. His father handed him the letter. "Read this."

Lukia's lips tightened as she shredded a small cabbage.

Alex examined the letter. "It's a summons from the government for you to appear at the Court of King's Bench, Wednesday, October 19, at 10 a.m."

"What else?" his father said.

Alex read slowly and haltingly, and stopped periodically to explain the meaning of words his father or mother didn't understand. Lukia's palms grew moist as she listened to her nephew.

When he'd finished reading the charge, Petro said with disgust, "I have no sister."

Lukia's throat constricted and her heart pounded with the realization there was no turning back.

Wide-eyed, Anna said, "Lukia! How could you?"

Petro said, "I didn't assault Egnat or Elena. I did not break the door down! I banged on it because he wouldn't come out and fight like a man."

"You threatened him, more than once," Lukia said, meeting his eyes. "You hit Elena before."

"There's more," Alex said, turning the page. "You will be given the opportunity to present your defence if you have one. If you do not have a lawyer, you may call the Manitoba Law Society for names of attorneys who can assist you in this matter. Otherwise, you are welcome to represent yourself at this hearing." He clarified the instructions, then gave the letter back to his father.

Petro waved it at Lukia. "This is how it is? I should've let you die in the hospital."

Lukia's hand flew to her chest. "Oy. I asked you to stop," she said, her voice cracking. "You wouldn't stop. Petro, he's my son. What was I supposed to do? Wait until you killed one another?"

He raised his hand as if to strike her, but stopped. He slapped the envelope against his palm. "I shit on this letter." He spat and left the house, slamming the door so hard the walls shook.

Anna said, "I asked you not to do this."

Lukia sat down on a chair. "I had no choice. I had no choice."

28

KING'S BENCH

Wringing her hands in her lap, Lukia sat beside Egnat on one of the black leather-padded chairs in the wood-panelled courtroom and waited for the judge to appear. Petro and Alex sat on the other side of the aisle. She kept looking over to get her brother's attention, but he kept his eyes forward. He'd kept his distance ever since his son had read the summons to attend the hearing. The judge, dressed in black robes over a white shirt and tie, came out of a side door. The clerk, who stood by a small table in front of the judge's bench, said in a loud voice, "All rise."

The people in the courtroom stood until the judge took his seat. As the clerk read the charges, Petro remained stoic. The judge told both Lukia and Petro to swear on the Bible that any evidence either gave would have to be "the truth, the whole truth, and nothing but the truth, so help me God." The translator, a young woman with glasses, made sure they understood.

Lukia, Egnat, and Petro gave their accounts of the fight. Lukia understood little of what the judge said, but the translator helped convey his meaning.

It took less than an hour for the judge to rule in her favour. Petro received a public rebuke and had to pay the court fees. Lukia left the courtroom feeling she'd made a terrible mistake. Perhaps she should have left the family dispute on the farm. Petro had refused to look at her while they were in court. She expected the outcome would affect their living together under the same roof. It would be rough, but she was thankful for one thing. Ever since Petro had learned about the charges, he had stopped insulting Elena and provoking Egnat. Her actions had brought about some change for the better, but she wished Petro understood the pain he had caused, the fear he'd created in the house. And the fact she'd had no choice.

For days after the court hearing, Lukia tiptoed around her brother, ignoring his frosty looks. He made it clear that he and his family would be moving out as soon as they found a rental home in Winnipeg. "The sooner we leave, the better," Petro said, his eyes blazing.

She understood it was a move he'd always wanted, but not like this. He had been waiting for his apartment building to sell in the old country before buying a place of his own. It pained her to hear the edge in his voice, the contempt he had for her and her family. Had she really thought they could go back to the way they were when they'd first settled in Rosser? Back then, she knew he wouldn't be easy, but she never suspected he'd go after her son.

She tried talking to Petro, but whenever the subject came up, he admitted no wrongdoing. As she reflected on her history with him, she realized he would never understand; he wasn't built that way. Her mother had said, on more than one occasion, that he had been a difficult child. Now, Lukia had to face the fact her brother might never forgive her for suing him.

As for the farm, the Mazurecs, Korneluks, and Karpinskys had tried to make a go of it, but the weather had beaten them. They were behind in their mortgage payments and taxes. When they weren't gazing skyward, praying for rain, they were figuring out

how to make ends meet. With wheat prices at an all-time low, they could not cover their harvesting costs.

With three years of crop failures in a row, many people had lost their farms. Those who hadn't given up had tried new crops, switching from wheat and barley to oats, rye, flax, peas, and alfalfa. Lukia and Egnat even experimented with different tilling methods. When Egnat suggested buying artificial fertilizer to improve their yields, Lukia refused, saying it was an expense they could ill afford. But that wasn't the primary reason. She rejected it because she didn't believe in bolstering their crops with unnatural substances. She was sure it would affect their quality.

In the old country, she'd blamed the government for their predicament, but here in Canada, with the government stable and no battlegrounds in sight, the biggest enemy had been nature. One natural disaster after another. Dust storms blew seed away, thunder showers drowned anything that tried to emerge, and the heat and mosquitoes seemed to be in a contest to see who could wear down the humans first. How could anyone grow anything in these conditions?

With debts piling up faster than grain in the granary, the Karpinsky family were the first to leave. Lukia knew it was more than their grim prospects that had forced them to quit their arrangement. They were likely fed up with the constant bickering and ugliness between her brother and son. The court case had put a stop to Petro's threats and name-calling, but the atmosphere in the house remained unchanged whenever Egnat and his uncle were in the same room. Added to the tension was Lukia's strained relationship with her brother. Until he and his family could afford to move, she'd have to endure the discomfort that hovered like an unmoving black cloud over the house.

When there was a fire under Petro, he moved fast. In a matter of weeks, he found a home in Middlechurch, northeast of Winnipeg.

Anna told Lukia it was rundown, but it would do until they found the means to move to Toronto. She further said Petro had talked about going east ahead of his family to see what work he could find. Because he couldn't afford the travel costs, he'd considered riding the boxcars that carried the feed cattle. Anna laughed as she told the story. "Petro thought that with his weight they'd hide him the best." Lukia wanted to add that her brother was too high and mighty to bed down with cows for the night, but since both her brother and sister-in-law had rejected the idea, she kept quiet. She'd said enough already.

Like a parade of strangers, the Korneluks hustled their goods out the door—even the radio Lukia and her children loved. At one point, Anna laid her hand on Lukia's arm and was about to say something, but Petro shook his head. Her sister-in-law wasn't about to cross her husband, not when she was leaving for a place without other adults for support. Despite their father's sour expression, the Korneluk children hugged their cousins before they left. Ted, Alex, Leo, George, and Rita even hugged their aunt. Lukia gave them some plum buns for the road, which they quickly hid so their father wouldn't see.

Standing outside the doorway, Lukia and her family waved goodbye as the Korneluks drove away, crammed into the jalopy that Petro had bought the year before.

Rattled by her brother's cold departure, Lukia turned to Egnat and said, "Why didn't I wait? Why did I take him to court? He never even said goodbye."

"Mama, if you hadn't charged him, who knows what would've happened?"

"He's a stubborn man, used to getting his own way. For once, I stopped him."

Dunya put her arm around her mother's waist. "He'll forgive you. Don't worry."

Lukia absorbed the sad looks on her children's faces. They wouldn't miss Petro's bellicose nature, but they'd miss the others. Lukia had never wanted her brother to leave. All she wanted was peace in the house. How had it come to this?

29

LILYFIELD

With both the Karpinskys and the Korneluks leaving in the late fall of 1932, there was no way Lukia could manage the farm alone. Outstanding taxes were due and the mortgage payments were in arrears. Three years was the limit the government had imposed. If you couldn't pay within that time, the bank came in and foreclosed.

The dread of foreclosure played on her mind. Whenever a car drove up their road, Lukia froze. She was sure it held the men sent by the bank to shut her down. When it was only her neighbours or hired hands looking for work, she breathed a sigh of relief. But one day, not long after the others had left, a black car roared up their road, the dust billowing out from behind. The closer it got, the more she sweated. Two men in dark suits sat behind the windshield. She froze on the spot. They turned out to be who she had feared the most.

She had no choice but to vacate.

She couldn't fathom losing all they had, and yet, it was happening. It was a small comfort to know it wasn't their methods that had sunk them. There were many others facing the same hell. It was the drought and another onslaught of grasshoppers that

195

had ruined their dream. The crop that year was so poor that even the threshing machine couldn't gather up enough grain, and she and her children had to rake the barley by hand.

Given less than a month to pack up and leave, Lukia asked Mike to search for another farm. This time, they would have to rent. Though beaten, Lukia couldn't think of doing anything other than farming. It was what had supported her family in the past. Perhaps they'd find a homestead they could manage on their own. After three years of eating dust, she, like the others who continued working the land, couldn't believe the dreadful weather would continue.

For the remaining weeks in the Rosser farmhouse, life was more peaceful without the other families, but Lukia and her children missed Victor Karpinsky's accordion playing. Their love of music was soon satisfied when Harry purchased a radio from a friend who charged little because it was cracked on the side. The radio served them well until Lukia learned that the batteries were expensive. Thereafter, she cautioned Harry and the others to use it only when necessary.

As Lukia considered her next steps, she tried to put the past aside. There was no point in dwelling on what might have been.

Mike found a 160-acre farm with a two-storey house for rent on a rise of land in Lilyfield, four miles from Stony Mountain. Egnat wasn't happy that Mike kept referring to the farm as *his* because he'd found it—another sore point added to his list of grievances.

The owner said they could keep two-thirds of the crop for themselves and give the remaining third of what they earned to him as rent. Lukia appreciated his confidence. Hopefully, there would be a decent enough harvest to make his offer worthwhile for them both. Egnat also bought an old truck, which they needed to haul the grain. It saved time, and time was money.

It was a smaller home than the one they had in Rosser. Egnat and Elena took one room on the main floor, and Lukia slept with Genya in a room off the kitchen. Dunya, Harry and Mike took the two rooms upstairs.

Besides the affordable rent, their new homestead had another advantage. Its location was only six miles from Stony Mountain, a federal penitentiary town with a thriving community, catering to guards and those who worked in the limestone quarry and their families. There were several churches—Anglican, Presbyterian and Methodist—a school, a barbershop and a grocery store where Lukia could buy basic staples without having to go the extra three miles to Winnipeg and deal with its traffic.

But there was also a disadvantage in living so close to a penitentiary. Not long after they'd settled in, Ihor stopped by to tell Lukia a prisoner had escaped. "He could be dangerous," he said. "We're advised to be cautious; he could hide anywhere. When you go to the barn, be careful. Best to take a rifle with you. You never know where he can be."

Lukia said, "If I find someone there, I'll invite him in to have a bite with us. If we treat him right, he'll treat us right."

"Mama," Egnat said, "he could be a murderer. You don't know."

"I know. People are people, no matter what." She hated being corrected by Egnat, as if what she'd suggested was foolish. Ihor showed his good manners. He acted as if he hadn't heard Egnat correct his mother.

After Ihor left, she filled a bag with a loaf of bread that she'd baked that morning and a container of cottage cheese and put it outside the door. "If he shows up here," she said to Egnat, "he'll know we mean him no harm."

She noticed her children's disapproving looks, but Lukia ignored them. Egnat followed Ihor's advice and took the rifle with him to the barn. Lukia was especially concerned about Dunya and made sure she didn't go out in the yard alone. In the morning, they learned the mounted police had caught the convict. Relieved, they returned to their usual way of moving about without fear of being killed or robbed.

After a while, they became used to the odd announcement from the prison. So far, no escapees had hurt anyone in their district. Lukia didn't dwell on what could be. Given the ongoing drought and the accumulating debt, she was more anxious about her family's survival than about some stranger with evil on his mind.

And as before, she leaned on her faith to get her through hard times. She expected peace in Sobor, but the worshippers seemed to argue about mundane matters. Mostly about who was going to do what and when.

The bickering among the church goers wasn't the only disturbing problem. The hostility between Wasyl Swystun, the choir director, and Father Sawchuk reached a boil that year. Swystun accused Father Sawchuk of being inappropriately ambitious and incompetent. He complained the priest was often unavailable because he was sick. It was a well-known fact that Father Sawchuk had suffered from tuberculosis and was in recovery, but the choir director would not accept that as an excuse. Wasyl organized a petition to have the priest removed. Lukia had had enough of conflict in her life and refused to take sides. Besides, she liked the priest and could see no reason for him to leave. But since she lived outside the city, her voice found few allies. Swystun convinced the congregation that Father Sawchuk had abused his power and had to go. Lukia was sad to see him move to a much smaller parish on the other side of Main Street. She considered moving with him, but Sobor was where those who'd emigrated from Volhynia practised their faith, so she stayed. With Father Sawchuk gone, perhaps the mood in Sobor would improve. This was God's house, a place in which to worship and not a place to fight.

The early winter months passed as before, with Lukia and Dunya working as domestics in Winnipeg during the week and returning home to the farm on weekends, where they huddled around the stove on cold days and nights. After supper, the family lingered around the table and sang folk songs. They didn't play instruments, but they had their voices. Gesturing with their hands, Egnat and Mike were the stars with their sonorous tones. They even tried a few Cossack kicks on the floor, competing as to who could dance the best.

The new year brought hope once again, the threads of which were almost severed by a few terrifying incidents. The first happened when Lukia was in the house and the chimney caught fire. She'd been baking bread when she noticed flames shooting out the top of the chimney. She grabbed Genya—who was playing with her doll on the floor—and wrapped her in a perina before she ran outside and yelled for her sons to put out the fire. Egnat, Mike, and Harry immediately stopped their work on the truck and ran for the ladder and a bucket. They put out the flames, but after two more scares like that, they learned to lessen the danger by cleaning the black and flaky creosote twice a year—the first at the start of winter and the second at the end. From a neighbour, they also learned how to warm up the chimney column beforehand with a torch held up toward the damper, allowing the smoke to rise freely and escape out of the chimney. Most important, they stopped using freshly cut wood and used only dry, well-seasoned wood from deciduous trees.

Lukia figured that if God had wanted to take them, He would have done so by now. There was a reason she was still on this earth and hadn't joined Gregory in heaven. Her work wasn't done yet.

30

THE PROMISE OF SPRING

Spring arrived as usual, its promise cloaked in warmer weather. Purple crocuses peeked out from the melting snow, brightening the days of all who passed by. With Easter around the corner, Lukia's sons removed the storm windows from the house and replaced a few spokes on one of the wagon wheels. Lukia, Elena and Dunya worked side by side all week making holupchis, varenyky, nalysnyky, piroshky, studenetz, and kishka. For dessert, they made a honey cake, a cheese cake, and sweet hrystyky—a sweet pastry made by deep-frying twisted strips of dough, then sprinkling them with icing sugar.

As Lukia kneaded the raisins into the dough for paska, the tall, round loaf of Easter bread, she breathed in the wonderful smell of saffron. It brought back memories of celebrations on the farm in Volhynia, where there were at least twenty members of her kin around the table. How they would laugh and sing! But then the wars came, one after the other, and the men left to do battle.

She pushed away the sad memories and set the kneaded dough by the warm stove to rise twice. Afterwards, she filled the tall, round, coffee tin cans two-thirds full and let the paska rise for a third time. While she waited, she filled the bowl she used to make the dough with water and asked Dunya to wash her face in it, just like she'd asked Hania. It was a tradition passed down through the generations. Washing your face in paska water improved your complexion and made you more beautiful.

Dunya didn't hesitate to wash her face in the saffron-scented water and followed it up with a look in the mirror by the door.

Lukia laughed. "You think your skin will show the change in minutes?"

"No, of course not," Dunya said, wiping her face with a towel. "I was just checking to see if I had any dough on my face."

"Yeah, yeah, yeah," Lukia said, smiling. She wasn't about to tell her daughter she was being vain. She appreciated that Dunya cared about her appearance. A young woman had to present well, if she wanted to attract a worthwhile suitor.

After the paska was in the oven and the main dishes and dessert were prepared, Lukia made dyes for colouring the eggs. She boiled beets in water with vinegar for a red dye and the skins of yellow onions in water for an orange dye and, together with Dunya, tinted at least a dozen eggs for the Easter meal.

Easter morning, the Mazurecs left early for church, because Lukia wanted the family to go to confession before the divine liturgy started. When Mike complained, Lukia said, "We only go once a year to confess our sins. This is not a hardship."

Before leaving the house, Lukia—as was the custom—went to each family member and asked for forgiveness. They replied, as was the custom, "May God forgive you." In turn, they asked her to forgive their sins. It was one way to address any past wrongs and heal wounds. She assumed her brother had given up this rite, now that he no longer believed in God.

The family dressed in their finest. The females put on their one good dress, and the men put on the suits they'd recently purchased—thanks to their dairy and egg sales and the work Lukia and Dunya had done in the city. Lukia considered her sons' suits an excellent investment, as they'd all stopped growing and the new outfits would last for years.

At the church door, a fellow parishioner greeted the family and pinned a fresh flower on their jacket lapels and dress collars. While they waited in a pew at the front for their turn to confess, Lukia prayed and asked God to forgive her for taking her brother to court.

When it was her turn, she went up to the priest, who had set up his open confessional to the side of the iconostasis, and knelt before him. He laid his brocade stole over her head and bent under to hear her confession. It was a simple exchange—no detailing of remembered sins. He asked Lukia if she'd sinned. She said she had. He asked if she was sorry for her sins. She said she was. And then he made the sign of the cross over her head and asked God to forgive her.

Having confessed, she felt lighter, as if her sins had been weighing her down. It was always like that—a peaceful feeling, signifying a fresh start. But before she returned to her pew, she lit candles for the deceased. Then back at her seat, she sang with the choir—along with the other worshippers—*Christ is Risen*, a joyous Easter hymn sung several times. It was a beautiful service, but with the priest's sermon, it lasted close to three hours. Mike and Egnat left midway through. She suspected they had gone outside to smoke, which annoyed her, but she let it go. She wasn't going to let their absence spoil her favourite time of the year.

Afterwards, the churchgoers gathered in a large circle in the yard, set their baskets on the ground in front of their feet, and pulled back the embroidered linens covering their food. Each basket had a paska or two—plain or decorated on top with a cross or little bird made of dough, or white icing with candy sprinkles. Like the other parishioners' baskets, Lukia's contained coloured eggs, a ring of kybassa, a large square of butter with a cross made of whole cloves, a dish of beet horseradish, and one peeled egg, sliced afterwards for lunch into pieces equalling the number in their family. She lit her beeswax candle, propped up between the dish of butter and the kybassa, and waited for the priest to come by with his censer to bless her basket. While the priest went around the circle, all those attending sang *Christ is Risen* again. It was a ritual celebrating the hope that Easter brought, but also a reminder of what they'd cherished in their homeland—faith, family, remembrance of those passed, and the food their land and animals had delivered.

Lukia had invited her brother and family for the Easter meal, but he refused to come, so she invited the Chimiuk family. Genya was thrilled, as Olga had a brother her age. While Lukia and Elena heated the food and Dunya finished setting the table, Genya and the Chimiuk boy ran around the living room, hiding under the tablecloth and getting underfoot, until his father told them to go outside to play.

The banquet started with the Lord's Prayer and the customary shot of horilka with the clinking of glasses and the toast "God willing." Following the cheer, everyone ate a section of the blessed, peeled egg—Natasha Chimiuk added hers from her basket for her family. The meal ended with the cracking of coloured eggs, always a fun activity for both young and old.

Egnat had a knack for picking the strongest egg by testing several eggs beforehand. He tapped the eggshell with his teeth to determine which was the strongest. Holding the one he'd chosen, he went around the table to where his mother was sitting. He held his egg up and said, "Christ is risen."

She replied, "Indeed He is risen."

Egnat licked his lips and struck the end of his mother's egg with his egg. "Ha-ha," he said, when her egg cracked.

Lukia chortled and turned her egg over for Egnat to strike the other end. It also cracked. Egnat moved on to Harry, who'd kept his egg intact after hitting Dunya's. After everyone had played, it was Olga who won the honour of having the strongest egg; both ends were as smooth as they were when she'd first picked the egg out of the bowl.

Teased about losing, Egnat said, "Next year, I'll be better prepared." The laughter and songs after the meal lifted their spirits and gave them strength to face another day of wretchedness on the prairies.

A couple of surprise additions to the farm uplifted the Mazurec household that spring. The first one showed up when Lukia was outside, laundering clothes in the metal tub. She had just finished washing half of the garments when their neighbour Ihor drove up their road in his truck.

As Ihor exited his vehicle, his collie jumped from the passenger seat to the driver's side and onto the ground after him.

"Good day, Lukia," Ihor said, taking off his hat and scratching his head. "It's a beautiful day."

"Yes, it is." Lukia wiped her hands on her apron.

"I came over to ask you something. Would you like this dog? He's a good pasture dog." Ihor bent down and gave the dog a massage around his ears.

"If he's so good, why are you giving him away?"

"Ha," he said, smiling. "I told Natasha you'd give me a hard time. We live too close to the main road. He's always running after cars. We're afraid he'll get killed."

The dog ambled over to Lukia. She patted his silky hair. "Are you sure about this?"

"Yes. Hate to give him up, but we have to."

Lukia shielded her eyes from the sun. "We'd be happy to take him." Egnat had come out of the barn and was walking towards them. She said to her son, "Ihor's giving us their dog."

"Is there a catch, Ihor?" Egnat said, stroking the dog's head.
"No catch."
"Their dog runs after cars on the main road," Lukia said.
"That's too bad," Egnat said. "Can I at least get you a bottle?"
"Not necessary."
"It's good and strong," Lukia said.
Ihor grinned. "All right, if it isn't too much trouble."
"Of course." Egnat went into the house and quickly returned with a bottle of horilka.

Ihor cradled the bottle. "Well, I best go." He petted his collie one last time. "Like my wife says, the work won't do it by itself."

Lukia held the dog until Ihor was farther down the road. She expected the animal to bolt and run after the car, but he didn't. He seemed to forget his previous owner the minute they gave him any attention. She'd always wanted a dog to help with herding the cows, but with all the commotion in the previous household and the dismal outlook, she'd put that wish aside. The collie could be a sign that life was taking a turn for the better.

Since Lukia had forgotten to ask the dog's name, Dunya called him Puppy, and the name stuck. No one in the family had a problem with the name until the day a man stopped by to see if they needed a hired hand. Lukia and Dunya were outside hoeing the garden and their dog began to jump around the man's feet, prompting Dunya to scold the animal. "Puppy, stop."

The man laughed. "That's not a dog's name."

Dunya crossed her arms and said snippily, "It's our dog. If I want to call him Puppy, I will."

The hired hand's eyes softened. "I didn't mean anything by it, Miss." Fingering the brim of his worn cap, he turned to Lukia. "Ma'am, could you use some help on your farm?"

Leaning on her hoe, Lukia said to Dunya, "What does he want?"

"Work, Mama."

"Tell him we're sorry."

Dunya bent down to caress her dog. "Sorry, we don't need help right now."

Lukia felt bad for the man. They needed the help, all right, but they couldn't afford it. She gave him two slices of bread and a couple of hard-boiled eggs for the road. Her stomach knotted as she watched him slump away. It was difficult turning away able-bodied men who came begging for work.

The other addition to their homestead was a wild horse Egnat bought at a farm auction to complete the four-horse team they needed. He told his mother that initially he'd been hesitant about buying the bronco, but the price was right and the seller said the horse had been sterilized to make him easier to handle.

Despite being neutered, the wild horse wouldn't keep still or allow a harness. He kicked up his heels when anyone came near him. Lukia viewed the purchase as a terrible mistake until she saw how much Egnat loved him. He called the wild horse Dan. She realized, as she remembered Egnat's boyhood, that he'd always had a special regard for horses. When they had to leave them behind in the old country, he was so broken-hearted he moped for weeks.

Though she admired Dan's powerful strength and silky, dark brown hide, this was an animal not easily bossed. It took weeks of Egnat's time, patience and courage to calm the beast and teach him how to walk with the other horses.

That Egnat had tamed the bronco was a testament to his natural ease with animals. But his faith in what he'd accomplished with Dan was soon sorely tested. Lukia was peeling potatoes for pancakes one day when Egnat entered the house after plowing, looking pale and distraught. He sat down on a kitchen chair and put his head between his legs.

She put her knife down. "What's the matter?"

He took off his boots and rubbed the soles of his feet. "I came in from the field and unhooked the four horses from the harness, like I usually do ..." He shook his head. "But I was tired, and I forgot to unhook one trace. It was Dan's. I didn't notice and told the horses to go." He sighed audibly. "What was I thinking? They ran off. The attached trace must've spooked Dan, and he took off with the plow, running like somebody was chasing him."

"Oy, don't tell me," Lukia said, sitting down beside him.

"You should've seen him. He did cartwheels, too. It's a miracle he didn't injure himself with that plow banging against him."

"Thank God."

"Yes, but will he trust me now?"

The Mazurec family hadn't had luck with the weather, but they had it with Dan. The horse continued to perform well for Egnat, who doted on him even more. He never made that mistake again.

31

A Chance Encounter

With plans to build a pig enclosure, Lukia and Egnat took the truck to Stony Mountain to buy some lumber. On the road up the hill to the town, they passed a large group of convicts chained together, weeding gardens outside the prison walls. They were hoeing the soil while guards on horseback monitored their movements. Some inmates were young, around her sons' ages. Maybe they had no parents to guide them, or maybe their parents had done their best and their sons had simply lost their way by getting mixed up with the wrong crowd. Seeing criminals slave like that had to be a deterrent for both young and old. She wished Mike had come along to witness the prisoners' labour.

If the penitentiary inmates didn't impress the locals with the lesson that crime didn't pay, then the formidable federal building should have. Its sheer size and the way it stood on a limestone outcrop high above the prairie offered a warning to all who passed by on the highway below. If you didn't follow the law, you could end up behind those walls.

At Dan Balacko's store, Lukia and Egnat selected the lumber they wanted. They'd been negotiating the price when a farmer who was waiting his turn interrupted. He said in Ukrainian, "I'm sorry, Dan, but I have to go. I'll come by tomorrow."

"That'll be fine. Have you met Mrs. Mazurec and her son? Lukia, this is Orest Parochnyk. He's a good man to know. He emigrated from Bukovina before the Great War."

Lukia regarded Orest with interest. Bukovina was an oblast south of Volhynia. He left before his countrymen became the enemy of the Tsar.

Orest took off his straw hat, exposing unruly light brown hair. Seemingly self-conscious, he ran his hands over his scalp as if to comb it somehow. "Lovely to meet you," he said, shaking her hand. She felt the hard callouses on his fingers, which she valued. It meant he was a hard worker, a man to be admired. His warm brown eyes crinkled at the corners, reminding her of Gregory. He was broad-shouldered, tanned, clean-shaven and not much taller than Lukia. Wearing trousers with a matching vest over a yellow, open-collar shirt, he looked like he belonged behind a desk rather than behind a plow. Only his rough hands and dirty fingernails gave his occupation away. And most unexpectedly, he wore cologne. It wasn't overbearing, but enough to suggest he was a man who took care of himself. Either that, or he had a good wife who made sure he didn't leave the house unless he was groomed.

"I'm sorry I have to run," he said. "I left a sick calf at home. Hope we meet again soon."

"That would be nice." She smiled.

He grinned in return and strode out of the store.

Dan said, "Looks like you've made an impression."

"Oh, yeah," Lukia said, dismissing his comment.

"You know, he's a widower."

"Never mind. How much is that wood going to cost us?"

While Dan figured out the price on paper, she hid her pleasure with the attention she'd received. With his warm, polite manner, Orest was the type of man she could be attracted to—that is, if she were ever interested in getting married again.

32

ART AMONG THE THISTLES

The harsh conditions continued in 1933, with another drought on the prairies. A plague of grasshoppers had come once again, swarming over the plants, whipping humans in the face as they rushed by.

That day, on a trip to the city to sell cream and cheese, Dunya hitched a ride, hoping to escape the hordes of insects and the blistering heat on the road. But the interior of the car was so hot and stifling, she had to crank open the side window just to get some air.

The driver, an overweight man in a crumpled cotton shirt and pants, said, "Not a good idea." His comment came too late. Dozens of grasshoppers rushed through the opening as if they'd been in line and were eager to get a seat in the car.

At first, she tried to fend them off, but they were too much for her. The insects jumped on and around the seats and obscured part of the windshield. The driver slowed and brushed what he could away with his free hand. She ended up scooping handfuls from the floor and dashboard and throwing them back out the window. The challenge was to close it before more came in. After a few tries, she got the window closed. For the rest of the ride, she clenched her teeth and tried to stay calm in the unbearable heat and stuffiness of a closed vehicle. She couldn't even enjoy the prairie vistas, as the windshield was filthy with grasshopper remains and excretions. The sweat grew under her arms, back, and legs, forcing her to wriggle in her seat to avoid sticking to the seat covers.

He said, sympathetically. "Either way, you're dealing with the devil."

He couldn't have spoken truer words. What they were going through was like the plagues described in the Bible. Some locals said it was God's punishment. She wasn't sure she believed that, but this was surely Hell.

As soon as the grasshoppers had flown off to other places, dust storms filled the vacuum—as they had done the years before—sweeping away any soil worth preserving. When Lukia went outside, she had to cover her mouth with a handkerchief. The dust was so thick, it was impossible to see the barn from the house. Even the air inside the house was heavy, making it hard to breathe. No matter how hard she tried, it was impossible to keep the dirt out.

When the weather returned to some semblance of normal, there was nothing left on the land except the hardy Russian thistles. Lukia could not comprehend such a disaster. Anything edible had been gobbled up by the grasshoppers, and the remaining remnants had been blown away by the wicked winds that followed in their path.

She could easily have lain on the ground and cried for days, but this was no time for tears. They had to re-seed. Fortunately, there were enough summer months left for the crops to mature. Lukia was also thankful they had stored enough hay bales from the year before for fodder to supplement whatever the animals could find on their own.

Weighed down by despair, the Mazurecs brightened when Ted Korneluk, Petro's oldest son, showed up at the farm for a visit. He arrived just after a dust storm had left Lukia and her sons swearing and praying at the same time. As Genya's godfather, he hadn't let the unresolved fight between his dad and aunt stop him from visiting. Ted, young and handsome, with raven hair and a style of beard he called a Van Dyke, told them he liked their new home and asked if they were planning any improvements. He said he loved painting anything that needed freshening up. When he offered to paint some scenes on the large, bare walls in the living room, Egnat thanked him but said they couldn't afford it.

"It's true, we can't," Lukia said, "but I have a little saved from my housekeeping job. I could pay for the paint."

Ted nodded in gratitude, but Egnat frowned. He did nothing to hide his displeasure, and when Ted went to the outhouse, he said, "Mama, we're eating scraps of bread and you want to buy paint?"

"Son, I understand, but it'll help your cousin. He'll take pictures of his work and maybe he'll get some jobs out of that. What's more, we'll have something beautiful to look at. As for the bread, so far we're managing."

Egnat grumbled some more, but Lukia would not be swayed.

By the time Ted had finished painting, her children agreed their mother had been right to accept their cousin's offer. On one long wall in the living room, he'd painted a tall ship in a stormy sea, and on the other, a green forest, with long grasses and a sparkling blue river that reminded them of Kivertsi. The seascape and landscape contrasted with the yellow dust bowl outside, giving them all a sense of wonder, a place they could imagine visiting at the end of a hard day's work. In the evenings, when Lukia did her handwork, she'd stop occasionally and admire Ted's art. His murals gave her hope that with rain, their fields could flourish like the land in the painting.

Much as she acknowledged Ted's gift and had encouraged his art, she couldn't see how painting pictures could be a fruitful occupation. Not in these hard times. When she worried out loud, Ted told his aunt he'd already placed an ad in the classified section of the *Winnipeg Free Press* and pulled a newspaper out of his brown paper shopping bag to show her. He flipped to the back section, and with his finger pointed to the ad. The first line was all in capital letters.

He read, translating from English to Ukrainian, "YOUNG ARTIST FROM RUSSIA desires work—all kinds of scenery, painting, decorating and sign-making for theatres; advertisement and show cards. 252 Manitoba Avenue."

"Hmm," Lukia said. "They have to write you. That will take time."

"Auntie," he said, "with no phone, it's the best I can do."

"Maybe you'll be lucky."

"Auntie, don't worry. Winnipeg is a big place. There are lots of wealthy people."

Lukia wished him good luck, but she didn't understand this new generation. Hardly anyone wanted to work on a farm. Yet, could she blame them? They'd seen the horrors their families had faced since coming to Canada. She had emigrated, hoping to keep her family together, but that had turned out to be some kind of joke. She and her brother were at an impasse. If she'd known what immigration would bring, she would have stayed home. But then again, she didn't want to live in a land where you never knew which enemy was coming next.

She sighed heavily. Perhaps Harry was right to choose another occupation. He was nineteen and working at an automobile service station in Winnipeg run by a parishioner at Sobor. After church one Sunday, Lukia had learned he was advertising for an apprentice mechanic. Harry, whose eyes lit up when any car drove by, jumped at the opportunity. Though good for him, his new job meant more pressure on Egnat. He now only had Mike to help him—the brother most likely to skip out of his duties than offer to do more.

Mike never left Lukia's mind. He had yet to show her and his older brother he could be trusted with both money and work. His heart wasn't in farming, but the prospects outside of it for an uneducated immigrant were even less viable. The country, with its unemployment numbers hitting an all-time high, continued to be in a state of unrest.

Lukia didn't have to wait long to share her concerns with her middle son. Several evenings later, when she was braiding a rug with rags from torn shirts, pants, and old towels impossible to mend, Mike sat down beside her on the chesterfield. He'd been quiet over supper, but now that he'd had a few glasses of horilka he appeared eager to talk. He filled a rolling paper with tobacco from a tin on the side table, lit it, and took a puff before he spoke. The smoke spiralled upwards over his head.

"Mama, I know you're worrying how to feed us all."

"Of course. All mothers worry." She took a long strip of brown gabardine fabric and braided it in with the other scraps of blue and green material. "Look at what the government's done. They've placed rations on flour, pork, even cocoa."

He took another puff. "I'm thinking of applying to get relief at the government camps."

"What? No." She stopped her braiding. "What nonsense is this?"

"It's not nonsense." He bent down to pick up the used match that had fallen on the worn wood floor. "The government is giving relief to single, unemployed men. They offer board and room, medical help if needed, and they find you work for twenty cents a day."

She laid the unfinished rug in her lap. "Listen, no one in our family is going to get relief. Since when do we ask for handouts?"

He pursed his lips and dropped the ash from his cigarette into the empty jar lid he held in his left hand.

When he didn't answer, she said, "You know what they do with immigrants who go into those camps? They force you to sign forms requesting to be deported."

"Where did you hear that?" His mouth twisted in disbelief.

"At church. One man got relief, and he had to sign a form. They don't give you the money for nothing. No, no, no. You have to pay it back. They can ask for it whenever they want." When he didn't reply, she said pointedly, "Nothing in life is free." She picked up another rag from the pile beside her. "Besides, your English isn't that good. How will you know what you're signing?"

Mike grunted. "I'd know," he said with an edge to his voice. He got up and stomped towards the front door.

"And remember, there's lots of work on the farm. We need your help."

Lukia didn't know if he'd heard this last part, as he'd already opened the door and was halfway out. She adjusted the light on the kerosene lamp and kept working. Why did he always look for the easy way out? Her sons could not be more different. Egnat was a worker. So was Harry. But Mike, who worked hard if he wanted to, was a dreamer. He was a wonderful singer and actor, but what was that? Singing and acting didn't put bread on the table. She examined the work she'd done on the rug. The colours were coming together nicely. If only the days ahead were that simple.

33

A Potent Drink

Everywhere she went, Lukia heard grim stories. That wasn't surprising, given that she had some of her own to tell. What was surprising was how many people dusted themselves off and kept going. To soften the blows that came with hardship, many made illicit alcohol; it helped to calm the nerves. Many even sold it. She'd made homebrew ever since she could remember, but she'd never sold any. She knew it was against the law, and with all the talk of deportation, she wasn't taking any chances.

However, she had no problem sharing what she brewed. For those neighbours who helped thresh the grain that hadn't been savaged by the grasshoppers, Lukia provided breakfast, sandwiches for lunch, a hearty supper, and a good shot of homebrew—a potent wine made from the succulent saskatoon berries she'd picked with Elena and Dunya. The homemade alcohol made her farm the most popular one in the district. Locals were told there would be a feast at the Mazurec house at the end of threshing—and more than a few stiff drinks. That promise kept the men working long hours.

On the last day of harvest, the men consumed Lukia's mouth-watering varenyky and holupchis with gusto and asked for second helpings. They swigged her booze until the moon was bright in the sky. When they could barely keep their eyes open, they got up and stumbled out the door. Lukia and Elena couldn't stop laughing at the sight of them.

Elena said, "Did you see them? They kept licking their lips. They drank so much they couldn't stand up. They had to leave on their bums."

"Yeah, yeah." Lukia laughed. "It's a good wine." It felt good to laugh. These were grown men who should have known better. But no one blamed them. They were good men who drank as hard as they worked.

One worker was so loaded when he got into his coupe to go home that, instead of driving down their road, he drove into the straw stacks in the barnyard. The fresh straw, being soft and loose, tumbled down, covering his car completely. Egnat, Mike, and the others had to haul him and his car out. He was quite the sight, with straw strewn all over, and some even sticking out of the neckline of his shirt.

Lukia laughed again. But it was a different story the month before when her livestock had accidentally swallowed too much alcohol. She'd made a brew from chokecherries and thrown the mash into the backyard. She'd completely forgotten about the potent mash until she saw her chickens and pigs staggering around. There was nothing she could do at that point except wring her hands. Now, as she looked at the inebriated men, she thought, *Better these men. Better these men than my livestock.*

One day, not long after harvest, Lukia had some unlikely visitors. Dunya was at the sink washing blueberry stains off of Genya's hands and face with a wet cloth and she was putting away the dishes from lunch, when a loud knock on the door made her jump.

"Who could that be?" she asked.

Looking bewildered as well, Dunya peered out the window.

Lukia opened the door to two tall, clean-shaven men in uniform—one thin, the other hefty—and a dog which she later learned was a German shepherd. She knew immediately they were the Royal Canadian Mounted Police. She recognized the dark trousers with the yellow stripe tucked into high, polished brown leather boots, the jacket with the brass buttons, and the tan brimmed hat. The police officer who gave Petro his summons wore the same outfit.

"Hello," she said, then turned to Dunya. "Talk to them. I won't understand." Her daughter's English wasn't great, but at least she could converse a bit and understand what most people said.

After a brief exchange, the officers left and headed for the barn with their dog in the lead.

"What did they want?" Lukia said, watching them from the open doorway.

"They were told we have a still."

"What?" Lukia swallowed hard.

"I said no."

Lukia frowned. "Who would say that?" Did one of their neighbours want them deported? Was she in any trouble?

"Did I say something wrong?"

"No, but who knows what they'll do if they find any horilka." She wrung her hands, then said, "Come."

Dunya took Genya's hand. "Where are we going?" Genya said.

Lukia said, "We're going to see what those nice men are doing."

Lukia stood in the barn's doorway with Dunya and Genya and peered in. Daylight cast a long, yellow rectangle across the interior's earth floor. Near the ladder to the loft, the hefty officer stabbed at piles of hay and straw with a pitchfork. The thin one searched under the horse blanket and behind a saw horse before moving to the place in the corner where Egnat kept the hand plow and various tools. All the while, the dog sniffed around the animals, upsetting them. The cows mooed and shuffled in their stalls, and the horse across from them stroked the ground with his hoof as if anxious to escape the intruders.

After a thorough search of the barn, the police went outside and inspected the area around the outhouse and the lean-to where Egnat stored more equipment. After they'd been out in the yard for about a half hour, they returned to the house and entered the living room. They pushed aside the rug covering the trap door in the floor, and the thin one climbed down the short ladder to the root cellar, while the hefty one went through each cupboard. The only time they conferred with one another was when the hefty officer came across a bottle of homebrew and some empty bottles behind a curtain on a lower shelf near the stove. He held the bottle of homebrew up to the window. It was three-quarters full.

Lukia assumed he was going to confiscate the horilka, but then he put it back on the shelf the way he'd found it. From his action, she supposed it wasn't a sin or a crime to possess homebrew—only to make it.

The two officers said a few words to Dunya, tipped their hat to Lukia, and left.

"What did they say?" she asked her daughter.

"They said they were sorry to bother us."

"Hmm," Lukia said. "At least they were better than the Polish officers who came to our house in Kivertsi, looking for guns. Those were pigs." She remembered the lustful looks they'd given Hania and the shameful way they'd treated her neighbour's husband. They threw him in jail because they found a rifle in his house similar to the ones carried by the Ukrainian army. "I'd like to know who complained about us." Lukia figured it had to be a neighbour. The horns of jealousy showed up in Canada, just as they had in Volhynia. Or maybe it was a not-so-subtle message to watch their steps in a country that kept its foreigners in line. The unexpected police visit had shaken her composure, but she was pleased they hadn't come during harvest, when she had plenty of bottles around. All the RCMP officer had found was a three-quarters full bottle of horilka. It was time to make another batch.

34

THE LETTER

The nights turned colder, signalling that winter was on its way. The below-freezing temperature the night before wasn't the only chill the Mazurec family experienced that October day. Dunya was carrying bowls of cabbage soup to the kitchen table when there was a knock on the door.

It was Mr. Chimiuk's nephew, Russell, a year older than Dunya. The fine, wispy hair above his mouth was a sorry attempt at a moustache. "Good afternoon, Dunya. I was at the post office and saw a letter for you." He took a light blue envelope from his jacket pocket and handed it to her.

"How nice of you." It was from her cousin Tanya in Volhynia. "Please, Russell, come in. Did you eat? We're just sitting down."

"Thank you," he said, taking off his tweed cap. "How could I pass up such a lovely offer?" He joined Egnat, Mike, Harry, and Genya at the table. Elena brought him a table setting and a shot glass. Dunya put the letter in her apron pocket and ladled soup into a bowl for Russell.

Egnat poured horilka into Russell's glass from the bottle on the table. "God willing," he said, clinking his half-full glass with Russell's. "How's your family doing?"

"You know, bad," Russell said, taking a slice of rye bread. "Father doesn't know how much longer he can hang on. He was joking he might end up holding his hand out like the men on street corners in Winnipeg."

Egnat slurped his soup. "It's like that all over Manitoba and Saskatchewan."

Mike said, "Even in the United States. I heard one guy say the farmers there have given up. They're roaming the country, most heading west towards California, looking for any work just to survive."

"Wheat's the lowest it's been," Egnat said. "Bad luck everywhere."

Russell nodded. "The drifters have it bad, too. The railway pressured the premier, so now the police are banning all free rides to the west coast."

"See," her mother said to Mike. "No free rides."

Mike grumbled. "I wasn't going to hop a train."

"Yeah, yeah, yeah."

Dunya sat down at the table and played with the letter in her lap, shuffling it from one hand to the other. Tanya hadn't written for a while.

Her mother said, "If you're so anxious to read it, read it. I want to know what she says, too."

"I will, I will. Right after lunch." The envelope was thick. She put it back in her apron pocket and took a spoonful of soup.

After Russell left, Dunya's family stayed at the table, waiting for her to read the letter. Months had gone by since they'd had any news from their homeland. With regime change a frequent occurrence, it was possible they weren't getting all the letters.

Dunya sliced the envelope open with a knife and took it near the window where daylight had not yet surrendered. She was pleased she could read her native language. *At least, there's that,* she thought. She blamed the teacher again for not showing her how to read and write in English.

The first part of the letter was about Tania's interest in some boy in Kivertsi. Dunya read that part silently. The boy had tried to kiss Tania. When she unexpectedly bent down, he tripped over her and landed on his face. Dunya giggled, picturing the silly scene.

"What's so funny?" her mother asked. "Why aren't you reading it out loud?"

"It's about some boy."

"She has a boyfriend?"

"It's nothing. Just a joke."

"Hmm," her mother said, making a face. "Nu, what else does Tania say?"

Dunya read silently for a few moments, then shuddered. "No!"

"What's the matter? Tell me, child."

"Oy, Mama."

"What? Has someone died? Is it Babcha?"

"No."

Her mother was beside herself. "Tell me already."

"I will. Let me catch my breath." Dunya sat down on the chair and sighed heavily.

Egnat said, "Everything is dramatic for Dunya."

"You don't know, so don't say," Dunya said, crossly.

Egnat gave her a look, then lit a kerosene lamp and brought it to the table. Elena finished tending to Genya and joined them.

Dunya cleared her throat and turned the letter to the light. She read, "It's hard in Volhynia, but it's worse in the east, where they have the collective farms. You are so lucky to be in Canada. We're managing, but every day it feels like another stone has been laid on our backs. You know how it is under the Polacks. They only give you so much land, and it better be productive. But in the east, under Stalin, it's become dangerous even to live."

"What does she mean?" Mike asked.

"Don't interrupt. Let me finish."

He glowered but gestured for her to keep reading.

"Stalin keeps up his propaganda. He says Ukrainians are subhuman. Imagine him saying that! He's never liked us. Maybe it's because we don't want to be under his Russian thumb. What he's doing is murderous! He's forcing families to give away what little grain they have. Soldiers visit each farm without warning and take away all their bags of wheat. They take away any kind of grain. They say the government needs to sell it because the yields have been too low. He says the farmers have to do it for the love of their country, that they have to help one another. If a farmer holds any back, he's sent to prison or even shot." Dunya cleared her throat before continuing. "People are dying from starvation, typhus, malaria. They say millions have already died. They're throwing them into pits. And those who are alive look like skeletons walking around, so thin. I heard some are so hungry they're eating corpses. Can you imagine, Dunya? I can't. I like awake at nights worrying the Communists will come to Volhynia and do the same here."

"Oy, oy, oy," her mother said. "That can't be. Aagh, what am I thinking? A man who doesn't believe in God thinks he can get away with the worst sin imaginable. To murder your own people! My God. But then again, these aren't his people. They're Ukrainians. To Stalin, we're nothing."

"How can people eat human flesh?" Mike said.

Her mother crossed herself.

Elena mumbled, "If you're starving to death, you would do it, too."

"Elena's right, Mama," Mike said. "If it meant life or death—"

"Shall I go on?" Dunya asked.

"Yes," Egnat said, "read the rest."

"I'm sorry to bring you such sad news. I hope your family is well. I walk by your old farm. It looks good, but you're not there. I miss you. Write soon. Pray for us. Love, Tania."

Dunya put the letter back in her apron pocket.

Her mother crossed herself again. "Oy, I thought there was nothing worse than what I went through. But this … this is unimaginable. Why haven't we heard of this horror in Canada?"

Egnat said, "People in power are very clever at covering up wrongdoing. It's always been like that."

Struck by the gravity of the letter, they sat in silence for a few moments before getting on with their evening chores.

While milking the cows, Dunya considered her own plight. It wasn't that long ago that she'd felt suicidal. Her desolation had arisen out of loneliness and hard work and not from unimaginable hunger, like many Ukrainians were facing in the old country. She pulled the cow's teat and tried to keep Tanya's kidding about boys in the forefront of her mind.

The tragic news from the old country left Lukia staring into the darkness for hours. *Imagine Stalin giving orders to expropriate farmers' grain!* It was one thing for him to say that Ukrainians were an inferior race to the Russians, but then to act on it—to treat them worse than animals, to starve them to death—that was unconscionable. That man had to be the devil himself.

Not that long ago, Gregory had fought for Russia. He'd been loyal to the Tsar. Yes, the Romanovs deserved to be overthrown because of their greed and disregard for their subjects, but they didn't deserve to be slaughtered. No one deserved that. She often said a prayer for Olga Nikolaevna, the Tsar's daughter, who had worked as a Red Cross nurse on the refugee trains. She saved Dunya's life. Her daughter had been only a few weeks old, when her belly button had become infected. If it wasn't for the princess's treatment, Dunya would have died. The royal was an angel, no question, and now she was dead. Dead, but not forgotten.

Life was strange. Those who fought against the Romanovs, shouting slogans to bring down the rich and reward the poor, now acted like they were tsars themselves. These Bolsheviks now declared themselves Communists but were no better than the Romanovs. They had turned out to be worse, at least for the Ukrainian people in the east.

Before falling asleep that night, she got down on her knees and set her eyes upon the icon she'd rescued from the Bolshevik fires. She prayed: *Please God, keep Stalin away from Volhynia, keep him away from the Carpathian Mountains, where my mother and brother live. Bless Olga Nikolaevna for her good deeds. May she rest in peace. And please take care of my family, here and abroad.* Crossing herself three times, she said with each cross, "In the name of the Father, the Son, and the Holy Ghost. Amen."

35

DREAM ON

The day Dunya had been waiting for had arrived—December 13, St. Andrew's Day, celebrating the first apostle to join Jesus. This year it fell on a Wednesday, a workday in the city, but because Hanukkah started the same day, she and her mother could leave their Jewish employers to their festivities and return to their farm.

The Bible mentioned that Andrew was the one who introduced his brother Peter to Christ. Dunya paid little attention to these biblical facts as presented by the priest on Sunday. She was excited about the day because that was when young people told jokes and played games and got their fortunes told. And best of all, this was the night that would determine who she was destined to marry.

She'd had marriage on her mind ever since she turned seventeen four months ago. She had embroidered linens for her hope chest—which is what the English girls called it. Besides a square tablecloth and an apron, she'd cross-stitched a fine wool wall hanging, depicting a colourful peacock of blue and yellow on a burgundy background, accented with a crocheted border. She used her mother's old blue trunk to store her handiwork, which lay beside her mother's good tablecloth, embroidered apron, and prayer book for the deceased.

She'd also begun embroidering traditional flower patterns on a white bedspread for a double bed. She smiled as she imagined lying under it in the arms of her husband. Though her family was poor, her mother had bought fine cotton broadcloth and thread to make a bed covering. While her mother excelled at braiding rugs out of rags and sewing clothing for the family without a pattern, Dunya and Elena were adept at embroidering and crocheting. Handicrafts kept their hands busy and their minds occupied during those cold, dark nights when the lamp flickered every time the wind howled outside.

At bedtime, her mother reminded her to put a stick of wood in a basin of water. "Dunya, whoever you dream of tonight, that'll be who you'll marry."

"Is that what you did, Mama?" Dunya said, as she slid the basin under the head of her bed.

"No. Your babcha never mentioned this tradition when I was young."

"It's too bad you never tried it. I wonder if you would've dreamt about Tato."

"Maybe." Her mother sat down on the bed. "We did other things in the old country. A group of girls would get together, maybe six or seven of us. Each one would bake some pompushky and put them on a bench. Then they'd call the dogs to see which girl's sweet buns the dogs would eat. The ones they chose signalled that she'd be the one to get married first."

"Was that true?"

"Yes. But sometimes, the boys in the village would hear of the girls' plans and feed the dogs so they wouldn't be hungry, then hide and watch the girls coax the dogs to eat. Of course, the dogs weren't interested because their stomachs were full."

"I like this way better."

After her mother left, Dunya couldn't wait to fall asleep. Tonight, she would dream about her husband-to-be. If she were still living in Kivertsi, she probably would have been married by now. Especially since she looked older than her years. She didn't know any married girls or boys in the Rosser district or in Stony Mountain. Maybe it was because no one had anything. Everyone was too poor to have a wedding.

Excited, Dunya tossed a while before she fell asleep. Images of the boys she knew popped into her head. She didn't know many, since she'd been too busy working to socialize much. Would one of them appear in her dream? He had to be young. She couldn't bear marrying someone old enough to be her father.

She needn't have worried, as that night she dreamt of a tall, dark, and handsome young man who took her by the hand and led her to the edge of a lake. His face was kind, a face she hadn't seen before. She woke up startled, wondering how she was going to meet the man of her dreams.

Lukia sat down on a stool by a large, round steel tub filled with hot, soapy water. She grabbed the washboard and began scrubbing the neckline of Mike's shirt. At least her children believed in the power of dreams. The fact their father had ignored her pleas to stay home because of a bad dream had made an impression. It underlined the importance of paying attention to the unconscious. They understood it worked even when they were asleep.

Dreams had guided her life, provided some direction; they had offered a warning when there was any danger. If only Gregory had believed in them. Maybe if he'd lived, she wouldn't have emigrated.

She had pleaded with him on the morning of his death not to go into the woods that day. She told him about her bad dream, about a big cow with swollen teats. The cow came to the house, and no matter how much Lukia drank, she couldn't drain the milk. It kept flowing and flowing. Amused, Gregory told her it sounded like a pleasant dream and didn't understand why she was fretting. That perhaps her dream meant they'd be rich. But she said no, that kind of dream meant the opposite. No good was in the forecast. He laughed it off, and when she begged him to cross himself before he left for the woods, he refused. She never found out if he'd been struck by a tree he had chopped or by one that was merely ready to fall.

And yet, even though she strongly believed in the symbolic meaning of her dreams, she wondered about the handsome man her daughter had dreamt of on St. Andrew's Day. The way Dunya had described him, he could easily be a movie star. Lukia had seen photos of good-looking men on the posters outside the Palace Theatre on Selkirk Avenue, but those were Hollywood actors in make-believe stories. Where was her daughter going to find such a man in a farming community?

Her daughter had a lot to offer some young man. She had long, auburn hair that shone like silk, hazel eyes that turned from brown to green in the sun, and full, kissable lips. Someone had told her daughter she had a figure like a Coca-Cola bottle. That made Lukia laugh. Only in Canada could someone describe a woman's body like a soda pop bottle, and it would be a compliment. Besides being attractive, her daughter was smart. There was no worry about her losing her virginity before marriage. She liked to flirt and tease the men, but she was too smart to let a man come between her legs without a ring on her finger and a commitment for life. Even so, where would Dunya find this tall, dark, and handsome man?

Lukia scrubbed Harry's socks and watched the grease from his work seep into the soap bubbles. It was too bad Dunya was such a dreamer. She'd always had her sights on something greater on the horizon, more than what girls her age or status in life could reasonably expect. She was the only one in the family who didn't cry when they left Kivertsi. Her eyes shone that day, as if she was expecting some reward on the other side of the ocean.

Standing up to relieve the ache in her back, Lukia decided to let the dream speak for itself. She wasn't about to quash her daughter's hopes. But how long could anyone wait for the right man to come along? She hoped her daughter wouldn't ignore other prospects because of a dream. That would be foolish.

36

THE UNEXPECTED

In the early days of spring 1934, farmers' eyes that had once shone with hope grew dull with the realization the next day would bring more of the same grim weather. Hoping to improve their lot, American farmers had gone on strike the year before. Their attempt at solidarity did nothing to improve the weather. Nature refused to listen.

On April 22, a wild dust storm arriving from North Dakota blew away topsoil and deposited up to six inches of dirt in the ditches and in ridges along the fences. The day was so grey, Lukia couldn't see the sun. Since they'd seeded early, she prayed the seeds had taken hold and hadn't blown away. Others in her district had to stop seeding. In some places, the dust had blown in before the snows had even left. As a result, farmers in both countries, with mortgage payments and rents overdue, lost their livelihood. Hundreds of thousands were on the move heading west—their bellies empty, their clothes threadbare, their shoes holey—hoping to lay their heads down in a place that promised enough work to feed and support a family. They'd sold their equipment and livestock for a pittance. This was their stock market crash. They didn't have shares in companies; they had shares in dreams shattered by years of unforgiving weather.

May brought more high winds and blinding dust. In some places, drifts of dust covered roads as deeply as snowdrifts. Shockingly, once the dust storms had abated, Lukia's crops showed minor damage. Some early sown wheat actually looked quite green, and she thanked God for the miracle. Egnat said it wasn't a miracle. They were just lucky to have seeded early. Others who seeded just before the dust storms hit had to seed again.

The summer that year was one of the driest on record, the worst since 1894. Egnat read that it was a continent-wide drought. Lukia and her family, as they'd done with other disasters in the old country, rode it out. Perhaps, having lived through the wars, the refugee camp, and losing four children and a husband, she was convinced this Depression wasn't as bad as what she'd experienced. She knew they had to be careful with the food they had. She wasted nothing. If there was a crust left over from a meal, she gave it to Genya. She wanted to spare the littlest one the agony of hunger.

Lukia continued to pray nightly on her knees, expecting that one day, God would answer her prayers. One of her prayers was for Petro. He and his family were living somewhere in the North End of Winnipeg. With no word from him, she resigned herself to living with the chasm between them.

What she hadn't expected was a letter from her other brother, Pavlo. Egnat had picked up the mail and, as soon as he got in the door, Lukia sat down anxiously at the kitchen table.

Egnat slit open the light blue envelope with its Polish stamps and air mail symbol. He read: "Dear Sister, I hope you and your children are well. How's Petro and his family?"

"Oy," Lukia said, interrupting. "We haven't written them in such a long time. They don't know about our troubles. Go on."

Egnat moved the letter closer. "When you wrote me of your joint venture, I was surprised. Petro wasn't easy as a boy, and he's been just as hard as a man. But family is family. We have to be there for one another. First, some good news. Antosha has delivered our first boy. Petro is a few months old and thriving."

"How wonderful," Lukia said, interrupting again. "He named him after his brother. That makes three children now." She counted them off on her fingers. "Elena, Mira, and now Petro. Keep reading."

"As for our dear sister, Panashka, her husband left her. He got angry she was doing her hair instead of cooking for him. He hit her across the face and took Tanya. Such a tragedy."

"Poor Panashka," Lukia said. "She had no luck."

Egnat stared at the letter in his hands.

"What?" Lukia said.

"Mama, Babcha died."

"No! Don't say!" Lukia's hand flew to her chest. "Oy, oy, oy. My God. What does Pavlo say? What happened?"

Egnat adjusted the letter in his hand, turning it towards the window. "I'm sorry to tell you, but our dear mama has died. She had been suffering with aches and pains; I didn't know it was that bad, because she didn't complain. When she took to her bed and didn't want to eat, we asked the priest to come. He prayed for her soul. You know how it is. She went peacefully in her sleep. We were blessed to have her as long as we did. We buried her in the Caucasus."

"Oy, Mama, Mama. Such a good woman. She helped so many. And now she's gone. That's how it is. Nu, what to do? I wasn't there. I should've been there." Lukia moaned. "Poor Mama. I wonder if Panashka was there beside her. We can't even phone. When did he say she died?"

"He didn't say. But they buried her already."

Lukia wrung her hands in her lap. "My God, my God. She had a good life. I think she was over a hundred, but who knows. The baptismal records were lost in the war. Still, what more can you ask of God." She crossed herself three times. "We must tell Petro. I'll talk to the priest. We'll have prayers."

Egnat handed the letter to his mother. She flapped one end of it in her lap, as if to banish its contents. She sat there until the sunlight left the room and it was time to make supper.

Finding Petro was a challenge. Egnat had to use a neighbour's phone to contact the priest at Sobor, who contacted a parishioner who knew where Petro was living. After a few tense days, the new priest, Reverend Mayevsky—who had replaced Reverend Sawchuk—assured Lukia that prayers for her mother could proceed.

Following the divine liturgy on Sunday, the Mazurecs and Korneluks gathered near the front of the nave to pray for Fedoshya. With no time to bake, Lukia had gone to KUB's bakery in a converted house on Stella Avenue to buy two loaves of braided bread, and to a grocery store to buy some apples. She set the food on the memorial table covered with her small embroidered tablecloth. The church's icon of Jesus in a gold frame along with some candlesticks completed the setting on the table.

Lukia handed Father Mayevsky her prayer book with the embossed Greek Orthodox cross on the cover, then stood between her sons, Egnat and Mike. Each mourner held a long metal tube candle while the priest waved his censer back and forth, blessing the food and those taking part. When he finished, he handed the censer to the deacon, who continued to swing the censer over the table as the priest read out the names of the deceased in Lukia's prayer book. Fedoshya's name was the last one he read. To end the service, the priest and deacon sang *Vichnaya Pamyat,* the mournful chant repeating the phrase Eternal Memory. The others joined in; their sad voices ringing through the mostly empty church.

Lukia recalled the last time she saw her mother. Watching her daughter and grandchildren leave Kivertsi, her mother had fainted in Pavlo's arms.

Mama, I'm so sorry. I'm sorry I wasn't there in your last hours. Lukia cried not only for her mother but also for those she'd buried and those she wouldn't see again. Dunya gave her another hankie to dry her tears.

Afterwards, Lukia invited Petro and his family back to the house for a bite to eat. The Korneluks all came, but Anna made it known to her sister-in-law the only reason they had come was out of respect for Petro's mother. Her unexpected death had done nothing to heal the rift between her daughter and son.

37

BARN DANCE FEVER

As the disappointing summer ended, Lukia fretted about their expenses. Where could she find the money for rent, for food, for feeding the livestock as well? She couldn't ask Petro, not after how cold he'd been at their mother's memorial. Besides, he had little himself. Ted told her the agent back in Volhynia still hadn't sent the money he'd collected on his father's apartment building.

The only ray of hope that summer was on the movie screens— that is, if you could afford to go. And somewhere in a small town in Ontario, a mother had given birth to five girls. The Dionne quintuplets had become an overnight sensation.

At church one Sunday, Lukia said to her friend Natasha, "So much fuss. It's as if no woman has ever given birth before." The Dionne family may as well have been in a circus—always on display, cameras flashing in their faces, strangers goggling at their every move. Lukia supposed the five little ones had become popular because no one wanted to think about their own lives. They wanted to escape. They wanted to avoid looking at what was right in front of them.

After a few evenings, during which Lukia agonized over their dire financial situation, Mike surprised his mother by suggesting they organize barn dances at their farm as a way of adding to the family income. They'd just finished milking the cows, and he offered the idea while they were standing outside the barn doors.

Lukia looked over at Egnat, who was brushing his horse's coat in the yard. "Did you mention your idea to your brother?"

"No."

"Let's ask him."

A cigarette dangled from Egnat's lips as he worked the brush through Dan's hide. "What now?" he said, when his mother and brother approached.

"Mike wants to put on barn dances, make some money. He said country folk would love them. A dance would take their minds off their troubles. They could let loose and kick up their heels for an evening."

Egnat stopped brushing and regarded his brother. "You want to do this?"

"Yes," Mike said. "I'll clean the barn and put up posters."

Egnat smiled. "You want to clean the barn, okay. Good idea, Mike."

"And another thing," Mike said, patting Dan, who eyed them all, as if he was part of the meeting and they needed his attention as well. "I think we should get a phone."

"A phone!" Lukia said. "What do we need a phone for? We hardly have enough money to get by and you want a phone?"

"We need to get the word out about the dance. People will call and want to know where it is. That way we can tell them."

Lukia hemmed and hawed, but Mike persisted. He insisted they could cover the cost with the money earned from the dance. She tsked some more, then reluctantly took the money from the glass jar over the stove to pay for the phone. She'd set aside the egg money for emergency repairs of any equipment. If Mike's scheme worked, she'd be able to restore the cash before there was a need to fix anything.

The day the phone—a rectangular wood box with a crank on the side—was connected, the Mazurecs gathered around the installer from the Manitoba telephone company to learn how to use the contraption. "To make a call, you have to call Central," he said. "The operator there connects you to the number you want." The man also said they had a party line, meaning any time they picked it up, there could be anywhere from five to twelve people using it.

"Five to twelve?" Dunya asked. She now knew enough English to converse. "If I say something private, will the people on the party line hear?"

He chortled. "Yes. You wouldn't believe what people say. They forget others are listening."

Mike's face twisted. He obviously didn't like what he heard.

"And the cost?" Egnat asked.

"You get one free call a day, but after that, you have to pay one cent a call."

Lukia found it confusing. She doubted she'd ever use such a contraption, but her children were eager to try it.

"It's modern," Dunya said. "The Chimiuks have one, and so do all the English."

In the days that followed, Lukia found herself staring at the phone, expecting it to ring, but it never did. Mike made some calls. She wasn't sure to whom, but the way he chuckled, she suspected it might be to some girl. Though unconvinced the phone had been a good idea, she was pleased to see Egnat, Mike and Harry work in harmony getting the barn ready for the dance. With plans to hold their first one in a few weeks, they built an outer wood staircase complete with handrails to the barn's loft. There was already a ladder inside, but none of them wanted strangers traipsing through the barn, scaring the animals. They also built wooden benches to line the walls in the loft, so that dancers had a place to sit.

Lukia was pleased that Mike no longer moped around the farm or complained when Egnat asked him to help with jobs. She hoped this scheme of Mike's succeeded. They were counting on the proceeds from the dance to add to their income. If the dances failed, Lukia expected her sons would return to bickering and blaming. With money in such short supply, she needed their cooperation more than ever.

All went according to plan. Her sons scrubbed the loft floor and arranged the benches against the walls. Lukia, Elena and Dunya planned the midnight luncheon, which Mike said was necessary. He'd been to a few dances in Stonewall, a town eleven miles from Lilyfield; the organizers always provided sandwiches and cakes. That excited Dunya, who loved to bake and had collected at least eight cake recipes—sponge, yellow, banana, poppy seed, honey, vanilla, chocolate and lemon. When Lukia voiced her fears about the cost, Mike reassured his mother again that the charge at the door would cover that and more.

As for music, he'd heard of a band that was just starting out and getting a lot of attention for their danceable tunes. Lukia praised Mike's resourcefulness, especially when a neighbour who stopped by on his way to the city said he'd heard the band play on the radio. He said that Andy Dejarlis was a popular Métis fiddler who had formed the group with his brother on drums, along with an accordionist and a saxophonist. How her son contacted Mr. Dejarlis and arranged for his band to play was a mystery to Lukia.

She began to believe Mike could make something out of his life. If he could organize a big gathering like a barn dance and pull it off, then there was no telling what he could do.

Excited about the upcoming barn dance, Harry and Dunya were happy to pitch in to advertise the event. They put up posters on telephone poles along the highway and hung notices in Dan

Balacko's store and the barbershop next door in Stony Mountain. And Mike placed ads in the classified section of the Lilyfield Gazette and even the Stonewall Argus. Their efforts paid off as word of the country party spread.

The day of the dance, the Mazurec family rushed around the property like chickens running from foxes. Mike and Harry had made two long tables for the midnight luncheon from sheets of plywood placed on wooden sawhorses. Lukia complained she had only one tablecloth made from oilcloth and worried about having a bare table. She didn't want the locals to think their family didn't know how to present food. She could've used her fine tablecloth with its beautifully embroidered border, but she saved it for special holidays, like Christmas and Easter. She couldn't afford to have it ruined by some stain impossible to remove. Fortunately, Natasha came to the rescue, loaning her an oilcloth one that could withstand any accidents by a boisterous crowd.

With all aspects of the dance covered, Dunya fussed over what to wear. She now had three dresses: her grey flannel, the bronze velveteen, and the newest one her mother had made. Since the first two were winter garments, she decided on the dark green rayon dress with a flared skirt. The colour of the fabric brought out the green in her hazel eyes.

"You'd better iron it," Lukia said. "You can't wear it like that. It looks like you slept in it."

Dunya pouted but got the iron out to heat on the wood stove. When she finished ironing the garment, she said, "What about you, Mama? Aren't you going to change?"

Lukia's polka-dotted house dress had a spot from last evening's meal on the collar, and she licked her finger before rubbing it. She didn't feel like putting on a different dress, but this was the family's first dance. The Mazurecs had to show they weren't ignorant or sloppy about presentation, nor could they look like they were destitute. She changed into the only other dress she had, the navy one she'd worn for Egnat's wedding and Fedoshya's memorial. She fixed her hair into a bun and announced she was ready.

Hungry for a good time, farm folk and townspeople from miles around arrived by bicycle, truck, car, and horse and wagon. Lukia said the cover charge of one dollar was too high, but Mike reassured her it was a good deal. He said that everyone would get a few hours of entertainment and a substantial snack, and where could you get that for one buck? To quench the dancers' thirst, they set out several pitchers of water from their well. Some brought their own alcoholic refreshments in bottles and flasks, from which they drank in the barnyard or in their cars.

The band did not disappoint. In no time at all, the dance floor became so crowded that Lukia said to Mike, "You couldn't have picked better musicians."

Dunya made a point of remembering the names of the songs and told her mother what Andy Dejarlis's band was playing. There were polkas, like "Bingo Jack," "Calico," and "Rolly's Polka." And there were waltzes, too; tunes named "Good Neighbour," "Apple Blossom," and "Rainy River."

Lukia had a hard time getting her tongue around some words. Since there had been little need to speak the language, she hadn't made learning it a priority. In the Rockwood municipality, there were many Ukrainian farmers, and when she shopped in Winnipeg, the merchants spoke Yiddish, Ukrainian or Polish. Even at Sobor, the young parish of mostly new immigrants spoke her native language. One of the few times she had to speak in English was when the Mounties showed up at her farm unexpectedly. But then Dunya talked for her. She was proud her children were learning English. As she'd told them many times, *the more you know, the better off you'll be in the world.*

After a full set, the band announced the next dance, a polka, would be their last number before their break. While the band played, Lukia and Elena set out dishes and cutlery for the midnight luncheon.

"Panye Mazurec," said a voice behind her.

Lukia turned to see Orest, dressed in a suit, his hair slicked back with pomade. It had been several weeks since their first meeting at Dan Balacko's store. Flustered at seeing him again, she pushed an imaginary hair behind her ear.

"How nice to see you again," he said, smiling. "Someone told me this is your farm."

"Yes." Composing herself, she pointed across the loft. "That's my son, Mike, over there, the one with the dark hair and moustache. He organized this dance." Mike was whirling a young woman in a red dress around the floor.

His eyes wrinkled. "He's got the right idea. What about you? Why aren't you dancing?"

"Ah. It's been a while since I danced."

"You haven't forgotten how, have you?" he asked teasingly.

"Of course, I haven't forgotten. You know how it is. There's been little to dance about."

The music had stopped and the dancers began to disperse. Some mingled in groups; others headed to the doors to have a smoke or take a drink from the flasks in their pockets. He turned to her. "Would you like some fresh air?"

"I wouldn't mind that at all," she said, smiling. "I have to head out anyway and get the food ready."

Outside, the sweet smell of freshly cut alfalfa hay was a welcome change from the odours of sweat and cheap cologne on the dance floor. A crescent-shaped moon hung on an indigo sky dotted with countless stars. Orest and Lukia came down the loft stairs; below them, a cow mooed and crickets chirped, punctuating the talk and laughter of a group standing in the barnyard. As they headed towards the house, a turkey flew up to roost in a poplar nearby and the chatter of the dancers faded with each step.

Lukia folded her arms and savoured the air and the stars above. "I love these nights. It's quiet and yet there's so much life. Even in heaven."

Orest murmured. "You're religious?"

"For sure. And you're not?"

"When I lost my wife, I lost my faith."

"That's too bad. How long ago was that?"

"She died giving birth to our second son. He's sixteen now."

"And you never married again?"

"No. I couldn't find anyone who'd put up with me," he said, smiling. "And you?"

"I've been a widow for twelve years."

"Twelve years? An attractive woman like you?" He crooked his head.

She laughed. "Flatter me, flatter me. Pan—"

"Please. Call me Orest."

"Orest, I'm called Lukia."

"Lukia." He said it softly, as if it was a name to treasure.

Unaccustomed to such tenderness, she turned away. "I better get the food. Are you staying?"

"I will, if you promise me one dance."

She beamed. He was the first man she'd given any attention to. But then again, he was the first one who'd pursued her like a gentleman.

Just before midnight, Lukia, Elena and Dunya spread the plates of ham and cheese sandwiches, sliced dill pickles, and various cakes—chocolate, vanilla, honey—on the two tables. Lukia stood back to examine the layout of the food. It was a generous spread. Out of the corner of her eye, she saw Orest standing in the loft's doorway, talking to a man about his own age. Every so often, he'd look over at her. Though flattered, she tried to look uninterested. She didn't want him to think she was desperate to find a man.

Dunya came up beside her. "Mama, is there anything else you need?"

"No, thank you. You can go." Dunya took a sandwich and a slice of cake in a napkin and joined her friend Olga and another girl sitting on a bench on the other side of the dance floor.

During the band's break, Lukia had a bite herself and sat down beside Natasha, who remarked on the honey cake, how delicious it was, and wanted the recipe. When the band played a waltz, Orest came over and put his hand out. "You promised."

Natasha raised her eyebrows and winked at Lukia.

Lukia took Orest's hand. It was warm and rough. She appreciated his firm grip, one that had come from years of heavy work. This was a man a woman could rely on. She'd forgotten what a pleasure it was to move across the floor in the arms of a nice-looking man. She and Gregory had only danced once, and that was at their wedding. Though a half-decent dancer, he would drink with the men at social events, while she sat on the side gabbing with the women. She hadn't minded, because after marriage, dancing was often left to the young. The older ones were too tired from caring for their children and toiling in the fields.

The last time she'd danced was at Hania's wedding. Both Mike and Petro had taken her for a spin around the floor. After dancing with them, a few widowers, hoping for a commitment, had asked her as well.

Orest adjusted his hand on her waist. She wondered if he minded that she was on the heavy side. He hadn't known her as a young girl, when her body was sturdy but slender. But what could any man expect of a woman who'd given birth to eight children? Still, how had she let herself go like this? Her mother had remained willowy her entire life. But it wasn't fair to compare. She and her mother had different builds. It was time to forgive herself. She found comfort in food and had indulged herself after losing one child after another. Losing Gregory didn't help either. Her habit was to have one good stiff drink at the start of the meal; it stimulated her appetite and made everything taste better. Even life.

"Nu, Lukia, you're deep in thought."

"I was just thinking how long it's been since I danced. It feels good."

He grinned and squeezed her hand.

What would Gregory think if he knew she was attracted to a man other than him? Would he be happy for her or turn his mouth down in disapproval? She tried to dismiss her reservations. He was long gone now. Dwelling on the past got her nowhere. And yet she would never forget how his moustache bruised her lips when he kissed her with passion. Nor the smell of tobacco and alcohol when he came to bed and nestled his warm body next to hers, caressing her and awakening her desire to have him deep within her. And now, she was feeling the same temptation in Orest's arms.

The resounding notes of the instruments at the end of the waltz jarred her.

Orest bowed. "I'm sorry, I'd love another dance with you, but I have to leave. I was up early. One of my cows gave birth."

"That's wonderful. Have a safe drive home."

"I'll be going hunting soon. If I'm lucky, I'll get a deer. I'll bring you some."

"You don't have to, but I won't say no."

After he left her side, Elena came up to her and teased, "You have an admirer."

"We'll see." She kept an eye on Orest as he said goodbye to a couple of men hanging around the barn door. One of them punched him lightly on the shoulder. Orest laughed, then glanced at her before disappearing out the door. She liked that he wasn't a big talker. The last thing she needed was a man in her life who needed a lot of attention.

While the band packed up, Lukia cleaned the tables with Dunya. "Thank God, there were no fights," she said. With so many young men inebriated on homebrew, there were bound to be a few who couldn't keep their fists by their sides. Suddenly, the sound of a ruckus outside sent a few stragglers in the loft to the doorway to see what was going on.

"Oy," Lukia said. "I spoke too soon." She and Dunya grabbed the dirty plates and went to look themselves. Stepping outside and onto the staircase, they had an unobstructed view of the ground, where two men were shouting and pushing one another in the chest.

Lukia climbed down the stairs as a curious crowd gathered around the two men. Before she reached the bottom of the staircase, she scanned the throng for Egnat or Mike to break up the fight. The only one she recognized was Ihor. She waved at him, and he pushed his way through the crowd towards her.

"Have you seen Egnat or Mike?" she asked.

"No."

"Do you know what the trouble is?"

"The tall, skinny guy with the freckles says he brought the young woman, but the other one, built like a bull, says he wants to take her home. Somebody told me the guy who'd brought her has a rifle in his car."

"Oy, we have to stop this."

Lukia searched the crowd again and spotted Egnat and Mike pushing their way into the centre where the two young men were jostling one another. Her heart pumped wildly.

Egnat's voice, loose with drink, barked, "Break it up. Go home!" The young men glared at each other, neither willing to give in. "Anything happens here, you won't be allowed to come back. I mean it. I'll call the police."

The young woman pleaded with the husky one, "Don't spoil the evening like this!" She said to both, "If you keep this up, I'm not going home with either of you."

The husky man grunted and whispered something in the young woman's ear.

"Hey!" the tall one said. "What's he saying?"

The young woman gave a grateful smile to the heavier man, but took the arm of the man she came with. She pulled him through the crowd towards his truck. With the argument over, the crowd dispersed.

Despite the fight, the evening was a tremendous success. Even after paying the band, Lukia had enough to cover the costs of the midnight supper, the phone bill, the staircase, and one month's rent.

That night, instead of praying for help, Lukia thanked the Lord for helping them add to their income. And for the lovely dance with Orest.

38

STEPPING LIGHTLY

Two weeks had passed since the barn dance. Dunya was in the kitchen with her mother, preparing cakes for the next one. Frustrated, she mashed the bananas so hard her mother looked over.

"What are you trying to do, kill the bananas?" Lukia said. "Take it easy."

Dunya grumbled. *It wasn't fair*. She'd been too busy with her mother and Elena—preparing the midnight supper in the kitchen and schlepping the food back and forth between the house and the barn—to get in all the dances she wanted. Her mother pointed out that that kind of help only took an hour at most, but Dunya complained anyway. She hated missing any dances. Her brothers and male cousins had romped to the music with no cares at all. She vowed that if she ever got married, her husband would not be the kind of man who would stand around while his wife catered to anyone who called.

Attempting to get her mother's sympathy, Dunya said, "Mama, you know how much I like dancing."

"Yes. I love it, too," her mother said as she spread icing on a poppy seed cake.

Dunya sighed. "Can't we get the food ready before the people show up?"

"How can we? You can't put the food out ahead of time. The bread will dry up; so will the cakes."

Dunya turned to Elena, who was stirring prune filling on the stove. "Elena, it's not fair, is it?"

"I don't know."

Undeterred, Dunya said, "Mama, you were young once. It's not fair my brothers can kibbitz around while I'm busy working in the kitchen."

"Daughter," her mother said, waving her icing knife, "listen to me. The men have their work; we have ours. You know how hard they worked to get the loft ready. Not everything is equal. Sometimes they work harder, and sometimes we do."

"I guess." Dunya mixed the mashed bananas, beaten eggs and milk into the flour mixture. "But please, can't we get things ready beforehand?"

Elena took the prune filling off the stove. "I can help. When the band has its first break, we can put the food out and cover it with tea towels."

"Yes," Dunya said, jumping up and landing with a thud.

"Oy. You're lucky there's no cake in the oven."

Locals began arriving early to park close to the barn and get a seat on a bench. The crowd was bigger than the one at their first barn dance. Word had spread as far as Teulon.

This time, Dunya got the dances she wanted. The first fellow who asked was their neighbour, Jerry Peeters, a Belgian man in his late twenties with a shock of blond hair that stood up on end as if it had a mind of its own. He owned a farm, which made him a good catch.

"You're looking lovely, Dolly," Jerry said, taking her hand.

"Thank you."

"The crowds keep growing. Your family has stumbled onto a real money-maker."

"What you mean?"

"Lots of people paying to come in." He rubbed his thumb and forefingers together to signify cash.

"Not so much money." She pointed to the band and made the same gesture. "Eating costs lots. Ham, cheese, baking. Not free."

For the first dance, a polka, he acted like a proper gentleman. An accomplished dancer, he twirled her around the floor with ease. But for the second number, a waltz, his hand moved down her back. When it got below her waist, she stiffened. Afraid he might do something even more embarrassing, she coughed.

"Are you okay?" He released his grip.

"Sorry," she sputtered and ran to the door. She stepped outside to clear her head. She was thankful he didn't follow her. When she returned, she noticed he'd latched onto a buxom blonde closer to his age. Her bright red-lipsticked mouth opened wide in a laugh as he tickled her under her arms. From the looks of how he fondled the blonde, he was only interested in seeing how far he could get with a woman. Dunya couldn't trust a man who made bold moves without permission. What kind of girl did he think she was? She was proud of herself. She'd stopped him before he'd made a fool of her. She pressed her lips in disgust and looked for a place to sit down.

Not long after the barn dance, Dunya got a job picking cucumbers on a farm three miles away. She had to be there just after sunrise, but the wagon was being used to move hay, so she rode bareback on one of the work horses. She hadn't ridden far when she came across Jerry driving his horse and cart down the road towards her. As he approached, he tipped his hat.

"Good morning, Dolly. Where are you off to in such a hurry?"

"Sicherski's farm for work, and I'm late."

"Is your brother having another barn dance?"

"Yes. We'll be putting up posters soon."

"Save me a dance," he said and tapped his horse to go forward.

She rode off, wishing she'd said something to discourage his interest, but he'd left so quickly. Dunya was sure Jerry would never bend for his wife. He'd expect women to bend for him. What could they possibly talk about? And even if they could talk easily with each other, he wasn't tall, dark, and handsome like the man in her dream. He had blond hair, squinty eyes, a bad complexion, and large ears. Just thinking of his leering face gave her a queasy feeling in her stomach.

She pushed Jerry's face out of her mind and considered where she could find the man she'd dreamt about. There had been no one even close to that description at the dance. He'd also have to speak Ukrainian, because her mother couldn't speak English. When her mother aged, she would naturally live with them.

She wasn't far from the cucumber farm now. She inhaled the scent of fresh manure that her horse trampled on the road. It was enough to make her animal hesitate, but she urged him on. He wasn't used to this kind of activity; her brother discouraged anyone from riding his horses. He said it was too exhausting for them to carry riders on their backs. They needed their energy for work in the fields. She'd seen Egnat's disappointed face when she galloped away from the farm. He would have preferred that she walk, but she had risen too late to do that. That was something she'd have to work on—her habit of being late for most things.

Focussing on the horizon, she envisioned her dream man walking towards her, getting closer with each stride. She was so caught up in her imagination that she arrived at Sicherski's farm road earlier than she expected. Again, she wished she'd stayed in school. Picking cucumbers wasn't a job she could brag about. She was sure Joan Crawford never had to pick cucumbers for a living.

Hot after a day's work and with no cars in sight, she pushed the horse to go faster on the gravel road. She loved the feel of the wind on her face. She felt free flying past harvested fields with only the company of a hawk overhead. Once more, she fantasized about life off the farm and the man in her dreams. She hadn't ridden far when a nearby gunshot caught her horse off-guard. He reared up, and she went tumbling to the ground. She landed on her side, bruised, but nothing broken except maybe her thumb. Hobbling and favouring her painful thumb, she mounted the horse again and rode home leisurely.

When she arrived back at their barn, Egnat was outside, checking the shoes on one of the other horses. Before she even dismounted, he said, "You could've left for work earlier. You put me behind by taking him." He came up beside her and ran his hand over the sweating horse's back. "Unless you're interested in doing the work this horse has to do, you'd better think twice about taking him again."

"I'm sorry."

His scowl remained as he stroked the animal.

She wanted to tell her brother about her accident, but, given his state of mind, she expected him to be unsympathetic. He would say she had it coming, so she said nothing. Her thumb was red and swollen and throbbed with pain. Probably broken. She was afraid she might also have broken her hymen in the fall. Sighing, she got the horse some water. Watching the animal quench his thirst, she vowed to never take him riding again.

39

THE LAST DANCE

Halfway through another barn dance, Lukia noticed her daughter's shocked face and near her, their neighbour Jerry Peeters stumbling and almost falling on the dance floor. She guessed the young man had had too much to drink. Curious, she made her way around the floor to avoid running into dancers and caught up with her daughter, who had taken a seat beside Olga on the other side of the loft. She beckoned Dunya to the corner where they stood away from the others.

"What happened between you and Jerry?"

"He's such a pig, Mama. He touched my tits, so I raised my leg and hit his dingle."

"What?" Lukia laughed. "Good for you. Once a pig, always a pig. Let's hope he doesn't bother you again."

Dunya smiled. "I don't think he will."

Since it was clear her daughter had no interest in such a man, Lukia relaxed enough to enjoy the music without worrying. When two grizzled farmers and a villager from Stony Mountain asked her to dance, she suspected that someone had sent word to all the available older men in the Rockwood municipality—which encompassed Rosser, Lilyfield, Stony Mountain and Stonewall—

to come and court her. She didn't think it was Mike who had spread the word, as he'd told her clearly back in Kivertsi he didn't need another father. And neither would it have been Egnat, who largely kept to himself, or Harry, who was even quieter. Regardless of how men knew about her widowhood, she wasn't complaining. It had been a long time since she'd had so much interest. It made her move around the floor like a younger woman.

The men were polite and fun to dance with. However, each one wore their past on their sleeves. One wept when she asked him how he was cooking for himself now that he was a widower. He said his wife had had tuberculosis and had perished in the sanitorium in Ninette. He'd also had a lot to drink, and Lukia wasn't sure if his tears had come because of his grieving or because he couldn't handle his liquor.

Another farmer had five children, two under the age of five— he'd married a young woman who died from complications at birth. He wanted a woman who'd gone through menopause, an assurance he wouldn't become a widower again. Lukia laughed at that. She told him he didn't want a wife or a lover to warm his bed; he wanted a housekeeper and a nanny.

The third man had a long handlebar moustache. From the way he twirled it and eyed her chest, she got the impression all he wanted was to fondle her in bed. She wasn't interested in sex on demand or sex without love.

She couldn't help comparing all of them to Gregory. Only Orest came close to being a companion she could warm up to. She had looked for him earlier in the evening, but then she remembered him saying he was going to hunt deer.

But what was the point of all the comparisons? Perhaps she was destined to be alone. Pleasuring herself gave her that release, even though having that thrill was better in a loved one's arms. And she was getting to the age where the will to arouse herself was becoming less frequent. It took longer and longer to reach a climax, the point where her body shuddered gratefully for the release. Would she want to lie naked beside a man again? Would another man find her attractive after eight children? Her breasts hadn't been pert for decades, her stomach was no longer taut, her thighs were dimpled, and her upper arms sagged. She wasn't optimistic about finding someone to love and grow old with. At her age, the only possible relationship would be with a man who would bring a ghost into the bedroom. His lost love would be under the sheets; her lost love would be there, too. That first love was always the sweetest; it was the one that left an indelible mark.

Lukia thanked the man with the handlebar moustache for the dance and while the band played a schottische, she went to the side table to quench her thirst. She had just put the pitcher of water down when she heard a loud noise from the middle of the dance floor.

The musicians stopped playing as dancers turned to see what had caused the commotion. Lukia made her way through the crowd blocking her view. Someone said, "She fell right through." Upon closer inspection, she found a young woman sprawled on the floor; her blue taffeta dress had ridden up her heavy thighs and her round, red face wore an expression of humiliation. It was Alesha Wasiliuk, a young woman Dunya's age. Her right foot had gone through the boards, splintering them into jagged pieces. While Alesha lay there moaning, a young man with acne on his face—whom Lukia assumed had been her dance partner—was trying to pull her leg out.

"Be careful," Alesha said. "I don't want you to rip my leg." Stepping around him, a middle-aged woman crouched and pulled Alesha's dress down to cover the beige slip underneath. After the young man helped the injured young woman up, she rubbed her arm and lifted her skirt high enough to expose a bloody, scratched knee.

Lukia said, "That doesn't look good. Does anything hurt?"

"No, Panye Mazurec. I'm fine."

Relieved, Lukia examined the floorboards. They were so badly split they would have to be replaced before anyone stepped on them again.

Mike came over to look. "Mama, is she okay?"

"She says she is. Thank God, no bones were broken. We can replace the floor. We can't replace a leg."

Mike and Alesha's dance partner placed some empty chairs around the splintered wood to keep others from falling through. Dunya brought Alesha a piece of cake, which she shyly took.

Lukia put her arm around the young woman. "Come with me. Let's take care of that wound."

Mike went up to the microphone and announced that because of the damaged floor, he was sorry the dance couldn't continue. The band began to put their instruments away. There were cries of disappointment from the crowd, but they understood. They slowly gathered their belongings and exited the loft.

In the morning, Mike and Egnat examined the floor again. When they found another weak spot, they determined it wasn't worth fixing. They had neither the money nor the will to put in a new floor.

Mike said to his mother, "What if she'd broken her leg? Or arm? Or cracked her head? I would've been sued. We could've lost everything."

The fear of losing what they'd worked for occupied their minds for days afterwards. Because of their fear, that was the last dance the Mazurec family held. On one hand, Lukia was sorry to see the parties end; on the other, she wasn't. It had been a lot of work, with all the baking, sandwich making, and cleaning up afterwards. There was also the added burden of policing those who couldn't hold their liquor. They had been lucky. No fight had broken out that had resulted in injury or death.

All in all, it had been a good family venture. The dances had brought each family member new friends, and the social gatherings had cemented their place in the community. Mike lamented it had to stop. Over the summer, his barn dances had attracted a lot of pretty girls from miles around, making him more popular than ever.

Dunya was perhaps the most devastated that the barn dances had ended. She told her mother, "I'll never meet the man of my dreams now."

There was nothing Lukia could say to console her daughter. She, like her older sister, Hania, was a romantic. They believed in some magical folk tale, where the woman lived happily ever after with the love of her life.

40

A DEER ONE

Lukia was coming out of the chicken coop with a basket of eggs when she heard a car drive up their road. Harry, who was at the pump filling a few jugs with water, turned towards the sound of the approaching engine. It was a car she didn't know. Her youngest son, always excited about any vehicle, picked up the jugs and hurried back to the house.

As the car came to a stop, Lukia recognized Orest behind the wheel of the shiny blue automobile. She was thankful that, having gone to church that morning, she had her good dress and beaded necklace on.

"Good day, Orest. What brings you here this afternoon?"

"I promised you deer meat."

"You didn't have to."

"Yes, I did."

He opened the trunk and pulled out a package wrapped in brown paper and tied with a thin rope. It was as neat as his dress. He wore a white starched shirt with a striped tie, wool gabardine trousers, and a matching tailored jacket; even his shoes were polished.

Lukia said, "Orest, this is my son. Harry, this is Pan Parochnyk."

Harry couldn't take his eyes off the car.

Smiling, Orest said, "It's a 1933 Chevrolet."

"Harry's learning how to be a mechanic. He's working as an apprentice at a garage in Winnipeg."

"Can I see the motor?" asked Harry.

"Harry, Pan Parochnyk's only arrived and he has his hands full. That can wait."

"It's fine," Orest said. He gave Lukia the package and opened up the hood for Harry to have a look.

Lukia clucked her lips, but Harry didn't notice. He was busy inspecting the engine.

"Will you stay for lunch?" she said. "We just got back from church. It'll only take a few minutes."

"Thank you. I could use a bite."

"Were you at church today?"

"No."

"You're so nicely dressed."

"It's Sunday," he said with a grin.

He followed her into the house, with Harry close behind, and took off his straw hat at the threshold. She took a quick glance in the mirror by the door. She fixed some strands of hair that had come undone from her bun, then went to the stove where a pot of borscht was simmering.

"Orest, please sit down at the kitchen table." She took the pot off the stove. "Harry, unwrap the meat Pan Parochnyk brought."

Lukia quickly wiped the crumbs off the oilcloth-covered table and got a bottle of homebrew out from the cupboard and some shot glasses. As she set the table for lunch, she noticed Orest glancing around the room. Breakfast dishes were stacked by the sink and a pot with bits of porridge on the bottom was on the stove. Tiny clumps of dirt speckled the floor by the door where they'd taken their boots off. She hoped he wasn't judging her too harshly. What with feeding the livestock and getting dressed for church, she hadn't tidied up beforehand, but that was the least of her concerns. Rather, she wasn't used to men calling on her. The last time she'd had a man come around was in the old country. Mike had become so agitated when he learned his uncle wanted to marry his mother that he'd stood in the doorway, shaking. Now her son was seeking a girl of his own, so surely, he wouldn't protest in the same way.

One by one, her family came into the kitchen either from outside or their bedrooms and met Orest. Lukia had expected some inquisitive looks from her family, but other than Elena, who smiled and raised her eyebrows before putting on an apron to help, the rest acted as if a male caller was an everyday occurrence.

Egnat, who'd met Orest at Dan Balacko's a month ago, was pleased to have some company to drink with and immediately poured them both a shot of horilka. Mike and Harry—his cheeks red with excitement from viewing the new car—joined them for a drink. The talk soon turned to the news of the new CCF party that had started in Saskatchewan and how it was gathering support. The opposition feared it was radicalizing farmers. Lukia half-listened as she sliced the roasted deer meat.

Orest said, "The CCF party is promising a lot. I don't understand how they think they can honour all those promises."

Mike leaned forward. "What does CCF stand for?"

"Co-operative Commonwealth Federation," Orest said in English. He then reverted to Ukrainian. "They have a lot of union guys in the party. The way they talk, we'll all be taken care of, whether or not we work. They want to put in universal pensions, health and welfare insurance, children's allowances, unemployment insurance, and worker's compensation."

Mike said, "Sounds good to me."

"It would sound good to you," Egnat said, rolling his eyes.

Mike frowned.

Lukia gave Egnat a look: this was not the time to be squabbling with his brother.

Egnat said to Orest, "What I'd like to know is, who's going to pay for it? No one has any money now. Maybe they expect the rich to contribute more."

"That'll be the day," Lukia said.

"I was thinking the same thing," Orest said, sitting back.

As Lukia set plates of thinly sliced deer meat, rye bread, and butter on the table, she recalled the many after supper conversations Gregory had had with other men in Volhynia. The talk had been of war and all the competing armies vying for a piece of Ukraine. She was sure men in her homeland were still sitting around the table, drinking and complaining about their military and government. It would always be like that. Ukraine's history was so tumultuous; the minute it got its independence, another country invaded its borders. There were no wars in Canada or the looming threat of a dictator purging the people, but there were dire threats due to years of drought. Poverty and starvation went hand in hand. How many years could those in need go on without losing all hope?

She knew little about the CCF party, but what she knew did not assure her of its future. Two years ago, when the federal government declared the Communist party illegal, the members searched elsewhere to spew their propaganda. They were attracted to the CCF, which wasn't a good sign for the new party. She couldn't trust any Communist. Look at what they'd done to her homeland. They raided manors, threw out the rich, stole their property, destroyed churches, and even slaughtered priests. And then they became much like those they'd thrown out—an elitist group with peasants under their feet, afraid to speak out.

Having had enough of such talk, Lukia interrupted, "Nu, let's eat." Elena placed a dish of sour cream on the table and a plate of sliced garlic dill pickles. Dunya ladled the beet borscht into each bowl. Standing, Lukia lowered her head and crossed herself three times. The others quickly stood and joined in to say the Lord's Prayer.

At the end of the prayer, Lukia said, "Eat, eat. Don't let the food get cold."

Orest swallowed a spoonful of borscht. "Very good," he said, smacking his lips.

"There's more if you want," she said, pleased with his praise. What pleased her even more was how comfortable he was with her children. Orest talked about his farm, his two sons, and how fortunate he was to have their help. Lukia kept glancing at Mike and Harry, who avoided her gaze. She sighed; there was no amount of shaming that would make them farmers. It was either in your blood or not.

During the meal, Dunya—who would be happy if her mother remarried—kept looking from Lukia to Orest, as if hoping to catch them in some illicit act. Lukia smiled. No one was going to rush her into anything.

After they'd eaten, Lukia gave Orest two sealers full of borscht to take home for his sons and walked with him to his car. As he drove off, Dunya came up behind her and took her arm. "Mama, he likes you."

"Maybe."

"I bet he'd want to marry you."

Lukia rubbed her hands. Until now, marriage had been far from her mind. She'd managed without a man for fourteen years. Perhaps if someone suitable had come along earlier—but then again, why would she want any man jumping on her? Even if he was an attractive man like Orest. She snorted. The desires she'd once had had come with her youth. She'd been more than satisfied with her husband in bed, even though there had been bouts of frustration. When he returned from the war a shell of a man, she hung on to the threads that held them together—threads woven through the shared pain of having lost four of their eight children and the agony of living through all the wars. They had suffered so much. Why would she want to take on another man's pain? Every man had his demons.

And then there were his two sons at home, grown men who would expect any new woman in their midst to cook for them, wash their clothes, and clean their house. She could never replace their mother, nor was she interested in taking on that role. She had her own brood to worry about.

And yet, as her eyes swept the land around her house, she saw only desolation. Orest at least owned his farm and his stock. Compared to the newcomers, he might be a man who could ride out anything else that God threw at them.

41

A PROPOSAL OF A KIND

Over the next few months, Orest continued to call. One time, she invited his family over for supper. When his sons arrived with him, they stood back a little, as if they needed the distance to get a good perspective on the new woman in their father's life. Dressed in overalls, they were a head taller than their father, and lean. She assumed their delicate heart-shaped faces, blue eyes, and thin lips had come from their mother. They were polite and didn't reach across the table for seconds until Lukia encouraged them to help themselves to more food. Her children behaved as well, but it wasn't an entirely comfortable meal. She felt Orest's scrutiny when she talked to his sons, as if he was assessing her ability to be a good mother. Not that they needed one. They were past that age and probably seeking wives themselves.

At another time, he picked her up in his Chevy and took her to his house for supper. In the car, he apologized for not changing out of the plaid flannel shirt he wore over a long-sleeved undershirt. He must have been working on his car or tractor, for she spotted grease on his pant leg. She told him she hadn't expected him to change, even though she had made some effort to be presentable—putting on her good navy crepe dress and the string of fake pearls Mrs. Hrushowitz had given her when she left her service. She'd also embellished her bun by placing two imitation tortoiseshell combs in her hair, one on each side. She could tell that her efforts had been worthwhile, as he kept glancing at her as they drove along.

Orest's house had three bedrooms, a luxury for a man with only two sons. The interior was well appointed, but it missed a woman's touch. There weren't any crocheted doilies, embroidered runners, or other handiwork. The living room had a burgundy chesterfield, a rectangular walnut coffee table in the middle, and two worn easy chairs. On the walls hung a couple of painted landscapes in gilded frames. On the other side of an arched doorway, a dining room with a fine mahogany table, six chairs, and a matching sideboard displaying a few family photos. One photo showed an attractive young woman, her hair softly curled around her face, her rosebud lips tender and moist, as if she'd just been kissed. She guessed the woman in the photo had been Orest's wife.

He didn't show her the bedrooms. Since there were no icons on the walls of either the dining room or the kitchen, perhaps he had one over his bed. He'd mentioned he was christened Greek Orthodox but no longer belonged to any denomination. She recalled him saying he had given up on his faith when his wife died.

Lukia teased him about his neatness and suggested he had some other woman on the side coming over to clean for him. He chortled good-naturedly and reassured her he was the one who did the cleaning and cooking. This surprised her, as she'd never met a man who was comfortable working in the kitchen.

He served studenetz, a jellied pork dish, and some stewed cabbage and tomatoes. When she complimented him on the food, he said, "Not as good as your cooking, but I do my best."

"Flatter me, flatter me. You'd make someone a good wife."

He laughed, but his sons exchanged disapproving looks. It didn't matter. She'd gone through too much in her life to care if she impressed the young.

They ate largely in silence. His boys ate with their heads down. She didn't mind. She wasn't much of a talker at the best of times. When Orest tasted the rhubarb pie she'd baked, he said, "This is delicious. Best pastry I've ever tasted." He gave his sons a look, obviously hinting for them to say something complimentary as well. He may even have kicked one of their legs under the table.

The younger one said, "Panye Mazurec, this is good pie."

"Thank you. I'm glad you like it."

The older one said nothing, but she was grateful Orest had at least prompted them. It showed his good manners.

Orest and his sons had had a shot of vodka before eating, but unlike the men in her family, they didn't hang around the table afterwards, downing one shot after the other. Of course, she reflected, that might have something to do with the alcohol they drank. Orest's was store-bought, and not as good as hers.

Afterwards, his sons went to the barn to milk the cows, and she helped Orest wash the dishes. Impressed with his self-sufficiency, she stole glances at him while she wiped the cutlery. In her experience, he was an unusual man. When the dishes were put away, he suggested a tour of his property.

He first took her to the barn where his sons barely looked up from their milking stools. It was as if they'd made an agreement beforehand not to give her any encouragement. Having weathered Mike's anger when she first entertained the idea of remarrying, she understood and smiled inwardly.

Orest had more than twice the livestock she had. His fields, already harvested, were in much better shape than hers. She bent down and picked up a handful of soil. It was soft and crumbled easily through her fingers. She wasn't jealous of any likely woman

267

in his life, but she was jealous he had fine earth. Having arrived in Canada almost two decades earlier, he had been lucky to secure a homestead with soil worth cultivating.

There was no question, he was a good catch. And she felt comfortable walking by his side. He said he admired her resourcefulness, how she had succeeded in making something out of nothing during these terrible years. He told her she stretched a dollar more than anyone he knew. He'd noticed that she made rugs out of rags and sewed her own clothes and her children's. He liked that she went berry and mushroom picking and preserved what she and her children picked for the winter and never wasted food, even meat bones, which she used to make hearty soups. And he said that the liquor she made was the best he'd ever drunk.

He finished his praise by saying, "There's no end to your talents."

"Stop already," she said, laughing. "I'll get a swelled head with all these compliments."

"I recognize a good woman when I see her."

They had come to his pasture, and, as was true of his fields, there was more substance here than on most farms.

"Now that harvest is over," she said, "I'll be getting back to my work in Winnipeg."

"It's too bad you don't have a husband who could take care of you. If you had one, you wouldn't have to scrub floors for other women."

She cocked her head. "That's how it is." She considered a life of leisure as they walked back to the house, the silence broken only by the crickets chirping in the grass. In the yard, they encountered a turkey, who snapped at their heels. Orest chased her away. Gobbling, she went back to pecking seeds off the ground.

In the car, instead of turning on the ignition, he turned to her. "How come you never married again? I wasn't kidding when I said you have a lot of talents. And you're so good-natured."

"Ha," she said. "You don't know me. I can be cross, too."

"Seriously, Lukia. Why haven't you married again?"

She stared out the windshield while he waited for an answer. "You know, after Gregory died, I thought about it. I had young children. They needed a father. But... maybe I didn't want to become attached again. When he died, something died in me."

"But surely, you had suitors."

She smiled and clasped her hands. "Men came around. I had offers, but it's not so easy to replace a father." She regarded him. "You must know. You haven't remarried, either."

"No, but now my sons are at a crossroads. I feel it. I don't know if they'll stay here or go. You can't control the young. It's not like it was a generation ago, when you could count on them staying and helping and taking over when you're gone. And this damn Depression. What hope does it give our youth? Why would they want this kind of suffering?"

"You've done well."

"What does that mean? Because I can feed my family, that means I'm doing well? I'm hanging on by the skin of my teeth. The only thing that separates me from the others is that I got a head start. I own my land—no mortgage, no rent, but I still have to pay taxes."

He took her hand. "Lukia, I like you. I like you a lot. We're both getting older; time is going."

"You don't have to tell me. I have so many grey hairs, I've stopped counting.

"What grey hairs?"

She chuckled.

He scrunched up his face. "We could be good companions for one another."

"Oy, I don't know."

"Tell me you'll think about it."

She mumbled she would, but did she love him? No. Did she

like him? Yes. But was that enough to change the way she lived? There were complications. She didn't know what his expectations would be. He had sons. And what would they expect?

On the drive back, she mulled over his proposal. He was right. She'd have a companion, someone to grow old with. And yet she wasn't sure if she wanted to sleep next to another man. She didn't know his sexual habits. Would he be rough? Would he be gentle? How demanding would he be? She'd managed without a man; she was used to her ways.

When they reached her place, the full moon was high in the sky, glazing the land with its light. He stopped the car and got out to open her door. She'd never had a man do that for her before. Though she questioned his beliefs, she couldn't criticize his manners. When he took her hand, he held onto it after she stood up. He gazed into her eyes and her knees buckled. A rush of longing swept over her. Then he kissed her, his warm lips on hers. She leaned into him. It had been so long. Maybe she could love him.

But as quickly as she'd allowed herself to feel some passion, she swallowed and said, "Thank you, Orest, for a lovely supper."

He held her arms and, for a moment, she thought he was going to kiss her again. Instead, he turned his attention to her farmhouse. She turned to look as well. Mike stood in the upstairs window, staring down at them.

"Have a good sleep," he said, getting into his car. He rolled down his window. "We'd be good together."

Would they? Her mind swam with the possibility. She stayed rooted until she could no longer see his car.

42

LOOKING FOR A MATCH

For the past couple of years, Dunya had been delivering milk and cottage cheese to various ladies in the district. She couldn't believe how many matchmakers there were among them. Each of her customers knew one young fellow who was unattached and looking for a bride. As she'd done ever since she had that dream a year earlier on St. Andrew's Day, she'd ask the women if the man they were suggesting was tall, dark and handsome. If the young man they were suggesting didn't come close to that description, she said, "Thank you, but he's not the one." Their faces showed concern or puzzlement or sympathy, as if she was a wounded creature in need of help. Dunya was unperturbed. Despite her mother's doubts, she was prepared to wait until her dream man came along.

Occasionally, her mother pointed out young men in their parish and praised how attentive they were to their own mothers or how educated they were or how bright their future promised to be, but none of her mother's suggestions interested Dunya. She understood her mother wanted her to meet a nice Ukrainian Orthodox boy, but what could she do if none matched the picture of the man in her head?

If a nice Ukrainian Orthodox man was so important, why wasn't her mother jumping at the chance to marry Orest? Her mother had mentioned his proposal, but since then, had grown quiet.

Curious, Dunya brought up the subject over tea when she and her mother were alone in the kitchen. "Orest is a fine man. He cares for you. Are you thinking of marrying him?"

Her mother murmured, "I don't know," and sipped her tea.

"What don't you know?"

"He has two sons. I have four children. How would he divide his property? Would you get anything if I should die? Or if he died first? Would there be anything for me and you and your brothers?

"Mama, I'm sure he'd be fair."

"Listen, I know of two widows in the old country who made the mistake of remarrying, only to discover their own children didn't count like they should've."

Dunya hadn't considered these complications. "Are you going to ask him about it?"

Her mother shrugged. "I can ask, but once you're married, it's not so easy to get what you want. You have to know the person. He's a good man, but his children are his children. He'll want to protect them. It's how it is." Her mother rose from the table. It was time to milk the cows.

Though her mother had explained her situation, Dunya didn't think her mother's fears applied to her own. She had no plans to marry someone who'd already been married.

The one young man who caught her interest was Doug Lawson. His family had been settled in the area for three generations; they were well-to-do and lived only a mile north of their home. She'd met him years before, when they were living in Rosser. He had even come to a few barn dances with some local girl. The first time she actually talked to him at any length was a week ago when she had cycled with her friend Olga to pick up the mail at the Rosser General Store.

She'd worn a new flowered dress her mother had sewn. The flared skirt floated around her thighs and lifted occasionally when the wind grabbed the hem as she rode her bicycle over the bumpy road. Olga, who cycled beside her, wore pants. She had raised her eyebrows on seeing Dunya's dress. She told her to be careful, as anyone could see up her skirt if she didn't hold it down.

"I know," Dunya said, irritated. She hated being criticized. She would have worn pants too, but she liked feeling the breeze on her skin. Besides, she felt attractive in a dress that showed off her curvy figure.

Dunya was hoping another letter from Tanya had arrived at the post office, but when she asked the clerk at the Rosser General Store to check the mail, the only letter was one from the phone company, a notice to pay their outstanding bill. It would be added to the other two phone bills on her mother's bureau. Already their phone had been disconnected. The money they had earned from the dances was long gone—the last bit used to put food on the table and buy some parts for their tractor. It hadn't occurred to her mother or Egnat to pay the phone bill, as it was a piece of equipment neither one used. Mike was the only one upset. Dunya guessed he was mad because he was missing this way of reaching girls he was interested in. She slipped the phone bill into her satchel and went outside, where Olga was talking to Doug.

Dunya and Olga talked to Doug for a good half hour, mostly kibbitzing around, but he also told them about a community picnic on the weekend and asked if they were going. It was the last one of the summer. Olga and Dunya shrugged at the same time, which sent them into a fit of laughter. When they'd stopped giggling, he grinned. "I hope to see you both there. You can bring anything—a pie, or bread, or a casserole."

Dunya furrowed her brow. "What's a casserole?"

He curled his mouth, as if she'd told him a joke. "It's a dish that's good for a meal. It can have meat, chicken or fish, chopped vegetables, and a cream sauce with a toasted bread crumb or cheese topping."

Impressed, Dunya said, "Do you cook?"

"Nah, but I watch my sister and mother put things together. So, are you going to come?" he asked, looking directly at Dunya, his warm eyes creasing at the edges.

"Maybe," she said, which prompted Olga to give her a puzzled glance.

"By the way," he said, "I really like your dress. Spiffy."

"Thank you." Dunya gave Olga an *I told you so* look.

"Hope to see you girls there."

Dunya and Olga watched him drive off in his red truck, the gravel kicking up under the wheels, sending a plume of dust into the air.

"He likes you," Olga said. "Did you see the way he kept looking at you?"

"Maybe," Dunya said, smiling.

"You're crazy," Olga said, getting her bike. "You know how rich he is? His family owns cattle, horses, sheep. And they have a ranch for foxes, minks and martens. They win all kinds of prizes for their animals. They have five breeds of dogs, six breeds of chickens, White Chester pigs, geese, ducks, turkeys, bees—"

"Okay, okay," Dunya said, interrupting. "Don't get so excited. Maybe *you* should go after him."

"Ha ha. Are you going to go to the picnic?"

Dunya pursed her lips. "I don't know. What about you?"

"If you go, I'll go, too."

Riding back home, Dunya reviewed her encounter with Doug. He was an excellent prospect, coming from a family with that kind of wealth. And he was pleasant-looking and tall, but he didn't fit her dream image. His type would play the friend of the movie star; he was the guy who didn't get the girl but was so nice you wanted him to find someone to love. She hadn't seen his type at the movies because she hadn't gone yet, but she'd seen his type on the newsstands. When she'd gone with her mother to Empire Drugs store on Selkirk Avenue to buy some Vick's VapoRub— good for rubbing on chests or the bottoms of feet for colds— Dunya had flipped the pages of the Photoplay movie magazine. She could tell from the photos who were the leading men and supporting characters; the photos of the leading men were always larger. And she was looking for a leading man.

But maybe her mother was right. She could wait forever for the right man to come along. In the meantime, she should give any reasonable young man a chance, and Doug was certainly that. She said goodbye to Olga at the crossroads a mile from her home and pedalled hard the rest of the way. Her skirt blew up, and the wind danced around her legs on the dusty ride home. She was sure that if Olga had been there, she would have been quick to disapprove. She'd told her friend she was going to go to the picnic, but now she wasn't sure. If she went, she'd probably bring a casserole— that is, if she could convince her mother to give up one of her chickens.

Her mother didn't want to encourage Dunya's relationship with an English boy, no matter how rich he was, but agreed to give up one chicken. The morning of the picnic, Dunya watched Mike hold a chicken firmly on the chopping block, keeping its wings tucked in, and then chop its neck off with an axe. He held up the headless fowl by its feet to let the blood drain. Its wings flapped briefly before he plunged the dead chicken into a large pot of scalding water she'd brought outside. Dunking helped loosen the feathers for plucking. He took the chicken out of the hot water after less than a minute and handed it to her. "All yours, Dunya."

With her mother's help, Dunya figured out a recipe for a

chicken, mushroom, and rice casserole. But the moment she put it in the oven to bake, lightning flashes lit up the kitchen and the following thunder made the poultry in the yard squawk and run to the henhouse. The sky opened up and rain poured down, quickly filling the empty bucket that sat on the ground near the house. More thunder and lightning followed, lighting up the sky. Sheets of rain pummelled the earth, creating puddles in the path to the barn.

Standing in the open doorway, Dunya scanned the grey sky in every direction, but no patches of blue were anywhere in sight.

Her mother stood beside her. "Oy, we killed a chicken for nothing."

"I'm sorry, Mama."

"Aagh. What can you do? We'll have chicken casserole tonight for dinner. We never had it before. Good to try something different."

Her mother returned to shredding cabbage for soup. Disappointed, Dunya picked up a pillowcase she'd started embroidering. She didn't mind not seeing Doug Lawson that day, but she minded missing the community picnic. It was where she might have met a man who looked like the one in her St. Andrew's night dream.

43

MORE OF THE SAME

Lukia saw little of Orest during the brutally cold months of winter for several reasons: her work in Winnipeg, the weather, colds (hers, his, their children's), and impassable roads. But each time he visited, the question of what Lukia wanted hung in the air like a fine spider web needing attention. He'd stopped asking for now. He wanted her to be sure, so he was willing to wait.

1935 had a promising spring, with warm temperatures and decent rain. The other bright news on the horizon was Elena's pregnancy. She'd announced in February that she was with child and expected to deliver in late summer. Lukia was excited for her son and daughter-in-law, but privately, she agonized about another mouth to feed.

The other excitement was about something they never had in the old country: the release of the new Eaton's catalogue, featuring clothing and household goods. Delivered in the spring to all the farmhouses in their rural municipality, it provided endless hours of pleasure. The Mazurecs thumbed through it out of curiosity; they enjoyed looking, even though there was nothing they could afford to buy. Once all the adults and Dunya had seen what the department store was selling, Genya had a turn. She liked to cut out the pictures of ladies' and girls' fashions for her imaginative play. Afterwards, the catalogue ended up in the outhouse where its remaining pages were put to good use.

The big news, though, was Ogilvie Flour Mill's plans to construct a grain elevator in Rosser. The locals buzzed for days, saying this could be a turning point, a sign that businessmen were willing to gamble on the future improving for grain. They latched on to that news like they were drowning, and the proposed elevator was a life preserver in the middle of an ocean.

That spring, the government took more action to ease the strain being felt on the prairies. Recognizing that thousands of families had left farming and more were on the verge of giving up, the Bennett government declared a national emergency. It came up with the Prairie Farms Rehabilitation Act to help farmers deal with soil erosion, drought and soil conservation measures. Farmers would get help to build a dugout to hold water for livestock and help to seed abandoned lands for pasture. The government also suggested strip farming of different crops to keep the soil from drifting away.

It was about time they got help, many said. With the new promises from the government, farmers began to believe good luck was just one harvest away. But the aid proved to be not enough to overcome what they were all fighting. The weather turned again, as it had for each of the previous five years.

Black blizzards, which was what locals called dust storms, descended later that spring, darkening the sky and land. Lukia and her family covered their faces when they went outdoors, to avoid sucking the dirt into their lungs. And as if that wasn't enough to contend with, the grasshoppers arrived again, seemingly on schedule.

Ihor Chimiuk told them he'd read in the newspaper that some

guy in Rhodesia—no one knew where that was—cleared the pests from his house and garden by playing the bagpipes. The writer of the article suggested farmers hire the Winnipeg Regiment to come out to the farms and play their bagpipes. His suggestion elicited a few laughs around the kitchen table but produced no immediate solution. It was anybody's guess what would work.

The grasshoppers didn't stay long but fortunately ate the sow thistles before they left. The cool, rainy weather also postponed the hatching of grasshopper eggs. This year, farmers had thought ahead and had seeded barley and oats early. That forethought resulted in much better crop conditions than in the last two seasons. Was their luck finally turning?

It was during this time that Petro and his family dropped in for a visit. He'd come to let Lukia know he was leaving for Toronto. There was no warmth in his words. He might as well have been a tax collector or a bank clerk giving the family the news they had defaulted on their loan. He barely made eye contact when he said to Lukia, "I need five dollars. Will you lend me five dollars?"

"Five dollars!" she said, shocked he would ask after so many months of ignoring her. "You think I have five dollars? I have nothing. I'm buying groceries on credit when I have nothing to barter. I'm sorry, Petro," she said, wringing her hands, "I wish I could lend you the money, but I can't. If I had it, I would gladly give it to you."

His eyes hardened. "And I thought I had a sister. When you needed money, I gave you without even thinking."

Frowning, she beseeched him, "Petro, please understand. There are days when we don't know how we're going to eat."

He twirled his cap in his hand and said, "So be it." He brushed past Egnat, who'd just arrived to say goodbye.

After Petro left, Egnat said, "He's still so angry."

"He wanted five dollars. I told him I couldn't give it to him."

"Mama, why didn't you give Uncle five dollars?"

"Where was I supposed to get it? Listen, we have nothing. We need it ourselves." She shook her head. "If he hadn't drunk his away, he'd have it, too."

Lukia wished she'd been less harsh. Could she have given him some? Maybe. Petro was right. He'd helped her out, but back then, he'd had more than enough. It was hardly a fair comparison. She could not afford to be generous when her own children and grandchild were hungry.

Lukia later heard that Petro found his money. He went to the Labour Temple and got a loan from the Communist association there. He let it be known that his sister had let him down.

Soon after, the Korneluks left Winnipeg for Toronto; only Alex and Ted stayed behind. Alex had never seen eye to eye with his father. Not a drinker, he couldn't stomach his father's taunts as to why he didn't drink. He was working at some job in the city, and Ted's ad had paid off, so he wasn't ready to move east. He visited the farm occasionally, surprising Lukia. Her nephew was always jovial, his brown eyes dancing. Dunya said he resembled that Hollywood actor Errol Flynn. Lukia had no idea who her daughter meant. As for her brother and Anna, Lukia had little hope she'd hear from him. Their family ties had been frayed beyond repair.

At the end of June, rain fell. At first, Lukia was grateful that finally their crops would be watered naturally. The unexpected downpour—five inches of rain—had broken the drought and wiped out most of the grasshoppers, but it also flooded the land. The humid weather on the heels of the rainstorm brought another unwelcome visitor—stem rust. It ruined all the crops—wheat, oats, and barley—except for straw. One farmer's brand-new green John Deere binder turned red with rust by the end of the summer.

The hot, dry winds further punished the wheat, resulting in low grades and a poor yield. Many farmers burned their ravaged crops, as there was no point in trying to harvest what had already been destroyed.

And what the cruel weather didn't get that summer, the gophers got. It got so bad that some municipal governments were paying one cent for every gopher tail. Egnat was against killing the little creatures that popped up from their holes and chattered at them. Lukia thought they were a nuisance, but agreed with her son that wasn't reason enough to kill them or mutilate them by cutting off their tails. At least those who did put a bit of iodine on their stumps so they wouldn't get blood poisoning.

During this time, a new fear arose, one that concerned the family's health and that of their livestock. They heard of horses dying of equine encephalitis, spread by mosquitoes. Out of caution, people working outdoors donned long shirts to avoid being bitten and catch what was ailing their animals. Egnat kept the horses in the barn during dust storms and checked their temperature. Lukia steeled herself and prayed that sickness wouldn't hit her family the way typhus had. She and Egnat had barely survived in the old country; this time they might not be so lucky.

It seemed every aspect of nature was against those who were trying to make a living off the land. It got so bad that farmers who quit couldn't sell their machines and tools. No one was foolish enough to invest their savings, if they had any, on a losing proposition. The only living thing that beat the dust was the Russian thistle. It sprouted up in the dry cracks of earth and along the gravel highways, as if to thumb its nose at those who rode by.

At least the Mazurecs had their dairy to sell; they had loyal customers at church who couldn't seem to get enough. They made cottage cheese by putting the milk on the back of the stove, heating it to lukewarm, then letting it sit for several days until it turned. They also made sour cream and butter to sell.

Lukia, Dunya and Elena took turns making blocks of butter from cream that was two to three days old. It was a tedious chore. They had to put the cream in the tall wood barrel churn, secure the lid which had a hole for the dasher to keep the cream from splashing, then churn non-stop for more than half an hour, agitating the cream until it turned to butter. If you churned too quickly, the cream stuck to the churn and didn't form the solid fat you wanted. And yet, you needed to churn quickly enough for the butter to become pale and soft. It all depended on the temperature, too. In summer, they churned more slowly so their butter didn't turn white, and in winter, they had to churn vigorously to keep the temperature up. The women developed muscles in their arms and hands, as strong as the men's. Churning steadily for a half-hour was not for the weak.

In August, Elena gave birth to Vera, another girl, and chose Dunya, now twenty, to be the godmother and John Slipchenko, Harry's boss at the gas station, to be the godfather. After the christening at Sobor, Lukia invited John, his wife, Father Mayevsky, and the deacon back to the house for lunch. Laughter around the table with some good-natured kidding from Egnat provided much-needed relief from the hardship playing out on the prairies.

Though laughing along with the rest, Lukia couldn't help noticing the lines on her eldest son's face. Now that he had another child, there was even greater pressure on him to succeed. And yet, she knew he'd never complain. Lukia had been so busy herself she hadn't stopped to think of the weight he was carrying—a load he'd taken on when his father perished on his sixteenth birthday. Not one to shirk his duties, he'd worked steadily alongside his mother, both in the old country and in Manitoba, where they felt the added burden of an unforgiving climate. With the farm deep in his soul, he couldn't blot out the dry and shrivelled crops any more than she could. He'd planted the grain as if each seed was a baby who had to be nurtured, watered, and fed. But year after year, the baby had been too weak to thrive. The new life was always on the point of dying. The constant fear of a poor harvest tore at him. Tore at all of them.

After the guests had gone home, Lukia left Dunya in the house to shred the cabbage they'd picked that morning to make sauerkraut for the winter. Lukia marched through the barnyard, past the clucking chickens, gobbling turkeys, and pigs rolling in the pen. Mike and Harry were so busy changing a flat tire on the truck, they never even noticed her as she strode by. *Good*, she thought. She wanted to see Egnat alone.

She found him pacing the fields, stooping down every hundred yards to examine the wheat that struggled to survive. A flock of birds flew overhead, identifiable only as black silhouettes in the bright blue sky. It wouldn't be long before the Canada geese would fly south and winter would be upon them again.

Egnat continued up the row, his back to her, unaware of her nearing presence. Every Sunday, he inspected the fields, making sure no plant escaped his scrutiny. It was a day of rest for many men, but not for her son.

"Egnat!" she called out.

He turned. "Mama, what are you doing here?"

"Nu, I wanted to talk to you."

His brow furrowed. "What's wrong now?"

She was close enough to smell the alcohol on his breath. She glanced down and saw a mickey sticking out of his pants pocket. *Oy, my poor son*, she thought, but she understood. Sometimes, there was too much to bear even for the strongest. At least he was wise enough not to drink when he was handling machinery, working the land, or handling the animals. So, she said nothing about the booze and instead nodded towards the wheat. "How is it?"

"You can see for yourself." He bent down and broke off some

dry stalks. "This is what we have." He crumpled the wheat into bits with his hands. "We'll be lucky to get enough to cover our rent this year." Choking up, he said, "I keep thinking if only I work harder, it'll come. But it doesn't."

She wanted to ease his pain; she wanted to hold him on her lap and comfort him, like she had done when he was little. Her eyes watered as she said, "We have to pray. Keep praying for rain."

"Pray? What good are prayers? You pray and the dust continues to blow. There is no God. Probably some big clown looking down at us, thinking: What a bunch of fools!"

"Oy, Egnat. Don't say." She put her hand on his shoulder. "We can't give up. We can't."

"Mama ..." He shook his head.

Putting her arms around him, she said, "Egnat ..." He put his head on her shoulder and cried. His body shook with sobs against her chest. Unable to stay dry-eyed, she cried with him, their sobs piercing the air like the unexpected cries of a crow. They stood for a while, joined in their sorrow.

They both understood what they could control and what they couldn't. As before, they got up every morning, fed the livestock and checked the sky and the sun overhead. She'd heard that Indians did a rain dance when they had to weather dry periods. She didn't feel like dancing. Instead, she prayed every night on her knees until she could no longer kneel.

44

NOT FOR ME

It was a beautiful late summer morning when Orest stopped by on his way to do some shopping in Winnipeg. She gave him a slice of blueberry pie and a cup of tea. They shared some local gossip until Dunya left the house to feed the chickens and collect some eggs.

The minute her daughter left, Orest said, "You know I've been patient, but it's been months since I asked you." His finger caressed the rim of the saucer. "Have you thought about marrying me?"

She'd thought of little else but didn't say so. "Orest, you're a wonderful man. Hard-working, a good father and a good provider. My problem is my children. I have four, a daughter-in-law, and two granddaughters. The family is growing. More will come. You only have two sons. If I marry you, what will that mean? Egnat's boss here; he'll be fourth in line at your place."

He cleared his throat. "I'll sign the property over to you."

"You would do that?" Her brow creased with surprise.

"Yes."

"And your sons?"

"You're a kind woman. I think you'd be fair."

Lukia massaged her thumb with her finger. "No one is that fair. These are your children. There'd be nothing but grief if something should happen to you. They'd fight me every step of the way in court."

"Lukia—"

"Listen," she said, "the only way I'd marry you is if you signed your property over to me now."

"What?" His voice pierced the air. "I'd be a fool to do that."

"Yes. And I'd be a fool to get into a situation that would bring me more trouble. I've had enough trouble."

A look of astonishment crossed his face. "So that's it? That's how you want to end it?"

She sat back. "Orest, I'm sorry, but I have to think of my family."

He shook his head and regarded her for a few moments before standing up. "If you change your mind ..."

"I won't change my mind."

"Thank you for the pie." He was already reaching for his hat on the chair beside him.

"Do you want to take a few pieces home for your boys?"

He shook his head, seemingly in disbelief. "Lukia, Lukia, I know now why you stayed unmarried for so long."

Though she'd done what she believed was right, she felt a lump in her throat. A good man like Orest didn't come by every day.

This time she didn't watch his truck pull away. She sat down again at the kitchen table and remembered what her mother had said after Lukia had rejected her brother-in-law Dmitro's proposal of marriage. "Why are you listening to your son? He doesn't know what you need. Your children won't always be with you. They'll find partners of their own, and you'll have no one."

Why had her mother been so critical? She hadn't remarried. She'd remained independent, getting all kinds of accolades for her work as a herbalist, curing people the local doctors couldn't cure. But her mother was right about her children. Mike and Harry were already drifting away. Once they found women of their own, they'd be gone. As for Dunya, it would all depend on who she picked for a husband. Lukia hoped her daughter would pick a nice Ukrainian Greek Orthodox boy. Perhaps there would be room for her in that home. Or maybe Lukia would stay with Egnat and his family. She couldn't consider prospects of her own until her children were settled. With the entire country in dire straits, how could any parent have faith in what lay ahead?

She missed her mother and her wisdom. What would she say now if she knew her daughter had rejected a good man and her son Petro was causing grief in the family? All Lukia wanted was a secure future for her children. Was that too much to ask?

45

WHAT THE HEN HAD TO SAY

At the start of the school year, Dunya accompanied Genya to the Lilyfield Schoolhouse, two miles from their farm. It was her niece's first day in Grade 1. Entering the schoolroom, Dunya noticed that nothing had changed. The divide in the community remained between those of British ancestry and those from elsewhere. It showed in the faces the English and Scottish children made behind the immigrant children's backs.

Dunya understood Genya's timidity at school. It came from growing up on the farm and not knowing the English language. Dunya sat at the back of the classroom for the first two days to ease Genya's mind. At recess, the slurs—*Bohunk* and *Hunky*—echoed through the playground. Leading the discrimination were the Stewarts, the children from the wealthiest family in the district. There was no way to protect her niece from the taunting. Dunya was sad to leave Genya there, but she had to get back to her work on the farm. At least her niece—who was starting school at age six like the other children—wouldn't have to contend with being different in age from the others in Grade 1.

But like her aunt, who got called Dolly at school, Genya got a new name—Jenny. Dunya wasn't sure if it was the teacher or the students who gave her the new name.

When Dunya asked her niece how she got her new name, she said, "The teacher gave it to me after she read the class a story about a donkey named Jenny."

Livid, Dunya wanted to scream at the teacher, but she knew it would do no good. It might even make things worse for Genya. Instead, she said, "Never mind. You have a beautiful name. You don't need a new one. I'll always call you Genya."

Genya adapted; the fact she was smart helped her deal with the ignorance. In time, the bullies left her alone.

Genya had another memorable incident that year, one that affected Lukia and Egnat, too. It had to do with one of their cows.

Lukia was the first to notice the Holstein heifer was pregnant. The cow had made her pregnancy known by giving the bull a head butt in the ribs when he came too close. It was her way of letting the bull know she was no longer available. That manoeuvre made Lukia smile. If women could adopt that tactic, they'd save themselves a lot of grief dealing with unwelcome advances.

Having a pregnant cow meant there would be another food animal or breeding stock to sell. Before long, the heifer resembled a large, round barrel with a head, tail, and four legs. Two months before she was due, Lukia stopped milking her to give her a chance to build up her milk supply for the calf to come.

When the pregnant cow went into labour, Lukia was the only witness to the birth. She had taken the cows to pasture because Dunya had gone to the city to sell milk and cheese. The cow lay down on the grass and her body began to heave. Lukia hoped she wouldn't have to run to get a rope to pull the calf out, because sometimes an animal in labour needed an extra hand. Fortunately, there were no complications, and soon after calving, the cow raised herself and began licking her newborn's hide. Within the hour, and with the help of her mother nudging her in the side, the scrawny calf, its skin wet and shiny, stood up on wobbly thin legs. The calf sniffed around her mother until she found the nipples on her udder and sucked. It was a sight Lukia never tired of.

The Mazurecs took delight in welcoming the new calf. The other cows huddled around protectively, as if to ensure the newborn didn't wander away. At supper that evening, there was more laughter than usual. Adding to their livestock naturally buoyed their spirts, especially after a grim harvest.

But next morning after breakfast, Lukia and Dunya went to the barn to milk the cows and found the newly born calf lying dead in the stall. The cow stood beside her dead calf, nuzzling her inert body and mooing with sorrow. The other cows, also distressed, looked on as they shuffled their feet. Lukia attempted to comfort the mother cow by stroking her back, but she jerked her head and body away. Lukia mumbled, "I understand. It's all right," and left the cow to grieve alone.

Standing behind her mother, Dunya said, "What happened? Why did she die?"

"I don't know. Maybe some infection after birth." Lukia bit her lip. Seeing the cow mourn reminded Lukia of her own losses. Childbirth was challenging for both woman and animal. There was always a risk.

Losing livestock was part of the drama of living on a farm, whether planned, like killing a chicken for a Sunday dinner, or unexpected, like a calf dying. Egnat buried the calf but her mother continued to grieve, loudly mooing and leaving the herd in search of her offspring. She refused to believe her calf had died.

Days later, Lukia was taking down the wash on the clothesline near the house when Genya skipped by. She was heading to the barn where her father was unloading hay into the loft. It was the weekend, and her granddaughter was happy she didn't have to go to school.

Lukia had just finished loading the clothes basket when she heard Egnat holler, "Genya!" Lukia looked over. The cow who had just lost her calf was charging Genya. "Run under the rack!" shouted her father. Genya ran, but the cow, with her head down, was gaining on her.

"Oy, my God," Lukia said, catching her breath. But then Egnat threw his pitchfork at the cow, grazing her. She halted in shock, then mooed sorrowfully at Genya, who was now safely under the rack.

Lukia clutched her chest. She put her basket down and ran over to her granddaughter. Egnat jumped down from the rack and led the cow back to the barn. As soon as the cow was out of sight, Genya scrambled out from under the rack into her baba's arms.

"Baba, the cow ..." Genya cried. "I didn't see her coming around the corner ..."

Lukia said, "Shh," as she stroked her granddaughter's back. She didn't want to think about what might have happened if Egnat hadn't been there to intervene. It was a sad situation for the animal, too. The mother cow was angry that Egnat had a child and she had none. Understandable. They'd have to watch her more closely for the next while.

Lukia took Genya back to the house and gave her a plum bun, then told her the folk tale of *The Speckled Hen*. An old man and an old woman learn from the hen not to cry when an egg breaks, because there's a better one coming.

46

THE ROCKWOOD DANCE

The fall dance at Rockwood School drew young men and women from miles around. As Dunya dressed for the occasion, she wished she could sew like her mother. Her two outfits were showing their age. Lukia had been too busy preserving fruits and vegetables for the winter to make anything new for anyone. That meant the only outfit Dunya could wear was a red crepe skirt and a Ukrainian embroidered blouse. Preening in front of the bedroom mirror, she fussed with the crimped waves in her shoulder-length hair, which she'd swept back and up in the latest fashion. She secured the style with bobby pins, then stood back from the mirror and admired herself. She liked the natural auburn glints in her dark brown hair, which had turned redder after the week she'd spent in the sun harvesting vegetables in the garden.

"Hurry, Dunya," Mike yelled from the floor below. "Ed's waiting."

"I'm coming, I'm coming," she shouted back with some irritation. Try as she might, she found it hard to be on time. She glanced through the window and saw her neighbour, Ed Burak, who must have been in his mid-thirties, idling his father's car. She was sorry Harry would miss this dance. The only time he came home was to get his dirty overalls washed by his sister-in-law.

"Have a good time," Elena said to Dunya as she rushed to the door. "You look lovely."

Her mother said approvingly, "Very nice," and continued cross-stitching some roses on a pillowcase.

"Maybe tonight, you'll find the man of your dreams," Elena added.

"Ha. Three years I've been looking. He's nowhere."

Because they were late, all the spots near the school had been taken and Ed had to park down the road. Mike grumbled under his breath and the two men hurried toward the school well ahead of Dunya. She knew her brother was eager to get to the dance and chase the girls. She stopped walking for a moment to savour the fresh country air and listen to the music wafting out the open school-room door. Nothing stirred in the flat landscape behind the building. The day had given way to twilight, with its soft orange glow hugging the horizon. This was beautiful, but she still hungered for what city life could give her.

Smoothing out her dress, she entered the building just as the last few bars of a polka were being played. Mike was waiting for her by the door. "What took you so long?" He didn't wait for an answer. His eyes were already scanning the room. "I paid the cover charge for you."

"Thank you," she said to his disappearing back. He moved so fast; he obviously had his eye on someone.

The dance organizers had pushed the wooden desks against the wall closest to the door. Above the desks, a blackboard displayed the alphabet, capitals and lowercase, and samples of good penmanship. Dunya wished she'd taken the time to understand what the teacher had meant by the exercises she'd given her. She didn't appreciate then that drawing circles would help her get into the flow of writing. She could sign her name now, but little else.

At the other end of the large room, the band—a violinist, accordionist and piano player—was taking a break. While most of the dancers returned to their seats, several young men headed out the door to sneak moonshine from the flasks they had in their pants pockets or in their vehicles.

Spotting a local girl, Sonia Goretsky, on the other side of the room, Dunya walked across the empty floor space with her head held high, despite feeling self-conscious in an outfit resembling a folk costume. She wished she had on a dress like Sonia's—rose-coloured rayon with covered buttons up the front. Her friend may have had a prettier outfit, but the poor girl had trouble with boys. She had a lovely figure, but was considered homely because of her broad face, prominent nose, and crossed eyes. Dunya was about to sit down when the band started playing again. Mike came up abruptly and grabbed her hand to dance. He always took her for the first dance to show the other men that his sister was not only available but a superb dancer, too.

It was when she stopped spinning on the dance floor with Mike that she noticed a tall, dark, and handsome young man standing by the opposite wall. He had all the attributes of the man in her dream on St. Andrew's Day, but his features were so well-chiselled he didn't look Ukrainian. She wrinkled her nose in disappointment. It wouldn't do to have an English husband.

Dunya sat down beside Sonia and noticed he was looking in her direction. When he started to walk towards her, her stomach flipped and her heart pounded as he came closer and closer. So what if he's English, she thought. One dance wouldn't hurt.

He smiled at Sonia. "Will you dance with me?"

Dunya's mouth flew open as Sonia stood and the tall stranger took her in his arms. Disappointed, Dunya tried to look elsewhere around the floor, but her gaze kept returning to the handsome man dancing with her friend. He and Sonia talked while they danced the foxtrot. Dunya had never known Sonia to be much of a talker, so what could they possibly be discussing?

At the end of the dance, he returned her friend to the bench and quickly left the building. She expected he'd gone to fortify himself with booze, like the other men.

"Well, aren't you lucky?" Dunya said.

"I don't know why he asked me. All he did was talk about you."

"Me?"

"Yes," Sonia said, rolling her eyes.

Unimpressed, Dunya said, "If he was so interested in me, he sure had a funny way of showing it."

"I'm telling you, he kept asking me questions about you. He wanted to know who you were, where you lived, if you had a boyfriend, and how old you were."

"If he wanted to know all that, why didn't he ask me himself?"

Sonia had no answer.

What was the good of all his questioning if he didn't have the nerve to ask her to dance? But as she was criticizing his behaviour, she saw him return to the dance floor. Dunya didn't want to stare; she didn't want to show him she was in the least bit interested. For a few moments, she pretended her attention went elsewhere, but curiosity won out and she took a second look. He wore a navy pinstripe suit and a white shirt with no tie. His collar was open and his raven hair, which he wore in the latest hair style—long on top and short on the sides—shone under the ceiling lights.

"He's a dreamboat," Sonia said.

He met Dunya's eyes. Feeling awkward, she turned her head towards the band.

"Don't look now," Sonia said. "Here he comes."

Dunya kept her eyes averted until she saw—out of the corner of her eye—his shoes stop in front of her. Her pulse raced as she considered what to do.

He cleared his throat, causing her to look up. His hazel eyes with glints of gold were on her. They were the warmest eyes she'd ever seen.

"Would you like to dance?" he asked.

For a moment, Dunya considered refusing, but she was curious about the man. She stood and took his hand. It was smooth, unlike the rough hands of the farm boys she'd met. Light on his feet, he guided her through a foxtrot, a waltz and a polka. He held her firmly with confidence, as if they'd been dance partners for years.

He said his name was Peter Klewchuk and his family was Ukrainian. They'd come over from Bukovina fifteen years before her family had set foot in Canada.

Thrilled he was Ukrainian, she almost yelped out loud. Containing herself, she asked, "Where do you live?"

"Stony Mountain."

"On a farm?"

"No. We live in town. My father works in the stone quarry there."

"Oh," she said. She wasn't sure if his father not being a farmer was good or not. With the hard times affecting them all, perhaps there were better ways to make a living.

Then, while she was still dancing with Peter, a short man tapped him on the shoulder and said, "C'mon outside."

Peter shook his head. "Not now, George. Not now." His friend's face fell. Dunya gathered that he wanted Peter to join him for a drink outside. When George left brusquely, Peter said, "I'm sorry I didn't introduce you."

"That's okay."

He looked down at her as they returned to waltzing. He must have been a good eight inches taller. His eyes twinkled as he said, "I've seen you before. At a barn dance. I went to a few at your farm."

"Why didn't you ask me to dance?"

He smiled. "You were too busy."

Perplexed, she wondered how she'd missed him, especially when she'd been on the lookout for a man of his description. But maybe she'd been running back and forth with the food for the midnight lunch. *That must've been it.*

They continued to spin around the floor number after number. Dunya was content to dance without talking. Since he spoke perfect English, she was intent on making a good impression and didn't want to hurt her chances by speaking poorly.

Peter hung on to her until the last dance. Neither excused themselves to get some air or a drink. At the end of the song, his green-gold eyes met hers and he said, "Boy, I want to kiss you right here."

His soft and inviting lips tempted her as well, but she knew boys didn't respect loose girls. She pressed his chest gently with both hands, keeping him at a distance.

"I hope to see you again," he said.

"Okay, Peter," she said, playing with the sound of his name. She knew that Peter was Petro in Ukrainian. A good Christian name. When they parted on the dance floor, Dunya immediately missed the comfort and security she'd felt in his arms. She kept glancing back as she searched for her brother's friend to get a ride home. Peter kept looking over as well until she'd left the school.

Riding back to the farm, she sat in the front seat between her brother and Ed, who pouted. "I should make you walk," he said. "You didn't have one dance with me."

She barely heard him. She only thought of Peter and his Hollywood smile.

47

DREAM MAN

The noise of the cow shuffling in the next stall prompted Lukia to look up. With her milk pail nearly full, she carefully stood up to see what the problem might be. Dunya was pulling at her cow's teats, but the milk wasn't flowing well.

"Dunya, are you paying attention?"

"Yes. Mama."

"It doesn't look like it. Where is your mind this morning?"

"Right here," Dunya said and pulled the teats in her usual rhythmic fashion. The cow settled down and swished her tail gently.

Elena chuckled behind her mother-in-law. She was milking in the third stall. "She found her dream man last night."

"What?" Lukia said. "Dunya, is that true? Is he tall, dark, and handsome like in your dream?"

"Yes."

Lukia chortled. "Don't tell me. Is he Ukrainian?"

"Yes," Dunya said, smiling. "He came with his family to Canada when he was only two. They live in Stony Mountain."

"What kind of work does he do?"

"Mama," Dunya said, with some annoyance, "I didn't give him a questionnaire. I don't know."

"Are you going to see him again?"

"Maybe. I think he likes me."

Lukia finished milking, picked up the pail, and approached her daughter. "Next time, ask him what work he does."

"I will, if I see him again." She frowned. "But Mama, lots of good men aren't working right now. It doesn't mean he's a bum or no good if he doesn't have a job."

"We'll see," Lukia said. "We'll see."

Lukia carried her pail to the milk house. Her daughter had sounded interested, but what could she know about a man she'd only met once? She'd said he was like the man in her dream. That was something. And yet there was a lot to be considered. She hadn't met his family yet. She didn't know if he was working, or whether he went to church. And who knew if this young man would even call.

With her mother out of the barn, Dunya returned to her daydreaming about Peter. When they were dancing close to the band, he'd bent his tall frame down and said, "Sorry, I couldn't hear you." That alone thrilled her. She'd never met another man who cared about what she said, but he did. So different from her brothers, who complained she talked too much. And when she repeated what she'd said, Peter listened with rapt attention. And then, he wanted to kiss her at the end of the dance, in front of everyone. She was glad she hadn't let him. She wanted to make sure he knew what kind of girl she was. A good girl. Not one to be taken for granted.

Peter visited Dunya a week after the Rockwood School dance and met her mother and brothers. Hoping they'd like him, Dunya's eyes flitted from her mother to her brothers, trying to gauge their reactions. They were polite, but nothing they said gave her any sense of what they thought.

As soon as Peter had gone home, Dunya asked her mother, "What did you think of him?"

Her mother shrugged. "Donya ..." (When her mother started with the word for daughter, it usually meant the beginning of a lecture.) "Yes, he's handsome, but looks alone won't put food on the table. How can he support himself, let alone a wife? He's not a farmer. He only does spare jobs. He has nothing to offer you."

Her brothers gravely agreed with their mother. Egnat said, "When I shook his hand, it was weak. He didn't grip it like a man."

Dunya was perturbed to hear the criticism, because she, like her brother, liked to show she was strong. A firm handshake was a quality to admire. "Maybe he didn't want to hurt you," she said.

Egnat guffawed. "At least he can drink like a man." Her brother didn't trust any man who wouldn't raise his elbow in a toast.

During supper, Peter had kept up with her brothers, but unlike them, his face reddened after a few drinks. She was thankful her brothers hadn't criticized Peter's looks. The last fellow who had come calling was a young man of English stock. He was pleasant enough, but Egnat and Mike found his freckled face amusing. After the young man's visit, Egnat had doubled up in laughter. "He must've been lying in the grass and some bird shit all over him." Mike roared as well. Dunya was sure they had criticized the young man just to tease her. She naturally got upset, which made them laugh even more.

Peter's lack of employment was a worry, but how could her family condemn him for not having a job? He was one of hundreds of thousands of unemployed across the country.

The second time he visited, he arrived on his bicycle—the tires well-worn, the leather seat scuffed and torn, and the back fender rusted. To keep his pant legs from getting caught in the wheel's spokes, he wore elastics around his shins, the kind men used to shorten too-long shirt sleeves. Dunya appreciated the care he took in his appearance. It showed he was intent on impressing her.

And he didn't seem to mind he had no car. Not like her brother Mike. Embarrassed he had none, he hid his bike in the ditch whenever a car went by.

Peter stayed for supper again and smacked his lips over a meal of borscht, kybassa, and potato and cottage cheese varenyky. For dessert, Dunya offered a slice of honey cake she'd baked. Afterwards, he dried the dishes, which surprised both Egnat and Mike, who considered that women's work. They also raised their eyebrows when Peter followed Dunya out to the barn and stood by a post while she milked the cows with Elena. Standing around was a luxury her brothers could ill afford, especially if it meant waiting for some woman to finish what she was doing.

Dunya didn't understand her brothers' disapproval. According to them, only 'skirts' belonged in the kitchen, and yet when they needed women to help cultivate the land, they welcomed them gladly.

After she'd deposited the newly expressed milk in the milk house, she went for a walk with Peter down the road. It was one way of getting him away from her family's critical eyes. The evening was cool, and the sun was about to vanish behind a row of trees in the distance. Puppy ran ahead of them, then doubled back to circle around their legs.

Peter bent down by the side of the road and picked a long blade of grass to chew on. "Your mother doesn't care for me, does she?"

"She says you have no work." She waited for him to say something, but he stared ahead, chewing on the stem. "How about Stony Mountain?" she asked. "No work there? They have a big jail. Must be something."

"No. They only hire the English or Scottish. We Ukrainians are back of the line. Two summers ago, I worked as a hired hand in the fields." He snorted. "Funny story. I worked with my shirt off and got so black from the sun the fellas called me *darkie*."

"Not so funny."

"Yeah. And this last year my brother, Bill, and I hopped a freight train and rode to Alberta. That was good. We found work in the lumber camps and I worked there the whole summer. Now, the railway guys are watching and arresting those who catch a ride."

"You go to school?"

He nodded. "I went as far as Grade 9. I was at the top of my class, but I didn't finish. I got in trouble for kicking a ball with a friend in the school basement when I should've been in class." He scrunched up his face, as if it was a memory he disliked returning to. "The teacher gave us a strapping after he caught us. It stung so bad I didn't want to go back." His voice dropped, and his face took on a faraway look. "I should've gone back." He bent down and patted Puppy, who took off down the road again after getting some attention.

The air had grown chilly. Dunya shivered and folded her arms across her chest.

"Want my jacket?" He had it off before she replied and put it around her shoulders. It was warm and smelled like some kind of flowery soap.

"Thank you."

"I should've kept going to school. When I refused ..."

She mouthed the word *refused*. Repeating words helped her remember.

"I was so mad. I didn't want the teacher to change my mind. Mr. Blackwell tried. He came over and talked to me and my father. Wanted to tutor me after school, but I wouldn't give in."

"That was nice he offered."

Peter grunted, then kicked a stone on the road. "My friend stayed in school. He's now an RCMP officer. His father told him, if he didn't keep going, he'd have to find someplace else to live. My dad didn't care if I went or not. Told me I should work with him in the limestone quarry." He picked another blade of grass from the side of the road to chew on. "He also fixes watches and clocks for the guards at the prison."

"Did you go work with him?"

His face clouded over. "I did. Worked in the quarry for a few years. Worked there until I almost died in the chute."

"What happened?"

"I was on top of this heap, shovelling, trying to dislodge a jam of crushed rock—"

"It was stuck?"

"Yes. The chute kept going. I was pushing the fine stuff toward the centre, trying to loosen it, and someone opened the top chute and I slid. The stones rained down on me, threatening to bury me. Thank God a worker saw me going under and stopped the machine. By the time they stopped it, only my hands were sticking up from that pile." He shuddered. "I wouldn't be standing here today if he hadn't seen me. The guy yelled and someone opened up the bottom chute and I fell through. The limestone stayed on my face for two days after that. I was pretty white." He laughed. "Must've looked like a ghost."

"You could've died."

"Yeah. Three minutes more and I would've suffocated."

"Suffocated?"

"It means something's covering your mouth and you die because you can't breathe."

"Oh."

"I couldn't work there after that. I don't miss the twelve-hour days, especially in the summer, with the sun beating on you, but I miss the money."

"Of course," she said.

He nodded. "After I quit the quarry, I found another job, working for the Perrys, a nice family. They run a boarding house south of town. They gave me decent wages to peel potatoes and do general housework. I don't do it anymore, but if something needs fixing, they call on me."

Her eyebrows knitted as she imagined him doing women's work. She didn't care what her brothers said. She did men's work, so what was wrong with men doing women's work? It showed he wasn't too proud, that he was willing to do anything to make a dollar.

They'd reached the end of the farm road, where it connected to the highway. It was so quiet you could almost hear the grass whispering. He squeezed her hand and turned to her. He bent down and kissed her—a sweet, slow kiss. His lips were soft; she responded, feeling her breasts against his chest. Her legs trembled, and when he kissed her again, she hungered for more. But it was happening too fast. She didn't want him to think she was easy. He tried to enfold her once more, but she untangled herself from his embrace. "No, Peter," she said. "We should go back."

His face showed disappointment. "Sure. If you want."

Around them, the darkness had taken over. The light from her house shone like a beacon from a lighthouse. They returned down the road holding hands, their silence broken by the sounds of Puppy's feet pattering alongside theirs. A hawk issued a lonely cry, and the wind rustled the oak leaves. It was a warning winter would soon be on its way.

48

NICE GIRLS

Lukia couldn't get to sleep. Why was her daughter encouraging Peter? He was a nice young man, but he had no drive. Was Peter really the one? He fit the description of the man her daughter dreamt of, but surely there were more tall, dark, and handsome men out there. Perhaps the one destined for Dunya hadn't shown up yet, and she would just have to wait longer. Lukia planned to talk to her daughter first thing in the morning.

The sun was barely up, but as usual, everyone was dressed and in motion, taking care of their chores. Lukia placed a few loaves of bread in the oven, then headed to the barn with Dunya to milk the cows. She took a deep breath of the crisp morning air, mixed with the smell of damp hay and cow droppings. Her daughter was silent. Maybe she was thinking of Peter.

Lukia broached the subject as they walked. "Soon, we'll have to get back to the city. We're fortunate to have work. How's that young man of yours? Has he found anything yet?"

"You know he doesn't have a job."

"And why doesn't he?" Lukia asked, opening the barn door. A stray cat scurried out.

"Mama, you know it's hard out there. And just before you ask if he's lazy, he's not. He's worked hard. He has almost Grade 9 schooling and—"

"He's not a farmer," Lukia said, interrupting. "Why didn't he stay in school?"

"He got in trouble. The teacher strapped him for throwing a ball when he should've been in class. He stopped going after that."

"That's not good." Her mother pushed the milking stool beside the cow at the far end.

Dunya positioned her stool by the cow next to her mother's. She began pulling on the teats. Once the milk started hitting the pails, one squirt after the other resounding against the metal, she said, "He worked for a few years with his dad at the limestone quarry in Stony Mountain. ... Poor guy."

"What? What are you saying?"

"He's a good man. He gave all his money to his father to save for him. His father owns the lot next to their house and he wants to buy it."

"Hmm. That's good. So, he'll have some property."

Dunya said nothing.

"As long as there's something there." Lukia pulled her cow's teats for a while, then said, "Is he looking for work now?"

"Yes, like all the men in the country."

Lukia considered her daughter's explanation. If what Dunya had said was true, she could eventually have a roof over her head. But having property was only a start. They'd have to buy materials to build a house and have money for food and clothing. And to accomplish that, Peter would have to get a job. But maybe Lukia was jumping too far ahead. He'd only come over twice. That didn't mean he wanted to marry her daughter.

Lukia continued to stew about Peter, even in the milk house. She dumped her pail into the tall metal can and said to Dunya, "I see the way he looks at you. He won't be content just holding your hand. He's going to want more from you."

"I don't know," Dunya said in an offhand manner.

"I know," Lukia said with some impatience. "You have to be careful. You have to keep your legs together."

"Don't worry so much."

"How can I help it? You're my only daughter."

"Mama, we haven't been seeing each other long." Dunya dumped her pail of milk into the can and put the lid on.

"Never mind. Boys are all the same. They want to get into your pants."

"Oy—"

"You can *oy* all you want. You know what they say about girls who have sex with boys before they're married?"

Dunya didn't reply.

"The boys want to get between your legs, but they won't marry you. Do you think anyone wants to drink milk that's spoiled? Men want fresh milk."

Dunya made a face.

Lukia raised her eyebrows. "You can make all the faces you want, but what I'm saying is true. Listen to me."

"I'm listening," her daughter said sharply.

"You wouldn't buy a cow if you could get the milk for free."

"Enough about cows and milk. You have nothing to worry about."

"I hope you're right," said Lukia, as they exited the milk house.

Dunya took both pails, and swinging them, went to the well to rinse them.

49

CITY BREAK

er mother needn't have worried, as there was little opportunity for Dunya to see Peter. She and her mother returned to Winnipeg in late October to work as housekeepers once more. While her mother resumed her work for the Bushbys, Dunya was pleased to get a position with Michelina Grobovetska, a fine dressmaker with two children, who lived on Pritchard Avenue near the Russian Hall.

The dressmaker was well-groomed, well-mannered, and fair. The only problem working there was the dressmaker's uncle, who slept on a hide-a-bed in the living room and fancied himself a Romeo. He was a despicable, stocky man, who wore dirty undershirts and belched and farted with no display of embarrassment. Because of his unsavoury advances, Dunya had to tell him on more than one occasion she had a boyfriend; she even lied and told him that Peter was her fiancé and they were planning on marrying as soon as they could afford to.

She'd done her best to convince the uncle of her unavailability, but then she made the mistake of going to a dance at the Russian Hall and returning with two young men by her side. Aware the uncle might wait up, she strode ahead of the men. As she'd expected, he was peeking through the living room curtains, watching her say goodnight to her escorts.

Afterwards, Michelina said he was so jealous, he chewed his pillow until the feathers came out. When he continued to lust after Dunya, often making lewd remarks, she complained to Michelina. The dressmaker talked to him and threatened to evict him, and for a while there were no further problems.

Dunya thought often about Peter, especially on weekends when she returned to the farm. But there were too many chores to even consider seeing him. Even if there wasn't so much work, it would have been difficult to arrange in the winter months. He had no phone, and neither did she. Nor did he have a car or even a horse and sleigh at his disposal. And as far as writing to her went, there was no point as she could barely read English.

Maybe she should have worried about his commitment, but she didn't. She figured that since he hadn't had a serious relationship until she came along, he'd show his interest again in the spring. She would just have to wait for the snow to melt.

That year, winter on the prairies was worse than usual. The blowing snow and frigid temperature on Ukrainian Christmas stopped Dunya and her family from going to church. The temperature had plummeted to thirty-five below Fahrenheit on January 7, 1936, making Winnipeg the coldest city of its size in the world. Thermometers malfunctioned, schools closed, car engines froze, and snow drifts blocked roads. Families huddled around the stove. The news announcer on the radio said it was the coldest winter since 1888. The unbelievable cold continued, culminating in a howling blizzard in late January, around the time King George V died.

Harry told his family the king's funeral would be broadcast all over the world. The Mazurecs didn't tune in, because Lukia reminded them batteries for the radio were expensive. The less it was used, the better. "Besides," she said, "he might be our king, but what did he do for us?"

In February, the temperature dropped even further. One fellow who continued to pursue Dunya—despite the weather— was Doug Lawson. Being the son of a rich rancher, he had no problem navigating the treacherous roads. He had a sleigh and his car had snow tires, a newly invented luxury item. Her mother viewed him as a desirable boyfriend, because he was a hard worker on his father's ranch (which someday would be his), and well respected in the community, largely because of his work as a caller at square dances.

During one of his visits, Dunya asked him to come upstairs to her bedroom, the only private spot in the house, so she could show him the bedspread she was embroidering.

"That's really beautiful, Dolly," he said, touching the embroidered roses. "You should enter it in the Spring Bazaar. It's great fun. My family's always entering our livestock and produce. We win all kinds of events. I'm sure you'd win a prize."

"Maybe I will," she said, smiling, as she folded her bedspread and put it back in the blue trunk.

"It's for your hope chest, huh?" he said, sitting on her bed. Something serious was on his mind.

"Yes," she said, closing the lid of the trunk. She was about to sit down beside him when her mother called them for supper. Whatever was on his mind would have to wait.

Later that evening, Dunya embroidered more roses on her bedspread and thought about Doug's visit. She was sure he'd been on the verge of asking her to marry him when her mother announced supper was ready. She imagined being Mrs. Lawson, the lady of the house, and never having to work the way she did now. Perhaps she'd have a domestic of her own. But then she frowned. He didn't speak Ukrainian, and whoever she married would have to speak the language, because her mother would eventually live with them in her old age. Being such a nice guy, maybe he'd learn to speak Ukrainian. She shut her eyes and thought about Peter. He was also sweet. What's more, he looked like the man in her St. Andrew's night dream.

A month later, as Lukia was heading home on the train with Dunya for the weekend, she noticed her daughter was unusually quiet. Knowing her daughter would speak when she was ready, Lukia continued to mend one of Michael's shirts. They were nearing the outskirts of the city, passing the industrial part, when her daughter said, "Michelina's kind and her kids don't give me much trouble, but ..."

"What's upsetting you now?" Lukia said.

"Her uncle stays with her. He's almost as old as you and he keeps bothering me to go out with him."

"Oy, the old fart. Tell Michelina he won't leave you alone." Lukia finished stitching the tear in Michael's shirt and snipped the thread with her scissors.

"I have. She's threatened to throw him out."

"Good." When Dunya made a face, Lukia said, "You can always quit if it's that bad."

"I like her."

Lukia nodded. As long as her daughter could complain, she was fine. She also knew if that uncle got too fresh, he'd be sorry. Her daughter would kick him in a place no man wants to be kicked.

Their train had stopped at a railway crossing where a long line of cars waited to cross the tracks. At the front of the line, two horses pulled a car without windows.

"Mama, look at that car."

A nearby passenger said, "That's a Bennett buggy. Thanks to our prime minister, gas is too expensive. People can't afford to run cars, so they take the engine out and convert them to wagons. They say as long as you can keep air in its tires, it's easier to pull than a wagon."

"That's really somethin'," another passenger said.

After Dunya had translated the information, Lukia said, "Where there's a will, there's a way."

An advantage of working in the city was the chance to go to the movies. Michelina let Dunya off one evening each week to see a Hollywood film. She couldn't believe her luck. After she'd seen one movie, she hungered for more. Entering another world made her forget her life on the farm and her work as a maid. Her mother said it was a waste of money, but Dunya convinced her it was a bargain after she explained she'd go only on "dish nights." That was when, for the price of a movie, the Palace Theatre gave away a dish from a plate setting of bone china decorated with roses and trimmed with gold leaf. Sometimes Dunya saw the same movie twice, just so she could get a bowl or a cup or a platter. And with a different dish offered each week, it didn't take long for her to complete a place setting.

On "dish" nights, Dunya would run four blocks down Selkirk Avenue to get there a half hour before the movie started; that way she'd be in front of the line and get the best seat. She couldn't wait to escape into a love story featuring an appealing actor like Gary Cooper, Clark Gable or Cary Grant, paired with an actress like Joan Crawford, Ida Lupino or Barbara Stanwyck. The actresses played smart, fashionable, strong women on the screen. They took nothing from any man.

She told her mother, "Going to the movies is a good way for me to learn English." That, her mother could appreciate. She even went once to the Palace Theatre with Dunya, but it was too hard for her to understand the story, so she declined the next time her daughter asked. Dunya understood, as she'd had similar trouble when the movie was a comedy. The actors talked too fast for her to get the joke. She also didn't care for musicals, which was a shame, as too often those were the only shows playing. Peter had told her they were popular because they lifted people out of the doldrums by giving them laughter and happiness on the screen. She preferred the dramas, as those stories resembled real life. The women were jilted, or had affairs, or were abused by men who should have known better. Dunya wasn't much of a crier, but when movies pulled at her heartstrings and she shed a tear, she thought that was the best experience a movie could provide.

One time, Peter came to the cinema with her. He'd moved to the city to seek a job (and to be closer to her, he said). He was staying in a rooming house on Higgins Avenue, but so far, he'd had no luck in finding employment and was now ten dollars behind in rent. He said he'd knocked on a lot of doors, but if you were Ukrainian, Polish or Jewish, a lot of those doors were closed to you. It was why a lot of young men who were trying to get ahead changed their names. He said he was proud of his name Klewchuk, and no "Limey" or Scotsman was going to make him feel ashamed. She admired his stance but felt sorry he'd had no luck in the city and would soon have to return home.

They sat in the back row of the Palace Theatre; it was where most couples sat and kissed during the whole movie. Much as Dunya enjoyed kissing Peter, she didn't want to miss what was happening on the screen. He had his arm around her and kept nuzzling her neck. At one point, his hand wandered to her breast, exciting both of them. She didn't mind his bold moves. She understood that men admired her large breasts and naturally were tempted to touch them. His caresses were not a problem—she enjoyed the sensation—but not seeing the film was, as they'd paid to get in. She kept turning her face to watch the screen.

Finally, she said, "Peter, I'm sorry, but I have to watch. How am I going to learn English?"

He gave a deep sigh and squeezed her shoulder. She was proud of herself for speaking her mind. They viewed the rest of the movie, *Next Time We Love,* with James Stewart and Margaret Sullivan, without further interruptions. Dunya got so involved in the story she murmured out loud twice during a few key love scenes. Peter must've got a kick out of her sighing because he squeezed her hand both times.

He escorted her back to the dressmaker's home, and on the doorstep, she said, "I wish I could pay your rent, Peter, but I'm saving for a fur coat. I've been saving for two years. Scrimping and saving."

"That's all right," Peter said. "I get it. I'm not blind. I see the women in line for the show. A lot of them have fancy fur coats. You should have one, too. I wouldn't want you to freeze to death."

"I wouldn't freeze to death," she said, giggling.

"If you can afford one, you should get it. This Manitoba weather isn't for sissies."

She laughed. She hadn't heard the word *sissies* before, and he had to explain it.

After he kissed her goodnight, she went straight to bed and mulled over her evening with Peter, her life ahead, and her desire for a fur coat. She liked Peter a lot, maybe loved him; she wasn't sure. Part of her struggle had to do with his poverty. They were both poor; life together didn't look promising.

As for the fur coat, her mother had balked at first at the idea of her daughter spending hard-earned money, but she also understood the need.

"It's crazy not to have a fur coat," Dunya said the next time she was home. "Look at our policemen. They wear those big buffalo coats and fur hats."

When her brothers said buying a fur coat was frivolous in these hard times, Dunya folded her arms across her chest and said, "Okay, I won't herd the cows anymore. It's boring work no one wants to do. It's hard sitting in the ditch for hours at a time, waiting for the cows to finish eating."

Her mother laughed. "No one can criticize you for not being determined." She said to Egnat and Mike, "Dunya never wastes money. Every chance she gets, she walks instead of riding. And she can stretch a dollar, just like me, through bartering and bargaining. She doesn't throw her money away on drinks and a good time."

Dunya knew her mother's argument was meant for Mike, who became quiet before she reached the end of her lecture. Egnat muttered but gave in. Neither brother wanted to herd cows. Dunya couldn't help but smile. She no longer needed her brothers' approval.

In January, at the height of the cold winter, she bought a muskrat fur coat on sale at Eaton's. She loved it so much she had a picture taken in the photo booth at Oretzki's. She thought the coat, along with a new felt hat, made her look like a movie star in Hollywood. A fur coat was what all the glamorous actresses wore when they played rich dames.

50

LILACS IN THE DUST BOWL

Lukia had hoped her daughter's work in Winnipeg over the winter would cool Peter's ardour, but it hadn't. He showed up on the farm the day after Valentine's Day, bearing a gift. Lukia invited him to stay for supper, and while the spinach soup was heating, she watched Dunya open the beautifully wrapped present at the kitchen table. Inside was a gold-plated vanity set: a brush, comb and mirror, embossed on the back with flowers that resembled lilies with stems.

"How much was it?" Dunya asked, looking at herself in the hand mirror.

He chuckled. "You don't ask someone that."

She twisted her mouth. "I like to know."

"$1.99. I ordered it from the catalogue."

Heaving a sigh, Lukia returned to the stove and ladled the soup into bowls, adding slices of hard-boiled egg on top. It was a beautiful gift but a foolish purchase, since he didn't have steady work. Most knew a fool and his money were soon parted.

Lukia couldn't fault him for his manners, though. He said "please" and "thank you." As before, he enjoyed her horilka, and kept up with her sons, though his face reddened after a few drinks. And as he'd done the last time he supped with them, he picked up a tea towel afterwards to dry the dishes. Lukia immediately took it out of his hands and said, "You go for a walk with Dunya. Elena and I will take care of the dishes." It was the least she could do. Having spent his money on such a lovely gift, that poor, infatuated young man deserved at least a little time with her daughter alone.

Since Peter hadn't seen her fur coat, Dunya made a production out of putting it on, then twirled in front of him. "Lovely," he said. "You look beautiful in it."

She appreciated the compliment but then felt bad. It was near freezing outside and he only had a thin wool coat over his pants and shirt.

They sauntered up the farm road, their breath like spurts of white smoke from a well-tended fire. Patches of snow in the dark ditches and fields bordering the road glistened in the moonlight. The air was still, except for the sound of their footsteps hitting the dirt and a wolf howling in the distance.

They hadn't gone far when Peter stopped. His face had grown pale. He mumbled, "Sorry," before abruptly turning to the side of the road and retching. She massaged his back, while she waited for him to finish heaving.

"I'm so sorry," he said, wiping his mouth with a blue polka-dotted handkerchief.

Dunya regarded the vomit. "All that nice food."

"If it's so nice, you eat it."

"Peter! How can you say something like that?"

"Your brothers kept pouring the vodka. I couldn't say no."

"Oh, yes. One brother tied you down and the other forced it down your throat."

By his pained expression, she knew he'd understood her message. It was his choice to drink that much. An awkward silence accompanied their steps back to the house.

He didn't kiss her goodbye and instead mumbled an apology again. "Please don't say anything about this to your mother or brothers."

"I won't," she said. Ordinarily, she might have said something to her family—it was hard for her to keep secrets. But since she'd heard enough complaints about Peter, she didn't want to add another to their list.

Egnat was kind enough to drive Peter home, another reminder her boyfriend didn't have a vehicle, or a job, or property. He had nothing to offer except himself.

Months passed before Peter showed up again. Dunya assumed his embarrassment over his last visit had kept him away. Maybe he hoped time had erased the unfortunate incident from her memory.

She spotted him through the kitchen window as he arrived one afternoon on his bicycle, carrying a grand bouquet of lilacs. Dressed in a suit, a freshly pressed white shirt open at the collar, and polished brown shoes, he was more handsome than she'd remembered. Her heart stopped for a moment. She quickly checked the mirror by the door and adjusted the tortoise-shell combs that held her wavy hair on each side.

She straightened her cotton blouse and stepped outside to greet him. As she walked towards him, he sang a popular ragtime song she'd heard on Harry's radio.

"Oh! You beautiful doll, you great big beautiful doll!
Let me put my arms around you."

He had a rich baritone voice and sang as if he was on stage, one arm holding the bouquet, the other arm sweeping to the side for emphasis.

"I could never live without you; Oh! you beautiful doll, You great big beautiful doll! If you ever leave me how my heart will ache, I want to hug you but I fear you'd break. Oh, oh, oh, oh, oh, you beautiful doll!"

He bowed and handed her the lilacs. "For you, Dolly."

"They're beautiful." She bent her head to inhale the heavenly scent of the bouquet. "Where did you find lilacs?" She'd only seen lilac bushes in the back yard of one of the wealthy families on Selkirk Avenue.

"In my father's garden."

She inhaled the fragrance once more and entered the house with Peter. She said to her mother, who was peeling potatoes in the sink, "Look what Peter brought."

"I see." Her mother stopped peeling to sniff the blossoms. "You'll stay for supper?"

"Thank you for asking, but I ate before I came."

"How about a pampushka?" She asked and removed a tea towel from a plate of plum buns, deep-fried and dusted with icing sugar.

"They look delicious."

Her mother put the plate of pampushky, a teapot, and three cups on the kitchen table. "I just brewed some tea."

While Dunya arranged the flowers in a glass sealer, she said, "Mama, did you hear Peter sing?"

"I heard him through the window. He has a nice voice."

Peter blushed. As Dunya placed the flowers on the table, she said, "You know all the words."

"My father has the recorda." He said *recorda* for record. Dunya couldn't correct him, as she didn't know the Ukrainian word for it. It was the way a lot of immigrants talked, saying *gara* for car, *telephono* for phone, and *storoo* for store. She smiled because she knew Peter said *recorda* for her mother's benefit.

"We'd love to hear them," her mother said. "We have a player." She pointed to the silver-horned gramophone in the corner. "Maybe you can bring some recorda to play."

"I'll bring some next time."

He never did. He said he didn't bring them because he'd heard the songs before. It was an odd answer. Then later he revealed his father wouldn't let him. Her mother didn't say anything when she found out the truth, but Dunya knew it was another bone of contention to add to the list.

51

HOT SPELL

The first five months of 1936 gave Lukia and Egnat hope again, the feeling their bleak days were finally behind them. World wheat prices rose, and because of the decent rainfall in May, the *Winnipeg Free Press* stated boldly that crop prospects in Manitoba were the best in seven years.

But then the heat wave started in June, stretching across the prairies, central Canada, and the United States. The unrelenting heat weighed on all of them. Lukia and her family didn't know whether to close the windows and keep the hot air out, or open them to catch the odd breeze. They quickly learned there was no breeze. What they experienced outside felt like a blaze from a furnace, which made them sweat even more. Their skin glistened with perspiration; droplets stayed for hours. After days of suffering, they took to not only closing the windows but covering them as well to keep out both the heat and the sun. To manage the extreme conditions without fainting from exhaustion, they baked and cooked in the early morning or late evening hours, because any extra heat in the house made it impossible to sleep. Even consuming extra alcohol to numb their senses did nothing to keep them from tossing and turning all night. When Mike suggested dragging the mattresses outside, Lukia and her children briefly considered sleeping outdoors. That idea was quickly scrapped when they realized they'd be tortured by mosquitoes, who weren't deterred by the heat.

Temperatures continued to rise over the next few months. July was the worst. For thirteen straight days, the temperature registered in the high nineties, with four days hitting over a hundred. Pavement buckled and cracked; steel girders twisted like pretzels. Horses dropped dead, grass crackled as if on fire, and over eleven hundred people died in Manitoba and Ontario—hundreds of them from drowning in lakes or rivers as they attempted to escape the scorching heat. You couldn't travel anywhere without the car overheating. Those who ventured out had to stop driving before they got to their destinations to refill their steaming radiators with water. You could easily poach an egg on the hood of a car or on the sidewalks of the city. It was a wonder anyone drove at all. Drivers drove slowly because the dust storms obscured the road. Sitting in a car was like sweating in a Turkish bath. You couldn't open the windows for fear of choking to death on dust.

When Egnat noticed it was too hot even for flies, he let the horses rest in the barn, the only place for the poor animals to shelter from the heat.

On July 11, the temperature hit 108 degrees Fahrenheit, followed by a wild electrical storm that blew trees down. Their neighbour's barn roof went with the wind, and if Egnat hadn't secured their outhouse, it would have gone, too.

During the peak of the hot summer, the booming thunder and lightning storms had everyone running inside. They expected a downpour, but the noisy sky brought rain in patches instead of the steady drink the land sorely needed. There were odd sections that had their thirst quenched by a sudden summer storm, but their farm wasn't one of them.

The heat was so oppressive, Lukia dragged her body from place to place as if carrying twice her weight. To cool off, she resorted to walking around the house and yard in her black satin brassiere. If men could go without shirts, she thought, then she could at least take her blouse off. Dunya did the same, and neither considered how provocative they looked, working in the garden or fields in their black satin brassieres, their cleavage on full display. The men who saw them either grinned or leered, and their English and Scottish neighbours gossiped behind their backs. One local's stinging words reached their ears: "What do you expect from uneducated 'hunkies' and 'garlic stinkers'?" Mike heard it in Stony Mountain from Dan Balacko, who said he'd heard the talk from a few locals gathered around his gas pump.

Lukia harrumphed when Mike told her. She'd put up with worse things in her life and wasn't about to change. She wasn't about to sweat under layers of clothes while she hoed just to please those who had their noses in the air. She said to her son, "They have their ways; we have ours."

Towards the end of July, temperatures returned to normal and the rains that came gave the late grain a second chance. It also helped that farmers had planted the new rust-resistant wheat. As a result, this year's harvest was better than the year before. Lukia crossed herself and thanked God for His mercy.

52

AN IMPOSSIBLE BROOCH

If Dunya had known Peter was so sensitive, she might've acted differently. What put her relationship with him in jeopardy was the brooch he gave her on her birthday. He must have asked one of her brothers when it was, because she'd never told him. Her mother had wished her a happy birthday in the morning after checking the date on the Hudson's Bay calendar hanging on the kitchen wall. But other than that, no special celebration had been planned; it was a day like any other day.

Dunya was returning to the house with a pail of water from the well when Peter rode up on his bicycle. He laid his bike down on the ground and said he was on his lunch hour but didn't want to miss wishing her a happy birthday.

"How nice," she said. "What kind of work did you get?"

"I'm helping a farmer with his harvest." He then stuck his hand in his pants pocket and pulled out a neatly wrapped gift. Grinning from ear to ear, he handed it to her. "Open it."

"What's this?"

She put the pail down and took the ribbon and tissue paper off the box. Inside was a gold filigree brooch in the shape of an eye with a light purple stone in the centre. "It's pretty."

He opened the clasp and pinned it on her shirt. Stepping back to admire it, he said, "Looks good on you."

"It'll look better on a dress," she said, smiling. She put her arms around his neck and gave him a deep, long kiss.

"That's better than lunch," he said, breathing hard. He ran his hands through his hair. "You make me want to stay." He reluctantly picked up his bike and climbed on.

"Thanks for the present," she shouted at his back as he pedalled away.

Picking up the pail, she rushed home. She couldn't wait to show her mother what Peter had given her.

When Dunya walked into the house, her face flushed with excitement, her mother and Elena were making another batch of varenyky.

Rolling out a round of dough, her mother said, "I see Peter was here."

"Before you say anything, he's working. As a hired hand."

Her mother pursed her lips and returned to rolling more dough.

Dunya said, with some annoyance, "At least he's working. And he brought me a present for my birthday." She unpinned the brooch and proudly showed it to her mother and Elena.

"That's lovely," said Elena, taking a closer look.

Lukia wiped her hands on her apron and examined the brooch. "What a funny brooch. The points are too spread out. It means you'll break up."

"Mama! What are you talking about? It's just a brooch."

"Yeah, yeah, yeah. Just a brooch." Giving it back to her daughter, she tightened her lips again. Dunya turned to Elena for support, but she stayed quiet.

Frustrated, Dunya resumed her chores. Ruminating on her mother's words, she examined the brooch and re-examined it, noticing the unusual design.

When her cousin Ted came over to touch up his paintings on

the wall and saw her brooch sitting on her bureau, he asked if he could borrow it. She had no problem letting him take it; she didn't even think to ask him what he wanted it for.

She forgot about the brooch until Peter brought it up the following Sunday. They'd taken their bicycles and gone saskatoon-berry picking in a bush a few miles from her farm. The sunshine and the sparrows tweeting on the neighbouring bushes made for an enjoyable afternoon. They worked side by side, both content to pick berries without talking.

It wasn't long before their pails were full and it was time to head back. As they were coming out of the scrub, Dunya tripped on a dead branch and fell. Peter put his pail on the ground and said, "Did you spill any?"

Irritated, she said, "I hurt my knee and you're asking me if I spilled any berries?"

"Don't get so upset. I didn't know you hurt yourself."

"Never mind." She lifted her skirt so he could see the cut. He took a handkerchief from his pocket, bent down, and dabbed the blood on her injured spot. He did it so gently she was sorry for snapping. She took the hankie from him, spit into it, and cleaned the wound as best she could.

When she returned his handkerchief, he met her eyes. She softened and moved towards him. He kissed her gently at first, but the more they kissed, the more ardent he became. He pulled her down onto the grass, where he pressed against her, his long legs covering hers. Aroused, he said, "Dolly ..."

She responded with a moan. He kissed her some more, planting wet kisses on her neck. When he unbuttoned her blouse, exposing her black satin brassiere barely containing her breasts, she tensed. "No, Peter. We have to stop."

"Why ...?" She placed her hand on top of his, preventing him from going further.

"I can't," she said, and quickly buttoned up her blouse.

Disappointed, he lay on his back beside her. "You don't know what you do to me."

She giggled. Having seen him aroused, she had some idea. She snuggled in the crook of his arm and they lay there for a while, gazing at the blue sky and listening to the sparrows sing.

When they got up, he brushed the grass and dirt from his pant legs. "That was nice," he said. Then his gaze turned serious. "Have you been wearing my brooch?"

"My cousin Ted borrowed it."

"What?" His face darkened. "Why would you give it to him?"

She shrugged. "He asked me. I didn't see a problem."

"He probably gave it to some girl."

"It's okay if he did. It wasn't a great brooch. My mother said the design was funny with a point on each side."

His mouth dropped, and she immediately regretted her words. He said nothing, but she knew he was angry because of the way his right cheek twitched.

She said, "Peter, I didn't mean to …"

He shook his head, as if he could shake what she'd said away. They rode their bicycles back one-handed, the other hand balancing the pails of berries in their baskets. They exchanged no words or looks during their ride, as if a curtain had come down between them,

After he dropped off the saskatoons at her house, she stood by his bike and said, "Peter, don't be mad."

His expression didn't change. He left without looking back once. A hollow feeling settled in her throat and stomach. He'd been seeing her off and on for about a year, and suddenly, she knew it was over.

Troubled by his reaction, she tried to dismiss it. She told herself he'd be back. But as the days went by with no word, she took the break-up as a sign her mother was right about the brooch.

Its odd design implied a dismal future. When she told Mike what had happened, he said she'd been too harsh. Maybe she had been. Mike also said a good man like Peter was hard to find. Why hadn't he said so earlier? When Peter was coming around, her family had nothing good to say about him. Well, almost nothing. But what was the point of reviewing what they said and what they didn't say? She'd lost her dream man.

53

A FAMILY PORTRAIT

Lukia regretted finding fault with Dunya's brooch. But like her daughter, she often spoke her mind, even if it meant offending someone. It was too bad he was such a sensitive type. A man like that would get hurt a lot in his lifetime.

Peter was gone, but it was only a matter of time before her daughter found someone else to marry. And then what?

Leaving Kivertsi had splintered Lukia's family. She had left her mother, sister and brother and countless relatives behind. She'd left the graves, too, and had nothing to remember them by.

What she needed was a family portrait, a picture to remind her of not only the sacrifices she'd made but also the threads that bound them all. The Chimiuks had a family picture proudly displayed on their kitchen buffet. Lukia had no intention of missing out.

That was why, on her next visit to Winnipeg, she dropped into a couple of portrait studios on Selkirk Avenue—Shapiro's and Vogue—to enquire about their prices. Inside their storefront, she studied the people in the family photos on display—what they wore and how they acted before the lens. They looked so dignified, sitting or standing erect, their faces pleasant and relaxed.

What settled her mind about which studio to choose was the photographer himself. When Shapiro came out of the back room, she quickly discovered he spoke Ukrainian. He showed her the backdrop he used: a wall made of imitation wood. He said that when the families stood in front of the wall with its vertical lines, they appeared taller than they were. That appealed to her since her family was short; there was no one over five feet, six inches.

Satisfied with the price he quoted and the studio portraits on display, she arranged for a family sitting the following week. She didn't expect any resistance from her children. She expected them to be as excited as she was. Getting your picture taken was not an everyday occurrence.

Lukia was right. Her family was eager to have their picture taken, but a few days before their scheduled sitting, Egnat developed a severe toothache. He was in agony. Lukia offered to pay for a dentist instead of a family photo, but he refused. He said, "Mike can pull it out."

She said, "Good, but be careful. Boil the pliers well."

When the tool had cooled, Egnat took a stiff drink of horilka, then went outside where the light was best. Lukia and Mike followed. Egnat sat down on a stump, gripped the sides, and opened his mouth wide.

"Which one is it again?" said Mike, joking.

"Ha, ha," said Egnat. "You pull the wrong one and you'll be missing a tooth, too."

Mike stuck the pliers in Egnat's mouth. As Mike pulled, Egnat grimaced and pressed his hands down so hard on the stump his knuckles turned white.

The infected tooth was out in seconds. Mike held up the plier's jaws with the tooth in it.

Egnat put his hand to his mouth and moved his jaw up and down. "I think you got it."

Relieved, Lukia sighed. She didn't have to cancel their family portrait.

The morning of their appointment, each family member ensured their clothes were clean and pressed, hair immaculately groomed, faces scrubbed, shoes polished and jewellery selected. Genya, now seven, sat patiently while her mother trimmed her bangs, fashioned a long braid down her back, and tied a white ribbon on the side of her dark brown hair. Lukia's sons wore three-piece suits, white shirts, and ties with ornamental tie pins to keep them straight. Mike, always the dandy, wore a cream-coloured vest instead of a matching suit vest like his brothers. Harry set himself apart by wearing a puffed-up white handkerchief in his jacket's chest pocket.

Since she'd had no time that spring to make suitable garments for something as important as a family portrait, Lukia had splurged on store-bought dresses. For the occasion, Dunya selected a belted gabardine dress with star-shaped buttons down the front of the bodice and a white bow at the collar. Elena chose a light blue rayon crepe dress with matching cloth buttons down the front, and for Genya, a velvet dress with smocking under the white lace collar. Baby Vera wore her white christening dress. And like the grandmothers in the studio photos, Lukia purchased a navy satin dress. She believed the dark colour made her look slimmer. The finishing touch for all of them was wave-setting lotion to control any flyaway hair and keep their hairdos in place.

Using both their truck and the car Harry borrowed from the garage where he worked, Lukia and her family arrived at the studio looking as neat as they did when they left the house.

Mr. Shapiro asked Lukia's four children to stand in the back and positioned the others in the front—Lukia and Elena with baby Vera on chairs and Genya standing between them. He directed them to look at the camera, then counted to three before the bulb flashed. The photographer took quite a few photos, reminding them to stand still each time.

Lukia left the studio feeling like a rich woman. She had little to show for all the years they'd been in Canada, but at least now she had a family photo she could frame and put on her bureau.

54

A LITTLE LIE

Since Dunya hadn't talked to Olga for several weeks, she hoped to see her at church. She wanted to tell her about breaking up with Peter. During the service, she strained her neck, scanning the congregation for her friend. Her parents were present, but not Olga.

At the end of the service, Dunya and her mother lined up in the centre aisle to kiss the cross in the priest's hand and receive a blessed piece of bread. Mr. and Mrs. Chimiuk stood right behind them.

Her mother turned and said to Mrs. Chimiuk, "How are you?"

"Not so good. Olga's in the hospital."

"What happened?" asked Dunya, her eyes widening.

Mrs. Chimiuk teared up. "She's contracted polio."

"What?" Dunya's mother said, alarmed. "How did she get it?"

"We don't know. She was taking care of a neighbour's child, who wandered away. Olga found her playing in the ditch by our house. There was dirty water in it. That's the only thing we can think of."

"Oy, tragedy," said Lukia.

"How's she doing?" Dunya asked.

"Not so good. She's tired all the time, her back hurts, and she has trouble breathing. My poor Olga."

"Can I see her?"

Mrs. Chimiuk shook her head. "I'm sorry, Dunya. You can't see her. She's in King George Hospital. That's where they're treating all the polio patients. They won't allow any visitors. It's contagious."

"Oy, Natasha, what misfortune! What are they doing for her?"

"They're giving her oxygen. What else, I'm not sure."

Mr. Chimiuk said, "They're giving her some kind of nasal spray. The crazy chemicals have turned her nose bright yellow. Doesn't seem right."

"Please tell her I'm thinking about her," Dunya said. "I hope she gets better soon."

"We'll pray for her recovery," added her mother, as she and Dunya reached the priest. They kissed the cross and took a piece of blessed bread from the plate on the altar, then walked down the side aisle to the exit. Stunned by the news, Dunya felt helpless. Her friend had a serious illness. And there was nothing Dunya could do except wait and pray Olga would get better.

The shock of what had happened to her friend stayed with Dunya for hours afterwards. In the weeks that followed, polio's reach was on everyone's mind. There were stories of babies becoming paralyzed. Some said there was a connection between equine sleeping sickness and polio. The fact no one knew for certain how polio was transmitted put everyone on edge. Dunya found herself looking at any still water with suspicion.

When the hospital discharged Olga, Dunya went to visit her at her house. She tried not to cry at the sight of her friend. The illness had damaged her spine. Olga now leaned to one side when she stood, her shoulders and hips uneven. How could she talk to Olga about Peter when her friend's entire world had changed?

They had tea and cookies in the living room, and talked about Olga's treatment in the hospital. Olga had just finished telling Dunya about the other children she'd met there when her mother came into the room. She said, "Olga, you have to sit up straight."

"My back hurts when I try."

"I understand, but you have to try," Mrs. Chimiuk said, a pained expression on her face.

Dunya quickly found out how much more had changed when she and Olga took a short walk by the farmhouse. Navigating past a flock of chickens pecking seeds off the ground, Dunya had to slow down periodically so they could walk side by side.

After they'd stopped a third time, Olga said haltingly, "I had a bad dream last night. I was in a dark tunnel. I kept running but I wasn't getting anywhere. I was running in one spot and there was no way out. It was so awful."

"Oh, Olga," Dunya said, taking her hand, "those kinds of dreams are scary, but my mother says a bad dream means the opposite will happen."

"I hope that's true."

Dunya tried to sound positive, but she could see how deformed her friend's body had become. "Maybe your parents are right. Maybe you have to keep exercising, working on standing up straight. It'll come. Don't give up. You'll see."

They strolled a bit more, through the red and gold leaves that carpeted the ground, and stopped to sit on an old bench near an oak tree. Dunya picked up a bright red oak leaf from the ground and played with it in her hands. Its edges were shrivelling, like the hope that Olga's body would return to normal.

Olga turned to her. "Dolly?"

"What?"

"How's Peter? I expected you to brag about his winning that whist competition."

"What whist competition?"

"He won first prize. His name was in the Stonewall Argus. You didn't know?"

Dunya made a face. She didn't want to admit she couldn't read. "He stopped coming to see me. He got mad because I let Teddy borrow the brooch he bought me for my birthday. I told Peter it wasn't a lucky brooch anyway, so it didn't matter. That made him angry."

"Of course."

"What do you mean, of course?"

"Well, you insulted him."

"I told him the truth," Dunya said, throwing the leaf down. "He should be able to take the truth."

"Who says? It's hard to take the truth."

Dunya remembered Peter's face when she told him about the brooch. He'd looked so desolate.

Olga whimpered as she got up from the bench and took Dunya's arm. "Is it okay if we go back now?"

"Sure."

On the slow walk back to the house, Dunya mulled over Olga's reaction. Perhaps she'd been too blunt with Peter. But what could she do about it now? She couldn't go running to him and say she'd been wrong. That the brooch was lovely when it wasn't. And what could she do about bad luck? Her mother had said it meant they'd break apart. And they did. Nobody wanted bad luck, but it happened to the best of people.

Feeling judged by Olga, Dunya blurted, "Doug Lawson asked me to marry him. He said he's going to make me the lady of the house."

Olga stopped walking. "What? I heard he was seeing a teacher."

Dunya's face fell, but she quickly recovered. "Well, yeah," she laughed. "I was just joking. Good for him." It wasn't good, but it explained why he'd stopped visiting.

They continued their walk back to the house. Dunya wished

she could take back her lie about Doug. But saying he proposed was only a little lie. She did it because she didn't want her friend to think she'd done anything wrong with Peter. She didn't want her to think she was so mean a man wouldn't want her. But maybe Olga was right; maybe she'd insulted Peter. Why had she said anything about that silly brooch?

55

ON THE RISE

King Edward VIII's abdication was the big news that December; King George V's son had left the throne for some American divorcée. As a result, his brother was crowned King George VI. For months, all the English in their community talked of nothing else. Lukia couldn't care less. What she cared about were the grain prices. They were on the rise, which meant this could be the last year she and Dunya would need to work in the city to supplement their income. It was such welcome news that Lukia began to think all the hardships they had endured these past eight years were finally ending. And yet, could she dare to hope?

Lukia knew Dunya brooded over how her relationship with Peter had ended. Whenever they drove with Egnat to Dan Balacko's store in Stony Mountain, she'd catch her daughter looking wistfully down the streets, hoping to catch a glimpse of the young man. So far, she had shown no interest in anyone else.

Again, Lukia hoped her daughter would find a suitable husband. She had little patience with Dunya's pining over Peter, but she admired her daughter's resourcefulness. She had convinced Michelina to make her a cream-coloured, three-piece suit in the latest fashion for a fraction of the retail cost.

"Why cream?" Lukia said. "Such an impractical colour. It'll get dirty."

"Mama, I'm not going to dig ditches in it."

Lukia said nothing more, but when Dunya brought the outfit home and modelled it in front of the bedroom mirror, Lukia couldn't help but be impressed with Michelina's tailoring. Lukia had constructed enough garments to recognize an artist at work. The hand stitching and design were beyond anything you could purchase at any dress shop. Over a gently flared mid-calf-length skirt, Dunya wore a three-quarter length jacket with filigreed metal buttons, a vest with bone buttons, and a neckline shawl, all in the same fabric. And to complete the outfit, Dunya had purchased an off-white blouse with a lace collar at Cliffords Ladies Wear, and a leather purse and oxfords with a stacked heel at Oretzki's. Lukia had to admit that no one would ever suspect her daughter, dressed in that outfit, was just a farm girl. She could pass for a young woman from high society.

To add to that surprise, Dunya announced one day that she and her brothers, Mike and Harry, were going to get a portrait done in their fine clothes. It was too much for Egnat. "Why do you need another photo? Isn't one family photo enough? Why pay Mr. Shapiro again?"

Dunya ignored her brother's reproach. It was as if she'd set her mind on some riches down the road and had to have a picture to show she'd qualify. She was peeling potatoes for varenyky when she told her mother she wanted to be one of those women, who dressed in the latest style and strolled down Selkirk Avenue on a hot summer night to stop at the ice cream shop by the Merchants' Hotel.

Holding her knife in the air, Dunya said, "Mama, you should see all the flavours. They have ten of them!"

"Ten? How wonderful," Lukia said, as she stirred the chopped onions in the frypan.

"My favourite is fruit. It has glazed fruit throughout. One day, I'm going to have enough money so I don't have to think twice about buying a cone."

"I hope you're right, but right now you're not the queen, and those potatoes won't peel themselves."

Dunya's expression soured, but she resumed her chore, attacking each potato as if it had something to do with keeping her on the farm.

Her brothers teased her as well, especially when they caught her walking in public. Mike had laughed with his brother about the time he went to the city with Dunya to sell their cream and cheese and caught her thrusting her breasts forward, a not-so-subtle trick meant to entice young men looking for a mate. He mimicked the way she walked, which got Dunya so mad she pouted for days afterwards. They considered her ways a joke, but they didn't laugh when she mentioned one evening during supper that she'd been dating a Russian fellow. She'd met Sergei when she attended a dance at the Russian Hall with Mike.

"How long have you been seeing him?" asked Egnat, buttering a slice of rye bread. He winked at Mike, which caused Lukia to send both of her sons a look.

"Three months. Pass the sour cream."

"Three months?" Egnat asked as he passed the dish. "How come you haven't brought him around?"

"He's been too busy." She put a dollop of sour cream in her bowl of borscht. "He works at the Grain Exchange."

"Oh, a fancy man," Egnat said, grinning.

Lukia said, "Well, good for you." She savoured a spoonful of borscht and thought about her daughter's impressive new boyfriend. He'd have to be educated to understand the Grain Exchange. It was just too bad he wasn't Ukrainian.

Egnat said to Mike, "What do you think of him?"

Mike gestured with his hand, like he had no opinion. "I didn't talk to him. I didn't know she saw him afterwards."

Lukia asked, "Is he Greek Orthodox at least?"

"Maybe."

"What do you mean, maybe? You better not rush into anything. Bring him around so we can have a good look at him."

"I will," Dunya said, unconvincingly.

Lukia slurped her borscht. She didn't want to get too excited about this relationship. Sergei might be another one rejected in time as well.

Another month passed by and Lukia still hadn't met Sergei. There was always some excuse why he couldn't visit. But knowing her daughter, Lukia believed she'd learn soon enough where their relationship was heading.

That time came only days later, when she was brushing her hair, preparing for bed. Dunya entered the bedroom and sat down beside her. She appeared troubled by something.

Dunya said, "Mama, the strangest thing happened to me today."

"What happened?"

"I'm sorry, you're not gong to like what I have to say."

"Oy," Lukia said, perturbed. "Tell me already. How can I know if I like something until I hear what it is?"

"I almost eloped today."

Lukia gasped. "What are you saying? With who?"

"Sergei. I was in Winnipeg today to see him."

"I thought you went to sell cheese."

"I did, but we arranged to meet at a jewellery store where he was going to buy me an engagement ring. And then we were going to get a license across the street at City Hall."

"Without a priest? My God, how have I raised you?"

"Don't get excited. I didn't elope." Dunya took a deep breath.

"Before I was supposed to meet Sergei, I ran into Peter on Main Street. I had to go to Eaton's first to buy some panties and Peter said he was going there, too. While he went to the basement in Eaton's to buy some socks, I went to buy the underwear. We planned to meet on the main floor afterwards, but there must've been some kind of mix-up because I couldn't find him, so I went on by myself to the jewellery store to meet Sergei. The clerk was showing us engagement and wedding rings when I looked out the window and saw Peter standing there. I ran out to talk to him, but he wasn't there." She sighed. "It must've been a mirage."

"A mirage," Lukia said, trying to digest what her daughter was telling her. "It was a mirage?"

"Then Sergei came out and asked me what I was doing and told me to come back into the store. He grabbed my arm, but a policeman came by and asked him what he was doing. Sergei said, 'I'm dragging my fiancée back into the jewellery shop.' The officer turned to me and said, 'Is that true?' And I said, 'I've never seen this man before in my life.'"

"What?" Lukia asked. "Why did you say something like that?"

"I don't love him, Mama. Seeing Peter again woke me up. He still cares about me."

"What about Sergei? And wasn't the policeman surprised?"

Dunya shrugged.

"Oy, Dunya, what do you want?"

"Are you mad at me?"

"I should be. I'm just thankful you didn't get married like that. It's a sin. You should get married in a church. Understand? And to a Russian? Oy. Daughter, daughter, what were you thinking?" They sat in silence for a few moments. Then Lukia shook her head and said, "Call Genya for prayers."

After saying a prayer to the Guardian Angel with her granddaughter, Lukia got off her knees, kissed Genya and sent her off to bed. "Goodnight, Baba," Genya called as she ran out the door.

Lukia sat down on her bed again. She didn't know what to think of her daughter's revelation. She had such a vivid imagination. Men found her attractive, but some of her stories were hard to believe. Lukia had never met Sergei. Did he even exist? If she took every word her daughter uttered as truthful, she'd believe every man was after her daughter. Doug was another one. Dunya had given the impression that the rich man's son was interested in her and would probably propose. When he'd visited a few times, he was friendly and courteous, but Lukia hadn't seen any sparks between them. And then he stopped coming.

What to make of Dunya's fanciful story? Who would blame Dunya or any girl for dreaming? Life wasn't easy. Who wouldn't want someone to take care of them? Lukia snorted. Well, better to have a daughter that confident than one who sat in the corner and moped, worrying about being a spinster.

But then again, maybe Dunya was telling the truth. Imagine her daughter planning on eloping! And that story of running into Peter, then seeing him again outside the window of the jewellery store. But Dunya also said he could've been a mirage, because he wasn't outside the store. Maybe it was a sign. Lukia believed in signs, strange as this one was. Maybe her daughter loved him. Maybe he'd come courting again.

Her sons were another matter. Egnat would be all right. He'd managed the drought when others had given up. And Elena had turned out to be a wonderful daughter-in-law, hard-working, and a devoted mother and wife. She never complained, so Lukia expected her son and wife would continue in harmony. Harry was settled in his livelihood, but it was Mike who remained the restless one. He was talking about buying his own truck and starting a delivery business, but how would he be able to do that? His drinking, his generosity with strangers, and his running after girls were problems. She spent many wakeful hours worrying about him, but what was the use? It hadn't helped in the past. For now, he'd continue to help Egnat on the farm.

As for herself, she was content living the rest of her life without a man to share her bed. Maybe marrying Orest would have worked out, but she had no regrets. She was sixty-two, too old to change. Her hopes and dreams now rested with her children. With wheat sales improving, she and Egnat could put some money aside and buy a farm of their own, one that would support them as their family grew. It was what they'd wanted when they immigrated.

"If it's meant to be, it'll be," she whispered. She picked up the family photo on the bureau. She'd have to mail a copy to her brother in the old country, but what to tell him? She'd tell him what she'd always told him. The truth. She'd mention her estrangement from Petro, Egnat's and Mike's arguments, Harry's work in the city, and Dunya's near elopement. Maybe she'd even tell him about Orest. She held the photo and gazed at each member fondly, as if that alone would keep them together.

In the morning, Lukia rose and headed to her garden. She wanted to tackle some hoeing before the sun was too high in the sky. Her sons and Dunya were already out tending to the animals in the barn, while Elena tended to the young ones in the house. Lukia hoed for a while, then stopped to admire the growth in the garden and the crops in the fields beyond. Abundant rains in May and June had kept the plants going despite the driest spring on record. Lukia and her neighbours hung onto the seed of hope that the promising conditions had brought them.

She bent down to pick up a handful of soil. After all their hard work, the earth crumbled easily through her fingers. Perhaps this was the beginning of the end of the Depression. With the decent weather, it appeared nature was finally extending her hand, showing she could soften her harsh ways. She leaned on her hoe and looked around, taking in all four corners of the farm. The prairie landscape looked like it had been painted a burnished gold by the sun. This land was now truly her home.

Glossary (Alphabetical)

Baba/Babcha - grandmother
Babushka – headscarf
Banyak – large pot
Bikasha – heavy coat made from cotton batting
Borscht – hearty soup made with beets, potatoes and cabbage.
Daye Bozhe – "God willing," the toast given before drinking
Djajo – Uncle
Holupchi – cabbage roll
Horilka – vodka
Hrystiky – twisted sweet dough, fried and dipped in honey
Hryvnia – Ukrainian currency
Junyou – vagina
Kazshook – a leather coat with a fur lining
Kishka – blood sausage
Kolomeyka – rousing Ukrainian folk dance
Kutya – dish of cooked wheat with honey and poppy seeds for
    Christmas Eve
Kybassa – ring of garlic sausage
Naymichka – maidservant, housekeeper
Oblast – region of the country, like a province or state
Pan/Panye – Mr./Mrs.
Paska – a sweet yeast bread made with saffron and raisins
Perina - comforter, filled with feathers or down
Perogies - dumplings filled with potato, cabbage, or fruit
Piyak - drunkard

Pich – clay oven with a brick shelf overhead, used as a stove

Piroshky – yeast dumplings filled with either fruit or vegetables

Pysanky – eggs finely decorated using melted wax and various
applied colours

Rushnyk – a tea towel, often made from white cloth and
embroidered

Smarkach – smarty-pants

Studenetz - jellied pigs' feet

Tato - father

Varenyky – filled dumplings that have been softly boiled,
sometimes called perogis.

Varenyka – one filled dumping

Vichnaya pamyat – eternal memory

Zloty – Polish currency

Author's Note

It was a gift to write this story. I shared the first fifteen years of my life with my baba, Lukia Mazurec, who came to live with my father, mother, and me, when I was a baby, but I did not learn from her what she'd endured as an immigrant. I suspect Baba didn't talk about her life because she didn't want to revisit the hard times, much like soldiers who come back from war.

I am grateful for all the tender care she gave me, and thankful my mother, a natural-born storyteller, shared her stories.

Writing biographical fiction is not for the faint of heart. I wanted to be true to the family I knew, but there was so much I didn't know. I had my mother's anecdotes of her family's immigration to Canada and the hardships they'd faced when they arrived, but I didn't have the details of that time. I spent many months researching the Great Depression in Canada and how it affected farmers on the prairies.

Though my mother, a gifted narrator in her own right, wanted her family's story published, I did not feel I could use the real names of those she and her family encountered in their journey to Manitoba and on the prairies. Therefore, most of the names in this novel—other than her family's—are fictitious.

ACKNOWLEDGEMENTS

My dear cousin, Jean Reid (nee Genya Mazurec), generously added more tales to the family history. And family members, though deceased, took me places I could only imagine. Characters and dialogue showed up on the page like gifts of rain on a prairie suffering from drought.

No author can write without the support of those in their corner. I'm thankful for the support from my Campbell River Writers Critique group, the notes from beta readers, Marie Seckler and Bob McClintock, and the cheers and encouragement from my family.

I'm most appreciative of my editor, Jocelyn Reekie—who's been a champion of my baba's story ever since I started writing it—my copy editor, Doreen Martens, and my publisher Peregrin Publishing for their faith in this biographical novel.

Most of all, I'm thankful for all the incredible support my husband, Robert, has given me. An avid reader himself, he provided editorial comment as well as meals and housework so I could write. What a guy!

A Note on
Historical References

The author gratefully acknowledges the usefulness of Bruce McManus, *Selkirk Avenue* (Signature Editions 1982); Barry Broadfoot, *Ten Lost Years 1929-1939* (Doubleday 1997); Pierre Berton, *The Great Depression* (Anchor Canada 2012); Christopher Dafoe, *Winnipeg, Heart of a Continent* (Great Plains Publications 2002); John Steinbeck, *The Grapes of Wrath* (Penguin Classics 2006); Edward R. Mills, *The Story of Stony Mountain and District*; (De Montfort Press 1960); Lisa Chilton, *Receiving Canada's Immigrants, The work of the state before 1930* (Ottawa: the Canadian Historical Association 2016); James S. Aberson, *From the Prairies with Hope* (University of Regina Press 1991); Lawrence Nkemdirim and Lena Weber, *Abstract: Comparison between the Droughts of the 1930s and the 1980s in the Southern Prairies of Canada* (Journal of Climate 1999 12-8); Don Aiken, *It Happened in Manitoba: Stories of the Red River Province* (Fifth House 2004); Brock Holowachuk, *Impact!: A History of Disasters in Manitoba* (Great Plains Publications 2009); Russ Gourluck, *The Mosaic Village, An Illustrated History of Winnipeg's North End* (Great Plains Publications 2010); James H. Gray, *The Winter Years: The Depression on the Prairies* (Fifth House 2004); *The First Hundred Years 1893-1993 Rural Municipality of Rosser* (Rural Municipality of Rosser 1993); Oleh W. Gerus, *The Reverend Semen Sawchuk and the Ukrainian Greek Orthodox*

Church of Canada, Journal of Ukrainian Studies, Vol. 16, Nos.1-12; and Rockwood, *100 Years of Rockwood History* (Rockwood Municipality 1982)

News of the day was gathered from the newspapers *Winnipeg Free Press, Winnipeg Tribune,* and *Stonewall Argus.* Information was also gleaned from the websites for the Manitoba Heritage Transit Association, Manitoba Historical Society, Orthodox Canada, Archives of Manitoba, Living History Farm, and St. Mary's the Protectress Cathedral in Winnipeg.

Special thanks to David Wyatt, historian at the Manitoba Heritage Association, and Jana Williams on the Stonewall Municipal Heritage Advisory Committee.

Book Club Questions

1. This book was completed during the Covid-19 pandemic. Some are saying the effect on the economy is the same as the Great Depression was on Canada and the United States. How much are present times similar to those, and how are they different?

2. Throughout the novel, there are many instances when excessive use of alcohol is mentioned. Alcoholics Anonymous had yet to develop a national presence. And alcoholism was viewed as a weakness, not an illness or addiction. Also, drinking in Ukraine is common, a part of the culture, much as it is in Ireland. What are your thoughts about the characters' reliance on alcohol to get them through the hard times?

3. Lukia chooses not to bring up the subject of excessive drinking with her sons. Yet she is aware of how much it's affecting her sons, especially Mike. What is your opinion on how she handled this problem?

4. Lukia gives up on a potentially easier life with Orest. Her children are older; before long they will leave. How much should children dictate what a widow or widower does the second time around?

5. This story brings up problems all immigrants face: dealing with strange language, different customs, and the hostile feelings of citizens who find it hard to accept differences in the newly landed. And yet, many countries need immigrants to build their workforce. How should a country deal with the opposing forces?

6. During the Great Depression, many gave up farming in the United States and Canada. What are the chances you would have weathered these times, given what you know about yourself? How much do you think this kind of endurance has to do with stubbornness, a strong will, or faith? Or is there something else at play?

7. One concern brought up by people in the book was that of economic relief. During the Great Depression, the government gave out handouts to help people stay on their feet. These came in the form of relief camps and breadlines. Lukia and many of her countrymen had a problem with government handouts. They believed it robbed people of their initiative. They thought it brought shame to the family. Today, there's discussion of a guaranteed annual income. What do you believe is the best way to support those in need?

8. One chapter is called "A Little Lie," which tells about the time Dunya told a white lie about Doug to her friend Olga. Are there occasions when lies are reasonable? How did it affect your opinion of Dunya?

9. Both Dunya and Lukia speak their mind, as they did regarding the impossible brooch. If lies are unacceptable, is truth in this instance better? Under what circumstances is it reasonable to tell the truth, even though it might hurt?

10. Lukia gives her daughter a lecture on keeping her virginity. She explains the importance of keeping her legs together so she can find a good husband. The world has changed. With the abandonment of the double standard, women today have more options. How has this freedom affected the idea of marriage and finding a suitable mate?

About the Author

Diana Stevan is the author of *Sunflowers Under Fire,* historical fiction and a finalist for the 2019 Whistler Independent Book Award, a semi-finalist for the 2019 Kindle Book Award in literary fiction, and an Honorable Mention for the 2020 Writers Digest Self-Published Book Award for mainstream /literary fiction; the well-received debut novel *A Cry From The Deep,* a time-slip romantic adventure; and the novel, *The Rubber Fence,* women's fiction.

Her varied background includes work as a clinical social worker, teacher, professional actor, and freelance writer-broadcaster for *Sports Journal,* CBC Television. She's had poetry published in *DreamCatcher,* a United Kingdom publication, a short story in the anthology *Escape,* and articles in newspapers and an online magazine.

Diana is currently at work on the third book of Lukia's Family Saga series, *Paper Roses on Stony Mountain.*

With two daughters grown, Diana lives with her husband, Robert, on Vancouver Island and in West Vancouver, British Columbia.

For more, visit her website: https://www.dianastevan.com

Manufactured by Amazon.ca
Bolton, ON

26682937R00213